Dawn —

Strong Women
inspire others —
I hope you enjoy
this book

Sincerely —

Sherri
Lipton
Hollatz

Cover designed by Lighthouse Studio Graphics
lighthousestudionc@gmail.com

"Bringing Light and Innovation to Your Images"

"Chrome Pink" is a work of fiction. The town of Leeward, North Carolina exists only in my heart and mind. The characters may sound familiar to eastern North Carolina but any resemblance to persons living or dead is merely coincidence.

First Edition December 2017 Trade Paperback
ISBN-9781979423168

Chrome Pink

Sherri Lupton Hollister

Finding your strength sometimes takes years.
For Rae Lynne, it took ten...

Rae Lynne Grimes still suffers from the torture of high school when the video of her being gang raped went public. Can she trust a man who works for one of her rapists? Can she allow herself to believe in love? When her dates start dying mysteriously, Rae struggles to prove her innocence while being the target of a madman.

Logan Birdsong is determined to prove he is not his father's son. Taking his step-father's name and continuing the business he built. Logan's greatest fear is failing his family. Torn between his need to succeed and his attraction to Rae Lynne Grimes he must make a difficult choice: protect Rae Lynne or do business with a sociopath.

"Rae, what's wrong?" He reached out to take her hand.

She pulled her hand away. "Nothing, what makes you think anything's wrong? It's just time..." Her breath shuddered out on a sob. "I can't—I'm okay with wham-bam-thank you-ma'am, but I don't know how to act with this." She waved her hands.

Logan leaned forward and asked, "Romance? Seduction?"

Rae blinked. "That's not my style."

"Why not, it's the fun part of sex? The build-up, the teasing and touching." He traced his finger along her arm.

She shook her arm and moved away, her body trembling. "It changes things."

"How's that?" He edged closer, resting his hand on her shoulder as he toyed with her hair.

Pulling away, she stomped to the dish washer and turned it on. "It makes it important."

Logan frowned. "Sex should be important."

"No, sex is a need, an itch that needs scratching."

Logan shook his head. "But it can be fun, or serious, or comforting..."

"Nope, it's just—"

"Wham Bam!" Logan turned away.

"I know, I'm seriously screwed up." Rae laughed. "Aren't you glad you'll be getting out of here tomorrow?"

Dedicated to all of those who have a dream but are afraid.
Don't let fear steal it from you.
This is my dream.

Acknowledgements

I am blessed with my own cheerleading squad. A group of people who believed in me even before I learned to believe in myself: my husband, David Hollister who worked as my research assistant, my time keeper during Nanowrimo and who always knew what to say to keep me from leaping off the nearest bridge whenever things went wrong, my little sister, Robina Norman who took me to my first Romantic Times Convention and then pushed me to apply for the Ann Peach Scholarship which I won, and my mentor MK "Marni" Graff who saw something in me and pushed me, molded me and convinced me I was good enough. To my Beta readers: Kay Wilson, Wayne Hollister, Diane Ruff, Merle Finch and Cindy Day who gave great feedback and read and reread the story to help hone my craft. To my friends and family, the Pamlico Writers Group, the Heart of Carolina Romance Writers Group and the North Carolina Writers' Read of Belhaven, your critiques, workshops, programs, conferences and fellowship have brought me this far.

To Jeffery Robinson of Southern Bank, David Kendrick and Mike Harmon of Aurora Police Department, and my mechanic extraordinaire David Hollister who used their expertise and experiences to help me with technical questions. *Thank you!*

Prologue
Twenty-one years ago

Mari staggered, her heels snagging the oyster shells covering the drive. The unforgettable scent of dying fish hung heavy in the humid air. She kicked off her shoes, the jagged surface of the weathered boards rough on feet no longer used to running barefoot around the docks.

What am I doing here? Malcolm's tense voice on the phone had the little hairs on the back of her neck standing up. *"Damn it, her cousin was one of the girls."*

Seeing her boss's Mercedes aglow in the moonlight made her stomach twist. She looked around, he'd told her he would make inquiries tomorrow.

Years of sore fingers, back aching from hours of being hunched over a metal table picking crab meat was a memory she knew would never truly fade. Buddy Grimes had saved her from that life, but her husband didn't think she was qualified for anything more than being a house wife. Marisol Grimes was no dumb Mexican fresh from the farm. Her job with Malcolm Bryant proved it. *Please don't let him be involved in Juanita's disappearance.*

Marisol Grimes tread slowly across the weathered boards careful not to get a splinter or make a noise. Voices raised in anger, their words ripped away on the wind, slowed her steps. She turned the corner by the cook house and the sound suddenly amplified, reverberating off the water. "You need to get rid of her." Mari slid between the cook house and a storage shed, she peered out at the loading dock. Two women lay bound and sobbing on the loading dock.

Malcolm's wife, Elva Bryant held a huge pistol pointed at an older man. She held her breath, releasing it slowly when she saw it wasn't Malcolm. She leaned out to get a better look, el Jeffe—Mr. Sawyer, owner of the seafood processing plant.

Sawyer hovered near two sobbing women. One of the girls could be Juanita. Mari fingernailed her palms as she watched Mr. Sawyer jerk one of the girls to her feet.

He waved his hands, arguing with Mrs. Bryant. Marisol couldn't hear his words but it Elva Bryant was not happy with what he had to say. An explosion shattered the stillness. Night birds flew up from the rushes.

A pop of sound, suddenly there, after the numbing silence. The echo of the gun shot like cotton in her ears. She was surprised to realize she was screaming.

Elva Bryant turned, her eyes hard and cold. Even from a distance, Mari could see there would be no mercy. People were shouting and running towards her. Mari stood frozen starting to hyperventilate. Malcolm leapt from behind a stack of canvas bags and pushed her across the boardwalk inconsiderate of her bare feet. She stubbed her toe and stuck a splinter in her foot. Malcolm clicked the fob on his keychain, opening the door he shoved her inside and hurried to the driver's side.

Bullets pinged the side of the car. Mari scream, several men rushed into the parking lot. Malcolm put the car in reverse, spinning tires. He slammed on brakes Mari braced her hand on the dash.

"What are you stopping for?"

He powered down his window and shot out several tires and a radiator. He rolled up the window and gunned the motor, fishtailing the car out of the parking lot.

"Oh my God, my car. I left my car and my shoes. Buddy is going to kill me." Marisol was shaking, her mind tripping over her thought. "You have to go back. I can't go home without my shoes and my car."

"Mari, you can't go home. Don't you understand?"

"What? I have to go home. I have two babies…"

The sadness in his eyes nearly brought her to tears. "They know who you are, they'll kill you."

She clutched her stomach, rocking forward. "That girl, was she my cousin?"

Malcolm gripped the steering wheel. "No, she was a new girl. Your cousin is gone."

"Dead?"

"Gone."

She blinked back tears. *My God, what have I done?*

Chapter 1

Present: Eastern North Carolina

Rae Lynne Grimes carried her black leather pumps in one hand and a half empty bottle of Jack Daniels in the other. The cool water of Bond Creek beckoned. She'd missed her morning swim—again. The water was all that had kept her sober since her return to Leeward three months ago. She'd come home to nurse her grandfather. She laughed and took a swig of whiskey letting the burn scald the tears from her throat. *I did a bang-up job, didn't I Pops?* She lifted her bottle to the sky in salute.

Reluctantly, she headed back to the house. The family expected her to act as hostess to those who'd come to pay their respects. Rae veered behind the boathouse to evade the hoard of free loaders who'd come to gorge themselves on fried chicken and the latest gossip. They were all wondering the same thing— *What's that girl going to do without her grandfather?*

Lifting her skirt, she yanked off her shredded panty hose. A burst of masculine laughter startled her. A group of men congregated at the edge of the patio. Their loud whispers hit her like a punch in the gut.

"With a rack like that, I'd give her a ten."

"Nah, only seven, did you see her face?"

Blood scalded Rae's face. She opened her mouth to tell them off but hesitated, realizing it was Dana they were critiquing. She ducked back behind the boathouse guilt adding to her shame. *I should have defended her, she's my best friend.* The fear was crippling, seeing those men who'd been part of Todd Bryant's gang—Former football players acting as if they were still in high school. Trembling, she prayed they'd not seen her. The fucking bastards still had the power to terrorize her. She braved another look.

Jorge Claudio stood off to the side looking uncomfortable. Memories of a drunken night spent groping in the backseat of his Chevy Nova filled her with dread. How many old lovers and one-night stands would she have to face today? Jorge no longer sported the Bruno Mars pompadour but still looked good, even in his khaki uniform. With his dark, bedroom eyes and full, sensual lips he should be on the cover of GQ, not playing cop in this hick town. Leeward, North Carolina wasn't the end of the world but it was surely a dropping off place.

Sprinting behind her art studio, Rae sagged against the rough wooden siding to catch her breath. A piece of paper pinned to the door fluttered in the breeze. Shoving the bottle under her arm she snatched it down. *Leave now, while you still can.* The whiskey burned in her belly. Crumpling the letter in her hand, she scowled wondering which one of the sick bastards had sent the note. She couldn't breathe. Todd and his gang had made high school a nightmare she'd barely survived. Rae rubbed the scar on her wrist as she concentrated on controlling her breathing.

Three months in Leeward managed to invalidate two years of sobriety and sanity. Determined to take care of her grandfather, Rae had ignored the snide comments from neighbors and family, believing she was strong enough to handle their scorn. They loved nothing more than to bring up her past, trotting out each of her sins as if she needed an introduction. Shame washed over her. Rae hadn't forgotten, she remembered nightly how she'd sold her soul for a few minutes of peace. The numbness the drugs offered was never enough. The sex, a tenuous connection as fleeting as smoke. She took another swig of the whiskey as the tears streamed down her cheeks. Her grandfather had been so proud to see her finally sober, a college graduate with a good job. *He wouldn't be so proud, now.* She smeared mascara and snot across her face as she crept up the back steps to her grandfather's office, praying no one spotted her.

The first note had showed up the morning after. *He's dead. Now go.* Rae hadn't seen who'd left it. The house was open and people were coming and going.

Anyone with an emergency scanner would have known when the rescue squad was called. They were all waiting like vultures, ready to swoop down and pick his bones.

Rae leaned against the doorjamb. Otis Grimes had retired from commercial fishing before she started school. He'd begun Grimes Outdoors so he could be home with his grandchildren after their mama left. He'd offered his expertise as a hunting and fishing guide, teaching Rae and her brother all he knew. She was an excellent shot but too impatient. Rae had learned to channel her energy into art instead. Her grandfather had been her friend and confident. She'd moved in with Pops when her daddy gave up and told her he couldn't deal with her anymore. Her grandfather was the only person who ever gave a damn about her. *And now he was gone.*

The office was just a small bedroom in the old Air Stream. Dark wood paneling from the seventies covered the walls. The only thing keeping it from being tomb-like was the big windows Otis had installed. She breathed deeply of his scent, pipe tobacco, Old Spice and—

"Well, ain't you a sight."

For ten years that voice had haunted her nightmares. The whiskey churned in her stomach as she looked into the dark, insolent eyes of her step-brother. Devin Kinnion eased his large frame onto the arm of her grandfather's chair and lit a joint. His broad muscular chest expanded with the inhalation of pungent smoke. The sweet allure of marijuana beckoned her closer. "What are you doing here?" The note shifted against the neck of the bottle. "Did you send this?"

"Send what?" He rubbed a hand over the dark stubble of his shaved head.

Rae waved the piece of paper at him. No longer the boy she remembered, this man was far more dangerous. Rae knew she should be concerned, but fueled with alcohol, she was determined to confront the man who'd instigated her ruin.

Devin took another hit off the joint. "Someone sending you love notes Rae Lynne? Must be Todd. He always did have a perverse sense of romance. You still spreading your legs for anyone with a bag of dope?" He shook the plastic baggy in invitation.

She lunged, the bottle of Jack Daniels raised. "Get out." She squeezed the words between clenched teeth, her body vibrating with anger and fear. Devin terrified her but she'd be damned if she'd cower. She wasn't fourteen years old now and he didn't have his friends to hold her down. "Get the fuck out of here!"

He snatched the bottle and tossed it out of her reach. "Such language." Their hot breaths filled the small space between them as each tried to stare the other down. Devin shrugged and flopped into her grandfather's chair. "Why don't you come over here and make me?" He propped a foot on the desk and ogled her, taking in the piercings and body ink. "You look like a carnival freak." He grabbed his crotch and grinned. "That's okay, I can do freaky?"

Throwing her shoes at his head, she shoved his foot off the desk. *God, how could I have ever thought I was attracted to him?*

Devin leapt from the seat, trapping her against the doorframe. He was nearly a head taller and fifty pounds heavier. Rae struggled to get free.

He sneered, countering her moves.

She brought her knee up. He grabbed her leg.

"You have a lot of piercings, little sister." He caressed her leg inching up her thigh. "You like pain?" He leaned into her, threatening. "I'll be happy to give you some. I owe you. Ten fucking years' worth."

Rae pushed at his chest. "Let me go. I'm not the one you owe." She fought the panic that threatened to turn her limbs to gelatin. The rape had left her broken and the only one who'd ever paid was Devin.

"I wouldn't have been there if not for you. Show me what else you have pierced?" He moved his hand up her thigh.

He was too big, too strong. *No, not again.* Tears pricked her eye lids but she wouldn't back down. She continued to fight.

"What the hell do you think you're doing?" Billy Ray shouted as he stomped up the stairway. His heavy tread caused the old trailer to sway and groan.

Shorter and broader than Devin, more like their dad, Billy was sandy-haired and freckled, built like wrestler. People were surprised to learn they were siblings. Rae favored their mother with her olive complexion and dark hair. They had the same arch of the brow, and dark almond shaped eyes. The slight pug to their noses was similar, though Billy's had been broken a time or two.

The men glowered at each other. Devin thrust Rae aside.

Rae Lynne stumbled.

Billy pulled her towards him. "Go." He pushed her into the hall.

Rae pitched forward, holding herself upright with help of the wall. Papa kept a revolver in the desk drawer. Worried, she turned back.

Billy crowded Devin, using his extra pounds to intimidate. "Stay away from my sister or you won't have to worry about prison, you'll be dead."

Devin met her eyes over Billy's shoulder. "Tell her to stay away from me." Billy turned to glare at her. Devin pushed past. On the stairs he whispered, "We'll finish this—later."

"Sober up before Dad sees you." Billy brushed past her and followed Devin out.

Shaking, Rae glanced at the ashtray hoping Devin had left the roach.

Chapter 2
One week later

Churning up a rooster tail in the parking lot of the Depot Café, Rae rode the 1957 Harley she'd just finished restoring.

"You finished it!" Dana's curly brown hair glowed copper and gold in the sunlight. She clapped and squealed like the excited school girl she'd been when they'd ruled middle school as the Fearsome Foursome. By high school they'd all begun to dim as they became the butt of Todd's cruel joke. Her smile faded, and Rae wondered if Dana was ever haunted by the past.

Rae's stomach fluttered. Todd had to be the one sending the notes. She glanced around the parking lot, the newest letter tucked into her pocket. She wouldn't let him frighten her away.

"God Rae, this is so perfect." Dana Windley was her oldest and dearest friend. She was a beautiful and formidable, six-foot tall warrior queen. Only her constant dieting was evident she suffered any doubts.

Dana, like her mother, was strong and confident. No matter what ugliness touched their lives, they still believed there was good in the world. Rae needed their faith for her own survival.

Rae fastened the helmet to the bike. It was painted to match with dark pink ribbons weaving between lighter shades. "What do you think?" She patted the upholstered leather seat with its pink ribbon embroidery. They'd bought the bike to raise money for breast cancer awareness and research, one of Dana's pet projects. She'd become obsessed after her mother was first diagnosed with breast cancer their freshmen year of college.

"Should you be riding it?" The license plate read TATAS. Dana's giggle burst like a bubble as she sobered. "I just don't want anything to happen to it after all we had to go through to get it ready."

"I had to test it to make sure it runs out okay. Don't worry, I'll give it the TLC it deserves before the Run."

Dana hugged her. "This is going to be the best Poker Run ever. We're going to raise so much money! We'll never be able to top this. I can't believe you got it done..." Dana placed a hand on Rae's arm, her warm topaz eyes filled with tears. "Rae, are you okay?"

Rae fought the swell of emotion, even with Dana, she couldn't allow herself to cry. "Wish Papa could have seen it finished." He'd rallied from his battle with lung cancer, excited to help them search for replacement parts.

Dana leaned against her, giving her a one-armed hug. "He'd get a kick outta people's reaction to a Pink Harley."

"Wow, is that the bike?" Jenna interrupted. She was the third member of the Fearsome Foursome and the new owner of the Depot Café. Jenna had returned home after her father's heart attack and taken over the McKenzie family business. After filing for divorce, she'd bought the café from her parents. With her runner's body, she looked more like a co-ed than the mother of a four-year-old. Her long rusty brown hair tied in its ever-present ponytail hadn't changed since high school.

The bike was just like the one her grandfather had bought when he'd returned from Viet Nam. Rae had grown up listening to stories of his adventures. When she'd found the bike at an estate sale, she'd talked fast, coming up with the idea to restore the bike and auction it off for Dana's Breast Cancer Awareness campaign. It was Dana who had convinced the old man to sell it to them, but Rae was the one who'd repaired and restored it.

It took months get the bike ridable, working on it only when she came home on weekends. After moving back to Leeward, the task had gotten a little easier. Rae worked whatever odd hour she could manage until her grandfather's health became too precarious. She'd hoped to finish it before he died. She had missed it by one week. One fucking week.

Forcing the sadness from her thoughts, she pointed out different features to her friends. "It turned out pretty good, didn't it?" Rae shoved her hands in her pockets. The note rattled, reminding her she wasn't wanted here. It seemed silly to be afraid of a few words printed on paper. She glanced around the parking lot searching for her tormentor.

"Pretty good?" Dana exclaimed. "It's amazing! I've gotta get some pictures for the advertisement." She wiggled her cell phone out of the pocket of her capris and started taking pictures. "I'm so excited. This is gonna to be the best fundraiser we've ever had. I owe you big time for this one."

"Good, you're buying my dinner." Rae linked arms with both women and aimed them towards the café. "I'm starved."

Dana said, "You got it. Anything you want." She paused at the door. "Is it okay to leave it out here?"

"You are not bringing that bike into my café," Jenna said.

"Maybe one of us should stay out here and watch it." Dana hung back.

"It'll be fine." Rae and Jenna dragged her inside.

"Come on, I'm starved. What're the specials?"

Jenna led them to a booth and spouted off the daily specials from memory. Rae placed her order and waited for Dana to decide. She made eye contact with the other patrons but only her neighbor, Phil Archer returned her smile.

"Okay, I'll take the grilled chicken, no sauce and a salad."

"What kind of dressing?"

"No dressing and water with lots of ice."

Rae and Jenna shared a knowing look.

"Who's the guy?" Rae asked as Jenna left with their orders.

"What guy?" Dana bounced up and hovered by the window keeping guard over the bike.

The older couple sitting there glared at Dana. After the third time, they tossed their napkins on the table and asked, "Would you like this table young lady?"

"Yes, ma'am." Dana beamed and waved Rae over.

The old woman rolled her eyes and stomped to the cash register, muttering, "Some people's manners."

Standing by the dirty table, reluctant to sit down, Rae said, "Back to my question. Who's the guy?"

"I don't know what you're talking about." The warm pink hue coloring Dana's face told a different story.

"All right, don't tell me, but you know I'll find out."

Dana began bussing the table. "How did the reading of the will go?"

"The way you'd expect. Uncle Clyde is the executor. Papa left me the fishing camp." Rae slid into the booth. "Connie and my dad want me to sell it." She sighed. "There's some kinda loan attached to it. Clyde is trying to help me keep it." She picked up a napkin and started shredding it. Dana put her hand out, tapping their fingers together. "It's the only real home I've ever had." Rae looked away, willing the tears to retreat.

"You're not going back to Raleigh?" Dana's fingers were warm and calming.

Rae shifted in the seat. "I want to do more with my art than design chandeliers." She'd spent the last two years working for a company that specialized in high design light fixtures. She liked the job, but it did not allow her own creativity.

"And what about the internship with Graphic Focus?"

Rae shrugged. "I blew that when I came home to take care of Papa."

"So, you're going to stay here and what? Paint cars?"

"And motorcycles." Rae grinned. It was hard to take Dana seriously with her hair curling about her face like Orphan Annie. Dana had played Annie in one of their school plays. Everyone believed she was destined for Hollywood or New York City, but that was before—Before Todd, before cancer. Dana had her own demons. She just seemed to cope with them better.

"You think you could paint a mural for me?" Jenna set down their drinks and a basket of bread.

Rae looked around the café. "Inside?'

"Yeah, I'd like a scene from when it was a train depot."

"Sure, I'll draw up a couple of ideas," Rae said around a mouthful of hushpuppies.

Jenna gnawed her lip. "Okay but I don't have a lot of money."

"I'm sure we can work something out. I like to eat, so how about a year of free eats?"

"A year?" Jenna frowned. "That would be what, about three thousand dollars or something?"

"It's a little less than I'd normally charge, but you're an old friend."

Jenna's green eyes bulged. "You charge more than three thousand dollars for a mural?"

Rae nodded. "Of course, if you just want one wall, then that would be about right."

Jenna blinked. "O-kay, I'll have to get back to you on that."

"Jen, can we use the Depot for one of the stops on the Poker Run?" Dana asked pulling out her computer to make notes. "It'll give you a little free advertising."

Jenna nodded. "Sure, but how are you doing all of this and opening a new business too?"

Dana had recently bought and refurbished the old gym. She was turning it into a dating club. "I like to be busy. Are you going to sign up?"

"I don't have a bike."

"No, for the dating club." Dana chuckled.

Jenna shook her head. "Between the divorce and refurbishing this place, I wasn't joking about being broke."

They turned to Rae Lynne.

Rae held up her hands, shaking her head. "Don't look at me. I'm not interested in joining any dating club."

"Come on, it'd be good for you to get out and meet some nice guys," Dana said.

Rae snorted. "Nice guys and me aren't a good fit. Wouldn't know what to do with one if I had one."

"Same thing you do with the bad ones, just less drama."

"Thought I had a nice guy once," Jenna said, shaking her head. "I'll go get your orders."

As the lunch crowd thinned, Dana and Rae pushed back their empty plates and began making plans for the Poker Run. Jenna joined them. Dark circles ringed her eyes. Rae didn't know how she did it, working from dawn until closing with a four-year-old at home. Money was tight after Mac's heart attack, but if Jen didn't hire some more help she'd be the one with health problems.

"How's your mom?" Jenna asked, stretching and groaning like a woman twice her age.

Making notes on the computer, Dana didn't look up. "She's got an appointment with her oncologist, but she said it's just routine."

A chill tickled Rae's spine. Sandy Windley was more to her than her best friend's mom. She could barely remember her own mother and her step-mother Connie...Well, considering everything with Devin, she guessed they were lucky they'd not tried to kill each other— at least not recently anyway.

"Rae Lynne Grimes, how serendipitous to meet you here."

The cultured voice held only a hint of southern accent. Swallowing the bile that churned in her stomach, Rae clenched the table to keep from fleeing as she looked up and met the curious stares of the businessmen shuffling impatiently behind her nemesis—Todd Bryant.

Ten years since the night he'd brutally destroyed her innocence. Todd was still too beautiful to be real, but Rae knew the monster that lurked just below the surface. "Taking a break from terrorizing small children and old people?" Her heart pounded. She was thankful her voice didn't crack.

"You won't be joking when you're out on your pretty little hiney and the fishing camp is mine."

"It's not worth anything to you. Why do you want it?"

He moved his eyes over her, making her skin crawl, but Rae refused to back down. She glared at him. "You don't intimidate me, Todd." She hid her trembling hands beneath the table.

He lifted his brows and grinned. "You want to make a bet?"

"Come on Todd, let's get some lunch. I've got to get back to work." Jorge's dark, sympathetic eyes met hers.

"Y'all grab us a table and order me a sweet tea. I've got business to discuss with Ms. Grimes."

The other men moved to the far side of the café but Jorge stayed. "I'm sorry about your grandfather, Rae. He was a good man."

"Thanks Jorge." The intensity in his eyes threatened to unnerve her.

"I came to the funeral."

"She doesn't care if you were at the funeral or not, wetback. Go, sit, I'll be there in a minute." Todd jerked his head towards the others.

Jorge's hand hovered briefly over his holster before clenching into a fist and returning to his side. "I'm not one of your flunkies, Todd."

"You like wearing that uniform, Whore-hay?" Todd sneered.

Jorge stiffened.

"You'll do what I say, sit."

Shame mingled with the anger in Jorge's eyes.

Rae felt sick as she watched Jorge walk away. Todd enjoyed humiliating people. She stared at the men gathered around the table: Banker Stanley Lyles, the local lawyer, Fred Rowe, and a couple of businessmen she couldn't call by name. "You're not getting my camp." Rae kept her voice down, not wanting to cause trouble with Jenna's few remaining customers.

"I always get my way. You should know that, Rae Lynne." His cold blue eyes peeled away her protective layers. He reveled in her discomfort. Leaning close, his hot breath against her skin. "If I want something, I get it. A little resistance makes the reward all the sweeter. Like the taste of your sweet little caboose when I finally took a bite." He shifted, making room in his pants for his growing erection. His hand hovered over her, not touching but invading her space. "Remember how you fought me, the memory still excites me—"

Rae exploded from the seat, slapping her hands against his chest, and shoved. "Shut up. Shut the hell up!" She gasped for breath as strong arms wrapped around her waist and pulled her away from Todd.

"Rae, stop, don't let him control you," Jorge whispered as she struggled in his arms.

"Let me go Jorge. I'm going to kill him."

"I can't let you do that, even if he deserves it."

Todd raised one golden brow. "Be careful Whore-hay."

Rae bit back a sob and eased back against Jorge.

Todd grinned. "Come on Rae, your whole family wants you to sell that land. Better do it quick before you don't have anything left I want."

Rae raised her fist and growled, "Let me wipe that smug smile off his face."

Jorge tightened his hold. "Don't, Rae, settle down. Don't give him the satisfaction."

"Go ahead sweet thing, I'll have you tossed in jail so fast—" Todd goaded, staying just out of reach. "I'll even have your friend here do the honors, wouldn't that be ironic?"

Phil stepped between them. "Enough. Todd, I think you should leave."

"Me, leave? Now, why would I want to do that? I've not satisfied my appetite, yet." He leered at Rae. "Perhaps we should ask Ms. McKenzie who should leave."

Rae recognized the threat in his eyes. She might save herself but her friends wouldn't be as lucky.

Jenna mumbled under her breath. "Stay, I have arsenic in the back."

"Mayor Bryant?" Stanley called.

Rae pulled from Jorge's embrace. "I gotta get back to work."

"You do that Rae Lynne. I'll keep an eye on your gal pals."

Rae shot Dana and Jenna warning glance.

Dana nodded and mouthed. "We'll be fine."

Rae brushed past Todd on her way out the door.

"I always get what I want, Rae Lynne."

"Not this time, not if I can help it," Shoving her hands in her pockets, Rae hurried out of the restaurant. She kept her head high. It wouldn't do to let Todd know he'd spooked her. *As if he wasn't dangerous enough, they elected him mayor?* Shaking her head, she sighed, "Only in Leeward, North Carolina."

Chapter 3
Later that day

"Polly, where the hell, are you? Come on Pol." The doorbell jangled her nerves as the door slammed.

Fueled by whiskey and anger, Rae Lynne stumbled through the front door of the little flower shop, a manila envelope clutched in her fist. Todd was calling in the loan on her property. She knew he would play dirty, but calling the loan in early...

"Polly!" Polly's Posies was pretty, pale and shiny, just like its owner. Rae glanced around the shop, everything tidy and in its place. It seemed a bit sterile for a flower shop, but what did she know? She was more comfortable in a garage.

Polly had once been part of the Fearsome Foursome—before Todd. "He's trying to do it to me again, Polly," she shouted from the center of the store.

Something fell. Rae pushed open a door and glanced in the back room. "Polly?" Rae frowned, confused by the metal tables and scientific-looking equipment. She'd not realized a florist's back room would look like a medical lab. The odor was vaguely familiar. She blinked away the dizziness.

Polly slid her phone into the pocket of her pale linen pants and scowled. "Seriously, Rae, keep your voice down." She pushed Rae back into the front of the store and let the door swish closed behind her. "Is all this really necessary?"

Rae held out the envelope. "Your husband is trying to rape me—*again*."

Polly paled and darted a glance out the big front window. Her translucent skin showed every vein. Her blush glowed like a road flare as she hurried to turn the *open* sign to *closed*. "Oh my God, this is going to be all over town. You've got to go."

Rae shouted at the curious passing by, flinging her hands in the air, "What are you looking at?" Not the best De Niro but it did the trick. Pedestrians hurried past the flower shop with their heads down and eyes averted.

"What is it you want, Rae?"

The exasperation in Polly's voice fueled her anger. Rae brandished the envelope under her nose. "This is what I'm talking about."

"I'm not clairvoyant, what's in the envelope?" Polly crossed her arms under her petite bosom.

"Todd is trying to steal my property."

"Steal it?"

Rae paced the small area in front of a spring display. "He's trying to force me to sell. I thought, maybe, you'd talk to him."

"I don't tend to Todd's business." Polly shifted towards the door, Rae's cue to leave.

Ignoring the hint, she fidgeted around the shop. Picking up one thing then another, Rae bit her lip. "I can't lose this land, Polly. It's everything to me." She clutched a delicate glass sculpture.

Polly snatched the figurine and held it out of reach in hands that were perfectly manicured and so unlike her own.

"Rae, I don't have time for this. I have a business to run."

"What happened to us?" Voice thick with emotion, Rae could barely speak the words. "We used to be friends."

Polly rolled her eyes. "Yes, well, that was a very long time ago."

"Don't you miss being a part of the group?"

Polly gave a delicate snort. "Truly, why would I miss what I never had?"

"We were like sisters."

"You and Dana were like sisters. I was just the token good girl."

"That's not true."

"Todd told me how you laughed about me behind my back. I was just your charity." Polly's pale eyes burned with anger.

Rae shook her head. "No Polly, he lied to you. It wasn't like that. We were the Fearsome Foursome. We ruled Leeward Middle School."

"You ruled."

Her denial fell like a stone between them. Rae tried again. "He's even got my dad and Connie on his side."

Polly let out a frustrated screech. "Just sell it to him. God, you don't want to stay here."

"How do you know what I want?" Rae's anger burned away the guilt.

"Why would you want to stay? No one wants you here. No one has forgotten what you did—"

What I did? "My days of worrying about what this town thinks are over."

"When have you ever concerned yourself with what anyone else thinks?"

"Unlike you, who worries what everyone thinks."

Staring at the numerous piercings and tattoos, Polly sneered. "It's obvious you don't care about anything, including your own appearance."

"You don't like my hardware?" Rae fingered her newest addition, an eyebrow stud. "No, I don't care about anything in this town, especially your husband. I am not letting Todd or anyone else screw me in the ass ever again."

"Is that vulgarity really necessary?"

"I would've thought you'd be used to it by now. Isn't that the way your husband likes it?"

"You need to leave." Polly pointed to the door.

"I am not a scared little girl any more. You tell your husband and his mama, I'm not going anywhere. I'm going to be a constant reminder of what he did to me, to you, to all of us." Her voice rising.

"We've worked hard to overcome the humiliation you put us through. I'm not going to allow you to ruin all we've built here. Stay away from me and stay away from my husband."

"I'll stay away, but you tell pretty boy to stay away from me." Rae plucked a daisy from a clay pot and sauntered out the door singing, "Pretty Polly's Posies, stick 'em up your nosies."

Rae staggered out of the shop, stumbling over a crack in the sidewalk. Someone gripped her arm and she came around swinging. Tears blurred her eyes.

"You all right Ms. Rae?"

Rae blinked at the homeless man, Ditchwater Pete. He'd drifted into Leeward a few months ago, surviving by doing odd jobs around town. He seemed to be everywhere and nowhere. She smiled at the twin images of him. "I'm fine Pete." She swayed against him, surprised at his muscular frame. "I'm making new friends and destroying old ones." She gave a bark of laughter, but her lip trembled. She bit it to keep from crying.

Billy roared up in his jacked-up truck. "Come on Rae, let's get out of here."

Pete helped her as she stumbled to the curb and climbed up into the four-wheeled beast. "She called you. Didn't she?"

"Does it matter?" He revved the motor. She barely had the door closed before he was spinning tires. "You want to tell me about these?"

The notes lay on the seat between them, even the balled up one from the funeral. "Someone doesn't want me here."

"Obviously," he grunted. "Why didn't you tell me?"

Rae snorted. "Really Billy, it's a little late to protect me now."

He flinched. "Fine, forget it."

"Sorry, it's been a really shitty month."

"Yeah? No kidding."

Rae let out a breath. "Okay, you didn't deserve that. It's just not high on my list of priorities right now."

"Someone's threatening you."

"It's not the first time."

"This could be serious." Billy slowed to turn up her lane. "You're going to the police."

She leaned against the window as tears blurred her vision. She didn't want Billy to know how much these notes frightened her. Heaving a sigh, she said, "Fine, I'll go to the cops." Her stomach churned. *But would they even believe me?*

Chapter 4
Two nights later

The Hard Hat Tavern, on the outskirts of Leeward, had Karaoke every Thursday night. Singing was one of the few pleasures Rae could still enjoy while trapped at the edge of the world. She missed the clubs and her friends. If not for Dana and Jenna, she'd go mad. The loneliness threatened her attempts at sobriety. Shrugging out of her jean jacket, she hung it on the stool and called for a lite beer.

Jorge Claudio entered the bar looking too good for her peace of mind in his faded blue jeans and rib hugging polo. Rae stiffened. Loneliness made him a greater temptation than the whiskey. Devin followed, scowling. Their eyes met in the mirror. The menace in his glare chilled her. She gripped her beer and forced herself to breathe.

She watched through the curtain of her hair as Jorge ordered Devin away. Rae breathed a sigh of relief. Devin tossed a last malevolent look over his shoulder, then stomped to the pool tables. Jorge stepped behind her. The spicy scent of his cologne stirred her senses.

"You singin' tonight?" He propped his hip on the stool beside her.

"Yeah, only thing to do in this town."

Leaning close, he whispered, "I can think of a few other things."

She glanced at his long-fingered hands. He'd always been good with his hands. Even knowing he was here with Devin, she was tempted. The loneliness was a physical pain. A few more beers and she wouldn't care that he was working for Todd. "Sorry Jorge, I'm not—"

"Rae, it's your turn to sing," Charlie interrupted.

She gave the old bartender a smile and slid from the stool.

A strong hand on her arm stopped her. She flinched. She didn't like to be touched without permission. Rae stiffened, her hands tightening to fists.

"It'll wait." His voice husky with promise.

Shaking her head, Rae hid the panic behind her attitude. "If you don't remove your hand, Jorge, I'm gonna remove it for you." She hoped he didn't see the trembling in her hands. She stiffened her knees to keep them from buckling. *It's just Jorge, he's a friend.*

He tightened his grip. "Why so mean Rae, you used to rip my clothes off? I promise, I'm better now."

She didn't doubt it, but she questioned his motive. Studying his dark eyes, she saw worry and fear, or maybe she just wanted to believe he was still one of the good guys. *Does Todd have something on him?*

Phil spoke quietly behind her. "It's your set, Rae."

"She's busy, call someone else," Jorge said. "Isn't that right Rae Lynne?"

She opened her mouth to deny it but Phil beat her to it. "Leave her alone Jorge. Can't you see she's trying to make a fresh start?"

Phil rarely spoke up. She was touched by his defense, twice in one week.

Jorge grumbled close to her ear, "I remember when she'd go on her knees for a pint of Jack. I'm sure you've heard the stories Phil. Did you ever give her a try?"

Heat burned her cheeks. Memories of those days haunted her, threatened her esteem and her sobriety. She'd only wanted the pain to end. Sex, drugs, alcohol and finally razorblades, but nothing stopped it for long.

Phil spoke with quiet authority. "We've all done shit we've regretted. I'm sure you don't want yours brought out for inspection."

Color filled Jorge's face. Swearing under his breath, he let her go. "I can't believe you're defending her."

Phil shook his head.

Swallowing her pain, she turned to Jorge, whispering, "I thought we were friends...you defended me—"

Emotions warred behind his dark eyes. The sadness was gone and only the anger remained. "That was before I was reminded of who you really are...you never cared who you hurt or who you fucked."

Rae flinched. "I hurt you?"

Phil took his arm. "That's enough Jorge. I think you should go."

Jerking his arm from Phil's grasp, he said, "We can't keep doing this. Hasn't she cost us enough?" His dark eyes glistened with tears as he stormed out of the bar.

Phil met her gaze. "You've opened a hornets' nest by coming back here. None of us are going to come away without getting stung."

"What do you mean?"

Phil shook his head.

Devin sneered at her as he hurried to catch up with Jorge in the parking lot. She watched through the grated window as Devin confronted him. Grabbing Jorge by the arm, he looked ready to fight.

Charlie whispered, "Sorry Rae, you still want to go next?" The librarian was on the last song of her set. "I can call someone else if you need a few minutes."

Rae turned away from the scene in the parking lot. "No, I need to sing." She guzzled the last of her beer and hurried to the stage.

Phil was already at the Karaoke machine. He gave her a reassuring nod. Rae was grateful for his friendship. Her numbers were dwindling, Phil and Ditchwater Pete were the only guys in town who didn't treat her like the Whore of Babylon.

She picked up the microphone and as the first strains of the song filled her everything else disappeared. The words came on the screen, she tossed her head back and opened her mouth. She didn't need the words. She knew this one by heart. A man came closer, listening. He was handsome in that clean-cut boy scout kinda of way. She sang to him. Forgetting.

She liked the classic hard rock chicks from the seventies and eighties: Joan Jett, Pat Benatar and Stevie Nicks were some of her favorites. Phil put on a second song for her.

She sang, searching the crowded bar for the Boy Scout. Head and shoulders taller than half the crowd, he wasn't difficult to spot. He looked like he'd be at home around a campfire or in a boardroom. His open, honest face looked almost boyish. In the dim light of the bar, she wasn't sure if his hair was brown or auburn. When he neared the lights from the pool table, his hair gleamed russet, reminding her of the bronze metal flake paint job on an old Mercury street rod she'd painted. He smiled and raised an eyebrow as she sang to him. *I wonder if I'll get lucky tonight.* She needed to get laid but just as the set was ending, he got a phone call and stepped outside. *Just my luck.* She sighed. *You could have had Jorge.* Sometimes it was just better to be alone.

Grabbing another beer, she waited while a few more singers took their turns. She kept a look out for the stranger but he didn't come back inside. Disappointed, Rae nursed the lite beer.

Phil put another set on for her. "I think you're going to like this one Rae. I picked these up for you when I went down to South Carolina last week."

Putting her head close to his, she read the label "Eighties Ladies" with a slash across ladies. It had all her favorites. She kissed his cheek and took her place on stage. Phil's kindness improved her spirits as she sang, "Holding Out for a Hero" by Bonnie Tyler followed by Pat Benatar's "Hit Me With Your Best Shot." She hated to relinquish the mic to the next singer.

"Last call," the bartender shouted.

"Aw man, really? Come on, Charlie, just one more song," Rae Lynne complained. She perched on top of the bar and took hold of the bartender's long, grey-blond braid and tugged.

"Don't you think you've had enough? Bar's closing." Nodding to Phil, he said, "Shut 'er down, Phil."

A look of regret crossed Phil's face as he started packing up.

"Like the song says, you don't have to go home but you can't stay here." Charlie moved down the bar and busied himself picking up empty bottles and cans and wiping things down. He glanced her way, expecting trouble.

Rae didn't want to go home. Being alone reminded her of everything she wanted to forget. She lingered, helping clean up.

Charlie popped her with the end of his bar cloth. "Go home, Rae Lynne."

"I can tell when I'm not wanted." She turned, and the room whirled. She staggered.

"Damn girl, you all right to drive? You want me to call your brother?"

Billy was last person she wanted to deal with. Straightening, she said, "Nah, I got the bike, I'll just take the West Road home. I'll be fine."

"Is that the same bike Dana was talking about? The one for the poker run?" Charlie asked.

"Yep, you going to help out with that?"

He nodded. "You better not let anything happen to that bike. Dana will kill you."

"That's why I'm taking West Road."

"Don't let the West Road light get you," he teased.

"Humph, I ain't afraid of no ghost." She snickered. "Besides, how can that old ghost find anybody wandering around without his head?"

Charlie watched her, his dark eyes concerned. "You sure you're okay to drive?"

"I'm fine, quit worrying. I haven't had that much to drink." She let the screen door slam shut behind her, then stiffened as a group of young guys barreled out of the bar behind her.

Rae fingered the brass buckle on her belt. The pretty butterfly came apart as a pair of brass knuckles, one of which also hid a one-inch blade. She refused to be a victim ever again.

One of the boys bumped her. "'Scuse me." He grabbed her to steady himself.

His friend pulled him off her. "Don't mind 'im, he's drunk. But I'm not. Why don't cha come with us?" The other two shouted pick-up lines and made lewd suggestions.

They don't look old enough to shave, much less drink. She couldn't be more than three years older but she felt ancient. "Thanks guys, but I got to get home to the husband and six kids."

They staggered to their truck, forgetting about her.

"Six kids?"

Rae reached for the buckle but recognized the Boy Scout as he stepped into the light. She shrugged and tightened her jean jacket around her. "It worked."

He gave her a charming grin that was sure to lead many women astray. "I know it's late, but would you want to grab a bite to eat somewhere?"

"I was told never talk to strangers." She buttoned her jacket and climbed on the motorcycle.

"We don't have to talk." He stepped closer. "You're riding a pink Harley?"

Rae Lynne smiled. "It's to raise money for breast cancer."

He shook his head. "Who would ride a pink motorcycle?"

"I would."

"Yeah, but damn, it's such a…it's pink?"

"Excuse me?"

"I'm just saying, Harley's aren't meant to be pink."

"This one is." She put on her helmet.

"You don't have to leave. We could still—"

She started the bike and kicked it in gear.

"At least tell me your name."

Rae pulled out of the parking lot, giving him a two-finger salute. She gave the bike some throttle and roared into the night.

The cool, humid air rushed past and she felt renewed. The roar of the motor and the wind in her face lifted the darkness from her soul. She was sorry the Boy Scout turned out to be a jerk. Maybe it was better to be alone. As she drove into the darkness, she became one with the bike. Nothing else matter, for this moment she was free.

Chapter 5

Rae slowed the bike as she left the highway. The dirt road was soft, and she kicked up dust as the tires slid before biting into the sand. When she reached the newly-paved West road, she let the throttle rev, giving the motorcycle its rein. It answered with a roar as it galloped through the night. A damp chill slapped at her face. Clouds, heavy and low, eclipsed the moon. The motorcycle's headlamp offered dim illumination as she drove deeper into the inky blackness. Fingers of fog slithered up from the swamp on either side of the road.

The road disappeared into a gray shapelessness. Rae slowed, straining to see through the thickening haze. A canopy of low-hanging branches draped in Spanish moss narrowed the road into a dark tunnel. The trees crowded around her. The night rustled with movement. A noise stole her attention from the road as a night bird took flight, its dark wings disappearing into the shadows of the midnight sky.

A blinding light roared out of the mist. Startled, she struggled to retain control of the bike. *The West Road light?* It was coming fast, bearing down on her. Fear short-circuited her senses. The bike jerked as the front tire struck a fracture in the pavement. The tire shifted, skidding towards the canal. Careening out of control, Rae flew over the rocky grade, managing to bring the bike to a stop a split second before hitting the water. Staggering under the weight of the bike, she stumbled but managed to keep her feet. Laughter echoed from the road. She looked up in time to see taillights disappearing.

"God how stupid can I be? The West Road light, really?" Angry tears blurred her vision. Shaking, she dismounted. "Oh God, just be okay." Swiping away the tears, she examined the bike. Flat tire, bent rim. "Okay, not too bad." She exhaled.

Looking around, her spirits plummeted. She'd come off the road on the rocky side. It was too steep to ride up. Across the canal there was a nice, flat, grassy glade but the tide was high and the canal was full. She groaned. *There was nothing to it but to do it.* Strengthening her resolve, Rae put her shoulder to the bike and tried to push it up the slope. Almost at the lip of the pavement, her feet skidded on the rocks and she started a rapid descent backwards. The bike gained speed as they rolled to the bottom of the ravine. Breathless, she fought to keep the bike from falling. The weight dropped her to the ground. The bike fell. She cringed, knowing it was going to end up on top of her. It didn't fall. She opened her eyes. A small boulder kept the bike upright. Rae crawled out from under it, shaking. Sitting amid the rocks, she crossed her arms over her knees and gave in to the tears. "Enough." Locating her cell phone, she hit the speed dial.

The phone rang several times. "Come on, come on." The night was starting to close in around her. She hated the dark. Things rustled in the woods. "Billy," she shouted.

"What?" He grumbled half asleep. "Grimes Towing."

Relief brought fresh tears, "Billy, I—"

"Huh? Rae Lynne? God, do you know what time it is?"

She could hear him fumbling, probably turning on a light. She blew out a breath, trying to reign in the fear.

"Everything okay?" he asked his voice low. "Are you drunk again?"

"I'm okay Billy, I'm not drunk. But-uh-I've had an accident. Somebody ran me off the road."

"What? You shittin' me Rae. You okay? Where are you?"

"Rae? Is she okay? What happened?"

Rae recognized Dana's voice. *Shit, when did they start sleeping together?*

"She's fine. She's on the phone. Now hush and let me find out what's going on."

"Well kiss my—"

"Damn it, Dana, let me find out where she is."

"Please tell me she didn't wreck the bike?"

Rae groaned.

"Let me handle this, okay? Rae, where are you?"

"West Road."

"West Road? Okay, do I need to bring the roll back?"

"Uh-huh." She bowed her head over the phone whispering a little prayer.

He exhaled. "And what will I be picking up?"

"Do I have to tell you that now?"

"Shit, Rae, not the bike. What were you thinking?"

"Billy, I really don't need this right now. Can you just come get me?"

"Sure, are you hurt?"

"She will be!" Dana's voice came over the phone.

The line went dead. Taking a weary breath, Rae struggled to her feet. Her legs threatened to fall out from under her. She grabbed the bike. It banged against the rocks, scraping its paint and falling to its side.

She wanted to sob. "Great, just frigging great." She picked up a rock and skimmed it across the canal, watching as the ripples spread over the surface. The full moon played peek-a-boo with the clouds. Eerie silence sent chills up her spine. A rustling in the woods had her scrambling up the embankment.

Back on the pavement, she struggled to catch her breath. Blinking back tears, she paced the black top, cursing her cowardice. "God, I hate the country, no street lights." What she hated was the dark and her fear of it. She kept a night light on at home. Fumbling in her pocket, she pulled her cell phone out and used it for a flashlight. *What if they see the light and come back?*

Shoving her hands into the pockets of her riding jacket she heard the crackle of paper. Another note. Rae pulled it from her pocket and with the light from her cell phone, opened it. Her hands trembled making the light unsteady. The words, in their big, bold print were easy to read. *Next time I won't miss.* She swallowed the scream and looked around, waiting for someone to jump out of the shadows. *Relax Rae, he just wants to scare you.*

"Yeah, he's doing a bang-up job of it." She crushed the note in her hand. Rethinking her plan to hurl it into the woods, she smoothed it and shoved it back into her pocket.

She'd left her denim jacket hanging on the back on of her bar stool while she sang. She'd gone to the bathroom. Anyone could have put the note in her pocket.

Devin and Jorge were at the bar tonight, but so were half the men from town. Could either of them be behind the notes?

Rae paced the macadam. Her head pounded.

A scream shattered the silence. Her heart sprang to her throat. "It's a bobcat, stupid." It had been years since she'd heard one. "Do bobcats attack people?" She couldn't remember.

Headlights turned onto Broome Road, a cloud of dust billowing behind. Rae strained to see if it was the rollback. They were coming fast. She felt vulnerable, and it made her angry.

The rollback slammed on brakes, coming to inches from her.

"You trying to run me over?"

"I didn't come near you," Billy yelled as he slammed the door.

Rae bursts into tears.

He pulled her into his arms. "Hey, hey, you're okay. Right, you're okay?"

Sobbing and trembling, she nodded.

"It's okay, don't worry, we can fix this." He patted her back.

"I'm okay." She said with a shaky laugh. Feeling foolish she slapped at the tears that continued to fall. "I'm really glad you came." Her voice cracked.

"Of course, I came, you're my pain in the ass little sister."

"I'm just so sorry to drag you out here this late."

"You're safe, that's all that matters."

Rae shivered, her teeth starting to chatter. "I know. I'm safe."

"Not for long," Dana said, stepping down from the truck. "I can't believe you."

"Dana, I'm sorry—"

"Where is it?"

Rae nodded to the canal. "Dana—"

Pushing past her, Dana walked to the edge of the road and glared down into the canal.

"I can fix it."

"I don't think you can." Dana turned away. "Why'd you ride the bike to the bar?"

"I just wanted to show it off." It sounded stupid. "Dana, I never meant for this to happen."

"I know. You never do." She paced. "I've heard it all before, Rae Lynne and I'm tired of it. I'm tired of cleaning up behind you. I'm tired of rescuing you from yourself. I'm tired of getting hurt for trying. You ruin everything..." Dana spun on her heel, scrubbing at her tears and shouting, "You know what this program means to me. This isn't just some charity to me. How could you be so selfish? You couldn't wait to have a drink?"

Rae ran behind her and grabbed her shoulder.

Dana whipped around and glowered.

"I'm not drunk. I was run off the road," Rae said.

"I smell Jim Beam."

"I drink Jack Daniels."

Dana sucked in her breath and screamed, "I don't give a flying...ugh—" She stomped away. "Just stay the hell away from me." She stopped, in a choked voice, asked, "Please tell me you didn't do this for the insurance? I know you need the money but—"

"After all I have done for you—you would think that? Well F-you. You think I would do this on purpose? I did all the work on your bike by myself. I painted it. I did the upholstery. It didn't cost you a fucking dime. You may have bought the bike but I paid for everything else. But I'm the selfish one. Bite me."

Dana crawled into the truck without saying another word.

Rae strode to the edge of the canal and watched as her brother secured the bike.

"You really effed up this time, huh?" Billy said, looking over his shoulder. "Damn it Rae, I can't believe you drove the bike out to get drunk."

"For the last time, I am not drunk. I drank a couple of light beers. Go ask Charlie, he'll tell you." Rae's voice rose. "Someone ran me off the road."

Billy studied her face and shrugged. "Doesn't really matter now, does it? The result's the same. Dana is pissed."

"Well, I am too."

"Come on, help me get this bike out."

Rae started the winch as Billy guided the bike up over the embankment.

Headlights flared as a car came barreling towards them.

Billy frowned. "Who's out at this hour?" The car skidded to a stop.

"It's Jenna," Rae said, recognizing the car.

"I called her." Dana stepped out of the truck, her voice raspy from crying. "I can't handle this right now. I'm sorry, Billy. I'll call you in a few days."

Billy hurried after her and pulled her into his arms. "Dana, we can fix the bike. It's not that bad."

She jerked from his embrace. "Yeah, it's that bad. Some things can't be fixed." She choked back a sob. "It will never be okay again. I can't do this anymore." She rushed to Jenna's ancient Caddy and dove in shouting, "Go, just go."

Billy watched until the tail lights were no longer visible.

"Billy?"

"Not now, Rae Lynne."

She stood in the middle of the road feeling shattered.

"Come on, let's get this bike back to the shop." Billy climbed into the truck. "The sooner we can get the bike fixed the sooner you can fix this."

Rae shoved her hands in her pockets. "She's obviously not my friend."

"Damn it Rae Lynne, not everything is about you. Not only did you wreck the bike, but Dana just found out her mother has another tumor. So, get over yourself."

Rae crumbled the note in her pocket.

Chapter 6

The headlights sped towards her. Laughing, Todd forces himself on her. She heard crying. It wasn't her. Someone else is crying. Rae came up sweating and trembling tangled in the sheets. She staggered to the bathroom to splash cold water on her face. *Someone else was crying?* The nightmares have plagued her for years, she should be used to them. Unwilling to return to bed, she jerked on clothes and stalked downstairs. "Damn it, I wasn't drunk. Call me selfish. After all the work I put into this project."

Rae plucked the truck keys from the ashtray on the kitchen counter. Her hand grazed last night's note. She glared at it, debated calling Mike. For a lawman, he was okay. She trusted him but doubted he'd take her seriously. She shoved the note in the drawer with the odd utensils and the other notes.

Her stomach rumbled, reminding her she hadn't eaten since lunch. She grabbed an apple and took a bite as walked outside. A light flickered in the woods between her house and Phil's. She shivered in the pre-dawn silence and hurried to her truck.

The garage echoed with emptiness, Rae let herself in and turned off the alarm. Every sound hung in the air like the last refrains from a forgotten song. The garage was different at night. She turned her attention to the bike.

Propped forlorn against the lift post, the beautiful paint job scratched, Rae felt the rebuke in the dented frame. "I can't believe she really thought I wrecked the bike on purpose."

Billy's words nagged at her consciousness. "… *she just found out her mother has another tumor.*"

She wanted to run but forced herself to stay. Squaring her shoulders, Rae squatted over her uncle's toolbox searching for a pry bar. What she found was Uncle Clyde's bottle of Ancient Age hidden in the bottom of the box. She put it back. *I don't need a drink. Well, maybe just one sip to settle my nerves.* It looked old, the label dirty and torn. She unscrewed the lid. The bold, sweet perfume of bourbon teased her senses. Her mouth watered, the smoky scent an irresistible lure. She took a swig and coughed. As the fire cooled, the warmth spread through her limbs, bringing that mellow mood she craved. She took another sip. This one burned a little less and relaxed her a little more.

Rae drained the gas from the motorcycle's gas tank and the liquor from the bottle. Pushing the gasoline out of the way she began sanding the paint from the tank. Yawning, she lit the torch to soften the metal so she could pound it back into place. *Just finish this, then go home and sleep.* Her eyelids drooped. Stifling another yawn, she heated the metal. Blinking, she listed to the side, and her eyes fell shut.

Chapter 7

"What the hell do you think you're doing?" The rumble of the metal doors crashing into the ceiling flooded the dim confines of the garage with morning light.

"What?" Rae blinked, the brightness like a knife through her eyes. "What time is it?" Squeezing her eyes shut, she grabbed for her head. She jerked in surprise, still holding the lit torch.

Billy snatched the torch from her hands and turned it off. "You're gonna set your fool head on fire."

"It feels like it already is," she mumbled, listing to the side.

"No, you don't! It's time to get up and get your shit together! Damn it Rae Lynne." He snatched his cap off and slapped his leg. "Are you trying to kill yourself? If you are I'll quit trying to save your ass. Just next time you try to blow yourself up, don't do it in my shop."

"I've been up all night working on the bike. I just want to rest."

Jamming his hat back on his head, Billy grabbed her and pulled her to her feet. "Oh, no you don't, we're gonna talk." He shook her.

"Quit Billy. That hurts."

"This hurts? This is nothing. You are lucky you didn't die, Rae Lynne—"

Rae groaned. "You're over-reacting."

"You were passed out drunk on the shop floor with gas, paint thinner and a torch. Do you not see something wrong with this picture?"

"I'm not drunk."

Holding up the empty bottle of Ancient Age he waved it in her face.

Rae shrugged. "It's only a pint."

"Only a pint, well hell, that's just fine then! I'm not sure what worries me more, Rae—that you seem to think it's all right to be drinking and working in my shop, or the fact that you believe drinking a pint of whiskey isn't a big frigging deal." He paced the garage. "You're an alcoholic, Rae. You need help."

"I'm not."

"Dana called this morning. She doesn't want to see either one of us right now."

Rae rubbed her aching head. "Are you serious about her?" He didn't answer. "She's not one of your hos you can poke and toss away when you're done. She's my best friend."

"We're not discussing this. She doesn't want to see me now so it doesn't matter." Wiping his hand over his mouth, he said. "I can't have you here, Rae. I think you need to pack your things. I'll hire another painter, one I don't have to worry about blowing up the shop in the middle of the night."

"You can't fire me, I'm part owner of this shop."

"Nope, I own my share of the shop, your share is still in probate and I'll happily pay you what yours is worth if you'll just go away." He sighed. "I'm sorry Rae, but if I can't trust you, I don't need you."

"Billy, that is so unfair. Nothing happened."

"Because you got lucky. I can't afford to take the chance that next time…"

"There won't be a next time," Rae said.

"I need someone who'll be sober."

"I have been sober. One night, one frigging night and you're gonna fire me."

"That's just it, Rae, it wasn't just one night. I know of at least three. How many more don't I know about?"

"You have no idea what I've been going through."

"You can't climb into a bottle every time things get a little rough."

"Papa died."

"He was my granddad, too."

"You still have Dad—"

"So do you."

Shaking her head, she muttered, "He hates me."

"He doesn't hate you."

"He never believed me about the rape."

"Damn it, Rae. That was ten years ago. Get over it." Billy kicked a tray of sockets across the cement floor.

Rae jumped.

Billy pinched the bridge of his nose and sighed. "I'm sorry. I didn't mean that."

Rae wrapped her arms over her chest, rocking back and forth, her toes curling in her shoes. "Just get over it? You think I haven't tried?"

"Rae…"

"You think I want to be this fucked up?" She swiped at tears that wouldn't stop falling.
"Every time I close my eyes I see them. I can't stand to be alone but I can't trust anyone." She shook her head. "I wish I could pretend it didn't happen. God Billy, some days—some days it's like it was yesterday."

"You need help Rae, more than I can give you," Billy said on a sigh. "I don't know what to do."

"No one asked you to do anything. I'm fine. So, I have a drink once in a while. You drink, too."

"Yeah, I drink, when I'm hanging with my friends."

Rae reached out and put her hand on his arm.

He jerked away from her.

She jabbed him in the chest. "I need this job."

"You don't act like it."

"How am I gonna save the fishing camp without a job?"

"Maybe you just need to sell it."

Clenching her fist, she shoved her face up to his and screamed. "I will never sell to Todd Bryant."

"Hey, hey what's going on in here? I heard you guys bellowing all the way out to the parking lot." Uncle Clyde swaggered into the garage with his bowlegged shuffle. His rheumy eyes missed little. "My bottle," he said without accusation, then looked at Rae Lynne. "What happened baby girl?"

"What makes you think I did something?" She crossed her arms over her chest and lifted her chin.

The old man snorted. "Because your brother looks like he's having a stroke and you, sweet cheeks, damn…must have been a hell of a night." He ambled over to the bike. "You better start explaining before your dad gets here. He's not as understanding as I am."

"Dad is not going to know." Billy pulled off his ball cap and ran a hand through his hair. "I don't need this." He looked to their uncle, his voice weary. "Can you take her home? I'll tell dad you're sick, Rae, this time, but one more thing happens—"

"I can carry my own self home." She grabbed her things and started towards the open doorway.

Clyde stepped into her path. "Not in your condition, little missy, you won't."

"Fine." Rae rolled her eyes and went around him.

Billy yelled after her. "I mean it Rae Lynne—This is your last chance."

Chapter 8

Rae stomped out of the garage and made a show of hurling herself into her truck. Clyde walked slowly to his and climbed in. He waited, his gnarled hands draped over the steering wheel. She scowled. He tipped his ball cap. With a roll of her eyes, she huffed and joined him. She slammed back against the seat and fumed.

Clyde's lips tilted upward wanting to smile, but he spoke without censure. "Well then, let's get you home." He eased onto the road creeping along ten miles under the speed limit.

The turtle's pace and silence grated on her nerves. Drumming her fingers on the armrests, she stared out the window. Colorful spring flowers rioted for attention. Rae was oblivious, leaning her forehead against the cool glass, she said, "He treats me like a baby."

"If you don't want to be treated like a baby, why do you sit there sulking?"

"What do you know about it?"

"I know you've been nursing that same old hurt for way too long." He squeezed her shoulder.

There was compassion in his eyes. She blinked back tears.

"I know you were hurt, baby girl. Even before—" He hesitated, obviously uncomfortable but determined. "I saw you nearly self-destruct but you found your way."

"I had Papa."

"This is how you honor his memory?"

She bit her lip. "No, but—"

"But nothing, Rae Lynne, this is about you." He slowed, turning to look at her. "You were always a fighter, getting into one scrape or another. Are you going soft now?"

"Todd is trying to take the fishing camp." She hated the whine in her voice.

"Yeah, and I'm doing what I can to stall."

"Even Dad and Connie want me to sell."

"So, you're gonna give up?"

"I can't fight everybody!"

"The only person you have to fight is that one you see in the mirror."

She rode in silence, the anger giving way to hurt. "Dana hates me."

"The bike?"

She let out a breath. "I'll buy you another pint of whiskey."

He chuckled. "Don't bother, that one has been sitting in my tool box for over five years."

"Did you forget it was there?"

"Nope, I remember it all too well." He passed her a five-year coin.

She examined the medallion. "You joined AA?"

"After your Aunt Suzy died, I wanted to follow her." His voice rasped with emotion.

"So why did you quit?" She turned in her seat as far as her seat belt would allow.

He gave a little cackle. "'Cause, I was drinking to forget her but she was everywhere. In the garden she loved, in the faces of our children and grandchildren. I won't ever stop loving her or missing her." He wiped his nose with an old bandana. "I nearly lost what really mattered—my family. I decided remembering was better. I got sober. It hasn't been easy earning back my sons' respect, but I am working on it." He sighed. "One day at a time."

She handed him back the coin. "You had something to live for."

"So do you."

"You heard Billy. He doesn't want me. Dana hates me. Dad, well, he hasn't known what to do with me since mama left."

"Honey, don't sell your family short. Dana and Billy will come around. As for your dad, why don't you give him another chance?"

"I don't know if I can handle more rejection."

He pursed his lips. "Fine, you do what you have to do. But this drinking…if you don't get a hold of it, it's gonna control you."

"Nothing controls me," she said. *I can't even control myself.*

"You can't let what happened define you."

"Now you sound like one of those talk show hosts."

He chuckled. "Yeah, well, sometimes they give decent advice. You gotta let go of the hate."

"I don't know if I can."

He reached over and patted her hand. "You can."

"How?" she demanded as she fell back against the seat crossing her arms over her chest. "They all hate me!"

"Yeah, since you're making it so easy for them?"

"Ugh! I get it. I screwed up. Dana was the only one who stuck with me and I messed it up. Royally."

"So, fix it."

"I'm trying!"

"No, you're wallowing. Self-pity is a useless emotion. Show them what you're made of."

"What am I made of?"

"You're the best of those who created you. Your mom, your dad, your granddad, even me."

Rae snorted. "Yeah, I'm so frigging special. My mom left me and my dad hates me and right now you're the only one who gives a shit about me."

"Watch your language, young lady. You know what your Aunt Suzy always said about cursing."

Rae blushed and parroted: "It shows a lack of education and breeding." She heaved a sigh, dropping her arms to her side. "I guess I really let her down, didn't I?"

Shaking his head, Clyde said, "You didn't let anyone down but yourself, Rae Lynne."

"Dad thinks I'm just like my mama."

"You remind me a lot of Marisol. Your mama wasn't a bad person. She was young and beautiful and lonely. Your dad," he paused, "your dad got caught up in trying to give his family more. Building the business Buddy failed to include Marisol. It got to her."

"She could have gone to work."

"She did. Against your daddy's wishes. She went to work in one of the offices downtown. She was hungry for attention and found it with the wrong man. A married man."

"She left us for a married man?"

"She'd planned to come back but things didn't work out."

"Why?"

"Because she left with Malcolm Bryant."

Straining the tension on the seatbelt, she turned to face her uncle. "Todd's father?" She stammered. "Is that why he hates me? She's the reason for all of this."

"Rae Lynne," he scolded, "Put the blame where it belongs. Todd hurt you. Not your mother."

She tightened her jaw. Her mama might not be to blame for the rape but she'd hurt her. She swallowed the heartache that threatened to choke her, "You've been in contact with her?

He kept his eyes on the road. "It's been a while."

"All these years and you never told me?" She'd trusted him, almost as much as her grandfather. The betrayal felt like a cold wedge between them.

"You never asked about her. I didn't think you were interested." Clyde shifted gears, speeding up to get over the one lane bridge before someone came around the curve.

Rae only had vague memories of her mother. Sometimes a song would come to her, the words in Spanish. She didn't understand the words, but the tune was comforting, like a lullaby.

Rae licked dry lips. Clearing her throat, she said, "Did she know?"

"Rae, you have to understand—"

Raising her voice, she demanded. "Did she know?"

He nodded. "Yes, but—"

Rae slammed her fist on the dash of the truck. "She knew? She knew the son of the man she'd run off with—"

"Rae Lynne, honey"

"No! She knew and she didn't come."

"She couldn't."

"She couldn't? Or she wouldn't. Didn't want to mess up the fancy gig she had for herself?"

"It wasn't like that."

"No? What was it like? She was too busy saving starving children in Africa? What was it, Uncle Clyde, why did she choose not to come to me when I really needed her?"

"When your Mama left she hurt a lot of people."

"Yeah? No shit, Billy and I were some of those people."

"Rae, I'm not your enemy. I'll tell you whatever you want to know, but I won't put up with you shouting at me."

"You're right. I'm sorry." She took a deep breath and let it out slowly. "Why couldn't she come?"

He turned down the lane and slowed the truck, down shifting as he tried to avoid the ruts and pot holes. "Your mama hurt a lot of people, but she angered and embarrassed someone very powerful."

She gave him a blank stare.

"Elva Bryant."

"Todd's mother?" She'd seen her at the trial. She was very remote and proper. The newspapers called her the ice matron in designer clothes.

"She is the Bryant Foundation."

"I thought it was her husband's—" Rae turned to look at her uncle.

"No, it was her money that started the foundation. It was actually started in her grandfather's memory. He was a Bryant. She and Malcolm are distant cousins."

He came to a stop at the back of the camp. The front faced the river. Three old trailers set up on pylons, not really much to look at, but it was home. It was her home.

Shaking her head, she put her hand to the door latch. "I'd hate to have to marry one of my cousins." Clyde had three boys. They'd played together as children but they were Billy's friends; she had nothing in common with them but DNA.

Clyde sighed. "That's money."

"Still, it's only money."

Frowning, Clyde said, "After what happened at the trial, you can still say that?"

Polly had chosen money over friendship. "Thanks for the ride." She leaned on the door, pushing it open, her mind shifting gears.

"Rae Lynne, you know I love you, right?" Clyde leaned forward to look into her eyes.

She met his gaze and nodded.

"You owe it to yourself to get your act together. You're tougher and better than you give yourself credit for." He gave her a sad smile. "You are loved. Know that! Don't let the demons convince you otherwise."

Rae ducked her head and stepped away from the truck.

He called before she shut the door, "Think about what I said, baby girl. I'll see what I can do about the land, but you gotta get control of your life. If you want, we can go to a meeting?"

Leaning into the truck she patted his bristled cheek and smiled. "I'll think about it." She slammed the door and ran up the two flights of stairs.

Chapter 9

"My family has a rich history in Leeward. We've been one of the leading families in this county for nearly two centuries. It's my duty, as mayor, to lead these backwater people into the new era." Todd droned on. The other members of the business lunch had already departed. Only Logan, Devin and Jorge remained. Todd's captive audience. "We've always felt a certain responsibility to these people. Heck, half of them were our former slaves. They look to us to lead them. There's a certain duty that comes with power."

Logan shared a glance with Officer Claudio, wishing he'd left with the others.

Devin, drinking through the better part of a twelve-pack, said, "And his friends pay the duty while he gets the power."

Jorge started for the door. "That's my cue to go."

Todd glowered at the officer. "I didn't tell you to leave."

The man's olive complexion mottled into shades of red. "I have to go on shift, Mr. Bryant. Surely you don't wish me to shirk my duties to the town?"

"Let Deputy Do-Right go," Devin yelled. "I've had enough of him watching my every move."

Todd frowned. "You need to sober up and get ahold of yourself."

Devin grabbed his crotch. "Oh, I've got ahold of myself."

Jorge smirked.

Devin leapt to his feet. "You think it's funny, Barney?" He crowded Jorge, puffing up his chest in challenge. "Ten years with only my own hand for relief. I missed those drunken frat parties with all those sexy coeds."

He grabbed the bottle off the table.

Jorge didn't flinch.

Hooting, Devin opened it and poured it down his throat.

"You've been compensated for your generosity," Todd said.

Devin snorted. "I've received nothing but promises and they don't spend very well."

"Trust me, in due time."

Devin slammed the bottle to the table and screamed, "I'm through trusting and waiting. I want what's coming to me."

Todd kicked back his seat and grabbed Devin behind the neck. He pulled them face to face. Devin, only a few inches shorter than Todd's six and a half feet, looked harder, with muscles defined by a life working out. The mayor was softer, his muscles honed by games not survival. Yet as they stood toe to toe, it was Devin who backed down.

"It's all good. We're good Todd."

Todd's predatory smile sent a chill down Logan's spine. The mayor patted Devin on the back, the friendly gesture seemed somehow threatening. "We've got big plans. You've got to be patient just a little longer. I take care of my friends."

Logan had a bad feeling about this deal. "I should be going, too. I've got a lot to do when I get back to the office."

"You really need an office down here. I'll have something set up. I don't want you being so far away when I need you."

Devin snorted, but the sound held an underlying menace. He reached for the beer the waitress set on the table.

With a quelling look at Devin, Todd insisted, "Stay, the night's still early." He continued his monologue on the Barton-Bryant pedigree. "My mother's family was one of Leeward's founding families. There are few families still here who can make the same claim."

"The Grimes family have been here just as long." Devin's words slurred as he lifted his head to give Todd a drunken grin.

Todd slammed his fist on the table. "The Grimes' aren't even worth considering,"

Startled at the burst of anger, Logan studied the two men.

Devin grinned. "You've sure spent a lot of time considering one family member."

"Shut up, Devin."

Devin patted the waitress on the backside, sliding his hand over her tight pants. She sidestepped but he caught her wrist and pulled her into his lap.

"Let me go." A look of panic filled her eyes.

Todd ignored them.

Claudio cleared his throat. "Leave her alone, Kinnion."

"Get your own girl." He wrestled with the girl. "Let's talk about whatever pops up." He giggled at his own crude joke. The more the waitress fought, the more excited he became and the less intoxicated. He shoved her shirt up, exposing her white bra.

Logan raised his voice. "I thought we were here to conduct business."

Devin released the girl. She stumbled from the room and nearly knocked over a homeless man in her haste.

Todd glared and nodded his head to Claudio. "Get rid of the bum."

Jorge glanced at the man. "Better move along, Pete."

Ducking his head down, the man shuffled towards the kitchen.

Logan rose and unrolled a map. "We really need to discuss the EPA. Are they going to allow us to build here?" He pointed to the map. "Isn't this area considered wetlands?"

"The whole fucking town is a wetland." Devin gave a one-fingered salute.

Todd waved away his concern. "Don't you worry about that, I can get the license and permits we need. Trust me, I know what I'm doing."

Logan didn't trust him. "I want to check with the EPA before I agree to go any further."

"I told you I would handle it. Now quit worrying. We're going to make a lot of money on this deal. I don't want word to get around until we have everything under contract."

"You don't want that bitch to cut a fuss," Devin grumbled.

Todd glowered at him but Devin was oblivious.

Logan decided he'd best follow his own counsel. He'd be checking those permits for himself.

Officer Claudio gave him a barely perceptible nod as if he'd read his mind.

"Just let me deal with the official stuff and you worry about getting a crew together."

Logan gathered his papers and shoved them in his brief case. "I'll draw up plans and make sure everything is approved—" He nodded to Jorge.

Todd said, "Just get your men together and be down here within the week. I'm anxious to get started."

"You can't get a project this size started in a week."

"If you aren't up to it, Birdsong. I have other contractors I can deal with—"

"I thought there were still some negotiations concerning the land."

Devin snorted and said, "No negotiations necessary, they'll be handing it to him on a silver platter."

Todd's look silenced him. "We all stand to make a nice profit from this project. Let's not blow it, shall we?"

Logan frowned, the niggling sensation at the back of his neck warning him this was more than just a risky venture. Only his fear of bankruptcy kept him from pulling the plug on the deal.

Putting his hand on Logan's shoulder, Todd said, "My wife has this little fund raiser she's been working on. Why don't you join us?"

Logan hesitated. "I don't—"

"I won't take no for an answer," Todd said, giving his politician's smile. "My wife would really like to have you there. I like to please my wife...with the small things." He guffawed. "Gives me a lot more freedom with the big things." He elbowed Logan as if sharing some inside joke. In a more serious tone he said, "I have to insist. This contract hinges on your commitment to the Bryant Foundation."

"Fine, I'd love to meet your wife. Will your mother also be present?"

"Good God, yes, Mama wouldn't miss a black-tie event. It is The Barton Mall Gallery opening, and the Bryant Foundation is one of the sponsors."

"Art gallery?" Logan wondered if he could schedule dental surgery for that night.

"Yes, an art gallery. We've been remodeling Main Street, one of those grants for gentrifying the neighborhood."

Logan forced a smile and said, "Sounds like a wonderful time."

"You do understand what is meant by black tie?" Todd asked.

Logan wanted to smack the arrogance off the asshole's face. Looking up from his briefcase, he said, "Yeah, no torn jeans and leave the *Bubba knows Best* T-shirt at home."

Devin spewed his beer.

The tension eased from Jorge's face.

Todd wiped spittle from his cheek. Narrowing his eyes, he scowled. "Don't embarrass me, Birdsong. You won't like it if you do."

Logan rolled his eyes. As he strode towards the door, he called over his shoulder, "If you're worried about being embarrassed, you might want to update your hairstyle."

"Looks like you belong in a boy band," Kinnion added, his laughter following Logan out of the restaurant.

Chapter 10

The old trailers looked like long-legged silver water bugs, beautiful only to another water bug. For Rae Lynne, the old Airstreams were home. Here, her grandfather had made her feel safe and loved.

Rae drifted through the rooms, viewing the photos, paintings, and sculptures she'd created. The memories filled her with longing. She picked up a paint brush. It quivered in her hands. She tossed it down. "I need a drink." She shoved the thought away.

Out onto the balcony the scent of the river calmed her. The smell of the pines mingled with the brackish water and lapped lazily at the rocky beach. She gripped the rail; the weathered wood bit into her palm. The twelve-foot wide structure was curved to connect the three trailers in a u-shape. Her grandfather had salvaged the old trailers and rebuilt them into private suites. Her grandfather's trailer was at one end of the horseshoe while hers was at the other. Billy's trailer sat in the center, rarely used.

Spring flowers perfumed the air. A bird called to its mate. A Great Blue heron flew up from the reeds, spreading its wings. Rae never tired of viewing the wildlife along the shore. She'd often painted scenes from the river for her grandfather. Tears streamed down her cheeks. *God, I miss you.* She felt rudderless without him.

Lifting her face to the sun, a gentle breeze dried her tears. Gasoline and a torch, she shook her head. She hated that Billy was right. She'd been stupid.

The ground floor was filled with more memories. Rae touched a cabinet her grandfather built and the antique table she'd helped him restore. Her graduation picture and diploma hung on the wall. He'd been so proud when she'd been accepted to UNC. Guilt churned her stomach. He wouldn't be so proud right now.

From under the sink in the kitchen she pulled a pint of black label Jack

Daniels. The thirst clawed at her like the talons of a raging beast. "One drink and everything will be okay." Uncle Clyde's words echoed in her head. *"If you don't get a hold on this thing baby girl, then it is gonna destroy you."* She could almost feel the cool sweet burn of the whiskey. Opening the bottle, she put it to her lips. The accusations and disappointment in Dana's eyes nearly choked her.

Rae jerked the bottle away and slammed it into the sink, screaming as the glass shattered. Tears and snot poured from her face as she turned the water on high and hot. She let it run until not even the smell remained. Carefully she picked the broken bottle from the sink and tossed it into the trash.

In a cleaning frenzy Rae exorcized the demon alcohol, pulling bottles secreted about the house. She tossed them into the trash, not even taking time to dump the contents. Rae cleaned, scrubbed and scoured until her arms ached and she was coated in sweat. Exhausted, she dragged the clinking and clanging garbage out to the metal trash cans.

Her arms quivered as she struggled to lift the heavy bag over the rim of the can.

"Hey, you need some help with that? What are you doing home so early?" Phil took the bag and stuffed it into the trash can.

Rae hadn't heard Phil approach. Her heart pounded, she fought to control her breathing. "Hi Phil, thanks, I wasn't feeling well. Uncle Clyde brought me home." She put the lid back on the can and fastened it to keep the racoons out.

"That's why your truck's not here? I thought maybe you'd wrecked it, too." His eyes widened, realizing he shouldn't have said anything.

"How did you know I'd been in a wreck?"

He looked down at his feet. "I had breakfast at the Depot this morning."

"And they were talking about me?"

He met her eyes, coloring. "Well, no, Jenna was just trying to make Dana feel better. I just happened to overhear." He shrugged. "You really wrecked the bike?"

Rae, hoping to make her escape, said, "Yeah, well, I need to get back—"

"I was just wondering..."

Not wanting to be rude, she waited.

"They're getting ready to open the art gallery? You know that new place at the old mall?"

Rae shifted her weight and tried to think of some way to avoid what she was afraid was coming. "Well, I'd—"

"You want to go?" He blurted. "I know you like art. You're an artist and all. I did some work for the owners and got a couple of tickets to the grand opening."

She'd heard about the gallery opening. The Junior Woman's League and the Bryant Foundation had acquired grants to remodel the old mall and turn it into a gallery and artisan center. If she was going to stay in Leeward then she would have to take the chance of running into Todd. But did she want to brave facing him on his own turf? Taking a deep breath, she said, "Sure Phil, I'd like to see the new gallery."

He grinned. "Great I'll pick you up Friday night around eight?"

Rae never let a guy pick her up. *Probably why I don't have many dates?* Shaking her head, she said, "I'll probably have to work. How about I meet you there?"

Disappointment marred his face. "Okay, yeah sure. Sure. Then I'll just... I'll see you there. Eight o'clock?"

Rae nodded and waited for him leave. She watched as he disappeared down the path that connected their properties. She went upstairs to shower and call her uncle. *I guess I'll give meetings another try.* Her hand hovered over the phone. There was another call she needed to make, first. She dialed the familiar number. "Ms. Sandy, hi, it's Rae."

Chapter 11

Rae stopped her truck at the end of the lane and yanked the mailbox door. It always seemed to stick when her hands were full of bills. It popped open with a sound like a vapor lock and a smell like methane gas. The mangled fur and darkened flesh didn't register, not at first. White bone gleamed in stark contrast to the blackening blood pooling in the shadows of the dented old mailbox. It was the sicky-sweet odor of decay that registered this was once a living thing.

A flash of a memory tugged at her consciousness. The smell of mold and decay and the overpowering scent of cologne. The truck rolled and Rae shook the memory, throwing the truck into park.

The paper, stuck in the congealing blood seemed like a label on some macabre package, the words in heavy black ink "Next time, this could be you." She choked back a scream and slammed the door. With shaking hands, she called Mike. It was time to report the notes.

The notes hadn't really frightened her, until now. Rae waited in front of the mailbox, the bills still clutched in her sweaty hand. Her mind whirled mixing the past and the present. She'd smelled dead things that night. She'd feared they were going to kill her. After the trial, she'd wished they had.

Mike pulled up beside by her. "Hey Rae Lynne." He nodded to the mailbox. "You want me to take a look?"

Rae blushed, dropped the bills onto the armrest and moved her truck to the other side of the lane. She got out and waited.

Mike parked the cruiser and got out. He pulled on a pair of latex gloves and opened the mailbox. "Damn." He stepped back and took a deep breath, then proceeded to bag the evidence. "Sounds like you have a fan."

Shifting from foot to foot, Rae looked away. "Yeah, I have several in town."

"You said there are other notes?" Taking off his gloves he put them in another bag and stowed the evidence in a cooler in the trunk of his car.

"Yeah, back at the house."

He nodded. "I'll follow you."

Rae led the way up the lane. They parked, and Mike followed her into the kitchen.

The kitchen was an eclectic blend of old and new. The Formica top bar doubled as a filing cabinet. Rae opened the drawer under the rotary-dial phone. The letters were tossed haphazardly inside. They seemed more sinister in the morning light.

Mike grabbed her hand before she touched the notes. Putting on a new glove he said, "Just in case there's any evidence left." He picked the notes up and placed them in a plastic bag. "Tell me everything you can about the notes."

Rae stared at the bag, her stomach churning. "I just thought it was a sick joke."

Mike nodded. "Yeah." He asked questions, made notes and then asked the same questions again.

Rae glanced at the old cuckoo clock she'd refurbished. The cuckoo was Poseidon on a seahorse. The clock house looked like something you'd see in an aquarium. The time showed she was late for work. "Mike, I really have to go. We've been swamped at the shop lately."

He closed his notebook and put it back in his pocket. "Fine but be careful and if you get another note, don't touch it. Call me first.

Rae rushed out the door, Mike on her heels.

"You might want to start locking your doors."

Rae retraced her steps and located the house keys they'd seldom used.

***

The scent of Polo permeated the interior of the sports car. The memory of Todd's cologne the night he'd invaded her body and damaged her soul gripped her by the throat. The notes, the dead thing in her mailbox and now this--she needed a drink.

Her lungs began to seize and blackness filled her head. Rae fell out of the car. Crouching beside it, she took deep breaths and tried to slow her pulse. She could see a half empty bottle discarded under the passenger seat. She closed her eyes and slowing her breathing, she practiced the relaxation exercises she'd learned in therapy.

"What the hell are you doing?" Her father demanded stomping into the garage.

Heat burned her cheeks as shame washed over her. "Just catching my breath," The scent lingered, taunting her. She felt in her pocket for the coin Uncle Clyde had given her. Rubbing it helped her to focus.

The notes were escalating, another one had been tucked under the wiper blade of her truck when she'd gone to lunch. "It'll be your fault if your friends get hurt." Running away would make her a victim again. She couldn't do it. Rae was starting to remember things about the night she was raped. She was determined to discover the identity of the third rapist and that could only be done in Leeward.

"We ain't got time for that. Let's get this get this piece of shit out of here." He lifted his ball cap and scratched his head. "I think every fool in town must be parked out in our lot. You got enough work here to last the rest of the summer."

Rae hid a smile. Uncle Clyde had called everyone he knew and told them to come in and get paint and body work done. His plan to help her save the camp. "Yeah, no problem," she said, taking a deep breath, she started to climb back into the car.

"Rae Lynne?"

She turned glad for the delay.

Buddy rubbed the bill of his dirty ball cap. "I heard about the bike." He nodded to where the Harley sat covered by a tarp in the corner.

Rae waited for him to yell and cut her down.

"You know I think this place is poison for you."

She didn't have the energy to defend herself.

"Clyde tells me you've been going to meetings."

Unsure how to answer, she simply nodded.

"Well, that's good, Clyde understands." He rattled the change in his pocket. "I think staying here's a bad idea, but if you can come up with the money for the camp,

I won't fight you. Sell it or don't, it's up to you."

It was the closest he'd come to accepting her. She stammered, "Thank you."

"Don't thank me, Pistol, I think it's a mistake…but, damn it Rachel, Rae—" his eyes were bright as if fighting tears. "I'm-uh glad you're here." He stalked away.

Something shifted inside filling her with an emotion she feared she'd lost: *hope*. With renewed determination, she pulled the bottle of Polo from beneath the seat and crawled back inside the sports car.

Chapter 12

Rae rammed her shoulder against the door, nearly spilling to the tarmac when the truck door finally opened. "No regrets." Papa's old Chevy needed some minor maintenance but it was a good truck, a classic. She missed her F150.

Late, Rae concentrated on putting one foot in front of the other without falling off her three-inch-heels. "These things should come with training wheels," she grumbled. Her reflection in the tinted glass doors surprised her. With her tattoos, mostly hidden by the wave of her hair falling across her shoulders, and her minimal body jewelry, she looked almost normal.

A glimpse of Ditchwater Pete mirrored in the window caused her to hesitate. He looked unwell. Worried, she turned, but he melded into the shadows of the shops across the street. Jostled by the crowd, Rae was carried along the swell like a leaf on the tide, Pete forgotten amid the glitz and glamor.

Men in dark suits escorted ladies in fashionable evening dresses. Rae's short red dress drew attention though she saw others in similar styles. She felt confident in her appearance. Her habit of morning swims kept her legs toned and her mother's heritage blessed her complexion. Though few in the small community would call being half Mexican a blessing.

Rae scanned the crowd for her date. The gallery opening attracted not only the elegant crowd, but also the up and coming young business types. She wondered if Dana would attend and if she'd say something about the bike.

A sea of bodies bottle-necked their way out of the main lobby. Rae had to admit, she was impressed. Several little shops sporting everything from pet clothes to jewelry filled the newly restored Main Street. It was part of a rejuvenation project the Chamber of Commerce and the Junior Women's League had been working on for several years. The Barton Mall Gallery's grand opening was 'the culmination of years of dedication'. At least that's what the brochure someone thrust into her hands said.

Rae spotted Jorge. He narrowed his eyes at her. *Will he tell Todd I'm here?*

"You're late." Phil suddenly appeared at her side.

Rae sucked in her breath and opened her mouth to berate him. Phil looked edgy and pasty. "Are you okay?"

"I'm fine." He swallowed. "A lot more people here than I thought." He looked her over. "You should have worn an evening dress. It's classier," he grumbled. "But—this looks nice."

"Yeah, well, thanks, I think."

"I'm sorry, I don't like crowds." He pulled at the collar of his shirt. "Is it hot in here?"

"We can leave if you want. We can always come back later to see the displays."

Hope filled his eyes, but quickly faded. He shook his head. "No, we should stay. It's important to support the town."

Phil looked good in his dark suit, if a little pale. His whiskey brown hair was still damp and curling at his nape as it dried. Rae wondered if he ever wore contacts as he pushed his glasses in place.

"Let's get out of the crush." He took her elbow and ushered her quickly though the first-floor exhibits.

Rae struggled to keep up. "Phil, I'd really like to look at the displays."

He heaved a sigh and slowed.

"Are you sure you don't want to go somewhere else?" Rae asked.

"I'm fine. Let's look at the art stuff." His attention drifted to something else.

Rae looked to see what had snagged his interest. She caught a glimpse of Jorge and the stranger from the bar. Heat burned a path from her breast to her thong as the dark red-head flamed under the pot lights. From the second-floor balcony, she could study the handsome stranger without his knowing. Phil repeated her name. Blushing, she murmured, "What?"

The stranger glanced up. From this distance, she couldn't see that his eyes were hazel but she remembered their color.

"Is something wrong?"

"No, no, I was just...you're not really interested in art, are you?"

Phil shoved his hands in his pockets and took them out as if unsure where he was supposed to put them. "No, not really."

"Then, why did you ask me to come?"

Phil led her away from the balcony, stopping in front of the next display. "You like art."

Rae squeezed his arm and smiled.

"Besides, I got the tickets for free. It seemed a waste not to use them."

Rae rolled her eyes and took her hand from his arm.

"Who's that with Phil Archer?"

"That's Rae Lynne Grimes."

"She's got some nerve showing up here."

The echo of whispers surrounded them. Rae felt the blood rush to her head.

"You heard about what she did to poor Polly?"

"I heard she attacked her in her own store."

Phil paled.

Rae stopped in front of a stained-glass piece, barely registering the vibrant beauty.

"I didn't think it would be a problem—bringing you here." He took a napkin from a passing waiter and wiped his brow. "You won't cause trouble, will you?"

She started to tell him to fuck off, but a waiter offered her a glass of champagne. She could smell the wine, feel the tiny bubbles bursting in her mouth. Rae forced herself to look away.

A crowd gathered around them, pushing and shoving and whispering.

Rae sidled away from the crowd and kept walking until she found a quiet spot. There was no sign of Phil. Tuning out the crowd, she refocused her attention on the exhibits. The world disappeared and for the first in a long time she enjoyed herself.

Rae looked up from a display of glass vases. The heavy-lidded gaze of the Boy Scout stared back at her, sending a rush of heat crashing through her. His slow smile sent shivers across her nerves. Rae looked away, unsure how to flirt.

"Fancy meeting you here and in such a pretty dress." His accent was a soft cadence. "I'm sure you didn't ride that Hog with those heels."

Looking him over from his polished cowboy boots to the tailored fit of his tux, she grinned. "You'd be surprised what I can ride wearing these heels." She blushed realizing that hadn't come out quite as she'd intended.

"Are you the entertainment tonight?"

Heat burned her skin nearly the color of her dress. *Did he think she was one of Todd's whores?* Turning on her heel she stumbled into another stranger. "Excuse me." She grabbed his arm to steady herself and glared into eyes the color of a midnight storm.

A slow grin showed beneath a long corkscrew curl of ebony. "I will accept whatever excuse has a lovely lady falling into my arms." He glanced behind her at Logan. "This man bothering you? I can have him escorted from the premises." He was her height, slight of build with a swarthy complexion. His dark eyes had a glassy sheen, his skin, a gray undertone.

Glancing at Logan she gave the stranger a tight smile and shook her head. "No, he...thank you, I should go."

He held her hand. "So soon? But we've not been introduced." His voice resonated with the rhythm of the Delta, smoky, dark with just a little twang.

"Back off Jack." Boy Scout stepped closer.

Rae Lynne looked up into eyes flaring from green to gold. "And who the hell do you think you are?"

He stepped back. "What did I say to piss you off?"

Straightening to her full height, Rae said, "Oh, I don't know, 'are you the entertainment'?"

Frowning he said, "Yeah? And the other night, you were singing at the bar..."

Rae snorted. "I was singing Karaoke."

He shrugged.

Yanking her hand from the vampire wannabe, she said, "You really thought I was a singer?"

He nodded. "You're real good."

She turned and feigned interest in a sculpture of driftwood and sea glass.

"You like it, cher?" The dark man insinuated himself into their conversation.

Rae recognized the Cajun accent. One of her grandfather's friends had come from Louisiana. "I'm still deciding, you?"

"Com se com sa. Some days I despise it, others I adore it." His dark eyes were like sunlight on the Mississippi, but the shadows underneath told a darker story. Rae knew what lay beneath his charm—one addict recognizes another. "C'est la'vie. I'm its creator. The artiste," he said it as if he were the only one. "Ezekiel La Port." He bowed with a flourish.

Biting her lip, Rae tried not to smile. He was being pretentious. She met Boy Scouts' frown and winked. She moved to the next exhibit, her entourage in her wake.

"Are you going to make me beg for your name, cher? It's a small town, I bet I could pull anyone over here and they would tell me your whole life story." Ezekiel waved a couple over.

Several others shifted closer. Rae narrowed her eyes and dared any of them to speak.

"Rae," she said as she stalked away.

"Ray? As in a ray of sunshine?" Boy Scout asked walking beside her.

Stopping short of the next display, she snorted. "Yep, that's me, just a little ray of sunshine." A chuckle rumbled in her throat.

"You have a lovely laugh."

Her body's reaction to his husky baritone was electric. She pushed that thought away.

"What's your name?"

"Logan."

She liked the way his eyes crinkled when he smiled. There were streaks of gold in his dark red hair. From a distance, he'd looked tanned but up close she could see his skin was just crowded with freckles. She wondered if he had freckles all over and yearned to play connect the dots.

Ezekiel grabbed her hand, startling her. He lifted it to his lips and brushed a kiss over her knuckles.

Jerking her hand free, she snarled. "Don't ever do that again."

Logan clenched his fists.

Rae's face burned.

Oblivious, Ezekiel said, "Come, tell me you find me charming."

"I find you annoying, Monsieur La Port. Go away."

Logan offered her his arm.

Sparing one last glare for the artist, she allowed Logan to lead her away.

Logan couldn't believe Rae was the same girl from the bar. The red dress was doing things to him that he'd not had to worry about since high school.

Rae slowed in front of a statue. Logan wasn't sure whether it was a scorpion or a woman doing a backbend. He tilted his head.

Laughing, she asked, "Not a fan?"

"I'm not sure what it is?"

"I think it's open for interpretation." She pointed to the tag that read *Scorpion Woman*.

"Okay, that clears things up." He shook his head.

"So, you're new in town?" Her soft alto held just a hint of southern accent like sweet tea on a hot day.

He shifted his weight to hide his arousal. A voice shouldn't have the power to make him into a randy teenager. "I'm a contractor."

"Just passing through."

Her dark eyes moved over him, setting him on fire.

Rae stepped to the next display. He was mesmerized by her grace. She moved like a dancer. She snagged her heel on a bit of carpet. He reached for her but she recovered, hiding her stumble with a little dance step. He smiled. She was amazing, he'd have gone head first over the balcony.

Logan felt more at ease as they entered the next exhibit, recognizing the traditional watercolor landscapes. He could now give a reasonable opinion without sounding like a complete moron. "My office isn't far from here." She glanced up and he rubbed his mustache off his lip, wary of making a misstep. "How about you? Are you from Leeward?"

"Oh yeah, I'm the prodigal daughter." Rae scowled at a group as they passed.

"…returned in disgrace," someone muttered.

Frowning, Logan looked her over. "You don't look disgraced."

With a soft, feminine snort, Rae nodded to the crowd. "They'd say my whole life has been a disgrace." Pink crept up her chest burning her cheeks, but her dark eyes were defiant as she walked down the hall. She pretended interest in a group of paintings of old barns, allowing him to catch up.

"They're just jealous."

Rae strode across the gallery to another exhibit.

"Hey, slow down before you fall off those stilts." He grabbed her elbow.

Rae smiled at him, her dark eyes luminous.

A frisson of awareness slid over his skin. There was more to her story than tattoos and whispers from the other patrons. He might owe Mayor Bryant an apology, this night was turning out much better than expected.

"She's not falling for me."

Logan, recognizing the voice of the Cajun, turned to order him to get lost, but La Port wasn't speaking to him. Someone stood just out of his sightline.

A raspy whisper replied, "I'm not paying you to fail."

A shiver of unease clanged a warning. Something was going on here and Rae was the target. She was already two displays away. Logan hesitated, trying to hear more of the conversation.

A group of young artists crowed into the alcove, talking too loud. He searched but the Cajun was gone. Frustrated, he hurried to catch up to Rae. She'd paused to study a group of glass sculptures.

Leaning close, Logan inhaled the sweet scent of her perfume. She smelled of sunshine and brown sugar. "You smell delicious."

"There you are! I've been looking for you."

Rae's face flamed. "Phil?" She glanced up at Logan.

He saw by her expression she would leave him. He glared at the newcomer.

Rae made the introductions. "Phil, I'd like you to meet Logan—"

"Birdsong." Logan held out his hand.

She smiled at him, her dark eyes softening, and nodded. "Logan Birdsong, my neighbor Phil Archer."

Phil accepted his handshake with a muttered, "Birdsong."

"Archer." Logan studied the smaller man.

Rae filled the awkwardness with chatter, describing the art work she'd seen here and how it compared to Raleigh.

"Mr. Birdsong?" A waiter handed Logan a note.

Logan frowned. *From Todd, who else?* Turning to Rae, he said, "I have to go handle some business. Can we get together later? A drink, coffee?"

Shaking her head, she said, "I'm here with Phil."

Phil gave him a smug smile and lifted his chin in challenge.

Logan forced a smile. "We keep getting the timing wrong."

She nodded. "Maybe next time."

"Third time's the charm." He sighed and watched as Rae disappeared amid the crowd.

Phil crossed the second-floor gallery at a quick pace. Rae didn't try to keep up. Other patrons came between them and she lost sight of him. As she scanned the crowd, it was Todd she found only ten feet away. Flustered, she ducked into the ladies' room hoping he hadn't noticed her.

"I can't believe you gave Phil tickets to the opening."

Rae recognized Polly's voice and retreated. Glancing out the door, she saw Todd with a group of business men. Rae debated her options. She could take a chance at slipping past Todd or stay in the ladies' room and become a target for Polly and her friend. Polly's barbs didn't frighten her half as much as Todd's malice.

"You said to give free tickets to all the contractors." A woman whined in one of the stalls. "How was I to know he was going to bring Rae Lynne Grimes?"

Rae stiffened.

Polly sighed. "It can't be helped, now. It's not as if we can ask him to leave."

The stall door opened. "I'm sorry Polly. If I'd known—" The woman spotted Rae and paled. She cleared her throat several times.

"You didn't know." Polly stepped out of a stall, straightening her gown. She met Rae's gaze in the mirror and stilled.

"Shall I call security?" The woman darted to the door.

Neither Polly nor Rae answered.

"What are you doing here?" Polly demanded. She moved with an economy of movements. Polly had always been calm and graceful, but now, it seemed she'd honed a different skill, that of avoiding conflict.

Polly had betrayed her by becoming a witness for Todd at the rape trial. News of their hasty wedding and the birth of their daughter just a few months later, and Rae understood. Polly was no longer that sweet, plain girl, easily susceptible to the charms of a conniving man. Her pale blonde hair perfectly coifed, make-up expensive and flawless, she was now the leader of Leeward's society.

"Quit the games Polly, you know I'm here with Phil Archer." Taking a deep breath, Rae said, "I'm sorry about the other day."

Polly stiffened. "I don't care about the shop. No one was there. I do care about tonight. The Junior Women's League has put a lot of effort into this gallery. I do not wish to be embarrassed."

"I'm not here to cause trouble. I'm an artist—"

Polly gave a delicate snort. "I don't consider spraying paint on old cars, art."

"I do have a degree in art."

"I don't care about your degree. If you cause a scene and upset Todd, I'll make sure you pay."

Rae sighed. "I'm just here for the art."

"You nearly ruined his life, I won't allow you to do it again."

"I'm not the one who terrorized him." Rae reached for the door. "But know this, Polly, I'll not be his victim again. I'll do whatever I have to do to survive."

"If you think we'll let you ruin our chances for the White House, you'd better think again. We know how to rid ourselves of trouble makers."

Rae yanked the door open, Polly could see the gathering crowd of eavesdroppers. Rae smirked. "Thanks for the warning. I'll just go find my date." Rae skirted the crowd and found a haven behind a wall of glass shelves.

Rae took a deep breath, allowing her heart to slow its staccato. She watched Polly join her husband and the group of businessmen. After few quiet words and a nod, they excused themselves. Todd's color heightened, he looked around, angry. His grip threatened to bruise her arm as he pulled Polly into a dimly lit corridor. Rae couldn't hear what they were saying but she saw the fear and pain on Polly's face. Her stomach cramped. She never thought her presence would put Polly in danger. Phil joined them. Todd stalked off, leaving Phil to comfort Polly. Rae slipped away and hurried to the gallery entrance, praying Todd didn't see her.

Ezekiel La Port stopped her at the door. "Leaving so soon?"

"I have to work tomorrow." He tried to engage her, following her out to the sidewalk. She hurried across the street to the parking lot. Rae was relieved when the truck started.

Backing out she caught a glimpse of Logan climbing into an old muscle car. She sighed. *Next time, maybe.*

Chapter 13

Rae Lynne stumbled to her truck with her to-go cup in hand. "I shouldn't have stayed at the gallery so late." She yawned, feeling more like sixty-four than twenty-four. She'd had too many sleepless nights working on the Harley. Between AA and the stress of trying to save the camp, it was all starting to take a toll. A box in the bed of her truck caught her attention. She hadn't put it there. A dark puddle oozed from beneath the package. Leaning over the side she flipped up the flap to reveal a pale pink nose covered in blood. She leapt back, knocking her coffee cup and splattering the contents on the ground. "Shit!" Fishing her cell phone from her pocket, she called Mike. Her hands trembled and tears pricked her eyes.

"It's Rae. The fucking psycho struck again. I've got another bloody one. Looks like it used to be a cat." She choked back a sob.

"Shit, you okay? I'm here alone until Jorge gets in."

"Yeah, I'm fine. I'm more mad, than scared. I can't believe this bastard killed a cat."

"Where are you?"

"Home. I found the cat in a box on the back of my truck." Rae looked through the dense copse of trees, wondering if her neighbor had anything to do with her present this morning.

"You on your way to work?"

"Yeah." Rae's hands trembled. She wasn't sure how she'd manage to hold a paint gun steady.

"Are there any tire tracks or foot prints around your truck?"

Rae looked around, but the drive was covered in rock-reject and didn't show foot prints. "There's no tire tracks. Unless they walked through the woods—" Her boots crunched as she trod over the gravel and examined the grass on either side.

"I don't see anything in the grass."

He sighed. "All right, drive it over to me."

Rae shoved her phone into her pocket and wished she had time to drive by the Depot before work. This is going to be a fun day.

Rae pulled into the gravel parking lot of the Leeward Police station. Mike stepped outside as soon as she parked. "Morning Mike," she said, stepping out of the truck.

"Rae Lynne." He went straight to the bed, popped his latex gloves into place and reached for the box.

Rae cringed. The note was soaked with blood and other fluids. Mike bagged it, then handed it to her to read. "You didn't heed my warning. Now, your friends and family will pay the price." She took a deep breath fighting the panic attack. "Oh god, is he serious?"

"What the fuck?" Mike pulled an engraved collar from the destroyed flesh. He wiped at the blood and read the tag. "Aw man, no."

Rae recognized the collar. It was the one Jenna's cat wore. "No, not Boots?" Turning her head, she spat in the gravel but that did little to relieve the taste of bile. "I didn't even know he was missing."

Mike frowned and shook his head. "Wouldn't Jenna put up signs or something if the cat was missing? She's had Boots since she was in school."

Rae stiffened. "I don't know. I should go. I can't stay here and let this maniac…" Her mind whirled, and she stifled a sob. "Oh God, I can't do this again."

Mike rubbed her shoulder but she shrank from touch. "If you run he wins."

"And if I don't?" She glanced in the back of the truck and blinked.

"Just a few days ago you were determined to stay and fight."

Shaking her head, Rae said, "What if next time it's not a cat, what if it's Toby?" Toby, Jenna's four-year-old boy with his big brown eyes and a thousand questions. She couldn't bear the thought of anything happening to him.

"I'll protect Toby and Jenna."

"And what about the rest of the people I love?"

"Rae," Mike said on a sigh. "Do what you want, but who's to say they'd be any safer with you gone? Get me a list. Let's put this joker behind bars."

Rae swallowed and took a deep breath. "The only ones I know who'd be this sick are Todd and Devin, or some of their henchmen."

Mike nodded. "Don't say anything about the cat until I know for sure it's Boots. For now, let's keep this quiet. Lock your doors, don't go anywhere by yourself. Do you still have your granddad's game cameras?"

Rae nodded.

"All right, we're going catch this bastard." Mike agreed to come by and help her set up a few of the game cameras around the house.

***

Rae and Mike put up the game cameras but there were no more notes or nasty packages. "It's like they know we put up the cameras," she told him after a week of nothing.

Mike sighed. "Maybe that means it was just pranksters."

"And the cat?"

"Boots died of old age. Phil and Jenna buried him in the back yard."

Rae frowned. "Phil knew the cat was dead and where it was buried?"

"You don't think Phil had anything to do with your notes?" Mike asked.

She shrugged. "He has opportunity."

"But why?"

"Todd?"

Mike shook his head. "Well, it's stopped and that's all I'm worried about."

Rae wasn't so sure. She left Mike in the parking lot and headed back to work.

It was nearing quitting time and Rae was looking forward to a swim in the creek and a soak in the hot tub. "Maybe tonight, I'll forgo the swim." She sighed stretched.

"You're covering the wrecker this weekend, I've got fire training in Raleigh," Billy said, wiping grease from his hands.

Rae nodded. She was punch-drunk with exhaustion and nerves. She'd been on edge all week waiting for the next message from her pen pal. She debated telling Billy but didn't want to worry him. It wasn't fair to burden him with her problems. As a volunteer fireman and taking over the body shop, it was difficult for him to keep up with his fire training. He'd just made assistant fire chief and this was sure to be mandatory training. "Will you drop the bike off to Dana before you go?" She straightened slowly, her body stiff; the smell of gas and sweat clung to her clothes like cheap perfume.

Billy nodded to the bike. "You finished it?" He walked around, studying it from every angle. "You did a good job, sis. Ya can't even tell it was wrecked." Draping an arm around her shoulders, Billy gave her a squeeze. "Dana is going to love it. Why don't you take it over to her? I think she's at the club."

Her words tumbled out in a rush, "I can't. She doesn't want to see me." Eyes downcast, Rae said, "Billy, I'm so sorry. I'm going to AA now and—"

"I know, Rae." He cleared his throat. "Anyway, the bike looks great."

Rae punched him on the shoulder. "You're just trying to butter me up since I have to pull wrecker duty this weekend." Tossing a shop rag to the floor, she said, "I'm going to home."

"Not until you help me load this bike."

Sitting alone at the café, Rae rubbed her finger through the condensation on her water glass. The smell of fried food lingered heavy in the air. Ditchwater Pete sat hunched in a corner all alone. She considered joining him but wasn't sure of her welcome. She kept her seat and tried to ignore the conversational barbs flying around her. Her neighbors, always so welcoming of outsiders, didn't hold the same for one of their own.

"She cost that boy his scholarship."

"Ten years of his life."

"You ask me she got what was coming to her, partying with those boys."

Jenna touched her shoulder and smiled. "Don't let 'em get ya down, Rae."

She smiled. "I'm good. Sorry about your cat."

Jenna frowned. "How'd you hear about Boots?"

"Mike mentioned it," she lied. She wasn't supposed to mention the cat. "Sorry, I know what he meant to you. How'd he die?"

"Old age, you know they don't live forever." She blinked away a tear and said,

"You finished the bike?" She drummed her fingers against the top of her order book.

Rae nodded. "Billy took it over to the club."

"That's good! What'll you have today?" She popped her gum.

"Still trying to quit smoking?"

Jenna nodded. "Yeah, patch makes me sick. The pill made me crazy. Now, I'm trying gum."

"Is it working?"

Jenna rolled her eyes.

Rae sympathized, quitting sucked. She placed her order and Jenna hurried away.

Jenna said the cat died of old age. Maybe it's not the same cat? Looking around at the packed restaurant, she wondered if any of them were her demonic pen-pal. Ignoring their frowns and stares, Rae studied the other customers. Most were loyal to the Bryant family. She couldn't blame them. The Bryants owned the phosphate mine and employed half the town. Her hand trembled as she reached for her water glass. She wished it were Jack Daniels.

"Hey," Dana said, "Billy dropped the bike off." She plopped onto the booth in front of her.

Rae looked down at the water ring searching for the right words and the courage to say them. "Dana, I'm sorry, I—" she whispered, wanting to explain, but she knew it was just excuses. Closing her eyes, she said, "I'm sorry."

Dana stared past her. When they both braved eye-contact, Rae was surprised to see Dana was crying too.

"The bike looks amazing." Taking a deep breath, Dana said, "You know I love you. We've been through some hairy crap together. You've been my best friend since, well, forever." She blinked and looked away. "You hurt me, Rae. I'm working on forgiving you, but right now, it's hard. I can't just forget it. Not this time."

Rae had learned in AA that asking for forgiveness was part of recovery but that didn't mean the other person would accept the apology. She swallowed the lump in her throat and managed to choke out, "I didn't mean to wreck the bike. I really didn't expect to get run off the road. I'm sorry, I just didn't think it would be a problem." She rose, hating public displays of emotion.

Dana put her hand over hers. "Don't go."

Rae shoved her pride aside and eased back into the booth. "I'll do anything to make this up to you, Dana. I just want us to be friends again. If you want me to be in charge of the Poker Run, I'll do it. I'll do a good job and I won't complain." She nearly choked on that one.

Dana tilted her head.

Rae blushed. "Okay, I won't complain much." She grasped Dana's hand, her heart pounding. "I can't lose you, too." Emotions overwhelmed her as she thought of the notes. Maybe Dana would be better off not being her friend, but Rae wouldn't survive without her. "If you want me to lead the band naked down Main Street, I'll do it. I will. I'll set my hair on fire and twirl a baton."

Dana's lip twitched and her eyes sparkled. This time with mirth.

Rae took a deep breath and let it out slowly.

Dana giggled. "I bet I could sell tickets. That might have to be our next fund raiser."

Rae felt the blood rise to her head. "I was only joking."

"But you did say anything, right?" She leaned forward, challenging.

"Aw Dane, you aren't really gonna make me walk naked down Main street? Are you?"

"I ought to—but no, I've got something else in mind."

The gleam in Dana's eyes didn't bode well. Rae frowned. She'd walked into a trap. "Um-okay." She took a deep breath and asked, "What do I have to do?"

"Goody. You'll sign up for my Cupid's Zone Dating Club and I'll consider us even."

"Cupid's Zone? What?" Rae's gasped in horror. "No, no Dana, I don't...You can't—" Rae's ears started to burn. She glanced around the dinner, people were watching. She started to slide from the booth.

Dana grabbed her arm and pulled her back. "Oh no, you don't. You're my best friend."

Rae Lynne groaned. "I'll march naked, Dana. I'll set my hair on fire, anything, but not that."

Dana crossed her arms over her ample chest and scowled. "Best friends support each other's projects and businesses. You are my best friend. Aren't you?"

Rae mumbled, "Maybe I don't need a best friend after all?"

"You need me Rae Lynne Grimes and you'll thank me, too." Excited, Dana explained, "I am just getting the Cupid's up and running, I need beautiful young ladies to join up."

Someone mumbled something about ladies but Rae barely heard. "You'll be perfect and besides, you'll meet some nice, interesting guys. What could be wrong with that?"

"What could be wrong with that? No God, you know that's like the famous last words in every horror movie. 'What could go wrong?' I'll tell you what can go wrong; everything! I am not dating material. I should probably come with a warning label." Her voice rose.

Dana crossed her arms.

"Do I have too?"

Dana nodded. "Five dates."

"Five dates?" Rae shuddered. "One date."

"Four."

"Oh, God no—three?"

Dana shook her hand. "Three dates and we're square. I'll have your contract all ready to sign tomorrow. Come by the club and get your pictures and your video done."

"You set me up." Realizing the rest of what she'd said, Rae gasped. "Video? Pictures? Uh-un, you said I had to go on dates. You didn't say anything about pictures and a video."

"How do you think we pick your dates?" Dana said with exasperation. "Now behave and quit bothering the other customers."

Rae glowered at the muttering customers and slumped back against the booth.

Dana started telling her how to dress and what to say.

"God, kill me now," Rae grumbled. When she mentioned the family and friends discount, Rae glanced up. "I've got to pay for this too?"

Dana said, "Don't worry about the money just now."

"Family and friends discount?" Jenna asked bringing Rae's drink to the table.

"You want to join my dating club, find you a decent man?"

"A decent man, do they exist?" Jenna shrugged. "I've had a man, now all I need is extra batteries and a cigarette."

"Thought you were quitting?" Rae glanced up.

Dana pulled her computer from her oversized-purse. "Cancer is not attractive."

Jenna shrugged and popped her gum. "Yeah, well, of the two, the cigarettes are better for me than the man."

"You just need a good one," Dana insisted.

"I thought I had a good one."

"You can have my spot. I don't want a good man," Rae said.

Dana frowned. "Yes, you do."

Jenna chortled, leaning on the table. "Yeah, well, I can give you a long list of the other kind."

Dana snorted. "She's never had trouble finding the other kind."

The bell rang. Jenna smiled. "Orders up, saved by the bell." Jenna hurried to get the order.

"Mom said you called."

Rae looked up and met Dana's eyes. She nodded. "How's she really doing?"

"She's okay."

"And you?"

"I'm getting there."

Chapter 14

"If I have to sit through another meeting with that obnoxious ass..." Logan knew if he was going to save Birdsong Construction from bankruptcy, he needed this contract. He needed Todd Bryant. He groaned and pressed his foot to the gas.

The delicate shifter protested the rough treatment as the gears growled. He forced his mind to relax. The performance car reacted best to a gentle touch. Music up, windows down, the scent of rain purifying the air, he pushed the muscle car around the coiled country road. The tension eased with the sexy purr of the well-tuned big block engine. The earthy smell of muddy water with its hint of brine washed away the cloying scent of cheap perfume.

Tonight's meeting accomplished nothing. Bryant can't see the necessity of permits. Kinnion's only interested was the girls hired for the evening. *Who the fuck hires hookers for a business meeting?* His gut warned him there was something wrong with the deal, but the contract appeared solid. *I need talk to Sam. This project has the potential to go sideways.*

Todd and Devin pushed at him to take one of the ladies to the backroom. He shuddered at the thought of sharing a woman with either man. Sensing a trap, Logan declined the offer. Only his powers of bullshit had convinced Todd his time would be better spent drawing up the new plans if they were going to keep this project on schedule. He hadn't been able to get away fast enough.

Lightning ripped a jagged gash in the darkening sky. Bruised clouds dumped rain onto the dark, twisty narrow road turning the tarmac into a slip and slide of muck as the canal overflowed. Logan down shifted.

"Great, just what I need." The fog came up out of the swamp. His cell phone chimed. Turning down the radio, he answered, "Birdsong Construction."

"Hey son, is your meeting over?"

Sam's deep, reassuring voice eased his tension. Logan took a deep breath. "Yeah Dad, I'm on my way back to the hotel." He stifled a groan. *How do I tell this man that I'm about to pin our whole future on a guy I wouldn't trust as pooper-scooper?* "I think we should pass on this project."

"Business being what it is, can we afford to say no?"

Logan's heart pounded at the thought of losing everything Sam had worked so hard to build. "I don't know, but I'm afraid dealing with Bryant might be worse than going hungry."

"You're running the business now. If you feel that we shouldn't get in bed with the guy, then I trust your judgment."

"Oh shit!"

A deer materialized out of the fog.

Logan swerved.

Lightning flashed.

The car hydroplaned. Logan pumped the brake.

The shoulder of the road crumbled beneath his tires.

The canal loomed as he sped towards it. Logan wrestled the steering wheel but there was no traction. His head slammed against the steering wheel as the car slapped down in the middle of the canal. "Oh God."

His step-father's voice, tinny and far away, called his name, "Logan? Logan. What happened? Logan!" His cell phone was just out of reach.

He released the seat belt and fell across the gear shift, groaning as it bruised his side. "Damn." He brought the phone to his ear. "I'm all right …just slid off the road." He stifled a groan. "Deer… in front of me." He took a deep, painful breath.

"Logan, you scared the daylights outta me!" His mother's shrill cry echoed in his head.

He winced. "Sorry, Mom, I'm okay." His parents were both talking at once. "I need to call a tow truck, okay?"

"You sure you're all right?" they asked in unison.

"Yeah, I'm fine, really. The car—not so much."

"Cars can be replaced. You call when you get settled, you hear?"

Logan grinned, picturing his tiny mama wagging her finger under his nose. "I will Mama."

"I love you," her voice cracked.

Logan hated to worry her. Lillie Birdsong had had enough heartache and worry in her life. "I love you, too." Ending the call, he glared out at the road. Lighting boomed, the hair on his arms stood up. He gasped. "Damn that was close." He dialed 9-1-1 and reported the accident.

"I've got an officer on the line, he says he can be there in about ten minutes and he's already contacted a tow truck. Do you need an emergency vehicle?"

"No, I'm not hurt, just my car."

"Do you want me to stay on the line with you until the officer gets there?"

"Thank you, no, it's fine."

The dispatcher wished him a good evening and disconnected.

Logan shook his head. "Good evening, my ass." He reached for his computer case and overnight bag pulling them into the front seat and stuffed his phone into one of the bags. The car shifted and water filled the floorboard. "Fuck." Thunder echoed through the trees and a brilliant bolt of lightning turned the twilight sky to pale lavender.

The car tilted. Scrambling, he gathered his things and crawled out the passenger window. He eased into the water and was relieved it was only knee high. Rain pelted him like rocks.

Logan took a step, dropped five feet and came up sputtering, holding his bags above his head. Finding a sand bar, he regained his footing. The rain eased to a steady drizzle. He trudged through the hip-deep water.

A blue light guided him to the road.

The officer in a yellow rain suit stood at the edge of the canal.

"Shit, shit, shit," Logan cursed as he plowed through the cold, murky water.

"Probably, but mostly it's just mud."

Logan wasn't amused.

"You okay?" The cop took his bags and reached out his hand to help him to shore.

"Fabulous," Logan growled, grabbing the proffered hand. "Lovely night for a stroll." The ground fell out from beneath his feet, plunging him into water over his head. The officer dragged him up. "Please, tell me the computer didn't get wet," Logan sputtered, clinging to the muddy grade.

The officer set his bags inside the police cruiser. "What happened?"

"Freaking deer in the middle of the road."

The officer nodded. "Suicidal deer, that's what I thought. I called the highway patrol but they're tied up on the other side of the county. So, I'll handle the report." He offered his hand. "Mike McKenzie, Leeward Police."

Logan wiped his muddy hands on his wet pants before taking his. "Sorry, Logan Birdsong." He pulled his wallet out of his wet pants and handed his ID to the officer. "Damn, it's cold, when's that wrecker gonna get here?" His teeth chattered.

Headlights flashed across the canal. "Speak of the devil."

The driver leaned out the window and yelled, "Didn't your Mama ever tell you not to play in the rain?"

Only a grin was visible beneath the ball cap but he looked young. Logan prayed he was competent. His hope of salvaging the Mustang diminished with each minute it spent submerged.

"You know how it is, some of us never learn." Mike stepped over to the truck.

Logan took his wet wallet and put it in his duffle bag, hoping it would dry enough that he'd be able to use it. He listened to the officer and driver banter like this was a social event. *Geez, just get my fucking car.*

"You think you can get it?" Mike motioned to the half-submerged car in the middle of the canal.

"Yeah, but he's gonna pay for getting me wet." The driver strode to the back of the truck.

"Ah, give him a break Rae, a deer run out in front of him."

"Funny, that's what they all say."

Logan glowered. "Funny? I'm wet, I'm tired and I really just want to get back to town. You gonna get my car out tonight or what?"

A lift of narrow shoulders and a smart: "Or what sounds good to me."

Logan's anger boiled. Turning to the officer, he asked, "Is there anyone else you can call?"

Rae spun around, hands going to her hips, the motion pulling the rain slicker open to reveal her gender. "Feel free to do it yourself if I am not doing it fast enough to suit you."

Logan nearly spit out his teeth as her hood fell back. Thick, dark hair curled about her shoulders and a streak of hot pink fell across her face. She was beautiful and sinister and looked like... "Ah hell, Rae? You're the tow truck driver?" He stepped into the glow of headlights.

She snorted. "Boy Scout!" She couldn't resist laughing. "I should have known. Damn man, we need to quit meeting like this."

Desire swallowed his anger. He cleared his throat and said, "My apologies, ma'am, it's been a hell of night. Can you please get my damn car out of the freaking water?"

Rae shook her head and pulled off her slicker tossing it over the side of the truck. "Yeah, I guess, but this doesn't count as a date."

Logan's brain turned to mush as other parts hardened to granite.

Rae waded into the water, pulling the cable.

Logan opened his mouth to warn her, but it was too late, she was already submerged. He rushed to the edge of the canal.

Bobbing back up, she sputtered, eyes narrowing, she said, "You're gonna pay for that one."

Logan felt his color rise.

Mike called, "Sorry, Rae, that first step's a doozy."

"Fuck you Mike!" She tossed her boots to shore and yelled. "Let out some cable."

Mike did as she asked. He'd obviously done this before.

She reached the car and dove under. Logan held his breath. She broke the surface, tossing her wet hair from her face. He watched, mouth going dry as she strode to shore. Her tee shirt was plastered against her skin, leaving little for the imagination. Her nipples beaded with cold, her bra offering little protection after her swim. Logan's thoughts drifted to ways he could warm her.

As she passed, she growled, "Big time."

She had him so heated steam was surely emanating from his body.

"You might want to close your mouth before you catch something," Mike suggested.

Logan looked away.

Rae lifted her tee shirt, wringing water. She revealed a stomach, tanned and firm with a jewel in her naval and a tattoo of a dragon on her ribs. She was nothing like the girls he'd dated, but she made him hunger like he hadn't for years.

"Don't go there," the officer warned.

"Your girlfriend?"

"No, just a very good friend."

Logan watched her. "What's with the tough girl act?"

"No act, she's worked in her dad's garage since she was in grade school."

Rae shivered. Logan picked up her discarded rain slicker and carried it to her. "You want your coat?"

She looked from his face to the coat and crooked her lip. She finished securing the car. "I think it's a little late for a rain coat."

Logan felt foolish. "Might keep you from getting chilled."

She ignored him and continued working.

Mike's radio crackled. He pulled it from his hip and ducked inside the police car. "Sorry folks, I gotta leave you," he shouted as he started the car. "Got a domestic out on Bay River Road—you got this, Rae Lynne?"

"Yeah, don't let Eula and Frank kill each other."

"No such luck." His tires spun as he sped away, siren blaring.

"Wait man, my stuff," Logan called. "Crap, my computer and clothes are in the back of his car."

"You'll have to wait until morning. Knowing Eula and Frank, Mike won't be back tonight."

He watched the tail lights disappear around a curve. "My phone! Man, my mom is going to flip if I don't call her."

"Mama's boy?"

"I was on the phone with my parents when the deer jumped out in front of me. My mom was upset. I promised I'd call." He forked his fingers through his wet hair.

"And how much did you have to drink with dinner?"

"What makes you think I've been drinking?"

Rae looked over at his car on the back of her truck.

"It was a deer."

She leaned in close and sniffed. "And the smell of Captain John's ribs on your breath. I bet you had a beer or six with that."

Logan put his hand to his mouth and breathed, he said, "I don't smell... You're making that up?" He scowled.

She laughed. Walking away, she called over her shoulder, "Guppy, fell for that one hook, line and sinker." She motioned a fishhook in her mouth. "The only thing down here for a tourist is Captain John's. It wasn't a difficult deduction."

Smart and sexy, with a streak of bitchiness. He hated to admit it, but he liked it. "I'm not a tourist. Right now, I'm a vagrant: no phone, no money, I don't even have my ID."

"Don't worry about it. The only one who could haul you in just ran off with your stuff."

Logan hurried to the passenger side of the truck.

"What do you think you're doing?"

"Catching a ride."

Shaking her head, she said, "It's not allowed."

"Ah, come on Rae. It's not as if there's anyone around to know. Didn't you just say the only one who could give either of us a ticket just ran off?"

She let out a breath. "Fine. Get in. But it's not Mike I'm worried about."

He shut the door and settled in the worn seat.

"Just what I need, to be stuck babysitting some rich dude's son."

"Where do you get that idea?"

"A completely restored '65 Mustang, designer shoes, rich kid attitude—"

He snorted. *If you only knew.* "I worked my ass off for that Mustang. My stepdad and I restored it piece by piece, took us three years. I deal with rich men, so I try to look the part. It keeps them from treating me like hired help." With his arms crossed over his chest, he glared out the window. "Sometimes."

They rode in silence for a few miles. "Did you and your dad really restore the Mustang yourselves?"

"Yeah. Sam and I kinda learned as we went. Damn, I hate to lose that car."

"Who's Sam?"

"My stepdad, he's the best." Logan chuckled to himself as he thought of what Sam would say about a female tow truck driver.

Interrupting his thoughts, she said, "You won't be able to get a rental car around here until Monday. Everything shuts down for the weekend."

She turned down a narrow street and he saw the sign for Grimes Auto Shop. Looking around, he frowned. "Are we in town?"

"You really are lost, aren't ya?" Rae got out, unlocked the gate and backed the truck into a fenced-in lot.

He got out and watched as she lowered the car and removed the cable.

"Do you think there is any chance it can be fixed?" He stared at the Mustang.

"Won't know until you tear it down. My suggestion would be to do that soon. Rust is not your friend."

"Looks like I'll be spending the night in my wet car. That has to be the cherry on top of my shit sundae."

"You can't sleep in your car, it's against the law."

"It's my car," he said in frustration.

"We have a locked impound, only authorized employees are supposed to be back here."

Logan frowned. "I guess that leaves the police station."

Shaking her head, she said, "Closed. Kids mess with things if Mike doesn't lock up."

"There's no one else at the station?"

"Small town," she explained with a shake of her head.

"Then what am I supposed to do?" He didn't like feeling vulnerable. He didn't know anyone except Todd Bryant and Todd wasn't someone you called in an emergency. He stuffed his hands into his wet pockets. "I got about forty bucks, is there a bar or all-night diner?"

"Get in, I won't leave you out here for the mosquitoes and the bobcats."

"You gonna let me sleep in the garage?" He was hoping for someplace with a shower, but he'd be grateful for anything that wasn't wet.

"No, my brother would have a fit if I let you stay in the garage. You can come back to my place. I got plenty of room."

He studied at her by the light of the open door. "You're kidding, right? What if I'm a serial killer or something?"

"Please, in tasseled loafers, not likely." She grinned. "I inherited my Pop's old fishing camp, there are three separate trailers. You can stay in one. I'll just add it to your bill." She backed out of the lot.

"Still, thanks."

She got out and relocked the gate. Getting back in, she said, "Oh and FYI, I sleep with a gun."

"I did not doubt it for a moment."

Chapter 15

Spanish moss clung to the trees lining the narrow, dirt path. The clouds blotted out the moon making the night eerily dark. "At least the rain has stopped."

Rae grunted.

Logan was starting to feel claustrophobic as they traveled deeper into the moss-lined tunnel. "You live back here?" He was beginning to wonder if he was the one in trouble. *If they start playing banjo music I'm out of here.*

Rae kept her eyes on the rutted lane. She was driving slow enough he could jump out and not even twist an ankle, but he had no idea how to get back to town.

"My grandfather left me the camp. It's been my home since I was teenager."

"Do you have to pipe in sunlight?"

She chuckled. "Almost."

Logan was startled when the headlights reflected off a shiny surface. He took a moment to comprehend the trio of antiquated trailers perched on pylons like long-legged herons. They were connected to each other by a series of bridges and balconies like a space-aged Robinson Crusoe. Beneath the trailers, the mirrored surface gave the illusion of a glass house.

Rae parked. "Home sweet home."

"Unique." The camp was nothing like he'd imagined. Logan climbed out of the truck. Three Air Stream Silver Bullet trailers, unpainted salt-treated wood decking, and tinted glass all came together to create a space-aged treehouse.

He followed Rae as she opened a sliding glass door and flipped on lights.

The interior of the house was as unique as the outside.

"My grandfather could build anything. He was born poor and learned to do a lot of things by necessity. Most of this came from stuff other people threw out."

She led him through an eclectic kitchen that looked like a Victorian farmhouse tagged by a New York City graffiti artist. Rae left him staring at the combination of shiplap walls and pressed tin ceilings.

"Hey, don't you want to get out of those clothes?" Rae called before leading him out to the patio.

Grinning, Logan rushed out behind her. He stopped short at the circular patio. "Oh wow, this is so cool." Several buildings circled the patio with the river curving around it to close off the circle. "What are all of these?"

Rae glanced over her shoulder. "Mostly storage, a smoke house, boat house, you know, the usual." She started up a set of stairs.

He followed.

"You can stay in my brother's trailer." She opened the door and hurriedly stripped off sheets and raised windows. "Sorry, no one has stayed here in a while."

He followed her down the hall. His steps were starting to falter as the evening caught up with him.

"Here are some clean clothes." She handed him a stack from a nearby chest-of-drawers. "I'm gonna wash up and fix something to eat. I don't know about you but I could eat a horse: hooves, tail and all."

Logan watched her leave. Not what he'd had in mind when she asked if he wanted to get out of his clothes.

Logan plowed his hand through his matted hair. Regret clung to him like the stench from the canal. The mustang was more than a car. It was the first project he'd shared with Sam outside of work. Sam had taught him the importance of a job well done. He felt he'd let him down.

He stripped off his sodden clothes. His shoes were ruined. Turning the water on scalding, he stepped into the shower. As the grime sluiced down the drain, Logan wished he could wash his worries away as easily.

Logan was under pressure to prove his capability as CEO of Birdsong Construction. He couldn't let his family down. His sisters were starting their second year of college and his mother and Sam had plans to travel.

Logan had been a half-starved, overlarge twelve-year old when he first met Sam. At nearly six-foot, Sam had mistaken him for a gangly sixteen-year-old. The job with Birdsong Construction meant he could buy the medicine his mother needed and pay rent.

Logan had started cleaning up around the job site. He'd run tools and supplies to the men without complaint. His willingness to work earned him the men's respect. He ignored the growl of his stomach and the pinch of his too tight boots as he outgrew his threadbare clothes. The men shared their food, brought him clothes they'd outgrown and even collected money to buy him new work boots. Their friendship was a luxury he'd never experienced.

When it neared time for school to start, Logan confronted his mother. He wouldn't be going back to school. He stood head and shoulders over her but she didn't shrink from him. *"Education is the only way to get ahead in this world,"* she'd insisted.

"It won't matter if we don't have food or a place to live," he screamed as he stomped out of the house.

Lillie Ryan, pale and weak from her illness, showed up at the job, determined. Logan, angry and afraid, lashed out at his mother. *"You ruin everything."*

Logan shoved his head under the shower the shame still fresh in his thoughts. He washed his hair and tried to shut out the memories.

Logan turned off the water. The lie about his age had seemed harmless and necessary. God, he'd grown up quick that day. Sam had insisted he tell the other men the truth. They'd been sympathetic but explained what his being on the job could have cost Sam.

Sam had hired Lillie to work in the office and do payroll. He'd kept Logan busy doing odd jobs until he got old enough to work summers. Then Sam married his mom and they'd became a family.

Logan dressed in borrowed sweats and wandered down the hall. The trailer was small. The furniture looked as if it had come from the streets, complete with graffiti. He liked it, black and gray with pops of color. Black and white photographs adorned the cement-gray walls. The subjects varied as did the angle. An upward look at a street sign challenged his depth perception and a shadowy image of an old woman in a rocker left him thoughtful.

The kitchenette, like the bath, showed signs of being remodeled though not recently. There was only a microwave, a coffee pot, a sink and a dorm style refrigerator, all painted a flat black with chrome accents.

"Come and get it," Rae called.

Logan opened the sliding glass doors and stepped out onto the balcony. Rae, standing on the patio, was backlit from the kitchen lights, leaving her in silhouette.

"What are ya offering?" His stomach tightened but his thoughts were not on food.

"Food! Bring your clothes down and I'll toss them in the wash."

Logan stuffed his shoes and clothes into a plastic tub that looked as if it was used for a laundry hamper and banged down the stairs in his borrowed flip flops.

He found Rae in the kitchen, setting out the fixings for subs. "Anything I can do?"

"Set your bag over there by the washer." She nodded to the room off the kitchen that housed the laundry. "What would you like to drink?"

"Beer?" Logan noticed the ink that adorned her skin. He'd seen the black rose with bloody thorns that wrapped around her throat like a noose. But the pink ribbon on her left calf surprised him, imprinted with the word HOPE.

"Sorry, no beer." Color stained her cheeks.

"Tea?"

"Don't tell anyone but I don't drink tea, how about a Pepsi?" Rae pulled out a couple of bottles and handed him one.

"Sure, fine." He chuckled and opened the bottle. He watched her put the sandwiches together, nodding when she asked what he wanted on his. After years of hunger, he'd learned to eat whatever was put before him. "So why can't I tell anyone?"

Looking over her shoulder, she grinned. "They'd call me a Yankee. He-eck, I might be tried as a traitor. You know how southerners are about sweet tea."

He laughed. "I'll keep your secret."

Rae didn't look any older than his sisters, scrubbed clean and dressed in thin cotton shorts and ribbed tank. He silently reminded himself that Rae was someone's little sister. It did little to cool his desire.

Her dark hair curled as it dried, the streak of pink at the widow's peak a stark contrast. Logan wanted to touch where it curled against her cheek.

She caught him staring and blushed. "Don't just stand there, cop a squat and let's eat."

Logan grabbed a bag of chips and followed, nearly colliding when she stopped to set the sandwiches on the table. As she turned to go back to the kitchen her eyes met his, igniting the energy shimmering around them. It was like being in an electrical storm. The intensity unsettled him. He'd never felt like this. He leaned in to kiss her.

"Get that look off your face!" Her growl sobered him. She leapt away from him.

"What?" He blinked. "I was just admiring your view." He turned his attention to the water barely visible in the moonlight. His ears burned. He felt like a horny teenager. "I bet the fishing's amazing here."

"Yep, fishing's real good, just be careful where you put your pole." Her lips pursed in a perfect bow.

Logan met her eyes and nodded in the face of her humor.

"Sit, eat," Rae ordered.

He dropped into a seat and picked up his sandwich.

***

Logan yawned and bid Rae good night. He found a landline upstairs in the bedroom and called his parents. "Hey, sorry it's so late."

"Logan, I have been so worried. I called your cell phone several times but it goes straight to voice mail," his mother chastised.

He felt a twinge of guilt. "Sorry, ma, my stuff is still in the officer's car. He left on another call before I could get it out."

"You should have called sooner, you know how worried I get."

Ashamed his parents had been the last thing on his mind, he started to explain. Sam's deep bass filled the line.

"Hey Logan, what's the status on the car?"

Sam's gentle distraction calmed his mother. Thankful for his interference, Logan explained about the Mustang. "Rae Lynne says we might be able to salvage it but we need to get the motor torn down soon, before it starts to rust."

"Rae Lynne?"

"Yeah, the tow truck driver. She's putting me up for the night."

"Uh-huh."

Logan could hear the smile in Sam's voice and felt heat sear his skin. "I'll see about a rental tomorrow."

"Tomorrow's Saturday son, you ain't gonna get much done out there. Those country folks roll the sidewalks up and shut the doors until Monday."

"It's hard to believe we're less than two hours from Greenville and just three from Raleigh."

"Yeah, it's a world away. At least you're not in Hyde County, their mosquitos have fireflies to escort them after dark. I ain't never seen a place where the night is so black."

Logan chuckled. "Maybe Rae will take me to get my stuff and I can check into a hotel. I'll let you know."

"Is she pretty?"

Logan grumbled into the phone, "She's a female tow truck driver. What do you think?"

"That hot, huh?"

"Yeah, but she's all business. She has several trailers her granddad left her, a fishing camp. She's letting me stay in one."

"Sounds like you're okay for the night. You need me to come get you or anything, you call. Call anyway and let us know when you'll be home. You know how your mama worries."

"Sure Sam. I'll call you as soon as I know what I'm doing." His mother came back on the line to wish him good night. Hanging up the phone he smiled, realizing he'd never doubted his mother's love for him, not even in the bad times. Exhausted, he crawled into bed.

Chapter 16

Logan woke disoriented, his body aching. He groaned, remembering the wreck. "What time is it?" There was no clock and he didn't have his cell phone. He climbed out of bed and stumbled to the window. Shoving the curtain aside revealed the time as the first hint of a new day flickered through the trees. A blush of the morning sun glowed pink with promise. As his eyes adjusted to the faint light, a movement below caught his attention. He pulled on a pair of borrowed shorts and stepped out onto the balcony. There was no one there. He sighed and turned to go back to bed.

A scream shattered the stillness. Logan rushed from the balcony taking the steps two at time. Stumbling onto the patio, he followed the sound of Rae's voice. The stench, reminding him of the meat packing plant they'd lived near as a kid, assaulted his senses. He found Rae tangled in a congealed mess of blood and intestines. She was cursing and crying as she tried to regain her footing.

"Rae?" Logan offered her his hand and pulled her to her feet.

"Get it off of me, please get it off of me."

Logan plucked the long greyish white string from her hair.

Rae was dressed only in a towel. She fumbled with the once white terry cloth, now stained with animal blood and innards. "Oh God, I can't believe the sick bastard would do something like this." Rae clutched his hand. "What kind of psycho does this shit?" Tears streamed down her cheeks and her hands trembled.

Streamers of pork intestines, and jellified internal organs covered the lawn in front of a weathered gray shack. Across the front, printed in blood were the words *Leave Whore*.

There was nothing fancy about the old shed her grandfather had built for her art studio, but it was the one place where Rae felt she truly belonged. Seeing the words

Leave Whore in big, bold letters on the front of it was an invasion akin to rape. Someone breeched the walls of her sanctuary. She would not roll over and hide, she would come out claws ready. Tears blurred her vision. She scanned the woods behind the shed but saw no one in the early morning shadows. A putrid stench filled the warming air, making her gag. The little porch was smeared with strings of entrails in varying degrees of decomposition. "Oh my God." Shaking with fear and rage she stood there, covered in gore.

"Rae, are you all right? What the hell?" Logan offered her his hand. "What's this all about?"

Rae straightened her towel and blinked back tears. "I was on my way to the creek for my morning swim." Her voice was surprisingly strong. Taking a deep breath, she choked back the bile that threatened. She stared at the mess, her fear turning to anger. How dare they invade her home, her studio.

"We need to call the police," Logan's calm voice penetrated her thoughts.

Rae shook her head. "The only one I trust is Mike."

"Then call him."

"I need to wash this off." Her voice cracked. She clenched her jaw refusing to give in to the tears and revulsion.

"Give me your phone. I'll call Mike."

"It's on the charger in the kitchen."

He followed her.

"Is his number in here?"

She nodded. "I'll have to burn this."

"Don't, Mike may want it for evidence." Logan found a trash bag in the pantry and handed it to her. "I'll call Mike and then take some pictures. Do you have any idea who did this?"

"Yeah, unfortunately, I do." She sighed. "I'm going to jump in the shower. Call Mike, please."

Logan took a couple of pictures and then moved back to the patio, up wind from the carnage. He punched Mike's number, listed in Rae's phone as Officer Goody-Mike.

"Hey Rae, what's up?"

"It's Logan. I'm on Rae's phone. Someone has turned her yard into a hog killing. I'm going to send you a couple of photos." Logan sent the officer the photos and redialed his number. "What do you think?"

"I think this is one sick fuck we're dealing with. He's escalating and I'm not sure how safe Rae is right now."

Logan frowned. "This has happened before?"

"Shit," Mike swore. "She didn't tell you, did she?" He sighed. "I'm still here with Eula and Frank," Mike's voice was weary. "I don't know when I can get free. I'll have to send someone else."

"She said she didn't trust anyone but you."

Mike let loose a couple more swear words. "Tell her it's Jorge or nothing. I'll call in a forensics team…"

"Is that Mike?" Rae asked joining him on the patio.

Logan nodded and handed her the phone.

"Hey Mike, my secret admirer has struck again." She sighed. "You're still with the magistrate?" She paced. Her hair was wet from her shower and she wore a pair of worn sweat shorts and an oversized jersey. "Mike, about Jorge?" Rae hesitated obviously not happy about the other officer. "Okay, sure, thanks. Yeah, Logan's staying until Monday. There's no way to get a rental car until then."

Logan waited for her to hang up. "Are you all right?"

She nodded. "Yeah, fine. Mike's sending over an officer."

"I saw something while I was taking pictures. Do you want to check it out?"

Rae followed him without comment.

The sun was up and the bright light illuminated the horror. The warmth began heating the air and the smell of death hung in the air.

"What are you looking for?" Rae asked coming up beside him.

"Broken glass, footprints, anything." He shrugged. "I don't know, I'm playing detective, I guess." He squatted and took a picture of bloody ice melting rapidly in the morning heat. Glancing at her, he noticed her sickly parlor. "Why don't you go back to the house and wait?" He straightened, worried she'd faint.

Rae shook her head. "No, I'm okay."

They wandered around the shed. "What's inside here?"

She frowned. "This is my art studio. My welder is the only equipment of any value inside."

"How many people would know this was your studio?" Logan felt a weight in the pit of his stomach. There was more going on that she was telling.

Rae lifted her shoulders in a shrug. "Probably everybody."

"Hey Rae, what's the problem? Mike said I needed to meet forensic guys here." Jorge Claudio narrowed his eyes at Logan and frowned. Turning his attention to Rae, he asked, "You piss off a butcher or something?"

"Fuck you Jorge, I'll wait for Mike," Rae stalked off towards the house.

"Hey, Rae, I was just funning. Crap." Jorge met Logan's glare and shrugged. His face paled and he brought his arm up over his nose but the shift in the wind brought the full impact of the decayed meat in his face. He ran to the woods and lost his breakfast.

"Are you having fun now?" She asked turning to glare at the officer.

Officer Claudio wiped his mouth on a white handkerchief. "Damn, that's gross and I hunt."

"It's the smell," Logan said feeling a little queasy himself.

"I'm sorry Rae, I shouldn't have made light of this, but my God, what kind of psycho does this?"

Rae shrugged and stayed where she was, in earshot but downwind.

Claudio frowned and pulled out his phone to start taking pictures. "Mike said you'd been receiving notes. Did you see or hear anyone?"

"I was going down to the pier for my morning swim, like I usually do. I didn't notice anyone. I smelled something and then I slid in the blood." She pointed to the place where she'd fallen. Looking to Logan, she asked, "You didn't see anything did you?"

"I thought I saw someone when I first woke up, but it was still dark out," Logan said. "When I got dressed and came outside, I didn't see anyone until I saw Rae heading to the water."

Claudio frowned. "And what time was that?"

"I'm not sure, the sun was just coming up but it was still dark."

"And you are?"

"Logan Birdsong, we've met." Logan raised a brow, surprised the officer didn't remember.

"Yeah, the contractor. What are you doing here?"

"He's my guest." Rae said.

"You're staying here with Rae?" Claudio asked.

Logan frowned.

Rae sighed. "Jorge, can we get to the investigation? I really want to clean up before this attracts something from the woods."

Jorge nodded. "Yes, ma'am." He made some notes. "The forensics team should be out to take samples, but I'm pretty sure it's pig's blood and guts. As soon as they get their samples you can clean up. If you can think of anything else just let us know."

"Is that it?" Rae demanded hands on her hips. "You're not going to do anything else?"

"What do you want me to do? I've taken pictures and your statement. Neither of you saw anything helpful. I have no leads and no suspects."

"You have suspects." Rae growled.

Officer Claudio said, "And without some kind of proof that gets us nowhere."

Rae stomped back up to the house.

Logan watched her go.

"What are you doing here Birdsong?" Claudio demanded getting in his face.

"Back off man." Logan explained about the wreck and Mike driving off with his things.

The officer narrowed his eyes. "And you're not here for any other reason?"

Logan glanced back towards the house. "Other than Rae Lynne?"

He frowned. "Did Todd put you up to this?"

Shaking his head, Logan said, "What? This? God no. Todd doesn't even know I'm here."

The Mexican shook his head and said, "He knows."

Logan frowned. "You think Todd had something to do with this?" He pointed to the carnage.

Claudio shook his head. "I wouldn't put anything past that maniac."

Logan sighed. "There's more going on here, isn't there?"

Jorge held up his hands. "I don't know anything."

"Yeah, does that include how to do your job?"

"I'm here. What more do you want?"

Logan rolled his eye. "The ground should be soft from last night's rain. Shouldn't there be some footprints. Those buckets would have been pretty heavy, twenty pounds?"

"More than like fifty." Claudio said.

Logan nodded. "They were frozen, I have a picture of some ice melting."

They wandered around the building and found the outline of where a bucket had been set. Claudio took pictures. "Looks like it sat here a while. May have been set here sometime yesterday."

"You think the rain yesterday stalled their plans?" Logan asked.

Claudio shrugged. "Could be."

The lab guys showed up. Claudio led them around, demanding samples of the blood used to paint the door. The intestines were all bagged up and tagged. The soil around the bucket imprint was taken for a sample. They dusted for prints. Checked doors and windows and peeked inside but nothing else was disturbed.

After the CSI guys left, Rae returned dressed in old clothes and carrying a couple of buckets. Together they scrubbed and bleached until they got rid of all but the faintest trace of the gruesome message.

Chapter 17

Logan showered and found his clothes stacked neatly on his bed. He shook his head. He couldn't believe Rae had taken time to launder and fold his clothes. He opted for another pair of borrowed shorts and a tee shirt instead of his business attire.

Down stairs he found Rae Lynne breaking eggs. She glanced up when he came into the kitchen. "I'm going to attempt a cheese omelet but no meat. I don't think I'll ever eat pork again."

He laughed. "No, after cleaning up that stuff I'm considering being a vegetarian."

Rae snorted. "I'm not joining that religion. Can you grab an onion from the pantry?"

The pantry/laundry was just off the kitchen. Logan found the onions in a basket and started out. His shoes he'd thought he'd thrown away last night were on top of the dryer stuffed with newspaper and coated in, he touched it, petroleum jelly.

He brought Rae the onion and asked, "You salvaged my shoes?"

She shrugged and started peeling the onion. "I come from a long line of fixers. Yours aren't the first shoes I've had to rescue."

He stared at her, her kindness stirred something dangerous inside him. He didn't want anything more than a weekend fling, did he?

Rae was mutilating the onions. He took the knife from her hands. "You're making a mess and if you don't watch it, you'll chop off your fingers. Don't you know how to chop an onion?" Taking half of the onion, he showed her how to slice evenly and precisely. "See, all of my cuts are uniform."

Rae rolled her eyes. "I didn't measure the eggs to make sure they were all the same size."

He chuckled. "Okay, sorry, my mom is a bit OCD, I guess it rubbed off."

Together they made the omelets and sat down to eat. Logan glanced at the clock and was surprised it was only nine o'clock. It seemed so much later.

Rae left him to his own devices, going out to her studio to work. Logan understood her need to immerse herself into her work after this morning's ugliness. The act of creating was her way of coping. Logan felt the same way. Sometimes physical labor was the only thing that kept a body sane. He missed being on his tools. Since becoming CEO of Birdsong Construction, the only tool he used was a computer.

There were no curtains on the glass doors that opened onto the patio, allowing natural light to filter into the kitchen. He could see Rae working in front of her studio. He busied himself making phone calls on her landline. He found paper and pen and made notes. It was busy work. If he had his computer, he could get some actual work done.

He wandered out to the pier and stared out at the water.

"You want a pole, there's some in the boat house," Rae called. Her helmet was perched on her head like an invitation.

He walked back up the incline. "I'm not much of a fisherman. I don't have the patience to wait."

She nodded and turned off her machine. "I can sympathize. I usually carried art supplies whenever I'd go out with my granddad and his friends. I would draw or paint or even take photographs while the rest of them sat with their poles."

He nodded to her statue. "What are you making?"

Rae blushed. "It's still rough." She sighed. "The Junior Women's League is searching for a statue to put in the town's Memorial Park. This is an idea from one of my granddad's stories. Papa was in Viet Nam. Have you ever heard the song, "He Ain't Heavy?"

Logan nodded and sang the title line. "He ain't heavy, he's my brother."

She smiled. "Not bad, you'll have to sing Karaoke with me next time."

"Does that mean you're sticking around?"

She frowned. "You mean my not-so-secret admirer." She sighed. "I can't let him scare me off."

"Mike says this has been going on a while. He thinks its escalating."

Rae busied herself putting the welding machine away and moving her half-formed statue back into the studio. "The notes started right after Papa died. This is the third one that has had body parts included."

"You don't have any suspects?" Logan wondered about Todd. Surely, he'd know trying to scare Rae Lynne would just make her more determined to stay.

"Too many."

He followed her back to the house. His stomach growled marking the passing of the morning.

Logan thought about the plans for Todd's hotel and spa. Rae's property fit with the plans. Officer Claudio had practically accused him of being in cahoots with Todd.

"Did Todd put you up to something?"

Logan struggled with the idea of mentioning his contract with the Bryant Foundation. Would Todd use something like pig's guts to try to run Rae off of her property? No, Todd wouldn't dirty his hands, he'd hire it done. Whoever sent this message wanted Rae to be afraid. Only a monster would use fear to control a person. He'd known monsters. Too often they smiled and said they loved you even as they taught you to hate them. He blinked his father's image from his mind.

Johnny Ryan had been the life of the party. He'd swept eighteen-year old Lillie Dail off her feet. After charming his way into her bed, he'd had found himself standing at the altar in a shotgun wedding. Johnny was a dreamer used to getting by on his looks and his charm. When that failed, the monster took over.

"Hey, you hungry?" Rae tapped him on his arm.

Logan nodded. "Sure, I could eat." People always commented on how much he favored his father. Logan's greatest fear was becoming his father's son.

Chapter 18

"Thanks for helping me clean up and thanks for giving me space." Rae grabbed the sandwich fixings from the fridge and dropped them onto the counter.

"It was the least I could do. You let me stay here and all," Logan said as he put everything on a wooden tray he found in the cabinet. "Do you want to dine on the patio?"

"People are always trying to put me in box and slap a label on it. It's like trying to put a square peg in a round hole. It'll go if you keep trying to force it but it'll never fit."

He left the tray on the counter and turned to her, frowning. "Labels make it easier for other people to relate to you. If you don't fit in one of their molds they're afraid because they don't know what to do with you."

Giving a little laugh, she went up on her tip-toes and kissed him.

"Thanks, what was that for?"

She smiled. "Are you afraid of me Logan?" She wrapped her arms around his neck.

"Should I be?"

She leaned into him and deepened the kiss. "Probably."

Logan pulled her against him, grinding his erection into her belly. He returned the kiss with a hunger not fueled by food. He trapped her between the wall and his body, pulling her long, muscular leg up to his hip.

She started to pant, her breathing becoming erratic. Rae pushed him away and slid from his embrace. "I-I" She shook her head. "I'm sorry, I shouldn't have done that." Backing to the sliding doors, she said, "God I'm sorry. I should go. I'll just go."

"No, Rae, it's okay. I'm a big boy. I can handle a little rejection. I get it. It was a thank you kiss and I tried to take it too far."

Rae growled. "God, quit being so fucking nice. Can't you see I'm screwed up. I gave you mixed signals. Damn it, can't you just get mad?"

He laughed. "Over being kissed by a pretty girl?"

Rae forked her fingers through her hair and rubbed her scalp. "I want you."

Logan grinned. "Okay, I'm fine with that." He started towards her.

Rae held up her hand. "I'm not. God, Logan, can't you see?" Taking a shuddering breath, she rushed on. "I'm scared. This asshole that's sending me these messages is trying to make me crazy. Hell, I am crazy." She sniffed. "I'm scared and it makes me angry. I've been afraid before. I can't live like that, not again." Her hands trembled. "Damn, I need a drink." She laughed. "I'm a newly recovering alcoholic." She paced in front of the glass doors. "I don't want to swap one addiction for another." Blinking back tears, she met his gaze. "Right now, I want to use you to forget all of this. I want to feel something besides fear. But I know it would be just a temporary fix.

"If I was still partying, it wouldn't matter. I preferred one-night stands, it's the only kind of relationship I'd allow myself to have." She looked up and he felt himself drowning in her dark, luminous eyes. "I'm scared Logan. You're a nice guy. I don't do nice guys."

She paced the kitchen. "Don't you see, I'm not the kind of girl you take home to your mama. I'm the girl you fuck when you've had too much to drink and you run out on the next morning in the sober light of day."

"No." Logan shook his head. He moved slowly towards her. With surprising gentleness, he linked his fingers with hers. "I've wanted you since the first moment I saw you." He stroked the tips of her fingers. "At first, I admit, it was just sex. You were sexy as hell up there singing and I wanted you."

She snatched her hand from his. "But now you know I'm so notorious I have a maniac trying to run me out of town with macabre love letters." She laughed. "I'm sorry, I just wanted to use you to forget." She rushed on before he could respond, "Since you won't be able to get out of here until Monday, I'll just—"

"Rae?"

She stared into his hazel eyes, now deep green with desire. Her hand, of its own volition reached out and stroked his bristled cheek. She like the rough feel of his beard against her finger tips. The electrical sensation sent pleasure to her brain. Closing her eyes, she blotted out the rest from her mind.

Logan leaned into her hand and kissed her palm.

Rae jumped back as if awakening from a trance.

Logan staggered back, bumping into the corner of the counter.

"Oh God Logan, I'm sorry." She lifted his shirt to check the damage.

"I'm fine, Rae. It's nothing, a scratch." He pushed her hands away and pulled his shirt down.

Embarrassed and confused, Rae stumbled towards the patio doors. "I'm gonna go to my studio. I'll stay away from you...if you need anything—" She didn't wait for him to respond.

Blinded by tears, she didn't see Logan move into her path. She crashed into him. His arms, so strong and gentle, held her. "Rae, you don't have to run from me." His voice rumbled in his chest. The vibration felt comforting as she pressed her face against him. "You're wrong, you know, I could take you home to meet my mama."

The tears came. All the pent-up pain and fear came pouring out in a torrent. "I don't cry. I never cry. God, I'm so crazy."

Logan whispered soothing words against her hair.

As Logan held her, breathing in the fresh scent of sunshine, metal and woman, Rae clung to him, dragging them both down to the cool linoleum. "Hey, it's all going to be okay." She stirred something primitive inside him. He rubbed circles on her back as he fought to keep his desire at a low simmer. Logan kept his hands on her back and his thoughts out of the bedroom.

"You want to talk about it?" he prompted.

Rae hid her face against his chest, shaking her head. "I want it to go away."

"Who is trying hurt you, Rae Lynne?" he whispered against her hair.

She pulled his face to hers and kissed him. The sweet gentle peck quickly turned to open-mouthed and dueling tongues. She groaned and slid up his body, straddling him, moving against him. "Make me forget, Logan."

Logan took a deep, shuddering breath and held her at arm's length. "You don't make it easy for a guy, do you?"

"I want you." She pushed against him.

"Yeah, but you don't want to." He tried to keep her at arm's length.

She lowered her head. "You don't know what it's like, living here. Everybody hates me." She scooted off him and made to rise.

Logan grabbed her hand. "Just let me hold you."

"You should run while you have the chance." Rae curled into his lap like a cat.

He wasn't sure how long he could resist as her nimble fingers traced patterns on his chest, then his thighs. He caught his breath. "I don't want to be another of your one night stands."

She gave a throaty chuckle. "You don't want to get involved with me, Logan. One night, maybe a weekend, but that's about all you could stand."

He cupped her face in the palm of his hand. "You'd be surprised what I can stand."

She pushed out of his arms and stood up. "I can't offer anything else." She shook her head. "Do you want to have sex with me or not?"

Logan pulled his legs up and propped his arms on his elbows. "You're afraid of me, aren't you?"

Lifting her chin, she glared at him. "I'm not afraid of anything."

He nodded. "I am."

Rae frowned. "What are you afraid of?"

"Losing you."

She snorted. "You don't know me. You don't know anything about me."

"I know you gave me a place to stay when you didn't have to. I know you're dealing with something scary with more bravery than most soldiers. I know you've suffered pain but you still hold out hope for the future."

Shaking her head, she demanded, "What makes you so certain?"

"It's written on your skin." He pointed to the tat around her neck, the noose of roses with the bloody thorns. "That tells me you have been so hurt you wished to die but got the ink instead." He pointed to her shin. Though he couldn't see it from this angle, he knew there was a pink ribbon with HOPE printed across it on her calf. "You got that for your friend who had cancer. The one you did the bike for?"

She nodded.

"It says hope. Not fight, not anything else, just hope." He smiled.

Rae turned away. Grabbing the plate of sandwiches, she said, "Let's eat."

Logan eased up off the floor and followed her out to the patio.

They didn't talk, just shoved food in their mouths, each lost in their own thoughts. Rae ached for something she never had, normalcy. She swallowed her sandwich, washing it down with a bottle of water. When they were done, she carried the half-empty tray back to the kitchen.

Logan followed. Taking the tray, he deposited the leftovers into plastic containers and stowed them in the fridge. "Are you going back out to your studio?"

Rae shrugged. "I guess."

"Don't think you have to entertain me."

Rae lowered her head. She knew how she'd like to entertain him. She'd been alone so long it felt like a physical ache. *"Leave, whore"* flashed through her thoughts. She shivered.

"Rae?"

She tried to smile. "I'll leave you be."

He touched her arm.

She trembled, her breath catching in her throat. "Logan, I'm not that strong."

"Neither am I." He pulled her against his chest.

"I just want to feel something...." she closed her eyes. "I need you."

"And you won't regret it later?" His lips traced the curve of her cheek.

"God, you're such a Boy Scout. Why would you ask that? Why would you even care?"

"I've never been a Boy Scout."

She moved her hands up his arms, her voice husky, "A Boy Scout is always prepared."

"We might have a problem."

Leaping to her feet, Rae disappeared down the hall returning a few minutes later with a package of condoms. "I think these are still good. I can't see the use-by date."

Logan raised his brow.

"My brother's." She lowered her eyes.

Taking the box from her hand, Logan asked. "Are you sure?"

"You're not?"

"About wanting you, no doubts. About taking advantage of you..."

She pulled her shirt over her head and pushed him to the floor. "Then just consider me taking advantage of you."

Logan didn't protest when Rae ripped his tee shirt over his head and put her mouth to his nipple. "Damn woman, keep that up and I won't be much good."

He tried to move her but she was determined to make him so crazy with need that he didn't notice her weird little habits.

His cock strained against the confines of his clothes. Rae traced the tip through the fabric, making a wet spot she touched the tip of her tongue to.

Sliding his hands up her ribcage, he pushed her sports bra up over her breasts and pulled her to him, his lips closing over the dark nipple as he shoved the bra over her head. Freed, he pushed both breasts together and licked her nipples, sucking them both in equal turns. He traced the inked rose over her plump breast. Rae shoved his borrowed sweats down and put her lips on him. He groaned, tangling his fingers in her hair.

Rae tore open one of the packets.

Logan reached for the condom. "I can do that."

Smiling, Rae shook her head and unrolled it over his cock. He twitched at every touch and she exalted in her power. Leaning over him, she flicked her tongue over the shell of his ear and sucked his lobe between her lips as she coaxed his cock inside her. Her eyes rolled back at the blissful sensation of Logan filling her. The walls of her sex urged him deeper. He filled all the empty places, completing her, at least temporarily. She welcomed him, gliding on top of him, pistons in an engine. They were fluid motion, performance cars, ready to race. The hair on his chest teased her nipples.

He caressed her thighs, kneading the strong muscles. Logan slid his big, callused hands over her hips. His long fingers encircled her waist then skimmed her ribs until he cupped her breasts. He rolled her nipples between his thumb and forefinger. Her head fell back and she arched, pushing them into his hand, begging for more. She rocked her hips, pressing down on him. Straining upward, he took one nipple into his mouth, still teasing the other, and sucked until she bucked and rode him harder. He moved to the other breast, his breathing labored. His cock pulsed inside her, each stroke bringing them closer to the finish line.

Rae clenched her pelvic muscles, beckoning him to let go. Logan rubbed her clit with the pad of his thumb and finally, she arched her back and screamed. He exploded inside her. She collapsed on top of him, too exhausted to move.

Chapter 19

Careful not to wake Logan, Rae slid from under his arm and quickly dressed. It probably wasn't a great idea to leave a naked man in the middle of her kitchen, but she couldn't deal with the awkward aftermath.

Rae usually spent the better part of the weekend working on her art. The rest of the day was for chores, but laundry and cleaning the toilets could wait, she needed to work, to create. She made her way out of the kitchen with one of the sandwiches and a soda.

The faint outline of the hateful words was still visible on the studio wall. She wished she could silence the words in her head. She needed a drink. Instead she fired up the welder.

Logan's strong and callused hands had been gentle. He'd made her wish she was a different kind of girl. The kind who believed in happy endings and picket fences...*Then why did you leave?* She glanced back at the house. *One of us has to be the first to go.*

Logan awoke alone and naked. He looked around for Rae Lynne, but he knew she'd run off to her studio. Dressed once more in his borrowed clothes, he grabbed a couple of sandwiches and contemplated his next move.

He found Rae in front of her studio, a welder's shield covered her face and an oversized man's dress shirt hid her sensuous curves. She was intent on her sculpture. He watched her work, awed by the smooth texture of her welds. He knew enough about welding to tack up something non-structural. Rae had a real talent.

"You could make good money as a welder."

Rae turned off the arc and lifted her shield. "Not many people want to hire a female welder."

"I would."

She smiled. "Are you offering me a job?"

He shook his head. "You don't need one, do you?"

She shrugged. "Depends on how crazy my brother gets next time I screw up."

He studied her face, his stomach twisting. "We okay?"

"We're great." Rae grinned and flipped her visor back down and turned on the MIG.

Being near Rae made everything vibrant. Logan didn't believe in love at first sight. He was being foolish, thinking there was something more between them than good sex and friendship. He turned away. The intensity of his attraction worried him. He'd never been one to fall easily. He'd never been in love before. It's just lust, he assured himself. But even as he fought against it, he knew this had the potential to be something more.

Leaning against the porch railing, he watched her work. Her hands trembled, proof that she was aware of him. "I want crazy," he whispered.

Rae's head came up, she switched off the machine and slowly lifted the face shield. Her dark eyes narrowed as she demanded, "What did you say?"

He stepped towards her, careful not to crowd her. His voice was rough with desire. "It wasn't just sex." That wasn't what he'd planned to say. *Shit, what am I doing?* God help him. She was twisting him around. He forked his fingers through his hair.

She backed away from him. "Of course, it's just sex. What else could it be?"

He cleared his throat. "I think we should find out."

She began gathering up her things, trying to ignore him. "You'll be leaving Monday. I don't think—"

"And if I wanted to see you again?" he interrupted, putting his hands on hers to still them.

Rae shook her head and pulled her hands free. "It wouldn't work. I told you."

"I could take you home to meet my mama." Logan stroked her arm.

"You don't know…there's things about me—"

"I don't need to know your past or even the future, just today and whatever days that follow." He pushed the strand of pink from her brow. He'd never planned to fall in love, hadn't allowed anyone to get that close. "My dad was a drunk who beat my mother. If he hadn't died, I'd have probably killed him."

Rae snorted, blinking tears from her eyes. "You're as screwed up as I am."

He chuckled and kissed the top of her head.

"I want to make love to you, not just have sex on the floor."

"Don't complicate things Boy Scout, let's just enjoy the time we have." With her hand in his, she led him to the patio.

"If you'd talked to me at the bar this could've been our third date," Logan teased.

"Oh? Then falling into bed on a third date is normal."

Logan pulled her into his arms and caressed her, careful not to frighten her away. He stroked the slender column of her throat and rubbed the tension from her shoulders. He massaged the muscles, soothing her with a strong, gentle touch. His lips followed. Logan took his time, touching and tasting her. With experienced hands, he undressed her.

Naked, she led him to the chaise shadowed in the eaves of the balconies, away from the brightness of the sun.

He eased her onto her back and came down on top of her, but she slipped out from under him changing their positions. "My house, my rules."

He bit her ear and suggested, "Let's just take it slow."

She grinned and yanked his clothes off with rough haste, kissing and biting and driving him wild. Rae took the condom he'd tucked in his pocket and put it on him.

He took her hands to hold them still. "Slow down, Rae Lynne, we have time."

Shaking her head, she insisted, "No, now, please." She didn't give him a chance to argue, impaling herself on his cock. She was wet and ready, and riding him hard. He forgot everything but how it felt to be inside of her. He gripped her firm, round cheeks and tried to slow her down. She bounced on top of him, her small breasts tempting him like ripe fruit. He licked her nipples, making them pebble. She tightened around him, drawing him deeper inside her. She increased her pace, he strained to hold out, wanting her to come first but the tempo was too quick and it was over too soon. He cried out as he exploded inside her, grabbed her arms and held her until the last tremors subsided. They collapsed together and slept.

Chapter 20

The slamming of a car door filtered into Rae's dream. She snuggled closer, savoring Logan's heat. *Car door, someone's here.* Logan shifted, exposing her bare skin to the cool river breeze. Rae shivered. "Someone's here." The words finally registered bringing her fully awake. "Shit!"

Leaping up from the chaise, she tangled her feet in the discarded clothes. Blinking away sleep, she searched through the pile. "Hurry, get dressed," she ordered, tossing Logan's pants in his general direction.

Logan snatched the pants from the air and pulled them on. He smirked as watched her frantic search. "Lose something?"

"Did you take my panties?" Distracted by how good he looked, she momentarily forgot her urgency. Logan stood six-feet tall, with a farmer's tan, well-formed and half-naked. "Get dressed," she said, but she couldn't hide the smile that teased her lips. He was a beautiful man.

Logan grinned, deepening the dimple in his chin. It made her think of classic movie stars. She wanted to take him back to bed. "You'd better get your clothes on or you're liable to have some explaining to do," he teased, swatting her on the bare behind.

Hopping on one foot, she pulled up her shorts. "I guess I'll have to go commando, I lost my drawers."

"You sure did." He snatched up the lost panties peaking from the cushion of the chaise and stuffed them in his pocket just as a shadow crossed the patio.

"Pervert," she muttered out of the side of her mouth.

"You say that like it's a bad thing."

Rae snorted.

Officer Mike McKenzie shuffled into view. He waved, but the arm seemed too heavy and it fell to his side like dead weight. "Hey guys, I sorry I'm so late. I was tied up with Frank and Eula all night." He yawned as proof of that statement. "Here's your stuff man, I'm really sorry." He held Logan's bags towards him.

"You just getting in?" Rae asked.

Mike nodded. "Magistrate Harris was on duty but his wife had a heart-attack and Miller was out of town. We finally reached Zebulon."

Logan took his bags from the officer. "There wasn't anyone to relieve you?"

"Afraid not."

"I really appreciate you bringing my stuff out here. But damn, you look beat."

"Yeah, it's been a long night." Mike blinked his eyes, widening them to keep them open. "I learned some interesting facts about your notes, too."

"Yeah? Tell me about it after I fix you something to eat." Rae led Mike to a chair and pushed him into it. "Sit, I'll get you some coffee."

"I've had a gallon of coffee," Mike groaned, "no more for me. I don't want you to go to any trouble, Rae." His stomach growled.

Shaking her head, she said, "Okay, how about a Pepsi or some milk with that sandwich?"

"Milk sounds good." His words slurred as he dropped his head on his crossed arms. "Wake me when it's ready."

Logan sat down beside him.

"You're a real popular fellow. Your phone has rung non-stop." He sighed. "Figured you might need it to rent a car or get a hotel room or something." Mike stared at him with bleary eyes. "If you want, I can give you a ride into town. Washington or Greenville would probably have a rental car place open and I know they've got plenty of hotels."

Rae set the plate of food in front of him. "He's fine right here. He's staying in Billy's trailer. Don't worry, I've not tried to use him for bait. Now, you eat up and you can use the other trailer."

"I'm fine." He yawned and picked up his sandwich. "I'll just eat and go."

"You were going to tell me about my pen pal."

He yawned. "Yeah, eat, talk, then go."

Shaking her head, Rae said, "I'm not going to let you kill yourself. You'll take a nap and a shower and then you can leave. Not before." She set his milk in front of him and sat down beside him.

"Yes ma'am," Mike said. "This is why I love you Rae Lynne, you sure you won't marry me?" He shoved half of the sandwich into his mouth like he'd not eaten in weeks.

"I like you too much to do that to you."

"Hmm." He ate the other half with his eyes closed.

Rae pushed a second one towards him. He cracked his eye opened and grinned. "Eat up and then go get some rest."

"Will you come up and tuck me in?" he asked, leaning towards her.

Rae grinning, said, "I'll send Logan."

"Not my type." They both grumbled in unison.

"I'm going to set some of Billy's clothes out for you to wear. If you leave your clothes outside the trailer, I'll wash them for you."

"You don't have to do that."

With her hands on her narrow hips, she informed him, "Yeah, I do. If your mama found out I didn't take care of her boy, she'd skin my hide. Now, I'll be back in a few moments. You eat."

Logan watched her walk away. She was a pushy broad. He grinned. He liked that about her. He wanted her again. He just needed convince her to slow down, to savor the moment.

"What's going on Birdsong? Why are you still here?"

Logan frowned. "I didn't have much of a choice after you took off with my stuff."

Mike frowned. "I seen the way you looked at her. You better not hurt her."

Logan glared at the officer. "Why would I hurt her?"

Mike shook his head, "You'd be surprised what people will do. She's good people." Mike waved his sandwich. "Taking care of you and me, that's Rae. She doesn't deserve the shit storm this town has put her through." He shook his head. "Wish I could catch the bastard who's messing with her."

Logan wanted to ask about the 'shit storm' but realized it would be better coming from Rae Lynne.

Shoving back his chair Mike said, "Just don't make me regret calling her to rescue your ass." He stood up and swayed on his feet. "Damn."

Logan stood. "You okay?"

Mike narrowed his eyes and nodded. "Yeah, do we have an understanding?"

Logan nodded.

Rae returned to the patio, the guys were doing the testosterone thing. She rolled her eyes and said, "Okay, you're all set, clean towels in the bathroom, sheets are on the bed and some of Billy's clothes are stacked in the chair. You finished eating?"

"Yes ma'am," Mike said with a salute. He teetered sideways Logan and Rae both put out hands to steady him.

"Then get your scrawny butt to bed before I kick it," she ordered.

"Scrawny, I have you know I get lots of whistles for my tight, gluteus maximums," Mike grumbled.

"Yeah, I hear they love you at the jail house," Rae teased, leading him to the stairs.

"Ha." He yawned. "Just wait until I've had my nap, then I'll have a snappy come back for you." He started up the steps. "I forgot. Jenna's cat was already dead."

Rae stopped beside him. "What do you mean, he didn't kill it?"

"It died, you know it was an old cat. She buried it about a week ago. Said Phil helped her dig a hole in the back yard." He took a step and paused. "Oh, and she left his collar on him."

"So, he didn't kill the cat?"

"So far the guy hasn't killed anything. The squirrel was roadkill."

"How do you know that?" Rae interrupted.

Mike yawned. "Tire tracks."

Logan repeated. "A road kill squirrel, a dead cat and frozen pig guts?"

Eyes widening, Mike asked, "You think they were frozen?"

"Officer Claudio and I saw where something had sat and thawed. It looked like one of those big plastic tubs you get from the butcher. I also took a photo of some bloody ice. After what you've said, it's a probable deduction."

"Don't use fancy words on the sleep deprived, Sherlock."

"We can talk about this after your nap," Rae said, pushing him up the first step.

"Not much more to tell."

"Go on, get some Zs, we'll talk more when you're coherent."

"I'm going. Would you mind if I wait until after my nap to shower? I think I might drown." Mike yawned and stumbled on the stairs.

Rae chuckled. "Yeah hon. No problem. There's nothing up there that ain't washable, just toss your clothes out before you crawl into bed so I can have them ready for you when you wake up." She watched, knowing he wouldn't appreciate her hovering.

He mumbled something unintelligible and stumbled up the stairs.

"He really thinks a lot of you," Logan said.

"He's one of the few."

Logan frowned. "Who wouldn't like you?"

"It doesn't matter."

"I cannot imagine anyone not liking you."

"There's lots of reasons not to like me, you just haven't gotten to know me yet."

"I want to get to know you."

Logan stared into her eyes, turning her insides to butter. "I need to work on my statue," she said, her tongue sticking to the roof of her mouth making her stutter. She flushed. "I've spent so much time working on the Harley, I've not had any time to finish my statue."

Logan smiled. "Why don't you work and I'll fix dinner. Do you have something in mind?"

They found chicken breasts in the freezer. Rae left him to plan the meal.

Rae stretched to get the kink out of her back. It'd been a good day despite its beginning. She smiled thinking about Logan. Good sex had a way of changing a person's attitude. She sighed. *Don't get used to having him around.*

"Do you have a commission for the statue?"

Rae turned and smiled at Logan. "The Junior Women's League is planning to commission a statue for the memorial garden. I won't get it but an idea came to me and I had to bring it to life."

"Why so pessimistic, it's looking good."

"I'm not a favorite in town. Let's just say that there are more than a few who could be considered suspects for my pen pal."

"That's too bad. I could see it in a court yard or garden. I think you're amazing."

Rae beamed. "Yeah well, the commission would make the difference in saving this place or losing it, but they won't give it to me." Her shoulders slumped. "I don't know why I put so much time and effort into this. It's just a waste of time."

"I'd choose it."

Rae glanced into Logan's eyes and for a moment almost believed it was possible. "You're not from Leeward. It doesn't matter how good it looks because I built it."

"Then why are you making it?" Logan asked.

Rae tried to put her thoughts into words. "It's like I'd already built it. After I sent in my plans, I couldn't help it, I had to build it. It was in my head."

"I can't imagine anyone being so narrow-minded they'd let petty animosity keep them from choosing your statue."

She snorted. "Never underestimate the capacity for people to be judgmental and vengeful." She fired up the welder.

"What's the deal about this place? Why do you need the commission to save it?"

"My grandfather borrowed money against the property. There's an annual payment due and unless it's paid, I'll lose it." She tacked on the face and began layering the metal, forgetting for a moment that she was having a conversation. She looked up at Logan, who was watching her intently. "Be careful you don't burn your eyes." She handed him a pair of dark glasses. "The rest of the family wants me to sell but I just can't. This is my home."

He nodded, his expression intent. "Have you thought about selling some of your art work?"

"Sure, let me just do that." She snapped her fingers. It was more of a swish in the heavy leather gloves she wore to protect her hands while welding. "You have to have buyers Logan, and so far, no one's been interested."

"Your work is really good. Mind if I take a few photos and send them to a friend."

"Knock yourself out." She tried to squash the seed of hope trying to spout in her barren soul. She forced herself to focus on her sculpture.

Logan took out his cell phone and began taking photos.

Rae watched him, wanting to believe but knowing it was pointless as Logan walked away, busily tapping on his phone.

Chapter 21

As the last rays of sunlight faded to ebony, the stars filled the sky with glittering jewels of pastel light. The evening was cool but the night's beauty lured Rae from the kitchen. She put a couple of hurricane lamps on the table, lifting their globes to light their wicks. A fire burned in the chimenea giving the patio a comforting warmth.

"Looks good?" Logan said, coming down the stairs.

"I wonder if Mike wants anything to eat."

"I think he's still out. You want me to go check on him?"

Rae nodded. "I'll put the rest of the food on the table."

"I'm up," Mike said, coming down the second set of stairs. "I can't believe you let me sleep so long."

"I called you twice and you mumbled, 'I will mom.' I figured you needed to sleep a little longer. Sit and I'll get you something to drink."

"Just water, my mouth feels like something died in it," Mike grumbled, following her into the kitchen.

"I got an extra tooth brush under the sink." She nodded to the bathroom.

"Do I have time for a shower?"

"Nope, eat first, we don't care what you smell like. We'll just put you at the end of the table." Rae pulled the salad from the refrigerator.

"I'm feeling the love," Mike complained.

They sat down to eat. Rae wasn't used to entertaining but she did her best to keep up a lively chatter.

After dinner, Rae broached the subject of the notes. "I don't understand putting all the blood and gore into the notes if he wasn't killing anything?"

"Makes it seem more menacing."

"It seems kind of lazy to me," Logan said.

Mike shook his head. "The squirrel might have been convenient, but the cat was buried."

"It doesn't fit," Rae said. "And the pig's blood and guts, that just seems a little Stephen King-ish."

Mike nodded. "Jorge learned Daniels' Meat Market had to throw out some tubs of offal after one of the power outages. They noticed a couple of tubs missing but thought it was kids pranking and didn't worry too much since it had already been counted and recorded for the insurance and health inspector."

Logan leaned close and asked, "So, does this mean the person doesn't really want to hurt her?"

Mike shrugged. "I don't know. The threats seem to be escalating."

"You think they're building up to it?" Logan demanded.

Mike took a deep breath and sighed. "I think the idea is to scare Rae Lynne away from Leeward. Using the macabre is most expedient. Jenna is Rae's friend. The cat was known to her. The bonus of my nephew Toby ratchets up the fear."

Rae paled. "If this sick bastard isn't just playing games, what's going to keep him from hurting Toby or someone else I love?"

Mike nodded. "Yeah, and how did he know about Jenna's cat?"

Rae frowned. "Well, it is a small town."

"Did you know the cat was dead?"

She shook her head. "No, Jenna hadn't said anything to me."

"Nope, with your granddad's funeral and all, she hadn't told you. She hadn't told me, either. My parents knew, but Toby told them. So, who else knew about the cat?"

"You said Phil helped her bury the cat."

Mike nodded. "Yes, he was working for her neighbor. She went over to borrow a shovel and Phil offered to give her a hand."

"Do you think it's Phil?"

"It could be anyone in town," Mike said. "But the cat had to have been dug up pretty quickly after being buried." At their confused looks, he continued, "Blood was used in the letter and the cat was several-days dead. Someone dug it up, froze it and then used it."

"They kept it fresh?"

"Aw gross," Rae pushed back her chair and stood. "That's sick."

"The whole thing is sick, Rae," Mike said.

"Are there any leads?" Logan asked.

Mike frowned. "Not so far."

Rae paced. "What you mean is there are too many suspects."

"Rae?" Mike started towards her.

Rae sniffing back tears, waved him away. "I'm okay."

"I'm going to make use of your shower." Mike patted her shoulder as he walked past her.

Slammed car doors and raised voices, interrupted their tranquility. Logan straightened from loading the dishwasher. Rae glanced at him and rushed to the window. "My neighbor must be having a party. You remember Phil. Funny, he rarely has any guests."

"They sound angry." Logan followed her to the window.

"Should I call Mike?" She asked with another worried glance outside.

"He's in the shower. Do you want me to get him?"

"Would you?"

He kissed her forehead and ran upstairs.

"Calm down Billy, let's find out what's going on before you blow a gasket."

Recognizing the voices, Rae rushed out to the patio. Billy barreled around the side of the house. Dana, behind him, grabbed his arm. "Don't make assumptions."

Rae smiled. "Hey, Billy, I didn't expect you back before—"

"What the hell do you think you're doing?" Billy demanded, grabbing her arm and shaking her.

"Stop, Billy, you're hurting me." Rae cried. choking down a knot of fear.

"Are you partying again?"

Rae shook her head. "I've not been drinking since I broke the bike."

"We got a message saying you could be in trouble," Dana said.

"We?" Rae asked.

Dana blushed. "I went to Raleigh with Billy, mom called and said she'd heard police were called to your house. We left early."

"So, Dana was the fire you had to put out?" she sneered.

"Damn it Rae, I got messages from everybody saying to come deal with my sister. I've heard everything from you're having an orgy to you were arrested for dealing drugs and soliciting."

Rae looked from her brother to her friend.

Dana shook her head. "I told him there was a reasonable explanation…"

"Hey Billy, I thought you were in Raleigh." Mike, still wet from his shower, stepped onto the patio. "Something wrong?"

"What are you doing here McKenzie?" Billy demanded, lifting his chin.

Logan came up beside Rae, leaning close, he whispered, "You okay?"

Billy's color mottled from red to purple. He glared at Logan. "Who the fuck are you?" To Rae, he demanded, "Is it true? Are you soliciting? Is this an orgy?"

Rae laughed. "You're kidding, right?" Shaking her head, she said, "Get out, go away, just leave." She turned on her heel, Logan at her side.

Mike stopped Billy from following her. "You owe Rae an apology."

"Just because you're sleeping with her, don't think you can defend her," Billy shouted.

Mike shook his head. "You don't know anything, Billy." He sighed. "I'm not sleeping with Rae Lynne. Listen, damn it, she's had a fucking maniac leaving her hate mail—"

"I know about the notes. She said they were no big deal. If you're not fucking my sister, why are you wearing my clothes?" He nodded at Logan. "And him, too. Somebody tell me what's going on here?"

Losing his temper, Mike, shouted, "Well, we could just go around naked, would you prefer that?" Mike grabbed the waistband of his pants.

"I'd prefer you not be here at all," Billy said, puffing out his chest.

Rae got between them. "Billy, shut up! Why are you giving Mike shit? I thought he was your friend?"

"Not if he's sleeping with my sister and interested in someone else," Billy growled, glaring at Mike.

"Jeez, hypocrite much?" Rae pushed against his chest. "You're one to be talking."

"If you're not sleeping with deputy dog, you doing this-this cowboy?"

Logan drew back his fist, but Mike stopped him. "You don't want me to arrest you and I'm too tired tonight."

"You're just now getting your shit together. You don't need to be bumping uglies with Officer Mike or some stranger."

Logan put his hand on her shoulder. "He's being an ass but he's just worried about you. If you want me to knock his teeth out, I will."

She laughed and leaned against him.

"Settle down," Mike said, "There's a good reason we're wearing your clothes."

Billy raised a brow. "And that is?"

Mike sighed. "Because, I ran off with his."

Dana raised a brow, a smile teasing her lips as she met Rae's eyes.

Rae rolled hers and shook her head.

Dana bit her lips to keep from laughing.

"That still doesn't explain why you're wearing my clothes." Billy crossed his arms and glared at Mike.

"You're an idiot. Your sister's life may be in danger. She has some maniac sending her bloody hate mail and you're worried about me wearing you cast off sweats." Mike shook his head. "Dana, take the asshole home before I come up with some reason to lock him up."

Dana frowned. "What's he talking about, Rae?"

Rae shook her head.

"She brought a stranger home with her," Billy argued.

Rae shouted, "At least I'm not sniffing around after a married woman."

"Damn it Rae, how many times have you turned to a man to help you get off the drugs and booze, only to end up worse than before?" He grabbed her hand and shoved back the bracelets covering the scars on her wrist.

Rae snatched her hand away. "I'm fine."

"If you're going to keep doing this shit, I'll have to insist Uncle Clyde sell the property."

"You would do that? You would use my home to make me do what you want?"

"You've left me no choice."

Fighting back tears, she held her hand to stop his protest. "I've learned in AA is there is always a choice. I'm not going to let you bully me, Billy. You do what you have to do." She walked up the stairs.

"Rae?" Billy called. "I'm sorry, I just don't want to see you hurt."

Rae looked down at her brother, her throat thick with unshed tears.

"Damn, you make my family seem like the Brady Bunch," Logan snarled.

"Rae, I'm sorry," Billy started up the steps after her. "I love you."

Dana put her hand on his arm. "Leave her be, you've done enough for one night."

"Damn it Dana, you of all people know how she is."

Dana glared at him. "Billy, shut up." She ran up the stairs after Rae.

Logan glared at Billy. "Congratulations, you hurt your sister more than either of us ever could."

"What do you know about it? Do you have sisters?"

Mike and Logan answered. "Yes."

Billy flopped into one of the chairs around the patio table. "So, she got another letter?"

Mike eased into one of the chairs and motioned for Logan to do the same. "She got a full-blown display."

Logan glared at Billy across the table, wanting to thrash him.

Mike launched into the story. "It's escalating. I can't be sure he won't try to do something to her."

Billy scrubbed his face with his palms. "Damn, she just needs to get away from here. Have you talked to Todd yet?"

Mike shook his head. "There's no evidence connecting him—"

"Bull shit, you know he doesn't need a reason to terrorize her." Billy shoved back his chair and paced the patio. "What about the spa and hotel he's trying to build? You know he wants this land. Isn't that reason enough for him to want to get rid of her?"

Mike sighed. "He holds the loan note, if she's not able to pay it on time, he'll have the land. Why should he go through all of this effort?"

Billy snorted. "The same reason he's messed with her for years, because he can." He flopped back into a chair and sighed. "God, he's going to do it to her again, isn't he?" He blinked back tears. "And I can't protect her."

Mike patted his shoulder. "We'll do what we can."

The three men sat in silence. Logan didn't know what the others were thinking but he was torn between his developing feelings for Rae Lynne and his need to save his company.

"Rae Lynne, can I come in?" Dana scratched at her bedroom door.

Rae rolled to her side and pulled her pillow over her head in attempt to ignore her friend.

Dana wouldn't give up. It was part of the reason they'd remained friends even after all Rae had put her through. "I know where the spare key is hidden," she called through the door.

Thrusting the pillow away, Rae stomped to the door and flung it open. "Come to chastise me some more?"

"No, I've come to apologize." Dana sighed and pushed past Rae into the darkened room.

With a huff, she slammed the door and flopped onto her bed. "What do you have to apologize for? I'm the screw up."

"Rae," Dana's voice was gentle but firm. She took a seat near the window in one of the padded chairs. Rae could hear her shuffling about and knew she'd taken off her shoes and was tucking her feet beneath her. This was going to be one of those talks. "We all screw up, that's life. Billy loves you, you know. He just doesn't know how to show it without being an ass."

Rae snorted. "He's just like Dad." She rolled over and stared up at the ceiling. It was a paler shade of dark, only the faint light from the moon filtering through the curtains offered any relief from the blackness.

"You want to tell me why the police were called to your house?" Dana asked.

Rae sighed. "Not really." She clutched the pillow to her chest and fought the urge to unload all of the ugliness into Dana's lap.

"Mom found another tumor." The words hung in the air, stifling like humidity before a summer storm.

Rae sat up, holding her breath.

"They're going to operate next week. She said it was nothing serious, just a little lump." Her voice cracked, and Rae was at her side, kneeling. She grabbed Dana's hands, squeezing, reassuring. They sat there, holding hands, neither speaking for some time.

"Do you want me to go with you?"

Dana laughed. "Just like that, I'm forgiven."

"Some things are more important."

"You're important, Rae. I want you to be happy." She sighed. "I don't guess you'll be signing up for the Cupid Zone now."

"Cupid Zone?" Rae asked moving to the chair beside Dana. She cut on the lamp.

Dana blinked, and covered eyes rimmed with fatigue. "The dating club."

"Oh, why wouldn't I? I agreed to two dates."

"Three, but I thought you were with Logan."

Rae shrugged. "He'll be leaving sooner or later."

Dana reached out and offered her hand. Rae gave it a quick squeeze and let go.

"It's okay, everyone leaves."

"Not everyone," Dana said grinning at her.

Rae rolled her eyes. "Oh-my-god, I know, I can't get rid of you."

Dana glanced at her watch. "Shoot, your brother's probably climbing the wall."

"Or trying to start another fight." Rae peered over her shoulder. She could see the men sitting on the patio. Billy leapt to his feet and paced, hands in the air.

Dana saw him and sighed. "I guess I'd better go."

Rae took hold of her arm. "Dana, be careful."

"Rae, what's going on?"

Licking her lips, she said, "Someone is trying to get me to leave. I'm worried they might target my friends. Just promise you'll be cautious."

Dana nodded. "Is that why the police were called?"

Rae sighed and nodded.

"You want to tell me about it?"

Rae grimaced. "You better go before Billy gets anxious. You know how impatient he gets."

They embraced, offering comfort and taking it.

Rae watched Dana leave and whispered a prayer to keep her friends safe.

Chapter 22

Dana rejoined the men on the patio and apologized. "I'm sorry we burst in here and made a mess of things." She smiled at Logan. "It was nice meeting you. I hope you stick around."

"I hope he doesn't," Billy grumbled.

"Come on buffalo rump."

Billy frowned. "Buffalo rump?"

She nodded. "Yep, you're too big an ass to be a donkey and if you keep angering the women in your life you're going to be extinct."

Mike snorted.

Logan turned his head to keep from laughing.

Muttering about big-mouthed broads and everybody siding with his sister, Billy followed Dana to his truck.

They listened as the roar of Billy's truck faded into the distance. Soon the night sounds returned and only the frogs and the cicadas were talking.

Mike interrupted the quiet. Shoving back his chair, he said, "I'd better get dressed and check in with dispatch."

"Are you on duty again tonight?"

"Just on call but I really hope no one needs me." He yawned, and with a half-salute, hurried up the stairs at the far side of the patio.

Alone, Logan tried to sort through his thoughts. *I need to get out of the contract with Todd Bryant.* He sighed, wondering if Todd would take him to court, then snorted. *Todd Bryant? Of course, he'd take him to court.* He shoved his fingers into his hair and cursed. *I wish I'd never met the man.* But if he hadn't met Todd, he wouldn't have met Rae Lynne. "Shit." He stood up and paced the patio, widening this path to the pier. *Billy seems to think Todd is the one responsible for the threatening notes. He and Rae have some kind of history. Did they date?* A bit of jealousy slammed into him and he shook his head. He was being ridiculous. Even if Rae and Todd had a thing years ago, she didn't want anything to do with a maniac.

Thoughts of his mother and the years she'd spent with his father nagged at him. He closed his eyes, trying to block out the images of the man who'd been his sperm donor. Dead now for more than a dozen years and Logan was still haunted by the things he'd witnessed, and worse, the things he imagined, heard only through the closed door. He was aware of what a woman would put up with in the name of love.

In need of a distraction, Logan pulled his cell phone from his pocket. He'd sent the photos of Rae's sculpture to his phone earlier. Scrolling through, he chose his favorite and texted it to his friend in Raleigh, tagging it, *"Perfect for your court yard."* He circled back to the patio.

Mike came downstairs in his uniform. "Well, I'm heading home, thank Rae for me."

Logan nodded. "Do you think her pen pal will strike again tonight?"

Mike shrugged. "I don't know but ask her if she put out her grandfather's game cameras. Maybe we'll get lucky." He bid him goodnight.

The night was still and quiet. Logan sat in front of the chimenea, its embers dispersing the slight chill in the air. It did little to warm his thoughts. He relived the scene with Rae's brother, wondering if he should have spoken up sooner. His worry over Todd and their contract preyed on his mind, and he poked the fire with a stick, watching as the sparks burst into the air as the flames rose higher. *I don't need this kind of drama in my life.* He would leave Monday. Logan covered the coals with sand and began turning off lights. He walked up to Rae's trailer and knocked. No answer. He turned away. *Maybe it would be best to avoid each other.*

Rae's door opened and she whispered, "Logan?"

His heart pounded. "You want to talk?"

She shook her head. "I told you, I'm pretty messed up." She tried to smile. "You heard my brother, I do this. I use some guy to help me get off the drugs and booze…" She blinked back tears.

Logan wasn't sure what to say. He touched her arm. "You're not using me.

You're a strong woman."

She snorted. "Oh yeah, so strong." She laughed.

"Mike wanted me to remind you about the game cameras. Have you already set them up?"

Rae's brow furrowed in concentration. Her eyes widened and she grabbed his arm. "Oh shit, I may have gotten a picture—" She dashed back into her bedroom and came out stuffing her feet into a pair of worn Nikes. "Come on."

"You want to take a walk?"

"No silly, well, yes, to check the cameras."

Rae dashed about the property, Logan wasn't sure how she managed to see where the cameras were hidden in the dark. They found ten cameras.

"I can't remember where I put the other two," Rae complained.

Logan was thankful. He leaned against a tree while Rae checked the cameras and tried to catch his breath. Only five of the cameras had photos. She removed their sim cards and put a new one in each.

"This one looks to have been triggered." She glanced in the viewer at the back and frowned. "Hmmm, we'll just take it back to the house. I think it may have malfunctioned or something." She unfastened the camera from its makeshift stand. They looked like a bird house with a deck. The camera was twist-tied onto the wooden frame. "I'll look for the others in the morning."

Logan followed her back to the house, his feet dragging. Rae bounced on the balls of her feet as if she were anxious to run. She'd run from one camera to the other while he panted behind her like a huge bear. He'd thought he was in good shape but he was going to have to step up his game if he was going to keep up with Rae Lynne Grimes. "Don't you ever get tired?"

She laughed. "I'm just anxious to see what we captured."

They went into the kitchen. Rae grabbed her lap top and set it on the breakfast table.

"I'm going to put on some coffee," Logan said.

She nodded and powered up the computer.

"You want cream or sugar?"

Glancing from the screen she said, "Just cream." She put in the first sim card and when the photos came up, she scrolled through them. A racoon, a squirrel and a blur in a hoody were the only images on that card. "Damn, I can't make out what color the hoody is much less anything else." She pulled out the card and put in another.

Logan set her coffee beside her and pulled a chair around so he could see the computer screen. "There, is that someone?"

Rae slowed down and scrolled back through the pictures. A dark gray hooded figure moved stealthily through the woods, head down. "Damn, I can't tell what he looks like."

"He looks thin, maybe a kid?"

Rae stared at the picture. "A kid?"

"Look at the height compared to that sign." He pointed to her "No Hunting" sign that was nailed about six-foot high on an old pine tree.

Rae got up and found a pen and a tablet, and made notations about height, sketching a brief picture and noting the location.

On the third card, they found a gloved hand holding a white plastic bucket and a great photo of one of the buckets, the butcher's name emblazoned on the front. She sighed. "I can't tell anything from the hands. Maybe a teenaged boy?"

Logan shook his head. "Maybe, or a woman?"

Rae frowned. "Those buckets of chitlins and livers weigh what, fifty pounds. I don't know many women who could carry fifty-pound buckets through the woods."

"So, we're back to a kid or a small man." He got up and refilled their coffee cups.

Most of the pictures were of local wildlife, namely squirrels, but they'd managed to track the path the pen pal had taken.

"They came up from the river." Rae drew a map from the canal that ran between her house and Phil's. "I need to call Mike." She glanced at the clock. It was nearly midnight. She frowned. "Maybe I'll wait until morning. I wonder if Phil could enhance the pictures enough to make an identification. He does computers and cameras for a living."

He nodded. "I guess I should head up to bed." He glanced at Rae hoping

S L Hollister   Chrome Pink   135

she'd offer something else.

"I don't think I can sleep," Rae said, closing the lap top and putting the sim cards in a drawer. "Would you be interested in a movie?" she asked, hope lacing her voice.

Logan nodded and followed her into the family room. The furniture was old, extra-large and overstuffed. "Just as long as it's not a chick flick, none of that romance and girl therapy stuff."

They agreed on a western they'd both seen a dozen times. They snuggled up on the big couch and as the commercials played, she began to talk.

Her words were a whisper at first. "My mom left when I was four." Between scenes they shared their stories. He told her things he'd never shared with another person. With only the light from the television, Logan was able to tell her the ugly truth about his real father, Johnny Ryan. "If he hadn't died, I would have killed him."

Rae put her hand over his and shook her head. "It would have destroyed you."

He wasn't sure he agreed, but he kept silent and watched as a young Kevin Costner bandied about with his guns. Rae snuggled against him. She didn't volunteer where Todd fit in her life.

Chapter 23

Rae woke before the sun. The press of warm male against her backside brought her fully awake. She couldn't believe they'd fallen asleep. The old couch was just big enough to sleep two. She slid away from Logan as Billy's words filled her head. Was her attraction to Logan just another of her addictions? It's not as if she hadn't thought it herself. She didn't want it to be true. She wanted to be free to be with him, to trust him.

Rae hurried to the bathroom. She hated being afraid. Afraid of her feelings for Logan. Afraid of going out to her studio or for a swim. She paced, feeling trapped. Staying in the same room, the same house enticed her to test her brother's theories. She wasn't sure what she feared more, her pen pal or her attraction to Logan. She longed for a swim. As she peered out the sliding glass doors the first glimmers of light crept out of the darkness. Giddy, she ran outside and searched the shadows as she made her way to her studio. *The swim will have to wait until daylight.*

She was deep into her sculpture when she felt Logan's presence. He was too much temptation in the early morning light. His dark auburn hair gleamed like a ruby, full of fire and warmth. He wore his own clothes and they clung lovingly to his body. His arms and chest were heavily muscled. His was not a body sculpted by the gym, but working muscles, chiseled over time.

He looked around. "No problems this morning?"

Rae cut off the welder and lifted her helmet. "Other than my own paranoia?" She shook her head.

"You're not paranoid…"

"If they really are out to get me?" She finished for him.

He smiled. "Have you got any more art you'd been interested in selling?

Maybe something for an office or a foyer?" He sipped one of the two cups he'd brought with him.

She nodded. "Sure, I've got a few pieces. You've seen some of it." He handed her the other cup. She sipped, surprised he'd gotten her coffee right.

"In the trailer I'm staying in, you did the paintings and photos?"

"Yeah, I've tried about everything." She blushed. "Well, in art anyway." Her eyes slid away from his. Her nipples beaded beneath her shirt and she wondered if he knew what his nearness did to her.

"I have a colleague who is interested in your art. I sent him some pictures last night."

Rae's eyes widened. "Really? You think he'll pay me for my art?"

Logan nodded and followed her up to the trailer where Mike had slept the day before.

She led him to the back room. It was crammed to the rafters with assorted art pieces: framed pictures, folders of painting and drawings, sculptures in assorted sizes and mixed media pieces. "Most of these are my earlier pieces, some of the oldest I use for lawn art."

"I really like this piece," Logan said as he picked up a warrior on a sea horse.

Rae smiled. She was proud of the detail in that piece. She had just learned how to use taps and dies to give the work texture and design.

"You really are talented."

She said, "The larger version of that piece is in the yard, down by the pier. I've always had a thing for sea and water mythology."

"You should have an art show."

She snorted, "Yeah right, where would I have this show?"

"How about the gallery that just opened."

Shaking her head, she said, "Not going to happen. The Bryants, as in the Bryant Foundation, and me are not on good terms. Besides, who would come to see it, much less buy anything?"

"Why do you work so hard at it, if you have no plans to sell it?"

She thought about that a minute and shrugged. "I guess it goes back to when I first learned to weld. I see images in my head and I have to give them life—I feel compelled to do it. Not that I'm against making money. Just no one has ever acted interested in purchasing any of my art."

"Whether you sell it or not, you still have to create. I get it, but you do want to sell your work?"

"Sure, I'd love to, my family is about tired of receiving this stuff as gifts and as you can see, I'm running out of places to store it."

"I just got a text back, my friend is definitely interested. Can I send him your phone number and e-mail address?" She rattled it off to him and he typed it into his phone. "Do you care if I take some more photos and send them out?"

Rae shrugged. "Help yourself, I'm going to get back to work on my sculpture."

"Did you do these paintings, too?"

The series of water scenes covering the wall were studies in landscapes, some done in oil, others in acrylic, pastel and water colors. "Those were done at a summer art camp I went to. They're all views of the river."

"They are really good. You should frame these and hang them in your living room."

"I never really thought about doing anything with them. They were just practice pieces." She shrugged and left him staring at the paintings pinned to the cork tiled wall.

She went back down to her studio and started up the welder. She studied the metal sculpture. *Could I sell some of my art? Would it be enough to save the camp?*

After lunch, Rae called Mike and told him about the pictures. "There's not much, just a few blurred shots of someone in a hoody. I wonder if Phil could enhance it and possibly come up with a recognizable picture?"

"It's worth asking him. Do you want to call or do you want me to?"

"I'll call him. If he's available maybe he can just come over here," she said.

"Okay, well, make a copy and email it to me but I really need to see the originals, too. If Phil can't do anything perhaps the guys in Raleigh can."

Rae hung up. "I'm going to see if Phil can come over and look at these."

Logan nodded. "Do you need me to get scarce?"

She frowned. "Why?"

"Aren't you two dating?"

Rae snorted. "Me and Phil, not hardly. Oh, you mean the gallery. He got free tickets and knew I liked art."

She looked up Phil's number and called. He didn't pick up; she waited for his voice mail. "Hi Phil, this is Rae. I have a problem with a digital photo I was hoping you could help me enhance. Give me a call or just come over, if you can help. Thanks. Bye."

"No answer?" Logan asked pouring another glass of lemonade into both their glasses.

"It's Sunday, he may just be screening his calls."

"Last night you said something about two more cameras, did you check them?" Logan asked handing her the glass.

Rae sipped the cold, tart liquid enjoying the fresh taste of real lemons. She'd almost forgotten they were in the refrigerator. She'd bought a bag thinking she'd make some grilled fish, but since her grandfather's death she rarely made the effort to cook. "I forgot about them. I'm not sure where I put them. You want to wander back through the yard with me?"

Laughing, Logan said, "Strolling with a pretty lady on a warm spring day, now who could complain about that?"

Rae was ready to give up. "I have no idea where I put the other two cameras." She shook her head. They both heard the whir and click of a photo being taken. Laughing, Rae located the camera. "It doesn't look like it has any photos except the ones it just took of us." She reset the mechanism and lashed it back in place. They didn't find the other camera. A phone call interrupted their search.

"Hello," Rae answered her cell. "Phil, yes, that would be great." She disconnected and started back towards the house. "Phil said he'd come over and check out my photos."

Phil was waiting on the patio as they wound their way up the lawn. He nodded in greeting and asked, "So what do you need me to look at?"

"Would you like something to drink?" Rae offered.

Phil shook his head. "I'm good." He set up his lap top at the breakfast table and Rae rushed over to the drawer where she's stashed the sim cards and handed one to him.

Phil glanced at the card and stuck it in the side of his computer. A few clicks and he had the photos uploaded.

Rae leaned over his shoulder and Logan watched, propped against the kitchen counter as she pointed out the photo she wanted enhanced.

Phil pulled it up and did some manipulation but no matter what he did, the photo still looked grainy and blurred. "Who is this?"

"That's what we'd like to know."

He frowned. "Is this person the reason the cops were at your house yesterday?"

Rae nodded. "Did you see what they done?"

Phil shook his head.

Rae brought the pictures up on her phone and showed him.

"Gross." He glanced at Logan. "Did you see anything?"

Logan sighed. "I saw someone but thought it was Rae. When I went to get a better look, they were gone and a few minutes later I heard Rae scream."

Phil frowned. "You were only minutes behind this person. My God Rae, you could have seen them and who knows what they would have done."

Rae glanced at Logan. "Well, at least I wasn't alone."

Pushing back his chair, Phil said, "I need to take this and put it on my computer at home."

Rae shook her head and held out her hand for the sim card. "I appreciate it Phil, but Mike said not to let the cards leave this house. It could be part of the investigation." She explained about her pen pal and the hateful letters she'd started receiving after her grandfather died.

Phil stood silent for a long moment. "I have better cameras that you could use if you want. What are you using, your grandfather's game cameras?"

She nodded.

"They're good for keeping up with where game are located but they're not good quality photographs." He rubbed his chin. "I think I have two I just refurbished.

Let me see if I can get those set to motion and you can use them."

"I hate to do that Phil, you use those cameras for your work."

"Not these, these are just some I took down when I replaced the cameras for one of my contracts. I went in and got them working. I thought I might put them up around my place. You're welcome to use them until the pest is caught."

She hugged his neck and he reddened. "Thanks Phil, you're a good friend."

Phil glanced at Logan and frowned. "Yeah, friend." He carried his computer across the lawn and over a tiny bridge that spanned the narrow end of the canal separating their two properties.

He returned a short while later and together, Rae and Logan helped set them up. Phil showed her how she could check them on her computer.

"There you go, I hope this helps. If you need it, I have some refurbished alarms we can set up, too."

She declined the offer but thanked him. "Would you like to stay for supper? I think Logan took some fish out of the freezer."

He glanced at Logan and shook his head. "Nah, but thanks."

Rae hated to admit it but she was glad he didn't stay. She was ready to be alone with Logan. At this point, she didn't care if he was simply a distraction from horror or another kind of addiction, she wanted to be with him and she'd simply deal with the rest later.

Logan cut the lemons in half and put them on the grill with the fish. He'd rubbed olive oil and herbs over the fish and then helped her make a slaw of cabbage, carrots and the same herbs. Warming it on the grill, he tossed the slaw with olive oil and lemon juice. He took ramen noodles and toasted them in a pan on the grill, breaking them into little pieces he added it to the slaw. Rae laughed. "I can't believe that's going to be good."

Logan kissed the tip of her nose and said, "You'll love it."

Rae poured them each a glass of lemonade and set the table on the patio. She turned on low music and lit the hurricane lanterns and the chimenea.

Logan brought out their plates and then held out her chair. Blushing, Rae sat and tasted the food. "My God, this is really good."

They finished their meal in whispered silence. The starry night and soft music cocooned them in an intimacy that was frightening and exhilarating. They skirted talk of work, family and all that had happened this past few days. Instead they spoke of music, books and art. Logan understood architecture and they agreed it was another form of art. Rae talked of the handicrafts prevalent in rural communities and how that influence was seen in many other art forms.

Rae stood and started cleaning up the table. "I wish I had some pie for dessert."

Logan taking the dishes from her hands, whispered, "They'll wait." Pulling her against him, he led her away from the furniture, at the edge of the patio, and began to sway to the music.

He sang along with Foreigner, "Waiting for a Girl Like You," his voice a deep rumble in his chest as she rested her head there, lulled by the music and the man.

Rae pulled out his arms, laughing to hide the lump in her throat. "I better clean-up before we have bears visiting on top of everything else." She hurriedly gathered up their plates and carried them into the kitchen, feeling Logan's eyes on her.

He followed, carrying the candles. "Would you like me to brew a pot of coffee?"

Rae shook her head. "I should go on to bed. Monday morning will be here before ya know it."

"Rae, what's wrong?" He reached out to take her hand.

She pulled her hand away. "Nothing, what makes you think anything's wrong? It's just time…" Her breath shuddered out on a sob. "I can't—I'm okay with wham-bam-thank you-ma'am, but I don't know how to act with this." She waved her hands.

Logan leaned forward and asked, "Romance? Seduction?"

Rae blinked. "That's not my style."

"Why not, it's the fun part of sex? The build-up, the teasing and touching." He traced his finger along her arm.

She shook her arm and moved away, her body trembling. "It changes things."

"How's that?" He edged closer, resting his hand on her shoulder as he toyed with her hair.

Pulling away, she stomped to the dish washer and turned it on. "It makes it important."

Logan frowned. "Sex should be important."

"No, sex is a need, an itch that needs scratching."

Logan shook his head. "But it can be fun, or serious, or comforting..."

"Nope, it's just—"

"Wham Bam!" Logan turned away.

"I know, I'm seriously screwed up." Rae laughed. "Aren't you glad you'll be getting out of here tomorrow?"

He turned to her, pulling her forcefully but not roughly into his arms. He kissed her with raw need and passion. Lifting her up onto the counter, he deepened the kiss. Rae tugged at his shirt. He took both of her hands in one of his. Smiling he shook his head. "Not so fast."

Logan nibbled down her neck, using teeth and tongue to make her whimper with need. She tugged her hands from his and twisted her fingers in his hair. He tickled her with his mustache. Raising her shirt, he kissed her stomach, tongued her breast beneath the edge of her bra. Rae tore it off, giving him better access to her breasts. Logan complied, giving equal attention with his mouth and placating the other with his fingers before switching sides.

He popped the button on her shorts and tugged them over her hips, lifting her with one hand and undressing her with the other. He dropped her shorts and panties to the floor and spread her legs. Stepping between them, he caressed with hands, tongue and teeth until she was melting. Logan freed his cock from his jeans.

"There's a condom in the pocket of my shorts," Rae panted.

He slipped it on and entered her swiftly, bringing her toward a fast climax as she clung to him as he stood before her. Rae grasped his shoulders, leaning over him as he held her ass in his hands and plunged deeper and deeper into her. She screamed and bit down on his shoulder, and he found his release shortly after.

Logan slid out of her and removed the condom. He'd wanted romance but she'd just wanted sex. He sighed. It was like having a burger without fries—it's still good but you're left wanting more. Rae started to jump off the counter but he pulled her into his arms. Holding her against his chest, her legs draped over one arm, her arms around his neck, he carried her into the living room and fell with her onto the sofa. "What do you have against foreplay?"

Rae shrugged and looked away. "It just makes it more intimate."

"Me being inside of you isn't intimate?"

Heat burned down her body. "It is, but it's only a small piece."

"Excuse me." Logan moved his hips reminding her that it wasn't that small a piece.

She chuckled. "I meant, it's only a small piece of me." She sighed. "I don't want to care about you, Logan. You'll be gone tomorrow. Let's just enjoy what's left of this weekend and let tomorrow take care of itself."

He stroked her hand. The tenderness in his callused fingers was nearly her undoing. "What if I want more than one weekend?"

Shaking her head. "I just don't think it will work."

"We could try."

"Why?" She pushed off his lap and paced the furniture-crowded room. "Why would you want more time with me? Didn't yesterday give you big enough taste of the craziness that is my life?"

"I like a little crazy," Logan said, smiling.

Shaking her head, Rae said, "You'd grow to hate me, just like everyone else does."

"Your friends Dana and Mike don't hate you. Your brother might be an ass, but he loves you. They came when they thought you were in trouble. That means something Rae. You may not realize this but you're one of a kind. You're strong, passionate, fearless…"

"I'm terrified."

He smiled. "Courage isn't not being afraid…It's doing things even when you are."

"Did you get that from a Hallmark card?"

He touched her hand, gently caressing her fingers with the callused pads of his fingers. He rubbed circles in the palm of her hand until she trembled and made to tug her hand away. Instead, he pulled, guiding her back to him.

"I'll get another condom." She tore her fingers from his grasp and rushed off to find the prophylactics.

Rae returned with three. She put them in his hand and he laughed. "You trying to kill me?"

She smiled and shrugged. "Are you too old to keep up?"

He growled and pulled her onto his lap. They managed to use two of them before falling into an exhausted sleep.

Chapter 24
Monday Morning

Rae Lynne, dreading the confrontation she knew was coming, white-knuckled the steering wheel as she drove into town. Her thoughts were on what she'd say to Billy. If her own brother didn't have faith in her, how could she expect anyone else to?

"Relax, it'll be alright," Logan insisted, rubbing her shoulder. "Billy was upset he'd hurt you. Sometimes big brothers behave badly when they're worried."

She forced a smile. It felt as if a herd of grasshoppers were tap-dancing on her spleen.

Logan reached across the seat and put his hand over hers. He rubbed her fingers. "Calm down, your brother loves you."

Rae held his hand. Logan inspired her to trust, something that didn't come easy for her. She felt a connection with him that frightened her while it intrigued her.

The sun was a bright promise. Through the windshield the sky was a perfect shade of Carolina blue. Rae inhaled a lung full of dew-laden air through the open window. It was heavy with the scent of wisteria and the whisper of hope.

Her grandfather had always told her she was strong. She would need all her strength to stay sober and fight her family and whoever wanted her gone. Rae hated confrontations. Fighting with Billy left her feeling out of sorts. Despite his hurtful words, he'd always stood by her. After their mom left, Buddy had drowned himself in work. It had been just the two of them. He'd tried to be her protector. She hadn't always made it easy for him. *If Billy hadn't been out of town, Todd wouldn't have hurt me.*

Rae fought the memories. She parked the truck in the shop's parking lot and sat staring out the windshield, garnering her courage.

Logan startled her by opening her door. He held it for her.

Rae looked around to see if anyone was watching. "I usually open my own doors."

He shrugged. "My stepfather taught me to always open a door for a lady."

Rae started walking. "I hardly qualify."

Taking her arm, he stopped her. Turning her to face him, he said, "You are a lady."

She chuckled. "Come on, before you start singing some old Lionel Ritchie song."

Rae led him to the office. Connie scowled as they entered. The fluorescent lights were not kind, revealing dark circles and thick patches where foundation clumped in frown lines. Rae was surprised at how old her step-mother looked. "This is Logan Birdsong. He took his car swimming Friday night. He needs a rental. You want to fix him up?"

The older woman pasted a smile on her puffy face and sneered. "Well, of course, my darling daughter, I live to do your bidding."

Rae rolled her eyes. "I gotta get to work. See you later?" She hated the sound of need in her words.

Logan touched her arm. "You want to grab some lunch later?" His hazel eyes showed his own need.

Rae smiled, relieved. "Sure, how about I meet you at the Depot Café?" She gave him directions and a kiss on the cheek. "See ya later." Glancing at her stepmother's open-mouthed stare, she said, "And Connie, you have a nice day."

"You musta got laid." Connie muttered raising one over-plucked brow at Logan. He narrowed his eyes, and she shrugged in response. "So, you need a rental and to settle your wrecker bill. Will you be storing the car with us?"

Rae pulled the door closed, and taking a deep breath, forced her feet to move in the direction of her brother's shop.

Billy was at his desk ordering parts. Rae waited until he hung up the phone. "I'll send out my resume`, but I wanted to know if you'd let me stay on until I get something else?" She bit the side of her mouth as she waited for his response.

Billy handed her an envelope.

"Is this my severance pay?" she asked, her heart pounding as she lifted the flap. "I was really hoping we could—" Frowning, she asked, "What is this?"

Billy stood, unclenching his hands, he rubbed his thighs. "It's all I could come up with. It's only a thousand dollars, not the ten you need, but I hope it gets you a little closer."

Rae Lynne realized this was Billy's version of an apology. Tears slid down her cheeks. "Thank you." She threw her arms around his neck. "I'll pay you back just as soon as I can."

"It doesn't mean a thing if you can't get that other nine." He disentangled from her embrace.

"Does this mean I don't have to send out my resume`?"

"We need a good painter." He shrugged. "I guess until one shows up, you'll have to do."

She punched his arm and said, "I'd better get to work then."

***

Rae glanced at the text on her phone. *Come to Gull's Pier, L.* She frowned. Gull's Pier was not her normal hangout. It was a little fancier than she was dressed for. She whipped the truck around and drove to the waterfront.

Giddy and nervous like a girl on her first date, she entered the dimly-lit restaurant. Rae tried to appear cool as she waited for the hostess to seat her. She looked around for Logan. The succulent aroma of fresh seafood cooking set her stomach growling.

"Takeout is at the back," the harried hostess said with a nod as she took the couple who came in after her.

Rae said, "I'm meeting someone."

The hostess frowned, giving her the once over. Rae was self-conscious in her worn jeans and paint-stained tee shirt. Lunchtime at the Depot, she would have gone unnoticed among the other blue-collar workers. At the Gull, which catered to doctors and lawyers and other office workers, she was severely underdressed. The hostess grabbed a pair of menus and ushered another couple to a table. People were staring. *Where's Logan?*

Rae stepped to the side and waited. Fifteen minutes passed. She was starting to feel foolish. Biting her lip, she looked around, easing from foot to foot. The spicy aroma of the day's specials perfumed the air, making her mouth water. "I must be early," she reasoned, glancing at the clock as she willed him to arrive.

Out of the corner of her eye she caught a glimpse of Logan coming from the conference rooms in back. She would tease him about getting lost. Todd Bryant, his arm draped over Logan's shoulders looked up at her and winked. *Oh God, no.* She stepped back, knocking over the decorative brass umbrella stand. It clattered to the tiled floor.

"Look who's here." Todd pulled Logan towards her.

Logan wrinkled his brow as he studied her. "Are you okay?"

"Rae Lynne Grimes I'd like you to meet Logan Birdsong of Birdsong Building Contractors. Logan, this is the former owner of the land we'll be developing." Todd mocked her.

Rae glared at the two men. "You work for Todd?" She was proud that her voice sounded strong even as her heart withered in her chest.

"You know each other?" The smirk on Todd's face said he was already aware.

Icy fingers chilled her spine. "You texted me?" *How did Todd get my cell number?*

Todd grinned.

Rae wanted to plead with Logan to leave with her. Instead she said, "Don't trust him. He'll suck you in and before you know it you'll be cheating old ladies out of their pensions."

Todd said, "That's a bit melodramatic."

Logan stiffened. "Rae, give me a little more credit—"

Blinking back tears, she whispered, "I did." She slid closer to the door, needing to escape.

Todd whispered. "Do yourself a favor Rae Lynne, sign the papers and leave, while you still can."

Logan stepped between them. "This is just business, there's no need for threats."

Rae managed to get the door open.

Logan grabbed her arm. "Wait."

Snatching her arm from his grasp, she hit the doorjamb and stumbled. Logan reached for her. She recovered, avoiding his touch. "I've got to go."

"Rae, this isn't personal..."

She nodded her head towards Todd. "With Todd, it's always personal."

"Rae Lynne, just sell the camp and say good bye."

"Fuck you Todd." She turned and bumped into Ditchwater Pete. Babbling an apology, she fell into her truck and jammed the key in the ignition. Blinded by tears, she shoved it in gear and stomped on the gas. Rae careened into traffic, ignoring the truck driver laying on his horn as he skidded to a stop inches from her bumper.

***

Rae stood at the river's edge skipping rocks across the water. Her heart and mind were in chaos. Blinking back tears, she couldn't help but wonder if Todd arranged for her to meet Logan. The thought made her stomach churn. She'd checked the text message as soon as she reached the wildlife boat ramp. The message came from Logan's number. *Could they have planned this together?* She was giving herself a headache. She threw another rock, watching the splashes with little gratification.

Picking up a large rock, Rae threw it like a baseball. Now she felt satisfaction as she watched it soar across the surface of the water, out to the channel marker. A croaker flew out of the water, the rock thwacked the fish, and it fell back into the murky river. "Ouch." Rae cringed. "Sorry."

Gravel crunched behind her. She turned to see Dana striding across the parking area. "You fishing?"

"Fish got in my way." Rae didn't want to see the pity in Dana's eyes.

"I bet he won't do that again."

Rae snorted, trying not to laugh. "I hate you. Let me be mad."

"Be mad, I'll be mad with you." Dana held out a white take-out bag.

Rae frowned at the bag. The scent of spices and savory meat tickled her senses.

"Not hungry." Her stomach growled, calling her a liar.

"Jenna sent you some chicken." She gave the bag a shake.

Ignoring it, she tossed another rock into the river. "How'd she know I didn't have lunch?"

"Logan came into the Depot looking for you."

Rae paused in mid-throw. "He came to the Depot?"

Dana nodded. "Billy told him that's where you'd go."

Rae snorted. "It's where I should've gone."

"He told us what happened at the Gull."

Rae shrugged.

"Eat!"

"I don't want anything." She wound up her arm to throw the rock.

Dana stepped in front of her.

Rae managed to stop mid-throw and cursed, "Damn it, Dana. Do you want me to bash you in the head?" She stomped away. "I can't deal with this right now." Tears streamed down her cheeks.

Unfazed, Dana slipped beside her. She tried matched her stride to Rae's, not easy in three-inch wedges. "I'm sorry you're hurting, but if you are going to stay sober, you have got to take care of yourself. It's especially important after something like this. You've not been sober that long and…"

Rae Lynne snatched the bag and stomped to the end of the public pier. She plopped on one of the wooden benches and opened the bag. Gulls, smelling the food, began to glide towards the pier. They called to her, hoping for a morsel.

Rae took a bite of the sandwich. "Spicy." She coughed.

Dana handed her a take-out cup with a straw at the ready.

Rae took a big gulp and winced. Pinching the bridge of her nose, she squeezed her eyes shut and waited for her brain to thaw. "Oh, that's good." The milk shake was a perfect blend of chocolate and coffee. Blinking back tears, she said, "Thanks, chocolate cures everything, huh?"

Dana studied her. "You okay?"

"Yeah, just feeling stupid." Rae hunted for a napkin and wiped her eyes. "What was I thinking? You don't pick up some strange guy off the road, fuck his brains out and decide he's your prince charming." She gazed out across the river, picking at her sandwich and tossing pieces to the gulls screeching overhead.

"Yeah, you don't know someone half your life and decide he's suddenly prince charming, either." Dana plopped onto the bench and leaned her head against Rae's shoulder. "We're a sorry pair."

"Are you talking about my brother? I told him he'd better not hurt you," Rae said.

"If I have a problem with your brother, I'll deal with him. What are you going to do about Logan?"

"Nothing, it was just one of those weekend flings. It's not my first."

"But Rae, he's—"

"Working for Todd Bryant." Rae jumped up and paced the pier. "How can I trust him?"

"Rae Lynne, He's just trying to make a living."

"You don't think Todd put him up to meeting me?"

"Do you?"

Rae sighed and picked up the last of her sandwich, tossing the crusts to the gulls. "No, I guess not. He wouldn't have sacrificed his car for Todd's scheme." The sun's caress was warm on her skin. The Wildlife boat ramp was one of her favorite places. The smell of the river's familiar perfume could bring her peace like nothing else. "You know how I feel about Todd."

"Yes, I do. Does Logan?"

"It doesn't matter."

"That's not what you thought this weekend." Dana stepped in her way.

"Yeah, well things change," Rae said.

"What else is going on?"

"What do you mean?"

"Tell me about the threatening notes."

Rae shook her head. "It's nothing, just somebody trying to scare me away."

"You sure it's not serious?"

Rae shrugged.

"If you don't want to keep your dates, you know, for the club. I'll understand."

"I'll keep the dates. We had a deal."

"Rae, perhaps you should give Logan another chance."

"I'd better get back to work." Rae gathered her trash.

"Rae Lynne?" Dana placed her hand on Rae's arm.

Shaking her head, Rae stepped around her. "No Dane, you can't fix this, not this time—"

Dana pursed her lips and chose her words carefully. "Okay, I won't try to fix it, but if you need me, you know where I am."

Rae hugged her., "Yeah, I know, you'd wrestle alligators for me."

"Well, maybe not alligators, they have too many teeth and really bad breath."

Rae linked arms with her and they walked towards the parking lot.

"You need to come down to the club Wednesday so we can do your video and photo album."

Rae stopped, her heart in her throat. She didn't have a good track record with videos. The thought made her shudder.

Dana patted her hand. "It'll be okay, it's just to let possible dates know what you're like."

"You did not tell me anything about a video or photos."

"It's part of the process and you know it. You *will* be at Cupid's Zone Wednesday afternoon at three or I will come looking for you. If I do, I'll put you in frills and ruffles and fix your hair like Curly Sue," Dana threatened, crowding Rae against her truck.

Rae fumbled with the door handle and leapt into the truck. As she is backed out she could hear Dana yelling, "Don't think you can run away. I can always find you."

Chapter 26

It had been two days since Rae had last seen Logan. He was still in town. Her friends kept her apprised of his activities. She knew he ate all his meals at the Depot and was driving one of two white work trucks with the Birdsong logo on the side. Every time she saw a light-colored truck, her heart sped up. Leeward was filled with light colored work trucks. So far, none she'd seen were Logan.

Wiping her clammy hands on her jeans, Rae tried the door of Dana's club. It was locked. She checked the time on her phone, three. "She tells me to be here but she's not even here." Rae checked her messages—nothing.

Rae stared at the Art Deco door and smiled with pride. It had been a real find. Dana had nearly ruined it. She caressed the repair, no one know the deep gouge Dana had put in the wood when, determined to help restore it, had proved that some people just shouldn't be allowed around power tools. Rae smiled, thankful there was something, Dana wasn't perfect at. The high gloss glowed in the afternoon sunlight and made the white and gold script on the window look like a jewel. The added architectural elements kept the old plain brick gymnasium from looking institutional.

Rae wasn't into the whole dating thing. Unlike Dana, who still believed in happily ever after, Rae knew, for her, there was no such thing. Logan's betrayal had hammered that truth home. She turned to leave, nearly stumbling into Dana in her haste to escape.

Loaded with an arm full of packages, Dana said, "Open the door for me." She shoved her keys into Rae's hand.

"Have you been shopping all day?" Rae opened the door and caught a couple of packages as they fell. Dana fumbled everything onto the nearest table.

Faint sunlight filtered into the room from windows near the ceiling. Dana strode to the wall and flipped on the overheads. The room's elegance was surprising: golden oak tables with chrome legs, matching chairs with beige upholstery. It had the feel of an upscale coffee shop with Art Deco and modern touches. The walls were painted in muted tones of beige and blue.

Dana crossed her arms over her ample chest and frowned. "I knew you wouldn't dress up, but did you have to wear dirty work clothes?"

Rae blushed. "I came straight from the garage."

Dana started opening packages. She held up a dove gray suit, laying another outfit on the back of a chair. "I like this, it looks sophisticated and I think the gray will look good with your dark hair and olive skin."

Rae shook her head. "It's not like anyone's gonna chose me."

"Not everyone who's joined Cupid's Zone is from Leeward." Setting the suit aside, Dana's expression softened. "If you don't want to go through with this—"

"I promised you I would." Rae didn't want her sympathy.

"That was before you met Logan."

"Logan isn't a concern." Rae wandered around the spacious room. The floor was a darker oak with area rugs set up in intimate conversation areas, each with colorful, eclectic couches, tables and chairs. It was very inviting. "I thought this was all online, what's with all the furniture?"

Dana looked around, smiling. "We have get-togethers each month. People can come in and meet and mix."

"Like a bar?"

"No alcohol."

Rae nodded.

"I know you care for him."

"I'm not discussing him."

"Rae?"

"No Dana, I'm here. You should be thrilled. Now quit busting my ass and let's get this show going."

"I just want you to be happy."

Rae snorted. "Why? It's not like I expect it anymore."

"Rae, that's not the attitude you should have. You deserve to be happy." Dana gave her a quick embrace. "We have each other and even your stupid asshole of a brother..."

"You still seeing Billy?"

"You mean the red-necked buffoon who thinks I'm just a booty call?" She shook her head. "No, I think I've decided to cut my losses on that one."

"If he can't see how awesome you are then he's an idiot."

Dana nodded. "Yep, he's an idiot." She grabbed a handful of clothes and started walking. "Come on, let's see if we can uncover the beautiful you under all that dirt and grease."

Rae followed her to the locker rooms. She and Billy had taken Tae Kwan Do here as kids. Dana kept the muted tones of beige and blue throughout the back, adding a soft green in the locker rooms/bathrooms to give it that beachy-spa look. Sea shells, sea glass and grass mats completed the look.

"Straight to the showers then to the green room."

"Green room?" Rae asked.

"It's the make-up room."

Rae hesitated at the door. The locker room looked much as it had when she'd last seen it. The paint and padded benches were a nice touch, and it no longer smelled of sweat and ammonia. "I could design some art deco mirrors."

Dana gave her a gentle push. "Later, right now shower and wash your hair." She opened a locker and handed her towels, shampoo and body wash. "I'll send someone in here in a few minutes to help you get ready." Dana shut the door, leaving her alone with her worries.

The door to the adjoining room opened. Rae clutched the towel to her chest.

"Hey, you decent?" Sandy Windley poked her head into the room.

Laughing, Rae said, "That all depends on who you ask." The two women embraced. remembering her lack of attire, Rae blushed. "You look great." Her voice cracked on the lie.

Sandy was still pretty, her smile vibrant. The ravages of cancer were evident. She was too thin, her make-up unable to hide the dark circles beneath her eyes. "Have a seat Lady Bug, let's show them how beautiful you are."

Rae sat in the beautician's chair while Sandy toweled her head. Rae was surprised at the strength in her thin arms. Sandy pulled the towel away, revealing a tangle of curls sticking up in all directions. Sandy massaged some sweet-smelling foam into Rae's hair and turned on the dryer. As Ms. Sandy fluttered around drying and styling her hair, Rae began to relax.

"I think we should just go with a natural look. Could we remove some of your-uh-decorations?"

"Don't you like my hardware?" Rae asked as she pulled out the eyebrow stud.

Shaking her head, Sandy chuckled. "Is that what you call it? Well, you are prettier without it."

Rae set the jewelry on the side-table and reached up, taking the older woman's hand. "Have I ever told you how much I appreciate all you've done, you know, since my mom left?" She met the older woman's gaze in the mirror. Rae blinked back tears.

Sandy stopped combing her hair, coming around to face her. "What's upset you?"

Rae took a deep breath and the tears fell. "I can't do this."

"You mean the video?" Sandy patted her hand.

Rae started to sob.

"Goodness, Rae." Sandy held her, rubbing her back and whispering words of comfort.

"I know about the tumor." Rae hiccupped. Accepting the paper towel Sandy offered, she wiped her nose.

Sandy blinked back her own tears. "Oh honey, it's just a little thing. The doc said it would be all clear with a couple of treatments." She met Rae's eyes. "Now you tell me the truth, what's really bothering you?"

The words tumbled out as Rae told her about Logan and Todd, the notes and her fear of losing the camp. There was more she wanted to say but the words stuck in her throat.

"Girl, you are wound so tight you're gonna spin off into outer space if you don't relax." Sandy sighed. "You need to stop worrying about things you can't change and focus on what you can."

"How can I not worry?"

"Listen to me, life is short. You need to allow yourself to be happy. Are you still doing your sculptures?"

Rae shrugged. "Yeah, but I gotta eat, too."

"Some sacrifices are worth it. Have you ever tried selling any of it?"

"Logan thinks-thought he could sell some to a friend of his." Rae ached for him. "I like working on the cars but, sometimes Dad and Billy make me feel like I can't do anything right."

"All families have their problems."

"I wish I'd had you for a mom."

"You have me for a friend. Now wipe those tears." Sandy smiled at her. "You know, an art deco statue in front of the building would help with its industrial look."

Rae nodded. "She needs some mirrors inside too."

Rae hardly recognized the woman in the mirror. Without her hardware, she felt naked, vulnerable. She touched her eyebrow, empty of its silver stud. It was her most recent piercing. After hospice had called, knowing her grandfather's end was near, she'd needed something to help with the pain. The tatts and piercings were all part of her personal therapy. It also made people treat her with caution. "I'm not this girl." Loneliness crept in. "Anyone seeing this video will expect me to be her." She pointed to the mirror. "But that's not me."

"It is you, just a different side of you," Sandy reasoned.

"No, she's who I might have been."

"Rae Lynne, she's as much a part of you as your piercings and tattoos."

Rae didn't agree but she would wear her *normal* costume to do the video. *What does it matter, it's all an act anyway?*

Half-sitting on the stool, Rae kept one foot on the floor. She calculated how far it was to the door as she planned her escape. Phil Archer greeted her from behind the camera.

"Afternoon, Rae."

"Phil." She clutched the seat until her hands hurt.

"Okay, let's get started," Dana said taking a seat off camera. "Relax."

Rae glowered. "This is as relaxed as I get."

"I'm going to ask you a few questions. Just be yourself."

Her pulse raced and she tried not to think about that other video. Remembering Phil with Todd at the gallery put dark thoughts in her head. *Phil had followed Todd and Devin around all through high school.* Rae frowned. *Anyone could run a cam-recorder, Todd didn't need a computer geek to do the job.*

"Show them who you are and they'll love you," Dana encouraged.

"Like that's ever helped me before." Rae shifted on the stool. "Let's just get this over with."

Phil raised his hand from behind the camera. "We're ready to get started. On three." He began counting, holding up his fingers.

Rae was afraid she might throw-up. Her mouth felt dry.

"Tell us your name."

Rae stammered out her name.

Dana asked a few questions. "What's your favorite color?"

"I don't know, I like them all."

"Rae?"

"I'm an artist. I love color, especially bright colors against black and white. I like contrast."

Dana nodded. "How about music?"

"Yeah, I like music." Rae shrugged.

"What kind of music?" Dana's voice held a note of exasperation.

"That depends on my mood. I like classic southern rock like Lynard Skynard but I also like Pavarotti. I don't know. Whatever moves me. Music should make you feel something."

"Do you have a favorite?"

"Rock, anything with a heavy beat, anything that can make me forget."

"Forget?"

"You know, the world, life."

"What are you looking for in a man?"

"I'm not looking for a man."

"Damn it Rae Lynne, this is a dating video. They need to know what you like and dislike," Dana shouted in exasperation.

"What I dislike is being trounced up in this normal suit and expected to perform like some trained monkey. What I dislike is phony people and right now I am the worst. This isn't me." She stood and pointed to the suit. "I want a man who likes me with my tattoos and piercings, torn jeans and painted tee shirts. I want someone who makes me laugh and listens when I talk. I want someone who doesn't judge me or others because we look and dress differently. But this girl..." Shaking her head. "I don't know this girl. I don't know what she wants in a man. Hell, I don't even know what she wants for dinner." Tears stung her eyes.

Dana nodded. "Cut. Phil take a break, we'll edit that later."

Rae shook her head. "Edit out the truth."

"No, but I doubt you want everyone to see that deeply inside you."

Rae nodded. "I think you made a mistake bringing me here. I'm not dateable, Dana. I pick up guys in a bar for a quickie and never see them again. I don't date. No man stays over and they sure as hell don't sleep in my bed." She ran her hand through her moussed curls, disrupting Sandy's hard work. She wiped her hands on her pants leg.

"Rae, if you want to make changes in your life, then this is a good step."

Rae rolled her eyes. "Learning to play nice with others?"

Dana nodded. "Who would you want go dancing with or out to dinner?"

"I don't dance and I'd go to dinner with you."

"Okay then, a male version of me," Dana said cheerily.

Rae snorted. "Great, just what I need—a man who'll bully me and make me do things I don't want to do. Nah, what I need is a really quiet guy who is used to taking orders and likes a woman with a bad attitude." Rae had not needed the psychologist to tell her she was using her bad attitude and sex to control men. She already knew that it was all about control. Falling for Logan meant losing control. It was a good thing they were over, she didn't need that kind of drama in her life.

Dana laughed. "Okay, tell us about your work." She motioned for Phil to hurry behind the camera.

Grudgingly, Rae muttered, "I work at Grimes Auto with my Dad, brother and an assortment of nuts from my family tree."

Dana put her fingers to her lips and spread her cheeks while mouthing *smile*.

Rae gave her a Cheshire cat grin and said, "Is this better?"

"Terrifying," Phil muttered.

Rae snorted. "I'm too scary when I try to be nice, Dana. I'm a bitch. It works for me."

Dana sighed. "Tell us about your art."

Rae felt more comfortable talking about her art. "I worked for a lighting company building one-of-a-kind chandeliers and sconces before coming back to Leeward. I liked the work but I prefer more freedom."

The video became easier and Rae was surprised when Dana called cut. "I think that's good. Thanks Phil, we'll view it later."

Phil left.

Dana draped her arm over Rae's shoulder. "You okay?"

"I'll live."

"You want to hang out a while, we can get a pizza?"

Rae agreed and Ms. Sandy joined them. It was nice to have some girl time with two of her favorite people. By silent agreement, they avoided all discussion of men and their faults.

Chapter 27

The sidewalk, still warm from the sun, had Rae feeling the perspiration pooling in her bra even as the evening breeze began to cool the city. The restaurant was one of those trendy places. A reclaimed storefront along Main Street where all the young and beautiful came to mingle after leaving their offices. Peering through the window Rae could see an assortment of business attire. Casual, business casual, not the faded jeans and vintage Aerosmith t-shirt she'd worn for her date. She considered sending a text with some excuse, but his video made her think of Opie from the old *Andy Griffith Show.* She wondered what was crueler—leaving or staying?

Taking a deep breath, she pushed open the front door. Sweet, spicy scents mingled with expensive cologne. She could feel the eyes of the other patrons and the wait staff as they turned to stare at her. She wasn't one of them. They knew it and so did she. Rae stepped to the hostess' podium and waited. The hands on the clock over the bar moved slowly, fifteen minutes passed and no one came to assist her. Rae made her way to the bar.

Rae stopped short of her goal, nearly colliding with a pretty, little bleached-blonde standing arms akimbo in her path. "May I help you," she challenged.

"Nope, I see him." Side-stepping the smaller girl, Rae walked up to the red-head at the bar. "Hey, Ralph?"

Ralph Evans turned and smiled, his face as open and honest as the son from that old sitcom. He was untouched and clueless to the world's cruelties. His was not a world where mothers left their children or a step-brother set you up to be raped by his friends. He knew nothing of drug-induced nights of madness, nor the alcoholic haze needed to find a few minutes' peace. *I can do nothing but corrupt him.*

His smile faltered, gentle brown eyes wary. She could see his mind shifting gears probably wondering what had happened to the girl in the video. "Rae Lynne?"

His voice quaked.

She almost felt sorry for him but before she could make an excuse and leave, he slid off the bar stool and held out his hand. Giving her a big toothy smile, his freckles glowing against the blush on his cheeks, he said, "It's so nice to meet you in person."

Ralph's smile seemed so genuine, Rae believed he really was happy to meet her. She returned his smile. "Nice to meet you, too." She wondered if he noticed the roughness of her hands. *At least I took time to wash and clean the dirt and paint out from under my nails.*

"Well, I hope you're hungry, they have the best food here. I love their shrimp and grits." His words came out a bit nervous. He took a deep breath and lifted his head. "I hate first dates."

She agreed. "I love shrimp and grits."

"That's why I chose this restaurant." He met her eyes and relaxed. Taking her elbow, he led her to the hostess' stand. Giving the little blonde a confident smile, Ralph said, "Michelle, we're ready to dine now."

Michelle gave her a vengeful glare before turning her attention to Ralph. "I'm afraid all we have left is the patio." She fluttered her eyelashes. "I hope that will be okay?" She narrowed her eyes at Rae, expecting trouble.

Rae noted several empty tables and met the girl's stare with a raised eyebrow.

Ralph shrugged, ignoring the lie. "It's a lovely evening, the patio will be nice."

Rae smiled at the hostess. "Yes, the patio will be nice. It's rather stuffy in here."

Michelle led the way out to the patio to a wrought iron table with a colorful umbrella. The sun in its descent painted the sky in shades of pinks and purples. The last glow of light silhouetted the tall pines across the river.

Ralph pulled out a chair.

Rae took the seat and awkwardly allowed him to push it under the table.

Leaning close to her ear he asked. "Would you like some wine?"

Startled, she shook her head and managed to blurt out, "Driving." Regaining control, she told the waitress. "Lemonade?"

Ralph smiled as he took his seat. "I'll have the same."

Michelle nodded, leaving them with menus.

Ralph asked a series of questions about her job.

Rae was saved from answering by the arrival of their server.

"Hi. I'm Tiffany, I'll be your server tonight. Do you know what you want to eat?" She rattled off the specials and set glasses of ice water in front of them.

After they placed their orders, Rae answered. "I drive a wrecker truck, do a little body work, but mostly I paint cars. My Dad owns the body shop."

"I like the pink streak in your hair."

Rae gave him extra points for trying to keep the conversation going. She decided to play nice. "I put it in for Breast Cancer Awareness. My best friend's mom was diagnosed with cancer when we were in college and I've worn the pink ever since."

"Did she beat it?"

"Yeah." She didn't mention the latest tumor.

"Do you participate in any of the fund raisers?"

"Oh, God yes. My friend, Dana, drags me kicking and screaming to banquets and bike-a-thons and everything in between. We're planning a poker run for this fall. She bought an old Harley that I've restored and painted pink."

"You painted a Harley pink? That's not the color I associate with a Harley." Ralph shook his head with a smile.

"It looks pretty cool." Rae pulled out her phone and showed him a series of photos she'd taken before and after restoration.

Leaning in close, he studied the photos. "I stand corrected."

"Now that sounded like a teacher," she said, teasing.

Ralph gave her a conspiratorial grin. "I'm only faking the teacher part. I'm really just an old athlete turned coach. I teach because it pays the bills."

"That's right, you're a runner. I read your bio, you've done five marathons?"

"No, I've done five half marathons and two full, but mostly I do the five and sometimes ten Ks."

"Five K, that's what, five kilometers, three miles?"

"Very good, yeah, I do the three and six mile runs for MS, Wounded Warriors, St. Jude's, if it's a good cause, I run. Of course, I'd probably run for free pizza and beer, too." He chuckled.

Ralph was not what she'd expected. He was nice and funny. She began to relax. He wasn't Logan. She didn't want to throw him down on the table and have crazy monkey sex with him, but she was enjoying his company.

"Hello little sister, what are you doing here?"

A chill seared her spine. Rae leaned forward poised to run. She steeled herself against the suffocating fear. It took all of her self-control to smile and pretend he didn't bother her. "Devin? I 'm surprised to see you out. Do they have you tagged with a GPS tracker?"

Devin Kinnion was movie-star handsome, his face a little harsher after ten years in prison. He was allowing his hair to grow back out and no longer looked like Lex Luther. Like Todd, Devin had learned to use his good looks to get his way: with girls, teachers and even the law.

"What? No puppet-master? Did you cut your strings? Do you think you can be a real boy?" Rae knew she was baiting the bear but she couldn't stop herself. When she was nervous, she went on the attack.

Devin glared at Ralph. "Did she tell you about her brother? We're very close."

Rae Lynne clenched her napkin in her fists. "He is not my brother." Narrowing her eyes, she said, "Devin, why don't you be a good little boy and go away."

"I did that already, thanks to you. Now, I'm back—to stay." He squeezed her shoulder, his grip bruising. "Todd will be building a new spa down on the waterfront. He's promised me a job with the new contractor, Birdsong Construction. But you already have intimate knowledge of Birdsong and his equipment, isn't that right little sister? Does Logan know you're on a date with another man?"

Heat rose in her face and she wished him dead. She refused to flinch.

The pretty, young hostess tapped him on the arm. "Mr. Kinnion, Mr. Bryant is waiting for you in the private dining room." She regarded him with open adoration.

Rae wanted to warn her but no words would come out.

Devin gave the hostess the full heat of his charm. "Thank you, Michelle. Well, we can't keep the mayor waiting." He whispered something to the girl. She giggled and slid her hand into the crook of Devin's arm.

He turned back to Rae Lynne. "I'll see you at the next family gathering." To

Ralph he warned. "Don't sleep with her unless you get her consent in writing first."

Rae scowled at his retreating back.

"So, he's *that* Devin?" Ralph stared after him.

"You know about him?" Rae met his eyes.

Ralph's face turned as red as his hair. "I Googled you." He licked his lips. "I'm new to the online dating and you hear horror stories."

"In that case, I'm surprised you showed up."

"I was intrigued by a woman brave enough to take on the Bryant family."

Heat seared her cheeks. "You're familiar with the family?'

"Anyone living on this side of the river knows of the Bryant family." His words held a hint of anger but he didn't elaborate.

"I didn't win the court case."

"You made a stand, something a lot of others are too afraid to do."

The river glowed, the last fingers of sunlight filtering through the pines giving the effect of fairy lights. She longed to be out there away from Devin and Todd.

"Well! Our food has arrived." Ralph spoke a little too loud, his relief obvious.

She gave him a tight smile and nodded to their server.

The shrimp and grits smelled heavenly, but her stomach churned. It was bad enough that Ralph knew her history but knowing Todd and Devin were in the dining room made her jumpy. She toyed with the food. Every time she tried to take a bite, her throat tightened and she felt as if she might be sick. Fear twisted her in knots making it difficult to concentrate on Ralph's attempts at conversation.

Ralph sat down his fork. "Would you like a doggie bag?"

Rae nodded, grateful for his understanding.

He paid the waitress and waited while Rae's food was transferred to take out plates.

"How about a walk?" He offered her his hand.

Rae attempted a smile and wished she could feel something more for Ralph than just friendship. "You're really a glutton for punishment." She let him escort her down the patio and across the tarmac to the river walk.

"It's a beautiful night." The moon was just coming up big and full in a sky filled with glitter.

The town had added rails and benches and widened the sidewalk several years ago creating a place for residents and tourists to stroll along the waterfront. During the day there were joggers, mothers with strollers and local business people having lunch, but in the evening, there were mostly couples. They passed young couples little more than children in their first blush of romance, and nodded to senior citizens married before they were born, still holding hands and whispering in the moonlight.

"I love the way the lights dance on the water. Like fairies." She babbled. "I always loved to go to the state aquarium and watch the moon fish and jellies. They remind me of ballerinas dancing in the water. I guess that's why I like the lights on the water, same effect, almost."

"You have a poet's soul," Ralph teased.

Rae snorted. A fish splashed in the river beyond the glow of the lights.

"I've had a nice time."

"Oh yeah, I'm sure, especially after Devin showed up."

He chuckled. "Yeah, well that was a little more interesting that I was hoping for but—" He shrugged. "—still, a nice evening."

Rae nodded. "It was nice meeting you." Her thoughts drifted to Logan but she forced that avenue closed. *It does no good to wish for what cannot be.*

"Perhaps we can see each other again."

"Sure, I'd like that. Maybe next time we'll go somewhere no one knows me."

He leaned in to kiss her.

Realizing his intent, she turned her head; his dry lips merely grazed her cheek.

Ralph shrugged. "Sorry, too fast?"

"No—I—" Rae couldn't explain the feeling of guilt. Ralph deserved someone who wasn't aching for another man.

"I'll blame it on the moonlight."

She chuckled. "It is a full moon." Ditchwater Pete darted between two buildings. She stopped walking to stare.

"Is something wrong?" Ralph asked.

Shaking her head, Rae said, "I thought I saw a friend of mine but I must have been mistaken." She smiled. "I must be more exhausted than I realized. I think I should call it a night."

Ralph escorted her back to her truck. Coming out of the shadows, they saw someone propped against the tailgate. Rae thought for a moment it was Pete, but as they came closer, her heart lurched and she realized it was Logan.

Ralph put his hand to her arm. "Should I call the police?"

Rae wanted to run to Logan and wrap her arms around him. Pulling away from Ralph, she blushed feeling as if she'd done something wrong. Embarrassed, she said "No, I can take him."

Logan pushed away from the truck, his hands in his pockets. "Ev'ning Rae." He nodded to Ralph.

Rae could feel Ralph measuring the situation. "Rae, what do you need me to do?"

She sighed. "It's okay, he's not going to hurt me." She offered him her hand. "Good night, Ralph."

Ralph frowned at her hand and shook his head. "Yeah, okay, I'm not a genius but I can see I'm getting the brush off. 'Night, Rae."

Rae watched as he walked away.

"A friend?" Logan asked.

"My date."

"You could do better."

She glared. "Who? You? Ralph's a nice guy."

"I'm a nice guy."

Shaking her head, she said, "Not for long if you're doing business with Todd."

"Rae, you don't understand."

"No, you do not understand, he destroys everything in his path. I can't be with anyone who doesn't see it."

"Your own brother works for him."

"Devin? Devin is not my brother."

Logan shrugged. "Stepbrother."

"He just got out of prison. Did you know that?"

Logan gave her blank face.

Rae rolled her eyes. "He's as bad as Todd."

"Damn it Rae Lynne, I don't have the luxury of riding that high horse you're on. I've got people depending on me. This is business. There's nothing personal about it."

Pinching her bottom lip between her teeth, she nodded. "It's personal for me, Logan. It's my land he wants."

"Then don't sell it to him."

She laughed. "You have no clue."

"He told me y'all used to be involved."

Rae clenched her fists. Between clenched teeth she said, "I have never dated Todd Bryant." Trembling she unlocked her door and set her take-out plate on the seat.

"Rae?"

Taking a deep breath, she said, "He bought my grandfather's loan, ten thousand dollars. If I don't find a way to pay it, Todd wins. So yeah, this is personal, Logan." Rae climbed into the truck and sat there gripping the steering wheel. The street was empty. She closed her eyes.

Logan reached for the door. "Rae, I wish—"

"Don't, Logan, we each have our dragons to slay." Rae pulled the door shut and started the truck. She watched him in the rearview mirror as she pulled onto the darkened street. She watched until she could no longer see him.

Chapter 28

"Damn that girl!" Logan slapped the hood of his truck. "She won't even listen." He watched as her tail lights disappeared. He knew what he needed to do but he dreaded what he might find. Cursing under his breath, he climbed into the truck, spinning tires as he pulled out of the parking lot. He clenched the steering wheel, straining to keep the truck at the speed limit as he drove out of town. "I've got to her out of my system." Being with her only made him want her more. He shoved his foot on the gas, rocketing the company truck down the dark, winding road.

The hurt in her eyes when she saw him at the Gull with Todd flashed through his memory. "Damn it, we were supposed to meet at the Depot. Why was she even at the restaurant?" *She said something about a text.* He slowed and pulled to the side of the road. Thumbing through his cell he checked his text history. Searching his phone, he found the text. "Fuck. That conniving bastard." He shoved the phone into his computer case and pulled back onto the road. *Todd's playing games. Why?*

Logan slowed the truck and made the turn towards Leeward. Todd said he and Rae had a history. He'd believed it was a romantic relationship but Billy and Rae both felt Todd could be her evil pen pal. "Oh God, please don't let me have chained my company to a psychopath," he prayed.

Birdsong Construction was in trouble. Logan had overextended his credit and bought more equipment and hired another crew but the jobs dwindled. He felt like that little boy trying hold back the ocean with his finger. He couldn't let the company go bankrupt. He couldn't let his family and his co-workers down. If Bryant was the only way to keep the business going then he'd just have to deal with the bastard. "Rae is just going to have to realize that this was business." *And if she couldn't?* A deer leapt from of the ditch bank. The stag stood like a statue in the middle of the road. Cursing, Logan slammed on brakes and swerved. He clipped the deer with the bumper on passenger-side. "Great, what a wonderful night this is turning out to be." The deer staggered to his feet and ran into the woods. Logan grabbed his cell phone and climbed out of the truck to check the damage. He wanted to scream at the deer. "Two deer in less than two weeks, that has to be a record." He sighed. The headlight was broken, his fender bent and the grill shattered. The damage was minimal. He snapped a few pictures. "Great, now I've got to call the insurance and deal with them." He crawled back in the truck. "I'll call them when I get back to the office." He yawned. Leeward was turning into a real nightmare.

Logan drove slowly through town. He was staying in the office trailer Todd had ordered for him. Why he needed to be here before they'd even bought the land, he didn't know, but Todd was insistent. Logan couldn't afford to argue, he'd sold his condo and rented out his office. The trailer was the only place he could afford to stay.

Seeing Rae with that guy tonight had gotten under his skin. He shouldn't care this much about a woman he just met. The guy barely looked old enough to shave. "She doesn't need a boy, damn it, she needs a man." He didn't like this feeling of jealousy nor insecurity that everything in his life was going to shit. He needed to forget about Rae Lynne Grimes and get his mind back on the job.

He turned the radio up and joined Dierks, with his off-key harmony as the truck bounced over the rutted, dirt road. "Five-one, five-O, this might be my new theme song." Thoughts of Rae in the throes of passion, dancing in the kitchen, smiling over the supper table... "This isn't getting over her." He sighed. "This is my new theme song." He needed to run a Google search on Todd and Rae, he needed to know what was going on with them. He'd run the Bryant Foundation and even looked up Todd. As a business man he'd won awards and been elected mayor. *Maybe I need to change my parameters?* Another deer came into view. He slowed the truck and glared at the creature until it's white tail disappeared back into the marsh grass. "Call the insurance company first."

Chapter 29

The drizzling rain and gray skies fit her mood. Rae felt emotionally drained. She sat in the Depot sipping a cup of coffee and nibbling on toast.

"How was your date?" Jenna asked topping off her coffee.

Rae sighed. "He was nice, too nice."

"That bad?"

She shrugged. "Devin showed up before our food, so I really didn't feel like eating."

"Oh no, did he cause trouble?" Jenna set the pot down on the table and eased into the booth across from her.

"Not really, I mean, he tried but Ralph already knew about him. He was really…"

"Nice?" Jenna asked.

Laughing, Rae nodded. "Yeah."

"Oh my God, the rain is doing awful things to my head." Dana slid to a stop at Rae's table. Jenna rose and Dana scooted into the seat she'd vacated. "Look at my hair!"

Rae smiled. "It's good to know you're not always perfect."

Dana blinked. "Perfect? Me? You've known me a long time Rae Lynne Grimes—"

"Yeah, and you always seem so put together and poised while I skulk around like a slug."

"Do you want coffee?" Jenna asked.

Dana nodded. "So how was your date?"

"Logan was there."

Dana stared wide-eyed and mouth open. "No, did you ditch Opie?"

Shaking her head, Rae said, "Ralph was a very nice guy, maybe too nice." She told her about Devin and Logan waiting for her. "I need to forget that man." She could still see Logan standing alone in the dark as she drove away. She wanted to trust him. She'd lain awake until dawn thinking of him.

"Oh my God, isn't that the school teacher?" Dana asked, snatching a piece of her toast.

"Where?" Rae looked behind her and back to Dana.

Dana waved the slice of toast towards the television. The Depot had two televisions mounted in the front corners of the restaurant.

Rae looked up and tried to make sense of the news report. A picture came on screen, a school photo. "Oh-my-God, it is Ralph." She shouted to Jenna. "Turn it up. Turn it up, Jen."

"Local teacher and track coach, Ralph Evans, was killed last night in a hit and run. Coach Evans was taking his nightly run on Bateman Road when he was struck down. Witnesses say they saw a light-colored work truck or van near the time of the accident. Anyone with any information is urged to call the Beaufort County Sherriff's department or Leeward's Chief of Police, Von Fleming." Phone numbers flashed across the bottom of the television screen.

"Hit and run? Ralph?" She thought of everyone she knew who drove a light-colored work vehicle. The number was staggering, including herself and Logan. *Logan?* Panic gripped her as she thought of last night. Logan had seen her with Ralph. Devin too. *That means Todd knew about Ralph, too.* "Shit. I gotta go." Leaping from the booth she ran out the door, praying. "Oh God, please let me be wrong."

Dana followed, shouting, "Rae, what's going on?"

The note plastered on her windshield was saturated by the light drizzle. Rae snatched it off and read it. "Leave before more of your friends get hurt." She groaned. "Oh God, no, please don't let this be my fault." She looked around, but there was no one in the parking lot except she and Dana.

Dana grabbed her arm. "Rae Lynne, what's going on? You're frightening me."

Shaking her head, Rae blinked back tears. "I'm not sure, Dana, please be careful. Someone..." Shaking her head. "I've got to go." She climbed inside her truck and gunned the motor.

Dana screamed. "Rae Lynne, get your scrawny ass back here."

Rae ignored Dana as she whipped the truck around. The power steering was stiff, and in her haste, she side swiped a light pole. She didn't stop. She sped down the highway, careening up on two wheels as she turned onto the dirt road. The Old Saw Mill road was filled with pot holes, Rae was sure she'd hit every one of them. She skidded to a stop in the muddy driveway.

"Rae Lynne?" Logan was coming out of the trailer with a travel mug in his hand. "What are you doing here?"

Rae sat there trembling, the motor still running. With trembling hands, she put the truck in park. Logan didn't look like a man who'd run someone over in a jealous fit. She turned off the key and searched for words. She needed to believe he didn't have anything to do with Ralph's death.

Logan propped against the door and leaned in the window. "Did you see the news?" He studied her, his eyes searching hers. "You saw it, too. I'm so sorry Rae. He seemed like a nice guy. You okay?"

The compassion in his voice was her undoing. She came out of the truck and into his arms. "Oh God, Logan—" She was breathing too fast, the panic and relief all mingled together to make her drunk. "I was so afraid." She clutched him tight, letting his scent soothe her.

Logan pushed her back, holding her at arm length, he asked, "Afraid, of what? Did someone hurt you?" He studied her face, concern in his eyes.

Rae bit her lip and she mumbled, "Your truck. It matches the one the witnesses saw. I just..."

"You thought I did it?" He stepped away from her. "Rae?" He shook his head. "You thought I was so jealous I went after this guy for having a date with you?"

She tried to get back into the circle of his arms but he stormed away. The rain turned from a drizzle to a shower.

"Damn it, Rae Lynne what do you take me for?"

She stumbled. "Logan, I—"

He said, "I'm sorry, Rae Lynne, I didn't kill a man for you."

With her stomach in her throat, she said, "Logan, it's not that. I was afraid

Todd might have—"

"No, don't bother. It's obvious what you think of me but let me ask you, sunshine, how about your own truck." He pointed to the damage she'd done coming out of the parking lot.

"I did that on my way here."

He nodded. "I'm sure the cops would love to hear how you had a date with the poor guy last night, and have damage to your truck this morning." He reached for his cell phone.

She crossed her arms over her chest and narrowed her eyes. "Call whoever you want it's not the first time I've dealt with the local cops."

"I'm not calling the cops, Rae Lynne. They don't need me doing their job for them." He closed his phone. "I was expecting a message." He shrugged.

Rae pointed to the truck parked beside the trailer. "Is that one yours?"

He nodded. "It's a company truck. We have several."

"There's damage on that one." She walked over and looked at the fender and felt her stomach churn. "There's blood and hair here."

"Yeah, I hit a deer last night." He looked up and frowned. "No, I was driving the other truck." He pointed to the one parked beside the trailer. Logan joined her in front of the work truck. "Shit." They studied the damage. "Someone probably hit another deer. The damned things come out of nowhere. They're all suicidal around here."

"Who has access to this truck?" She asked staring at hunk of red hair stuck to the grill.

He glanced in the cab. The keys dangled in the ignition. "No one should have been driving it last night."

"You might want to call the law yourself, before Todd does."

"Why don't you just call them? You're so tight with Mike, I'm sure he'll be happy to take me out of the way."

Rae put her hand on his arm. "Mike is the only one I'd trust. The rest are part of Todd's good ol' boys club. And you can bet this isn't going to end well. If Todd can blame me, he will and if he has to use you to do it, oh well. Don't think that he'll be loyal to you just because you're working for him. He believes everyone is expendable."

He threw his hands in the air sloshing coffee. "I think you're being paranoid. This is a coincidence. If you ask me, someone hit a dog or deer and just didn't want to get in trouble for driving the company truck."

"Logan, just be careful, okay? You don't know him like I do." Her tears mingled with the rain as she trudged back to her truck. Bile churned in her stomach. *Maybe if I told him about the note?* She shook her head, Logan seemed to think Todd could do no wrong.

Chapter 30

Logan couldn't shake the feeling that Rae's assumption was right. Ralph's death was too much of a coincidence. He called the police station and asked for Mike. They put him on hold while he stared at the truck and waited.

"This is McKenzie." Mike's voice sounded tired and distracted.

"Mike, Logan Birdsong, I need you come out to the office. Here at the building site."

"Man, I'm kinda swamped, can I call you back later. There's been a hit and run—"

"Yeah, that's why I'm calling, I may have the truck that hit the coach."

"What?" Mike lowered his voice. "What are you talking about?"

"One of my company trucks hit something. It had to be last night. Keys are still in the ignition but no one was supposed to be driving it."

"Joy riders?" Mike asked.

"Maybe." Logan hesitated not sure if he should tell the officer what Rae Lynne believed. "There are more coincidences."

"I don't like coincidences," Mike said. Logan could hear something in his voice.

"I met the coach last night." He tried to think how best to phrase the next part. "He was on a date with Rae Lynne. I was at a meeting with the Bryant Foundation."

"Fu—, great, of course you were." Logan could hear him calling to someone, but the words were muffled. "This rain is going to mess up any evidence that might be on the truck."

"I'll take care of it," Logan said. "I've got a tarp."

"Don't touch anything," Mike warned.

"I know, I watch CSI."

Mike snorted. "Yeah, wish we could solve this in an hour."

"Oh, and Mike, I hit a deer on the way home last night. I called the insurance company when I got back to the office..."

"Anything else?" he demanded.

"No, I think that's enough to incriminate me."

Mike hung up.

Logan would have laughed but the very real possibility of being accused of killing a man stopped him. "She's right, it can't end well."

Mike and two other cops came within the hour. Logan took them to where the truck was parked. He'd covered the hood of both trucks with a tarp.

"You touch anything?" the fresh-faced officer asked.

"No, I just pulled the tarp over it to keep the rain off."

The young officer looked skeptical but nodded. "Good."

"He's with the county," Mike explained, "part of the investigative team. This here is Detective Rodman."

Rodman shook his hand; he was older, harder. He met Logan's eyes. "The tarp was a good idea, probably kept the evidence intact."

"You really think it's evidence?" Logan asked. "I thought maybe it was a dog or deer."

The detective glanced over to the tech and they exchanged a glance. "It's evidence."

"Shit," Logan said and stomped away.

Mike caught up, he said, "The truck that hit the deer?"

Logan turned and showed him the damage.

Mike made notes. "You'll need to get a statement from the insurance company. Ask them to run a transcript of the call and the time. You may need an alibi."

Logan shook his head. "Beautiful."

The officers set a tent up over the truck and began processing it.

Logan paced. "You really think this truck was used to kill that guy?" he asked Mike after the tech guy started packing up. The other officer was arranging for the truck to be transported to the state facility, but for now, it would go to Washington.

Mike led Logan away from the other officers and said, "Yeah, I do." He exhaled. "Listen, since you called it in it looks better, but you're still going to be a suspect and if Todd is behind this…"

"Why would Todd be behind this? I don't get it. I know he's an ass, but murder?"

"I've known Todd most of my life and I wouldn't trust him if he said grass was green."

"Because he's a politician?"

"Because he's a sociopath." Mike ran a hand through his hair, weariness like the rain clung to him. "He's done stuff…"

"Rae Lynne?" Logan felt his stomach cramp. *I don't want to know.* "What happened?"

Shaking his head, Mike said. "I can't…Rae needs to tell you."

"Mike?"

"Let's just say that he's let others take the fall for him even when the evidence was there to convict him. Rae's been through hell because of that asshole."

"Why would he want to frame me? I'm working for him."

Mike shrugged. "If I understood how his mind worked I'd be terrified."

"What now?"

"Come down to the station, make a statement. We'll get Rae Lynne to come in and tell her part in it. Maybe we can get the real killer before anyone else gets hurt."

"You don't think this was a onetime thing?"

"If Todd's involved, no, I don't." He rejoined the other officers.

Logan didn't like the way that sounded. *Surely, they won't try to pin this on me?*

But he had a really bad feeling as he went to his truck and followed Mike to the Leeward Police Station.

Chapter 31

Rae entered the police station with clammy hands and a stomach that felt as if she were on a carnival ride. There was no receptionist or dispatcher on duty. She shuffled her feet, hoping Mike would come out of his office and they could do this outside.

She started down the hallway looking for Mike's office. The first door was open. Logan and Jorge were deep in discussion. They glanced up, and seeing her, Jorge stood up and shut his door. Her cheeks burned, and with her head down, she kept walking. The building smelled musty, like it needed a good cleaning. Rae felt the need to cough. The town had moved the police into the old doctor's office after the former station flooded when the water tower collapsed. They'd barely taken time to move things in before hunting the group that had sabotaged the tower.

She found Mike's office and handed Mike a plastic baggie with the latest note.

He looked at the soggy mess and frowned. "Why didn't you call me?"

"I'd just heard about Ralph and I wasn't thinking too clearly."

"You thought well enough to go warn Logan."

Rae looked away. "I was on my way when I saw the note."

"So, you touched it?"

"It was raining. The paper was already turning to mush."

"All right." Mike shoved his hand through his hair. His eyes were glassy with fatigue.

"Take me through the events of last night all the way up to where you first heard about the coach's death."

She did, starting with picking Ralph out of the videos at Cupid's Zone. "I really didn't think he'd pick me. That was my strategy you know, choose guys who wouldn't choose me. I think Dana's gotten wise to my plan, though." Rae gnawed her bottom lip as she realized she was babbling. "Sorry, I'm a little nervous."

Mike nodded. "It's okay, just tell your story and I can get a better idea of what's going on."

"Do you think my pen pal did this?" Her eyes were dry, too much time spent worrying when she should have been sleeping. "I think we need to tell Jenna and Dana, if this guy killed Ralph. He might go after one of them."

"We don't know he killed Ralph. It may be like the squirrel and the cat. He took advantage of the situation and used it to freak you out."

"Well, it's working."

***

Rae and Dana sat eating takeout in Dana's office at Cupid's Zone.

"Was it bad?" Dana asked. "Being questioned by the cops?"

Rae shrugged. "Nah, not too bad, I just had to talk to Mike." She picked at her food. "Mike said I may have to go to Washington and talk to the sheriff, but he's hoping I won't."

Dana nodded. "So, what else is going on, you told me to be careful. You said something similar when Billy and I went out to your place. Is this about what happened out at your place?"

Taking a deep breath, Rae told her about the notes and her fears. "I'm afraid if I don't leave, he might start hurting my friends. Ralph may have been killed because he went out with me."

Dana set her food down. "Then, you really don't think Logan had anything to do with Coach Evans' hit and run?"

Rae Lynne took a deep breath. "No. I don't. He seemed genuinely worried about how I felt. I can't see him doing it. And he did call the station to report the damage to the truck. According to Mike, it wasn't long after I left."

"They said on the news it was probably kids joy riding."

Rae snorted. "Yeah, Todd even went on camera and said they're looking into the coach's grade book to see if anyone might have a reason to kill him. I mean, really, who would kill a guy for a bad grade in PE?"

Dana nodded, nibbling on sweet potato fries. "It doesn't sound like a reason to murder someone. But you remember that case of the mom who murdered the girl that beat out her daughter for cheerleader?"

"That's an urban legend."

"No, it really happened back in the eighties."

"I still think Todd had something to do with it, but I doubt there's evidence to support it." Rae tried to imagine Todd as her pen pal. It just didn't fit. He might send her threatening notes and dead cats, but he'd kill the cats himself. And she was pretty sure he'd like it.

"You think Todd is behind your threats?" Dana toyed with her food.

Rae shrugged. "I don't know, it's just so weird. He has the note. If I don't pay it off, he gets the land. Unless he's trying to hurry me out, I can't understand the purpose. Why waste his time?"

"Maybe he thinks it'll make it more difficult for you to raise the money?"

"I don't know, and this thing with Ralph—"

"It was probably just an accident. Some kids got scared and ran off. The notes sound kind of like a bad prank. Did you get any dessert?"

Rae looked in the bag. "I thought you were on a diet?"

"I'm drinking a diet soda."

"There are a couple of pieces of carrot cake."

"See, that isn't even real dessert, that's a vegetable, so I'm good." Reaching into the bag Dana pulled out the cake. She tasted a dollop of the cream cheese frosting and moaned like she was having an orgasm.

Shaking her head, Rae laughed. "Yeah, you're good all right. Don't come crying to me when you can't fit into those new clothes you just bought."

Frowning, Dana pushed the cake away and stuck out her tongue. "That reminds me, you have another date. I took the liberty of accepting for you." Dana sorted through photos and papers on her desk. Finding the one she was looking for she held it out to Rae.

"Not another date," Rae whined. "Dating me is not a good idea, just ask Ralph."

"You had nothing to do with Ralph's demise. I'm sure it was just a tragic accident. The timing stinks but he <u>was</u> running on the highway. Aren't you going to ask about your date?"

"Okay fine, who is it?" Rae took the printout and seeing the photo, groaned. "Really Dana?"

"Ezekiel La Port, you know him? He's an artist."

"Yeah, I met him."

"When, where, how?" Dana leaned over and studied the photo. "What did you think about him?"

Rae looked down at the photo. His dark eyes were mesmerizing but she'd seen something else there. "Arrogant, talented, I don't know. I think he can be charming when he wants to be and the rest of the time he's an ass."

"Then the two of you should get along just fine."

Rae rolled her eyes.

"You're supposed to meet him at the Gallery coffee shop for supper tonight."

"Aw Dana, I'm not in the mood to be social."

"Yeah, so what else is new, think of it this way, you're almost done with your commitment. Tonight, and one more date and I won't bother you anymore."

Rae pushed away from the desk and paced. "Like I really believe that." Staring out the window, she blinked, seeing Logan across the street talking to a woman. "Fine," she said, her heart plummeting. "I'll go. Maybe I can get it over with quickly."

"That's the spirit. The "pull it off fast like a crusty old Band-Aid" plan," Dana teased, coming to stand behind her.

"What do I care who he sees?" Rae Lynne muttered under her breath.

Dana placed her hand on Rae's shoulder. "You can come back here and shower and get ready."

"Sure, whatever—" Rae shrugged.

"Try to keep the enthusiasm down, Rae. I don't know if I can handle it."

"I gotta go back to work." She balled up the paper and tossed everything in the trash including the tasted piece of carrot cake.

"You could have given it to someone," Dana called. "No reason to be wasteful."

"I got the other piece to take to Uncle Clyde." Rae watched as Dana frowned at the cake in her trash can. "Don't do it Dane. Once on the lip—"

Dana looked up and scowled. "Shut up bean pole." She slammed her office door.

Chapter 32

"Leave work early, I found the perfect outfit for you," Dana squealed into the phone.

Rae held it away from her ear. "I'm working. You do understand the concept, right? I like to eat and other luxuries, you know like lights and gas."

"Okay, so who licked the red off your sucker? No don't tell me, I already know. Come on Rae. Shut the torch down early and come see what I have for you. You'll look amazing and I have it on good authority that Ezekiel is anxious to go out with you. He's even called to confirm."

Rae rolled her eyes. "Fine, I'll be there as soon as I can."

"Now Rae, hurry up, we need time to make you look amazing." There was a pause. Dana said, "I didn't mean it like that. I think you're pretty amazing but you know what I mean, right?"

"Bye, Dana." Rae closed the phone and raised her arm to throw it.

"Don't do it sis, you'll regret it later when you have to replace it," Billy laughed, entering the body shop. "So, who has you in such a mood?"

Rae Lynne growled, stuffing the offending phone into her pocket of her jeans. "Your girlfriend is a pain in my ass."

"Girlfriend, since when do I have a girlfriend?" Billy frowned.

Rae tilted her head and frowned at her brother. "Dana, sleepovers at your house?"

"That's more friends with benefits."

Rae shook her head. "And you had the nerve to call me a whore? Damn it Billy, she's my best friend. Don't go screwing her around."

He grinned, waggling his eye brows. "But she likes it when I screw her."

Rae Lynne walloped him upside his head with a dirty air filter.

"Damn it Rae, that's gross."

"Yeah, so are you."

"Aw come on Rae, how is what Dana and I have any different from you and pretty boy? At least we've known each other longer than a weekend." Billy wiped dirt from his face.

Rae frowned. "He wasn't your best friend and I knew what I was doing. It was never meant to be anything but sex. Is that the way it is with you and Dana? Is that what she thinks this is?"

He shrugged. "We haven't exactly talked about it but, well, we just kinda fell into bed together and you know?"

"Yeah, I get it." Shaking her head, Rae ignored him and began banging on the fender of the latest in a long line of light-colored trucks that had come in to the shop to be fixed recently.

"Women," he said and stomped away.

"I need to leave early, I got a date," she called after him.

"Bite me."

***

Rae Lynne pulled to the curb and parked. A folded piece of paper fluttered on the passenger seat. She picked it up. "People get hurt when you're around." It was different than the rest. The pen wasn't as bold and the paper was different. Searching the mess in her glove box, she dumped the owner's manual from its plastic pouch and stuffed the note inside. *I'll have to get this to Mike.* She decided the morning would be soon enough. He was still working on the coach's case. She couldn't shake the feeling of guilt that threatened to overwhelm her.

"I should probably call off tonight's date." She glanced at the sign glittering in the window. Dana wasn't going to let her off the hook. With resignation, she stepped from the truck. Pete was busy digging a flower garden across the street. Rae waved. He stopped to wipe sweat and held up his hand in silent reply. She smiled, glad to see he was finding work. She sympathized with the man, remembering all too well the months she'd spent on the street. She watched as Ms. Barbara brought him out a glass of tea. The retired bank teller didn't wave but Rae didn't expect her to. She sighed and hurried into the club. Breathless and grubby from work, she ran into a glaring Dana and said, "I know, I know, I'm late. What can I say, we've had an influx of light-colored work vehicles suddenly in need of fixing."

Dana pointed the remote at the television behind the coffee bar. "They're still not saying whether it was Logan's truck that hit that guy but Fleming is insinuating he's guilty. Do the police have any other suspects?" Taking Rae by the elbow she rushed her to locker room.

Rae gave a humorless laugh. "Besides me, you mean? I don't know. Mike said he'd come by and review my statement with me but I've not seen him. I wonder if I should go to the station again. The thought of dealing with Von Fleming again makes my skin crawl." Rae toed off her boots and stripped off her sweaty and stained work clothes. "Do you have anything to take ink off my hands?"

Dana handed her the can of hairspray. "That's because he busted you for under-age drinking."

"And trespassing, and loitering, and something else, I don't remember. He's such an ass. Does this work?" She sprayed it on her hands and the ink started coming off. "Hey cool."

"I'm beginning to think all men are." Dana handed her a paper towel.

"What? A-holes? Problems with Billy?" Rae asked coughing. "Damn that stuff is strong. I think this must be left over from the fifties and beehive hairdos."

"Did you say something to him?"

Rae flushed. "Why, what happened?"

Dana shook her head. "Nothing, it's no big deal." She looked as if she were about to cry.

"Hey, you want to talk about it?" Rae put her arm about her shoulders.

Pushing her away, Dana said, "Ewe, no, you're naked and you stink." She grinned. "I'm fine. Get your shower." The door slammed behind her.

"Okay Billy, what stupid thing have you done now?" Rae climbed into the shower, wondering if she was going to have to kick her brother's ass before he came to his senses. Or Dana came to hers.

***

Rae was already late but she didn't care. She didn't want to be here anyway. Dana had insisted on fixing her hair and dressing her up like Biker Barbie. The suit was cute but not something she would have chosen for herself. Skinny jeans with leather trim on the pockets and down the legs paired with a cropped jacket decorated with Mexican inspired embroidery and leather. *At least Dana agreed to let me keep my jewelry on this time.* She stopped to read the brass plaque at the front of the gallery: *Barton Mall Gallery, a cultural gift to the town of Leeward.* Rae snorted. "Pretentious ass." She pushed open the glass doors. The gallery was nearly vacant. Those rambling around seemed lost in their own thoughts. She let out a pleased sigh and began absorbing the displays. Her blood zinged with each piece she studied.

The community of Leeward was mostly blue collar, a combination of fishermen, farmers, timber men and a few small businesses. The only corporation of any size was the potash company owned by the Bryant family. Most of the culture in Leeward came from the high school: Athletics Booster Club and PTO, an occasional band concert, and the annual high school play. Around here, art consisted of home crafts. People barely scraped out a living, whatever time or money they had went into family, church and a few civic organizations. Art was whatever appeared on the water tower, most commonly a rendition of the Leeward Warriors. She'd painted one herself during her delinquent youth.

Yet art had changed her life. When her grandfather introduced her to an art professor friend of his, she'd found a way to redirect her emotions. Her grandfather had understood her need for an outlet. As a child, she'd shown an interest in painting and drawing, but it was during her troubled teens that her sculptures had become her salvation.

Rae was in no rush to meet her date. *It's a good collection.* Some displays made her want to rush home and work on her own projects. Logan believed she could make money from her art. *Jenna mentioned a mural, it would be great advertisement. I wonder if Jenna and Dana would be willing to display some of my work.* She contemplated the possibilities.

Rae made her way to the Gallery's coffee bar. The tiny cafe was full of energetic, young business people and artists. She recognized many of the artists but most of the business men and women were strangers. She saw Ezekiel with a group and waved. He flipped his hair and gave her his back. Rae bit back a laugh. *He's snubbing me? How cute.* She rolled her eyes and maneuvered through the crowd. "I'm here now, Bubba, we're going to do this date thing and then I'm out of here." She wanted to be done with her commitment. If Ezekiel La Port wanted to play games, she could care less.

Rae propped on the bar and ordered a latte. A seat opened up near the balcony. Taking her coffee, she sat down and gazed at the art displayed on the floor below. The view was unique, an excellent overview of the different displays. The fusion filled her eye with a kaleidoscope of colors and textures. Rae sipped her drink and let her mind wander, allowing herself to relax and enjoy the ambience.

She stiffened at the sound of footsteps behind her.

"You're late," Ezekiel said.

Rae glanced over her shoulder, pretending a calm she didn't feel. "I wanted to take another look at the displays."

"Did you look at mine?" he asked, grinning like a kid as he glided into the seat across from her.

She wasn't sure what game he was playing. Returning her attention to the gallery, she said, "It looks different from up here, doesn't it?" She avoided answering his question. Something about Ezekiel made her cautious. She was thankful for the taser in her pocket book.

He wiggled nervously in his seat. "You liked my driftwood sculpture, didn't you?"

She shrugged. "How did you find out about Cupid's Zone?"

He stilled. "What?"

Rae turned to him, focusing her attention on his eyes. "Who put you up to dating me? Who sent you to Cupid's Zone? Who told you I was signed up?"

Sweat beaded his forehead. "I don't know what you're talking about."

"How did you find me?"

"I asked around. I found out about your friend's club." He shifted in his seat.

"Who did you ask?"

"Are you in witness protection or something? Why the third degree?" He stood up, his chair crashing to the floor. "I should have known better than to try to get to know a freak like you. You're not even a real artist, are you?"

"Rae Lynne is a very talented metal artist." Logan's deep, familiar voice cascaded over her senses like water on an arid plain. Rae caught her breath as she looked up into his fierce gold-green eyes.

"No one invited you," Ezekiel snarled.

Logan's smile wasn't friendly. "Public place."

The Cajun artist waved his pale, thin hands. "We're on a date."

"You insult all of your dates?"

Ezekiel narrowed his dark eyes. "You are interfering where you are not wanted."

Logan turned his attention to Rae Lynne. "I have some news for you."

She leaned back in her chair and shook her head. "I think you've already said enough."

Logan frowned. "I'm sorry. I was angry. You accused me—"

"Yes well, I was just trying to protect you." She fumed.

He nodded and touched her shoulder, staring intently into her eyes. "I realized that about five minutes after you left. I'm sorry Rae."

"You'll have to work out your issues some other time. You're messing up our date." She says this? Or E does??

Logan said, "You did that all by yourself."

Ezekiel's face bloomed crimson and he stalked off.

Rae mused, "You're my hero."

Shaking his head, Logan said, "I wish that were true."

"What do you need to tell me, Logan? I'm on a date."

He glanced at Ezekiel across the room. "Looks like you're having a great time."

She snorted. "Okay, so I really don't want to be here but I am, so spill it so I can get back to annoying Ezekiel."

"I have a buyer interested in your wounded soldier sculpture."

"A buyer?"

"The office building, I just finished in Raleigh has a large courtyard. The owner offered three thousand for the statue."

She felt her breath catch in her chest. Breathing deep she nodded, she said, "Five, it's worth five thousand."

"So, you want to sell some art?" He grinned.

Coming out of her chair, she threw her arms around his neck. "I can't believe it. I might be able to keep my home!" Tears seeped past her best attempt to contain them. "You're not joking, are you?"

"I'm not joking. Here's his contact information, call him." He handed her a business card.

She took the card. "Why did you do this, Logan?"

He touched her cheek and smiled his eyes heavy with regret. "I should go, you're on a date."

Taking his hand in hers, she held it, reluctant to let him leave. "My first impression about you was right."

Giving her a lopsided grin he said, "Your first impression was that I was an asshole."

Nodding, she said, "Yep, that's right." *No, it was that you were a Boy Scout.*
He released her hand. "G'night."

Rae watched him walk away with her heart.

"Shall we go?"

Rae glanced up, Ezekiel stood beside her expectantly. Rae frowned. "Go where?"

"I'm going to take you home."

"I've got my truck."

His eyes were blurry and there was a sweet odor about him. He leaned against her and draped an arm over her shoulders. "Then you can take me home."

Rae stepped out of his embrace. "I don't think so."

"Don't tell me you're going to let me drive home in this condition." He lurched towards her.

"I'll call you a cab."

"Forget the cab." He grabbed her arm. "I said, you're taking me home. Now let's go."

She glowered at the hand gripping her upper arm. He was bruising her. "Unless you want to lose that hand, I would remove it before I remove it, permanently."

He snorted. "I'd like to see that."

She stepped close. Putting her weight on her back foot, she caught her shoulder under his solar plexus and flipped him. In another quick move, she whipped a knife from her pocket and held it against his hand., "Your call." Years of Tai Kwan Do finally paid off.

Shoving her away, Ezekiel crawled to his feet. "You stupid cunt! You don't have enough sense to know when you should be thankful. I'm doing you a favor. You think the others would treat you this good?" He staggered down the stairs, still muttering.

Rae waited a few minutes then made her way cautiously out of the gallery.

A white van pulled up to the curb. Phil Archer and someone in a hoody stepped out and helped Ezekiel to the vehicle.

As she watched them drive away, she remembered the latest note. Her stomach twisted with the image off her game camera, someone in a hoody. Shaking her head, she dismissed the idea. *Lots of people wear hoodies.*

She called Mike and climbed into the truck, locking the doors behind her. She agreed to stop by the station on her way home. As she pulled out of the parking space she contemplated Phil picking up Ezekiel La Port. *Maybe they're friends?* Phil and an artist, it didn't fit.

Chapter 33

Rae dialed the familiar number and waited. Her dad's phone number was the same one they'd had since she was a kid. A herd of butterflies danced in her stomach. *I should've just called Billy.* But she was mad at her brother, treating her best friend like some girl he picked up in a bar. Pacing the balcony, Rae admitted the truth. She wanted to be the one to tell her dad she'd made the first real sale of one of her art pieces. Biting her lip, she waited as the phone rang.

"Good morning, Grimes residence." The bimbo's sing-song voice came over the line. They still didn't have caller ID.

"Hey Connie, can I speak with my dad?" Rae tried to keep her tone neutral. She didn't want to fight.

"Your dad is getting ready for work. He doesn't have time to deal with whatever crisis you have going on now." Gone was the voice of Snow White and in its place, the wicked queen.

Rae clenched her teeth. "Please Connie, I really need to speak with him."

"I got it Connie." Buddy Grimes deep bass came over the line. "You can hang up, now." He waited for the click. "What's wrong Rae Lynne?"

"Hey, Dad, nothing's wrong. I've got some news I wanted to share."

"They're arresting you for that teacher's death?"

Rae gave him a nervous laugh. "No, of course not. I sold one of my statues." Sitting down at the glass and wicker table she made a few notes in the notebook she'd started for cataloging her art.

"You're not hung over?" He sighed, sounding weary.

"No Dad, I've not had anything to drink in a couple of weeks now. I'm good. Really."

"Are you sick?" His voice changed to concern.

She chuckled. "Daddy, I'm fine. Really, I sold some of my art and I've got to get it wrapped for shipment. It's supposed to be picked up this afternoon."

There was a pause.

"Dad?"

"Well, okay, that's really—great Rae." A shuttering sigh filled the line.

Rae wanted him to be thrilled for her but she resigned herself to the fact that at least she wasn't bringing him bad news. "Okay, see you tomorrow?" She swallowed the tears that threatened. "Anything new come in?" she asked, not wanting to lose this tentative connection. *Tell me you love me. Tell me you're proud of me.*

"Nah, nothing new, looks like you're all caught up for now."

"Okay, well, I'll probably come in tomorrow anyway. If nothing else I can clean up." She blinked back tears.

Buddy said, "Okay, baby girl, I'll see ya tomorrow, oh, and Rae, congratulations on selling your art."

Rae Lynne held the phone, listening to the dial tone. He'd called her baby girl again. She swiped at the stray tear and picked up her book and her half-finished cup of coffee. Looking out over the balcony, she whispered a prayer. "God, please help me not screw up again." Squaring her shoulders, she hurried down the stairs to wrap up her first sale.

Rae was struggling to tie a cord around the statue. A noise behind her caused her to drop the cord. She whipped around to find Logan striding towards her. She tried to slow her breathing. "Damn Logan, you scared the shit out of me."

"Well, hello to you, too. I figured you'd be at work." He grinned and picked up the cord.

She concentrated on regaining her calm. "I took the day off."

"Are you okay?" Logan put his hands on her shoulders. "Rae, did I scare you that bad?"

She burst into tears and he pulled her against his chest.

"What's going on? Have you had more letters?"

She nodded and told him about the one she'd received the morning she learned of Ralph's hit and run, and the latest one that didn't match the others.

He held her, whispering words of comfort until she'd regained control.

"I'm sorry, I don't usually blubber like this."

Logan handed her a handkerchief to wipe her face and blow her nose.

"You carry a handkerchief?" She started laughing. "I thought that went out with my grandfather."

Shaking his head, he said, "Sam got me in the habit of doing that."

"I think it's sweet, thank you."

"Yeah, just what I was going for."

The sun reflected off his hair, burnishing it to copper. It made Rae think of a sun god bringing the gift of morning light. Her heart misfired, stuttering in her chest like an old clunker. Lowering her eyes, she said, "What happened to the cord?"

Logan handed it to her and together they re-wrapped the blanket around the statue. "I guess you didn't need me after all. You got it all wrapped up by yourself."

"I can't believe you came to help." She stared into his eyes until the intensity became too much. She took the cord and wound it around the blankets.

Logan grabbed one end of the cord, sending tingles through her as his hand touched hers. His hazel eyes darkened. Clearing his throat, he twined the cord around the statue and tied it.

Rae asked, "Why aren't you at work?"

"I've not decided what to do about Todd."

She pursed her lips, his words as effective as a bucket of ice water. She stepped back, putting a little distance between them.

"Rae, I've looked him up online, I've tried to find anything for why you don't trust him but there's nothing. If you want me to know about Todd, you're going to have to be the one to tell me."

Rae lowered her eyes.

Logan cleared his throat. "Let's get this thing ready to go." He picked up the big roll of plastic bubble wrap. He raised his brow. "You act as if this thing is made of glass."

Rae shrugged.

"Give me a hand here."

She reached out and took the roll as he wrapped it around. Each time his skin touched hers, Rae's nipples puckered and it took all her self-control not to lean into him.

Rae was relieved when the tape ran out and Logan declared it ready to go.

"The guys should be here in a few minutes. They'll have the statue in Raleigh this evening."

"Mr. Crompton will wire the rest of money as soon as the statue arrives," Rae said, trying to keep a clear head. "Thank you for doing this."

He brushed her cheek with his knuckles. "All I did was take a few pictures."

"You did so much more than that, thank you." Rae put her hand over his, holding it to her face. Logan opened his hand and she kissed his palm.

Logan leaned down, then touched his lips to hers, a gentle caress. "The statue will look good in Ryder's courtyard."

Rae closed her eyes, longing for more but afraid to take the risk. "I'd like to see my Brother/Soldier in its new home."

"Just say the word and I'll take you to Raleigh."

Rae bumped her shoulder against his chest. "You'd have made a great Boy Scout."

Logan put his arms around her. "Yeah? I told you, I'm a nice guy."

"You know what they say about nice guys, don't you?"

His voice, low, whispered against her skin. "Yes, we finish last."

Before she could think of a reply, they heard voices coming around the side of the house.

"This is the place, Joe."

"Hey boss, is this the statue you want us to move?"

Logan smiled and waved the two men over. "Hey guys, you got here just in time." Logan oversaw the loading and securing of the statue.

Rae stepped back and watched they loaded the statue into the van. Blinking back tears, she turned away, embarrassed by the crazy emotions churning inside of her. She was happy to be selling her statue but it almost felt as if she were losing her grandfather all over again.

"Hey, you okay?" Logan turned to her.

She nodded looking out at the river.

"We're all done, boss. You want to check it out before we go?" Joe interrupted.

Logan rubbed her shoulder and walked over to examine the tie-downs.

Rae swiped at the tears and went to check for herself. "It looks secure." He handed Joe an envelope and patted him on the shoulder. The men waved and drove away.

"What was the envelope?" Rae asked.

Logan shrugged. "Just the address and all."

"And all? Did you pay them to take the statue to Raleigh?"

Logan put his arm around her shoulders. "I'm starved, what do you have to eat?"

"Logan?"

He shrugged. "Crompton will reimburse me, don't worry."

"Fine, I guess the least I could do is feed you."

Logan followed Rae up to the house. "Ryder is also interested in some of your paintings. I sent him some pictures. Did he email you?" He'd been compiling a list of customers and associates he wanted to send pictures to. "You need to set up an online catalogue of your work. It'll make it easier to sell it. I can help you with some of that, but my sister is more tech savvy. I can ask her about setting up a website where people can purchase your work and all you have to do is package it up and send it out."

Rae pulled lunchmeat and cheese from the refrigerator. "I need to give you a broker fee for all of this."

Shaking his head, he grabbed the bread and a couple of knives. "I don't want your money."

"But I thought you were in a bind? Isn't that why you're working with Todd?" She juggled everything towards the table.

He relieved her of some of her burden, setting everything down. The company was still in jeopardy but Todd seemed less like the solution. "I'm not in that big of a bind," he lied.

"Logan?" She turned to face him, her eyes narrowing.

He sighed. "I don't want your money. I want you to do everything you can to save this place."

Her eyes shimmered with emotion, staring up at him with a vulnerability so raw it made him ache. "Todd won't let that happen, Logan." She swallowed. "He's made it his mission to keep me down since I started high school." Closing her eyes, she clutched the high-backed chair. "He and Devin arranged for me to be left behind after a party." She blinked and glanced up at the ceiling. "They drugged me and took turns with me, then left me on the highway."

Logan dropped into one of the chairs. "Oh dear God, that's why Devin went to prison?"

She nodded. "He was the only one I could really remember. I was almost positive Todd was there but my memory was shaky. After the trial, Todd made sure that I knew he was there. He sent me a copy of the DVD of them raping me."

Logan leapt to his feet. The chair slid across the floor and toppled but didn't fall. He thought of their weekend and her insistence of being on top. Her reaction to being held too tightly. "How old were you?"

"Fourteen, I'd just started high school."

"Oh Rae, I'm so…" He wanted to touch her but he wasn't sure she would welcome his touch.

"They emailed the video to everyone in school." Her voice cracked. "The jocks, mostly football players, began harassing me. Some tried to get me alone—"

He touched Rae's hand, needing a connection to her but afraid of frightening her.

"I became known as the town whore, the party girl who'd take on three guys…"

"Three?"

"Oh yeah, there was a third guy I can't even remember being at the party. They all wore masks." She laughed and licked her lips. "Todd was a senior and I thought once he was gone people would leave me alone." She shook her head. "He kept coming back and he got other guys to do stuff. He paid guys to take me out and bring me to parties. They tried to force me to have sex but I fought back. I got a reputation as a bad ass and crazy. I started doing drugs and then I did do things but it was my choice." She blinked. "I realized I could make the pain go away for a little while with drugs or sex or alcohol, then I discovered razor blades."

Tears were streaming down his face. He pulled her close and kissed the top of her head. "How did you survive? My God, why aren't you crazy?"

She laughed. "I am crazy. Don't you know that by now?"

"You're beautiful."

"You're the one who's crazy."

He laughed. "For you. God, you make me crazy, Rae Lynne. I admire you. You not only survived, you have become an amazing woman. Todd did not beat you and he's not going to beat you now."

She clung to him laughing and crying. "Give me a minute, I'll be right back. You want to fix us a couple of sandwiches?"

Logan watched her walk down the hall to the bathroom. Shaking himself out of his thoughts, he washed his hands and fixed sandwiches and poured lemonade.

Rae smiled when she joined him. "Thank you."

The silence was oppressive, Logan blurted, "Rent me one of your trailers."

Rae glanced up from toying with her food. "What? Why? Are going to work with Todd?"

"If you save the land it won't matter." He reached for her hand.

"Logan no, you can't keep working with Todd and stay with me. You don't know what he's capable of."

"My being here might be a deterrent. If I stick around, he can't hurt you."

"You'd stay for me?" She shook her head. "And what if you get arrested? Fleming is a Bryant tool. Logan, if you're smart, you'll get as far away from Leeward as you can."

"I can learn more on the inside."

Rae gripped his forearm, digging her fingers into the muscle. "No Logan, I'd rather give up my land than risk anything happening to you."

"I have a contract. If I try to get out of it, Todd will tie me up in court until I'm toothless and blind. Will you rent me one of your trailers?"

Rae hesitated. "If Todd suspects you're helping me…" She let out a breath of air. "He's not someone you want to trifle with."

Logan felt as if he'd started this dance one step behind. "Yeah, I'm starting to get some idea." The mustang, the text message and the hit-and-run were starting to feel like machinations in some twisted game.

"Did anything come of the truck?" Rae began putting stuff back in the refrigerator.

Fleming hadn't cared what Mike said about his cooperation. He'd insinuated Logan was his number one suspect. Shaking his head, he said, "They still don't know who was driving. The truck was wiped clean of fingerprints."

"Do you have any suspects?"

"Too many." Logan sighed. Sam had insisted on calling a lawyer.

Chapter 39

Rae's phone pinged as she was finishing laundry. She read the message. It was the bank transfer. "Woo-woo!" She danced around the tiny laundry room and out to the kitchen. "Logan," she called running up the stairs to Billy's trailer. He was busy putting his stuff away. "I just got a whopping infusion of moola into my account!"

Looking up from his unpacking, Logan grinned. "Sounds like a reason to go out and celebrate."

"What if Todd or one of his friends see us together?" While she was sure Todd had already made Logan a target, she wasn't sure of his end game, but she knew it wasn't going to be pleasant.

"It's not like he doesn't know we've been together." Logan rubbed her arms.

"And that worked out so well for us."

Pulling her close, he swayed with her and hummed. "We can't let fear keep us from being together. If we do, he wins."

Rae shivered and burrowed closer. "Then we'd better be prepared to handle whatever he dishes out."

Logan smiled. "Good, now where should we go?"

Rae suggested The Governor's Palace, the new restaurant built in New Bern overlooking the Tryon Palace. Logan called to make reservations. "Okay, they have us down for eight, does that give you enough time to get ready?"

Laughing, Rae kissed him and rushed out to the balcony and crossed over to her own trailer.

"Dana would gloat if she could see me now," Rae told her reflection as she poured scented bath oil into her tub. The hot water filled the room with steam that would hopefully freshen up the red dress she'd worn to the gallery opening. She didn't have time to press it.

Rae eased into the garden tub and lay her head against the rim, allowing the heat of the water and the scented oil to relax her. A bath was one of her guilty pleasures, a luxury she didn't often indulge in, but tonight was special and she wanted the works.

The ocean scented candle burned on the edge of the tub, the fragrance a complement the bath oil, both a gift from Dana she rarely used.

Rae closed her eyes and gave in to tears that had been threatening all day. She grieved the loss of her grandfather more at this moment when he was no longer with her to celebrate her success, her first real art sale. "You would like Logan," she whispered, her throat filled with emotion. The water lulled her, memories of her grandfather comforted her. She finally relaxed.

Rae awoke to cooling water and the pounding on her bedroom door. "Are you all right in there?"

Pulling the plug, she yelled, "Yeah, I'll be out in a minute."

"We're going to miss our reservation."

His heavy footsteps sounded outside her bathroom door. She wrapped herself in a towel and grabbed another for her hair.

Logan pushed open the door. "You aren't ready yet?" He was handsome in his dark gray slacks and jade green shirt. He'd even donned a tie.

Rae stood in the center of the bathroom, mesmerized by the heat in those eyes. Logan filled the space with his presence. Rae was very aware of his virility. He was all man and his masculinity warred with this space that was her homage to femininity.

In a small voice, she whispered, "I fell asleep."

Logan chuckled. "Your excitement is overwhelming."

She laughed. "Sorry, I haven't taken time to enjoy a bath in a very long time." She sighed and sat down on the cushioned vanity. Logan watched her with his bedroom eyes as she went through her routine of smearing lotion on her face and combing the tangles from her hair.

The bathroom was the one room where she allowed herself to be a girl. It was a bit over the top. The vanity was black and chrome with a bright pink cushion on the seat. She'd built it from an old vanity someone threw away and pieces of scrap metal. Her grandfather had taken it and had it dipped in chrome. The tiles around the tub where black and white squares in various sizes with an occasional bright colored tile of pink, green or blue randomly thrown in for contrast. They were all samples and rejects but they made a beautiful pattern. The tub was pure luxury, a white garden tub with black trim and brushed aluminum fixtures. Scatter rugs in bright colors covered the floor and black and white prints adorned the walls.

Logan examined the room before returning his attention to Rae. He smiled. "You've been holding out on me."

Rae blushed. "What do you mean? I've not..."

He leaned down and brushed his lips against her ear. "You're a bit of a girly-girl."

She shrugged. "I was just having my own private celebration."

He raised a brow. "It would've been more fun with two." He lowered his tall body onto the closed toilet and watched her in the mirror.

Rae met his eyes, her body responding to him even without him touching her.

"Would you rather order take out?" Logan asked his voice husky. He shifted, his desire evident in the strain of his pants.

Her nipples beaded in response. She said, "I want to go out and celebrate."

Logan nodded and stood. "Then I think I'll just wait outside." He hurried to the door, his hands fisted at his sides.

When the door closed, she let out a sigh and smoothed her hair. With shaking hands, she applied a swipe of lip gloss and a touch of eyeliner. The eyeliner took two attempts. Her hands weren't as steady as she'd have liked. To her reflection, she asked, "What are you gonna do?"

She opened the door and knew there'd be no going back. Rae joined Logan at the window where he stood staring out at the darkening sky.

He turned to her. "You're still not dressed?"

Rae let the robe slide to the floor. Lifting her chin, she met his eyes.

His voice ragged, he whispered her name.

She licked her lips and blurted out the first thing that came to mind. "I appreciate what you did for me."

Logan shoved his hands in his pockets and looked away. His voice was quiet and strained. "You want to have sex with me because I found a buyer for your statue?"

Chewing on her lip she looked at him in confusion and nodded.

"Damn." He marched to the door muttering under his breath. "I didn't do it to get you into bed," he said. "Get dressed. Let's go celebrate. I'll wait for you downstairs."

"Logan?" Her skin burned with shame, tears burned her eyes. "Don't you want me?" She raised her chin and refused to back down.

"Sheesh, Rae, want you? Hell, yes I want you." He shouted and shoved a hand through his hair. He heaved a breath. "But not like this. Not as payment for something I've done in friendship. Put on the robe, please, or my noble intentions—" He took a deep breath and turned away. He leaned his head against the open door. "Have mercy Rae, I'm a man, not a saint."

"Please don't go."

"I am trying to do the right thing here."

"I know and it's sexy as hell." She stepped towards him. Pushed the door closed. "You're right, Logan, I don't want to thank you. I just want to fu-sh-it-oot," she sighed, "I just want to have sex with you." Swallowing the fear in her throat, she realized things were about to change. *Are you really ready for this?*

"I want to make love with you, Rae," he said, staring into her eyes he leaned against the door.

"I-I don't know how." She looked away, blinking back tears.

His big calloused hands rested lightly on her shoulders. With a gentleness that was surprising, he stroked her neck with his thumb as he touched his lips to hers. "We can figure this out together."

"I'm scared."

Against her lips, he whispered, "Together."

She wrapped her arms around his neck, leaning into him.

His lips sought hers.

A piece of her soul slipped free and entwined with his. It was frightening and exhilarating, like the downhill ride on a roller coaster. She clung to him.

He nibbled her bottom lip, sucking on it and caressing it with his tongue. His big, callused hands stroked her, his lips followed, licking, nipping and turning every inch of her skin to an erogenous zone. "You are so beautiful," he praised, tracing her tattoo with his tongue. He knelt in front of her, lifting her leg he tasted her skin behind her knee, gliding his tongue up her thigh.

She cried out and pulled at his head, her control evaporating. "Logan?"

"Trust me." His breath tickled her skin as he drove her mad with his tongue.

Squeezing her eyes shut, her heart racing, Rae cried out as the first orgasm started to crash through her. She clung to him, pulling at his hair. She threw her head back and growled deep in her throat. "Oh God Logan, now."

"Slow Rae, you won't regret it." His words shimmered with promise against her skin. His finger replaced his tongue, delving into her core. Her muscles clenched, she rocked on the balls of her feet thrusting her hips in rhythm with his hand. She exploded in a burst of light as sensations swept over her.

Lifting her in his arms, Logan carried her to the bed to continue their quest.

"You have on too many clothes," she complained, reaching for his zipper.

Laughing, he shed his clothes, stopping occasionally to kiss, touch and tease, and to cancel their reservation.

Chapter 40

Logan came awake, the scent of smoke drifting through the open window. The room was filled with the stench of charcoal and the acrid scent of gasoline. He stumbled from the bed and shoved the curtain aside. Smoke filled the predawn with an ethereal glow, a tiny sun burning the blackened sky… "Oh shit, fire?" He grabbed his cell and called 9-1-1 as he yanked on his pants and shoved his feet into his shoes minus his socks. He gave the dispatcher the information and realized he was alone in the room.

"Rae?" The bed was empty. Another glance out the window and he knew where she was. The studio was on fire.

He screamed her name as he ran.

He stumbled and slid down the last few steps. "Rae." Logan followed the smoke across the patio to Rae's workshop. Throwing open the door, smoke billowed black and hot, blinding him and scorching his lungs. Tears filled his eyes as he choked on the acrid air. Searching the darkness, he prayed, "Please God let her be okay." He dropped to the ground and crawled under the smoke. "Rae Lynne, Rae?" He fell against her. She lay unmoving on the floor. "Can you hear me?" He touched her head, his hand coming away sticky with blood. "Rae, baby, we've got to get out of here." Timbers creaked overhead, a sharp crack and pop. Logan threw his body over hers as a whoosh of air brought a beam down on top of them. The weight of it knocked the breath out of him, but the rafter wedged atop the smoldering remains of her work desk and shelves, stopping short of crushing them. He crawled through the maze of falling and burning debris. He feared he'd pass out before they reached safety. He slithered on his belly, dragging them from the building. In the wet grass, Logan collapsed, only half aware of the hands that lifted and pulled them away from the heat.

Someone covered his mouth with an oxygen mask he pulled it away and demanded. "Where's Rae Lynne?"

"She's with the other EMTs." Strong hands pushed him back onto a gurney. He felt them lift him into the ambulance.

Logan twisted his head and tried to see her. "She's alive? Please, I've got to see her."

"What happened, Logan?" Billy's face came into view.

Logan's voice was hoarse and rough as he replied. "I smelled smoke, it woke me."

"Has Rae been drinking again?" he asked.

Logan shook his head.

The EMT said, "There was an empty Jack Daniels bottle beside the shed."

Billy cursed. "She's lucky you were here."

Logan pulled at the oxygen mask and struggled to be heard over the noise of the fire trucks. "She wasn't drunk."

Billy gave him a pitying look. "It's not the first time she's done this, Logan."

A second EMT joined the first. "Mr. Birdsong, we're going to put the oxygen back on you now. You need to quit fighting us."

He nodded but held the EMTs hand. "Is Rae Lynne okay?"

"She's on her way to the hospital but her vital signs are good."

He could see the firemen battling the flames as they loaded him into the ambulance. The spray of the water glittered and exploded like fireworks as it cascaded over the fire, refracting the light like a prism shooting tiny shards of rainbows into the ebony sky. He closed his eyes thinking how ironic that fire could be both beautiful and tragic.

Chapter 41

"Logan, where's Logan? I want Logan. Logan." Rae's screams and sobs could be heard throughout the emergency room.

Logan pushed past an orderly and a couple of nurses. "I'm here Rae," he said as he forced his way into the treatment room.

"You can't be in here," the young physician's assistant said.

Logan ignored him as he hurried to Rae's side. With both his hands bandaged he had difficulty gripping hers. "I'm here Rae. It's okay, baby, we're okay."

Rae fought the nurse covering her face with an oxygen mask. She gripped his arm. "Ezekiel's dead. I heard the nurses talking. He O.D'd. Everyone I've dated is dying. You can't die, Logan, promise me." Tears streamed down her face, making streaks through the soot. She started coughing. She was shaking with shock and fear.

"You need to put the oxygen mask back on," the nurse said.

"Put the mask on, Rae, I'm not worried. We haven't gone on a date yet."

She pulled the mask down. "You are not funny." She sniffed back tears. "If you die, I swear, I'll kill you."

He kissed a clean spot on her forehead. "I'm not going anywhere."

"Now, can we clean your wound and get it stitched up?" The doctor came at her with a syringe but Rae stopped him. "What's in the syringe doc? You're not knocking me out. I want to be awake."

"It's just a local, honest. It will numb the skin for me to clean and stitch your head but it won't knock you out."

Rae looked at Logan, her eyes pleading. "Can you tell if that's what it is?"

Logan glanced at the shot, and at physician's assistant. "I'm not sure what it is, Rae."

The PA picked up the bottle from the desk and handed it to Logan. "She has a concussion. I would not sedate her."

Logan remembered seeing the medicine before and thought it was just as the PA claimed.

"Don't trust them, Logan. Todd has people everywhere. Stay with me." She replaced the mask before the nurse scolded her again.

"It's going to be all right, Rae. We're safe here."

"We don't know who's working for Todd."

"It might not be Todd," he whispered against her ear.

Staring into his eyes, she demanded, "Who else could it be?"

"I don't know, but I think it's dangerous to assume its Todd."

She looked down at his hands. "You got hurt because of me." Tears streaked down her cheeks, exposing pink skin amid the soot.

"I got hurt because some asshole tried to hurt you."

They became silent when an efficient woman in a lab coat entered the room. "Ms. Grimes, we need to do a blood test." She carried a plastic box by its handle with boxes, vials and tubes for taking blood. Pulling a fresh needle from a box she reached for Rae's arm.

Rae didn't fight her. "They think I was drunk. That I started the fire."

"You need to stop talking," the tech said. She darted a glance towards the PA.

Rae frowned and nodded to Logan.

Logan straightened her mask and raised his eyes to the nurse. "I told them you weren't drinking."

"The blood test will prove it, one way or another." The nurse took two vials of blood and raised her eyes towards the PA. "Now quit talking and let the doctor stitch you up."

"Are you done yet?" The young man growled at the older woman.

She stepped back but stood at the door watching.

The PA shaved the back of Rae's head and cleaned the wound. He noticed the tech watching. "Don't you have something to do?"

The woman met Logan's gaze. She nodded and left the room.

Rae whimpered.

Logan growled, "You gotta be so rough?"

The PA glared, his hand trembled as he prepared the sutures.

Logan said, "You want the nurse to take care of her?"

The PA paled and allowed the nurse to administer the shot.

"I can't work with him in here, threatening me," the PA said.

The nurse rolled her eyes. "Why don't you go on your break, Barry, I'll finish up here."

He looked ready to protest but turned on his heel and left.

The nurse managed to suture the wound without drama.

She was just finishing when the efficient nurse returned. "No alcohol or drugs showed up in the blood test," she said. "I've already contacted the authorities and put the information in your file."

The tone of the nurse's voice alerted him. Logan watched as she slipped a thumb drive into Rae's hand. The two women held each other's gaze in silent communication. Logan didn't know what was going on but it was obvious the efficient nurse was on their side.

Rae clutched the devise in her hand.

"Be safe." She met the other nurse's curious look with a stern expression and left.

"Well, let's get you moved to a room," the nurse said. She turned to look at Logan with a question.

"Birdsong, Logan Birdsong," he said. "I'm her fiancé."

"Very well, Mr. Birdsong," she handed him a container of handy wipes, "you work on cleaning her up and I'll see about finding Ms. Grimes a room."

He waited for the nurse to leave before he began wiping at the soot and grime from Rae's face and hands. Rae started to doze. "Hey, I don't think you're supposed to go to sleep. Rae. You've got a concussion."

"I'm awake," she mumbled. She handed Logan the thumb drive. "You might want to hold on to that."

"What is it?"

She shrugged. "Probably my test results." At his frown, she said, "She was the same nurse who took care of me after the rape."

Rae frowned at the IV drip. "What's in it?" she demanded, fighting the oxygen mask.

"It's to hydrate you along with an antibiotic," the nurse explained.

"Can I have water?"

"A little at a time, it may make you sick. I'll bring you a pitcher of ice water if you promise to take it slow."

Rae agreed.

"You should drink some as well," she told Logan as she went past.

"Rae Lynne, what in the hell is this about you setting the fishing camp on fire?" Buddy Grimes demanded, barreling into the hospital room, nearly knocking over the nurse on duty.

"Calm down Mr. Grimes, she's okay," Logan said, stepping towards the older man.

"Calm down? Who the hell do you think you are, telling me to calm down?" He shoved past Logan and stomped towards the bed where Rae lay ensnared by the IV and oxygen mask. "Were you drinking?"

Rae shook her head. "No Daddy." She pulled down the mask. "I was hit in the head."

He stopped at the foot of her bed. "Billy said you'd been drinking."

"They did a blood test, no alcohol nor drugs." She pointed to her head. "I got twenty stitches."

He paled. "Someone did this to you?" He dropped into the chair by the bed and put his head in his hands. "I thought after you were raped that it would be the worst thing we'd have to go through." He clutched her hand. "I am so sorry Rae Lynne. I've not done a very good job of taking care of you."

"Daddy, I'm all right. I'm here." She started crying, holding onto her father's hand. "It's okay, we're okay."

"I've failed you, again." Buddy Grimes bowed his head over his daughter's hand, tears sliding down his weathered cheeks.

"You're here and that's all that matters."

Logan poured a glass of water for each of them. "Remember what the nurse said, only a sip and then put the mask back on."

"What happened?"

Rae started to pull the mask back off but Logan shook his head. Her voice was muffled by the mask. The men moved closer to hear her better. "I couldn't sleep. I went down to the workshop. Someone hit me in the head."

Logan picked up the story. "I woke up to smoke. I saw the workshop on fire and called 9-1-1. I yelled for Rae but she didn't answer."

Buddy scrutinized him. "What were you doing at my daughter's house?"

Rae sighed. "He was sleeping, Daddy, didn't you hear that part."

He grumbled under his breath. "Sleeping my ass."

Logan finished. "Rae was unconscious when I found her."

"What happened to your hands?" Buddy asked.

"The workshop was on fire. I had to get her out." He didn't elaborate.

"You saved my girl?" Buddy looked at him with tears in his eyes.

"Well, I owed her. She kind of saved me first," Logan said.

Rae snorted. "You were already out of the canal when I got there. It was nothing compared to going into a burning building."

"Yeah, but if I lost you, who'd be there to save me next time?".

Chapter 42

Billy erupted into the room, a full-blown explosion of fear and anger. His face was streaked with soot and tears and he smelled strongly of smoke and sweat. "Damn it Rae, I can't sit by and watch you self-destruct." His face and eyes were red and watery. Seeing their father, he turned his attention to Buddy Grimes. "Make her sell the camp. Fire her from the shop and send her back to Raleigh or Timbuctoo. I can't deal with her killing herself."

Buddy shook his head. "Calm down son, Rae's not going anywhere."

Billy whirled on his sister, lying defenseless in her hospital bed. "If you're intent on killing yourself, you need to do it away from here. I mean it Rae. I want you gone. I can't do this. I can't go on a call and find you dead." Tears streamed down his cheeks. He slumped into a chair beside his father.

Buddy patted his shoulder in sympathy.

Logan's anger was tightly leashed, between clenched teeth, he said, "She wasn't drunk."

Billy glared. "They found a Jack Daniels bottle beside the studio."

"She was hit on the head," Buddy stated.

"I was with her Billy, she wasn't drinking."

Billy shook his head and stared at his sister.

"The blood test was negative for alcohol or drugs," Logan added.

Confusion shadowed Billy's face. "Someone attacked you?" He closed his eyes and rocked in the chair. "When I saw the bottle, I just thought…"

Buddy placed his big hand on his son's shoulder. "Once again we've bulldozed into the situation without understanding the facts and come out looking like a pair of asses." Buddy shook his head. "I swear son, of all the things you could've inherited from me…"

Billy got up and stood by her bed. He took her hand in his and just stood there shaking his head, tears streaming down his face.

"Billy." Rae fought the oxygen mask. "I love you Billy, but as soon as I get out of here I'm going to kick you in the nuts!"

He laughed and wiped his face on his dirty sleeve. "You know, I'm always gonna bluster and say the wrong thing and try to tell you what to do."

Rae nodded, as tears slid down her cheeks. "You've been doing that since I can remember. Why would you stop now?"

The nurse came into the room. "If you don't keep that oxygen mask on your face, I will remove your visitors and put you on lock down."

Rae rolled her eyes and replaced her mask.

"See that it stays that way." The nurse checked her vitals, made notes and stopped to examine Logan's hands. "Are you in pain?"

He shrugged. "Not terrible."

"You need to keep those clean and dry. I'll bring you some antibiotic cream to put on when you change your bandages."

He thanked her and as she started out the door, she had to step aside for more visitors.

"Logan!" His mother launched herself into his arms. She stumbled back when she saw his bandaged hands. "Oh, my darling, what happened?" She wiped at tears that flowed prettily down her porcelain cheeks.

"I'm fine Mama," Logan leaned down to greet her with a kiss. "Sam." He nodded to his stepfather.

"Boy, you been causing your mama an awful lot of worry lately." He gave Logan a one-armed hug and smiled down at Rae. "And this pretty girl must by your friend, the lady tow-truck operator?"

Rae blushed and smiled up at Sam.

Logan nodded. "Not what I'd planned for a first meeting. I'm sure I'll hear about it from Rae but yes, this is my lady, Rae Lynne Grimes. Rae, these are my mom and dad, Lillie and Sampson Birdsong."

Rae started to remove her mask but caught sight of the nurse lingering in the doorway. She waved and nodded. "It's nice to meet you."

"I'm sure it will be," Lillie said, worry in her hazel eyes. "I'm so sorry you were injured."

"Thank God we lived to tell it." Logan patted Rae's shoulder.

Mike stepped through the door and accessed the room. "I need to ask everyone to step out of the room."

Everyone started talking at once.

The nurse ordered, "Officer, get these people under control or escort them out."

Mike shook his head and said, "Calm down or I'll send you out permanently." They quieted. The nurse scowled. "I'll be back."

Mike waited for the door to close. "I need to get a statement from Logan and Rae," he explained as he looked around the room.

Rae pointed to Lillie and Sam and motioned to Mike.

Logan said, "Mike, these are my parents: Sam and Lillie Birdsong."

Mike didn't even raise an eyebrow at the sight of the tiny white woman beside the mammoth black man. "Fine, let's get your statements."

"Maybe we should go," Lillie said. She handed Logan a bag. "There are some clothes and things I thought you might need." She hugged him.

Sam gave him a hug and slipped him some cash. "If you need anything, call my cell. We'll be staying at the Black Beard Inn."

Buddy stood up and shook Sam's hand. "Your son saved my girl's life..." He blinked back tears.

Lillie put her hand on his elbow and smiled through her own tears. "We were both lucky tonight."

Mike gave Buddy and Billy an expectant look.

Buddy said, "I ain't going nowhere."

Billy said, "As assistant fire chief I'll need a statement, too."

Mike waved his hand. "Fine, Logan you want to start since Rae's doing her Darth Vader impersonation."

"Ha ha." She rolled her eyes.

Logan took her hand. He told Mike about smelling smoke. "It woke me. I called for Rae but she was in the studio. When I found her, she was unconscious, and the workshop was filling with smoke. The roof fell and thankfully the beam wedged and we were able to crawl out."

Rae removed her mask and started talking, "I woke up and couldn't go back to sleep. I was staring out the window and thought I saw something—"

"And you didn't wake me?"

Rae shrugged. "I wasn't sure what it was. I didn't see anyone. I went outside and smelled something, gas I think. I heard a noise but when I turned to see what it was, I just remember a movement and then an explosion inside my head."

"There was a Jack Daniels bottle beside the shop," Billy said. "I believed she'd been drinking."

"That's what you were supposed to believe."

Logan put Rae's mask back on and glanced at the men. "The blood test proves she wasn't under any influence."

She struggled with Logan, refusing the mask. "Someone set that fire, but it wasn't me." Logan tried once again with the mask but she turned her head. "Someone is out to get me, and my money is on Todd Bryant."

Mike said, "There's no proof that he had anything to do with tonight's events."

"No proof? My shop has been torched. I have a concussion. Logan was hurt. What more do you need, my body in the morgue?"

"You could have been hit by a falling beam. How can we prove someone hit you?"

"Because I said so."

"And who was it? Did you see anyone?" Mike crossed his arms over his chest.

Rae huffed. "What about the bottle—were there any fingerprints on it?"

Mike nodded. "Yours and Billy's."

"Billy's?"

Billy nodded. "I thought it was yours. I wasn't careful with the evidence."

Rae slammed her head against the pillow. "I threw out all my liquor after I wrecked the bike." She hated how crazy and out of control she'd felt. "That was the day Phil came by. When I was throwing the trash out. He asked me to the gallery opening." She blushed. "I agreed to get him to leave. I was embarrassed."

Logan squeezed her hand.

"Did he say anything?" Mike asked.

"Phil? No, I mean other than to ask me to go to the opening. Oh, and he knew I'd wrecked the bike." She frowned. "He asked me why my truck wasn't home. He must have seen Uncle Clyde bring me home."

"You think he took one of those bottles and used it to frame Rae?" Billy asked.

"He wouldn't do something like that," Rae said, "We're friends."

"He's also been on the fringes of Todd's gang since high school." Mike pointed out.

"But so were you and Billy and half the guys we went to school with."

Mike shook his head. "I just played football."

"Phil was a victim of Todd's pranks," Rae said.

Billy said. "He would do anything Todd asked him to do. I always wondered if he was the one with the camera."

Rae glanced up at him. "You mean the third rapist?" Shaking her head, she said, "anyone could run a camcorder, even a dumb jock. They didn't need a computer geek. The video wasn't very good quality."

"You've seen the video?" Buddy asked, his voice heavy with emotion.

Rae pursed her lips. "I received a copy in my locker at school."

Billy and Buddy made sounds of anguish and anger. "Why didn't you tell me?"

Rae shook her head. "I couldn't." She looked away. "I was stupid."

"If anyone was stupid, it was me." Buddy took her hand and gave her a gentle squeeze.

"Mike, have heard anything about Ezekiel La Port?" Rae asked.

"The artist?" Mike frowned. "Yeah, he overdosed, did you know him?"

"I met him at the gallery opening," Rae said.

"Rae had a date with him the other night," Logan said.

Mike studied Rae over his phone. "Two dates dead? Rae, that has to be some kind of record."

Rae nodded. "Yeah."

Mike frowned and glanced at Logan. "You're not with Logan?"

Rae looked up at Logan and sighed. "Dana coerced me into joining her dating club. It was penance for wrecking the bike." Taking a couple of deep breaths from the oxygen mask she continued. "Ezekiel joined Cupid's Zone but he didn't live here. He was just here with the art tour." She started coughing and put the mask back on.

"I heard him tell someone that she wasn't falling for him," Logan told them.

"You were there?" Mike demanded.

"This was at the opening but yeah, I stopped by to give Rae some information."

"Damn! This just gets better and better." Mike shoved his hand into his hair. "You know that makes both of you look complicit in his death."

"But surely, it's a suicide or accidental overdose," Buddy argued.

Billy shook his head. "Too much of a coincidence at this point. It wouldn't surprise me if Todd didn't find a way to spin this into something that points to Rae Lynne."

"Do you think this is all related? The fire and the threatening notes?" Logan asked.

"What notes?" Buddy asked.

Mike interrupted, "I don't believe in conspiracies." He was making notations on his phone and looked up. "I don't see how they could be related. The coach was run down while jogging. The artist, a known drug user, overdosed."

Logan offered Rae a sip of water. She nodded and took a drink.

"Two of the guys I've dated recently end up dead."

Mike met her gaze. "Makes you look like a suspect."

She nods. "And my shop burns right after I sell one of my statues?"

Mike shook his head. "Todd's an entitled SOB. I wouldn't put it past him to try and burn you out but why kill your dates?"

"To frame me?"

"Then why set the fire?" Billy asked.

"Maybe it's not just Todd? We know he has an agenda but what if someone else has another agenda," Mike said.

"Someone is trying to get rid of me. They threaten me, try to scare me and then attack me?" Rae whispered.

"Who besides Todd would want to get rid of Rae?"

Rae glanced at Mike and said, "His wife."

He nodded. "Or his mother, but I can't see her digging up a dead cat."

"A cat?" Billy and Buddy asked. "What about the cat?"

Mike swore. "The person in the hoody."

Logan said, "Not a teenage boy but a woman."

"Polly Bryant."

Mike shook his head and started pacing.

"And what about Logan? It was his truck used to kill Ralph."

"Fine, fine, it's a fucking conspiracy!" Mike ran a hand through his hair.

Logan said, "But what if it isn't Todd?"

"He's right," Billy said, "we can't be sure Todd's behind this."

"Yes, we can." Dana slipped into the room carrying a couple of shopping bags. She darted a look over her shoulder before shutting the door. "Jenna and I heard Todd talking. He's on his way here with Chief Fleming. He plans to arrest Logan for the coach's murder and you for Ezekiel's."

"But Ezekiel's death wasn't—"

Dana interrupted, "There's evidence it was a forced suicide, something about a designer drug. The SBI are on their way here, Jenna called someone she knew in the bureau. We've got to get you away from Fleming and see if they'll help us."

Rae shoved the blankets off. Logan reached for her and helped her off the bed. "But I don't understand what a designer drug has to do with me. Why does the SBI care? I'm sure they got bigger fish than Todd."

Dana turned off the IV, slid the needle out and placed a bandage over the puncture.

Logan lifted a brow.

Dana shrugged. "Candy Striper and I took care of my mom, you know, the cancer."

"What's this about a designer drug?" Mike asked. "Wouldn't DEA..."

Dana shoved the bags into Rae's hands. "It doesn't matter, we've got to get you guys out of here," she said. "If Todd and Fleming are worried about the SBI then they are our hope."

Mike shook his head. "I should've been notified they were arresting Rae and Logan."

Logan helped Rae to the bathroom to change. They could hear Mike and Dana arguing.

Dana said, "Because you are honest, Mike. Geez, we don't have much time."

Chapter 43

Billy sidled up beside Mike. With a glance at his dad, he asked, "You think Devin could be involved in this?"

Mike shrugged as Rae and Logan rejoined them. "He's out of control. We've had several complaints from women about him being aggressive. There's been rumors of him being drunk and fighting, I don't think he has the capacity to plan a conspiracy."

Logan shook his head. "No, you're right, but what if he accidentally ran down the coach?" Logan explained his theory. "He knew where I kept the keys. Todd insisted I hire him. He confronted Rae and Ralph on their date."

Buddy said, "He'd expect Todd to bail him out."

Rae explained for Logan's benefit. "The rape kit taken at the hospital had only shown evidence of Devin. He'd kept his mouth shut about Todd and whoever else was involved. He went to prison and never betrayed his friends. He would expect compensation."

"We don't have time to debate this," Dana insisted. "We've got to get Rae and Logan out of here before the chief arrives."

The nurse entered and started to protest when she saw Rae up and dressed.

Rae pleaded with her, "You know what Todd and Fleming are like. I can't stay here and pray for justice. If they arrest me, I'm as good as dead."

"But you just can't walk out of here." Reluctantly, the nurse said, "You take the service stairs after you take the elevator to the next floor, they'll take you down by the cafeteria." She began laying out a plan to secret Rae away.

Rae put her hand on the nurse's arm. "Why are you helping us?"

The nurse licked her lips, her eyes full of remorse. "My sister was one of Todd's girls. She killed herself last year." She blinked back tears. "At least that is what I was told."

It was obvious the nurse believed it was something else. Rae had heard about Todd's girls. Girls he kept drugged and used for sex. She squeezed the nurse's hand. Rae wasn't the only one who'd been hurt by Todd and the Bryant family.

The nurse returned with a gurney. "Ready?"

Rae wasn't sure she liked the idea, playing dead was a little too close to her recent reality.

Logan lifted her onto the gurney.

She gave him a reassuring smile.

The nurse handed her an inhaler. "Just in case." She gathered the troops and set off the alarms, yelling, "Code blue."

A second nurse rushed in with the equipment. "Better hurry before they figure out it was a diversion."

As Logan pushed the gurney down the hall, Rae could hear the nurses setting up the room. Dana began weeping.

"We've got to hurry." Logan draped the sheet over her face and caught the elevator.

It was early morning shift change, everything was a bit chaotic. They could hear people coming and going in the hallways. They took the service elevator, punching the number for the morgue but stopped it on the second floor. Logan hid the gurney where the nurse suggested and taking Rae's hand, hurried to the stairwell.

Logan pulled Rae down the stairs, pulling her against him as she fell, slid and stumbled as quickly as she could in his wake.

The nurse told them these stairs were seldom used by patients and visitors. They passed one orderly on their descent. He barely acknowledged them, rocking to the music blaring from his iPhone. It was so loud, even with his earbuds in, they could identify the song.

Rae felt as if her lungs would burst.

Logan slowed.

Breathing hard, Rae fumbled with the inhaler, dropping it on the stairs. Logan retrieved it and helped her take a few puffs. "Do we need to stop?"

She refused to stop. "I'm fine." She panted but it was obvious, she was not. Her skin was clammy. Her heart pounded. She felt light-headed and sick to her stomach.

Logan half carried, half dragged her down the last flight.

Propping her against the wall, he ordered, "Wait here." He went to the glass door and looked out.

Rae slumped against the wall and tried to catch her breath.

Billy's truck came into view. "Okay, here he comes." Logan took her hand and pulled her through the door. As the started across the blacktop, Billy eased forward.

From the corner of her eye, Rae saw another truck coming fast. She screamed but it came out more as a croak.

Logan grabbed her about the waist and rolled with her across the median. The truck plowed over speed bumps and curbs coming towards them. Logan lifted Rae to her feet and shoved her behind the brick wall where the trashcans were stored. The truck careened into a post, bounced off and sped away. The stench of the trashcans was overpowering but Rae welcomed the scent. It meant she was still alive.

Billy called to them. "You guys okay?" He came around the dumpsters, waving his arms. "Come on, let's get out of here before he comes back." In the truck, Billy said, "I think that was Devin."

"Whose truck was he driving?" Rae gasped, her hands trembling as she struggled to fasten her seat belt.

Logan leaned over and helped her. "Go, just start driving."

Billy pulled cautiously out onto the highway, "I don't know, maybe one from the body shop? Rae, this is getting a little scary."

"It's been scary!"

"Where are we going?" Logan asked.

Billy shook his head. "I don't know. I can't think of any place that wouldn't be obvious to Todd or Devin."

Rae shook her head. "You're the only one Todd hasn't known forever."

Logan reached into his pocket for his cell phone, thankful it had survived. He hit speed dial and was relieved when Sam answered. "Dad, I'm in trouble."

Chapter 44

Billy pulled into the hotel parking lot and drove around in a circle.

They'd spent the past few hours driving around, trying not to get caught by the law or Todd's people. They were all running out of patience and Rae was still suffering from the smoke she'd inhaled.

Just two days ago Rae had been full of hope. She'd sold her first statue and it looked as if Todd couldn't touch her land. Now she was on the run and dragging Logan down with her. Rae was afraid her life was doomed to be a series of nightmares. Nothing would ever turn out right for her.

"Billy what are you doing? Just park the truck already," Rae complained. Another round of coughing and she spit up more dark mucus.

Billy continued to drive through the parking lot, looking at each car, "I don't recognize any of these vehicles. I don't think Todd or Devin could've found us."

"Of course, they didn't find us, we didn't even know where we were going until an hour ago."

Billy frowned. "Are you sure you can trust this guy?"

Rae sighed. She knew she was being a bitch. but she was scared. Taking Billy's hand, she gave him a reassuring squeeze. "No, but I trust Mike and Logan trusts his dad."

"I don't like this, what if Chief Fleming found out about this meeting?"

"Then we're screwed."

Logan pointed. "There's Sam."

Mr. Birdsong and Mike McKenzie stood with a man in a worn, dark suit.

"Just put us out here," Logan said as he reached for his seat belt.

"Logan, that's Pete, the homeless guy." Rae put her hand on his arm.

"Ditchwater Pete?" Billy started to pull into a parking space. "I'm going with you."

"What about Dana?" Rae said, "If Todd wants to hurt me he'll target the people I love. You need to protect Dana and Ms. Sandy and Dad, and tell Uncle Clyde to stay with one of the boys." Her voice rose as her fear escalated.

He grumbled. "Fine, I'll go, but damn it I don't like leaving you. Why don't I call Dana, get her to come get me? I can leave you the truck so at least you'll have transportation."

"And you don't think someone might decide to follow her, my best friend?" Rae stood in the doorway, leaning across the seat to look at him.

He reached across the seat and grabbed her hand. "Be safe sis? I know I've not done a great job taking care of you but," he said, "just be careful, okay?"

Rae blinked back tears. Afraid she might never see her brother again, she crawled over the seat and wrapped her arms around his neck. "You too, okay, don't be macho." She didn't wait for a response but crawled quickly out of the truck and slammed the door. Knuckling the tears from her face, she waved as Billy drove away.

Logan touched her shoulder. She turned in to his embrace. "Come on, let's not stand out here drawing attention to ourselves."

"I'm scared." She slid her hand in his.

He nodded as he led her towards the hotel room where the men waited. "Together we can handle anything."

She laughed and leaned into his side. "Sounds like a Hallmark card."

He chuckled. "It might be my next job if we go into witness protection."

Rae elbowed him. "Not funny."

"Let's get you guys in here out of sight," Pete said. Stepping away from the door, he studied the lot and the surrounding area.

Rae gave a nervous laugh. Logan squeezed her hand and led her into the dimly lit room. His touch was reassuring.

"Dad thanks." He reached for Sam with his free hand, hugging the big man. "I appreciate this. Where's mom?"

"I sent her home. Your sisters are with her and I feel better knowing she's safely out of the way."

Logan agreed and gave his stepfather's hand a squeeze, wincing when he forgot the burns that hadn't had time to heal. "Me, too."

The curtains were closed and the wall sconces did little to alleviate the shadows in the room. The sun was setting, adding another layer of gloom.

"I think all this cloak and dagger stuff is ridiculous," Mike said, plopping down in one of the chairs by the window. "We should just go to the sheriff and straighten all of this out. I'm not convinced these incidents are related and I don't believe in conspiracies."

Rae crossed her arms over her chest. "Fleming was coming to arrest me."

Mike sighed. "I'm not convinced of that, either."

"You told me you didn't believe in coincidences. How can you not believe all of this is related?"

Logan and Mike started to argue, but the agent cut them off. "I have information that proves all of these events fit together." Pete stepped forward and shook Logan's hand, then Rae's. "Jake Monroe, special agent State Bureau of Investigations."

"I don't guess we need to introduce ourselves, mind if I call you Pete?" Fear and weariness made Rae surly.

"Why don't you try Jake instead."

She dropped into the seat next to Mike. "Why have you been in Leeward pretending to be a homeless guy?"

The agent met her eyes and said, "We came here to prove there was fraud in local government and law enforcement, but we've uncovered so much more. I believe we're looking at drug and human trafficking."

Rae choked back a laugh, then started coughing. Tears streamed down her cheeks and she struggled to catch her breath. Logan moved beside her, putting his hand possessively on her shoulder. She leaned into him and tried to control her breathing. She was thankful for his support. She leaned against him. The shadow of a memory teased her thoughts but wouldn't gel into a real thought.

"She needs to be in the hospital," Logan said, rubbing her back.

Rae shook her head. "I'm okay."

Monroe shook his head and took the seat across from them. "It's not safe. I have an agent on the way. He has medical training. He'll bring oxygen and other medical supplies."

"Drug and human trafficking, isn't that a job for the FBI?" Logan asked.

"Right now, we're working this inhouse." Agent Monroe studied their faces. "I'm here on a government task force to gather data, not make an arrest."

"What the hell does that mean?" Logan growled.

"It means they can't do anything but give reports," Mike said. "Typical."

Monroe shook his head. "It means I need to get the intel on the Bryant family in order to bring in the FBI and DEA. The drug that killed Ezekiel La Port has a unique chemical signature. One we've seen before."

Rae shrugged. "What's a chemical signature?"

"It's like a fingerprint or DNA."

"Don't all drugs have their own unique signature?" Rae asked.

"This drug is unlike any other date-rape drug we have ever come in contact with."

Rae reached up and grasped Logan's hand. "Date-rape drug?"

"The drug that killed Ezekiel La Port was the same as the drug that was used in the alleged rapes of you and two other women," the agent explained.

She let go of Logan's hand and leaned in close to the agent. "Alleged? There was no alleged about it." Rae stabbed her finger into his chest and said, "Todd Bryant drugged me, raped me and videotaped the whole fucking incident! It happened and I relive it nightly. There's no alleged about it!" She had a spasm of hard coughing.

Mike stood up and grabbed a bottle of water for her. "Easy Rae." He turned to the agent. "You're here because of the drug?"

Monroe eased back as far as his seat would allow. "I'm sorry Ms. Grimes, I'm afraid I've been reading legal transcripts so long I forget there are real people involved." He shook his head. "The drug is a newer development. I'm looking into the complaints of several victims and families who claim they or their relatives have been coerced into the sex trade by the chief of police or the mayor. The drug may have been used on these victims, but we have no proof."

"Whoever gave the guys the drug they used on me sold some to Ezekiel? I knew when I met him, he was an addict."

"It's not just that, Rae, we believe the drug is being manufactured here. We want the guy who's making it. It's been used in at least two other rapes and possibly a murder."

Rae blinked and shook her head. "You think Todd and Devin had something to do with these other crimes?"

"Todd maybe, Devin was locked up," Monroe said. "But my guess is, that even if Todd and Devin didn't commit these crimes, they know who did."

"The third rapist?" Rae asked. She felt suddenly ill. Blood drained from her head and she started to hyperventilate. She put her head between her knees and concentrated on breathing.

Logan rubbed her shoulders. "Does this mean there's a chance to catch the third rapist?"

"Murder?" She raised her head. "If they'd been convicted when they raped me, maybe, dear God—"

Monroe eased forward in his seat. "What do you remember about the third guy?" He asked, his tone gentle.

With her head in her hands, Rae said, "You've seen the video?"

"Yes."

She looked up and met his gaze. "That's all I remember."

"You don't remember him being there before seeing the video?"

"I don't think so, maybe. I thought there were three but the only ones I could bring into focus were Devin and Todd. The fact that I couldn't remember a third guy, coupled with Todd's alibi is why people didn't believe me. Physical evidence linking Devin to the rape is the only reason he served any time. He swore the whole time that we had consensual sex and then I left him. He said I must have met up with the other guys afterwards." She blinked back tears. "It's amazing really, that he did time at all. It was only because of my age that he did. The whole town thought I'd made it up." She wiped angrily at the tears. "In the end, it was his own admission that we had consensual sex that sent him to prison. I was only fourteen."

Logan pulled her head against his shoulder and draped his arm protectively around her. "So now what do we do?"

"We build a case."

"We didn't build a case the first time around, what makes you think we can do it this time?"

"We find the drug."

"How?" Logan asked.

"Yeah and what about us? What happens to us while you're searching for your drug dealer? I mean, the cops are looking to pin all this on Logan and me. We can't go home or even out in public."

Logan put his hand over hers. She took a deep breath and tried to bring her nerves under control. She turned her hand over until they were palm to palm and took a deep breath.

Rae looked up to see Sam studying her. She met his appraisal with chagrin. "I'm sorry Mr. Birdsong I can't imagine what you must think of me, of all of this?"

Deep grooves marred his dark complexion. In his sultry southern drawl, he said, "Darlin', you call me Sam and you got nothing to be apologizing for."

"For getting Logan mixed up in all this?" She blinked back tears.

Sam chuckled, his deep bass almost musical as it rumbled in his barrel chest. "Logan has been his own man since he was twelve years old. He's capable of making his own decisions." He smiled and nodded his head. "Don't you worry Ms. Grimes, I'm sure we'll get this all figured out."

"I don't know how." She exhaled. "I don't remember much about that night. It was amazing that I wasn't charged. By the time the defense attorneys finished shredding my testimony I'd started to believe I had done something to deserve what they did to me." She closed her eyes and squeezed Logan's hand. "They kept saying beyond a reasonable doubt. I was as surprised as everyone else when they found Devin guilty."

"With all that has come out, it's starting to look like your rape was just the beginning," Mike said with a sigh.

Monroe disagreed, "It started long before that. The Bryant's have been covering up stuff for a very long time."

"What do you know?"

"I have been told that Elva Bryant had something to do with your mother's disappearance."

Rae's stomach twisted. "My mother left with Elva Bryant's husband. That's what she had to do with my mother's disappearing act."

"Rae, your mother wasn't romantically involved with Malcolm Bryant. They found something."

"Oh, great and what did they find that was worth leaving her husband and children for?" Rae sneered, breaking away from Logan she paced the tiny hotel room.

"Something that put both their lives in danger."

Rolling her eyes, Rae demanded, "How is it you know so much about my mother and Malcolm Bryant?"

"I've talked to them."

"You've spoken to my mother?" Rae frowned. "Well, then you've done something I haven't." She turned her back to them.

"Elva Bryant is a powerful woman," Monroe said.

Rae snorted and spun on her heel. "She's a rich bitch who used her money and influence to keep her spoiled son out of trouble. But that's hardly a mafia mom."

"There is some belief that she may have control of the date-rape drug."

Rae trembled, her mind whirling with what that statement meant. "Why would an old woman want a date-rape drug?"

Monroe nodded. "Why indeed."

A burst of static shattered the silence. Mike's radio chattered, startling the group. "Excuse me." He stepped outside to listen to the call.

Rae said, "So what do you want from us? How do we fit in with all of this?"

Mike pushed open the door and yelled, "I gotta run—Todd's dead."

Chapter 45

"Todd's dead?" Rae clutched Logan's hand. She was afraid to believe it. "It's over?"

Logan turned to agent Monroe. "Turn on the television."

"The victim has been identified as Todd Bryant mayor of Leeward." The newscaster announced.

Rae started to cry. "It's over, it's finally over." Trembling, she was thankful for Logan's support.

Logan and Monroe exchanged a look.

Rae looking from one to the other demanded, "What? What are the two of you thinking?"

Monroe sighed. "Todd wasn't working alone. Someone killed him..."

"Devin or Polly?" She asked looking at the two men. "They had plenty of reasons to kill him."

"We don't know who killed him or why. It could have been a partner, a victim or as simple as a B and E." Monroe pulled out his cell and started punching numbers.

They returned to the television, watching Mike drive up in front of Todd's house. The house looked similar to the rest of the Pearls in the circle, the part of Leeward devoted to historical homes. Pearl Circle's youngest house dated 1913, a lovely Victorian until the Bryant money convinced the historical society to allow Todd to build his mansion there. They'd given in to the coercion of the Bryant family but even Elva Bryant wouldn't go against the society over the look of the house. The outside harmonized with the others on the circle, and while Todd's home was modern on the inside, the exterior looked like a Greek Revival to equal Tara.

One brave journalist shoved a microphone in Mike's face, demanding details of the murder. Mike replied, "No comment."

Logan switched channels. The journalist was interviewing a neighbor. Rae recognized the woman as a retired schoolteacher. "I was walking Hemingway."

The journalist interrupted, "Hemingway?"

The older woman blinked myopically. "My bulldog." He motioned for her to continue. "The vehicle nearly ran us over when it sped out of the driveway. I don't think he even looked to see if anything was coming. He just plowed out into the street like he was the only one on the road."

"Did you get a look at the driver?"

Shaking her silver head, she said, "I was too busy keeping Hemy from getting run over."

"Can you describe the vehicle?"

She frowned. "I wasn't paying much attention until he nearly run us over. It was a reddish truck, not real new but not an antique. I really don't remember much else. I went up to the house to protest and saw the door open. When I called out no one answered. I was worried, so I went inside...oh my dear Lord, it was awful! I've never seen...I called 9-1-1." The old woman was visually shaken.

Monroe closed his cell and said, "He's not dead. He was shot in the head but he's still alive. Polly and the kids are missing."

Rae shivered. "Do you think the shooter took them?"

Monroe shook his head. "I don't know. We're waiting for information."

Rae licked her lips. "I want to go to Todd's, see what's going on."

"Chief Fleming is there!" Logan and Monroe warned.

"I can't just sit here." Rae paced.

Sam said, "I can go, no one knows me."

"No, I'll go. Mom would never forgive me if I let you get tangled up in this mess. Besides we may need you to bail us out if this thing goes sideways." Logan raked his hand through his hair.

Rae moved into his embrace, wrapping her arms about his waist. "They could arrest you for Ralph's murder."

Logan kissed her and pulled away. "Fleming's busy and Mike will be there. I'll be fine. I'll try not to let anyone see me, okay?"

"I bet you wish you'd just kept on driving right past this place."

He kissed her forehead. "I wouldn't miss knowing you no matter how this turns out."

Sam wouldn't go back to the hotel. "If anything happens to you, your mama would skin my hide."

Logan knew that went for both of them. He hated putting his dad in danger.

They drove to the circle but rescue vehicles, nosey neighbors and the media made that route too congested. Police tape and a couple of auxiliary officers were in place to keep everyone at bay.

Sam drove to the street parallel and found a house with a realtor's sign posted in the yard. "I'll wait here for an hour."

Logan shook his head. "You're a black man waiting at a vacant house in the dark? This is the south."

"Those cops are too busy to worry about me," Sam argued.

Logan frowned. "But the neighbors might not be. Drive around and check back in an hour. If I'm not here come back in another hour. If I'm still not here, go stay with Rae Lynne."

"Your mother will kill me if I leave you."

"Please Dad, I'll be fine, but I need to know Rae is safe."

Reluctantly, Sam agreed.

Logan eased the door shut, glancing around the neighborhood. He was relieved when no one shouted for the police. He hurried behind the house, taking a narrow path through the shrubs. The spring air was filled with the sweetness of new blooms and the night sounds of small critters.

As he came upon the backside of Todd's mansion, the flash of the strobes from the emergency vehicles added an eerie glow and enough illumination Logan was able to avoid stumbling around in the dark. Circumventing windows and security lights, he edged around the side of the house. Two auxiliary officers stood sentry on the colonnaded portico. Three volunteer EMTs were off on the grass talking and smoking. One young volunteer was losing his dinner in the bushes. Chief Fleming came up to the front porch grumbling to anyone who'd listen. Logan ducked back in the shrubs, his heart pounding. *Damn that was close.*

"It's that damn Grimes girl, I'll bet. She always threatened she'd finish him off. She nearly succeeded."

Mike argued, "You know Rae had nothing to do with this. She was in the hospital with smoke inhalation."

Logan hadn't seen Mike on the porch; he must have been in the doorway. His heart beat frantically as he ducked back into the shadows.

Fleming snorted. "Yeah and she faked her own death to avoid being arrested. You sweet on that girl? You need to be careful McKenzie, she'll have you mixed up in her mess."

Logan had seen enough re-election posters to know that Fleming had once been handsome, but he'd gone soft. His square jaw fleshy with bloat. The broken veins on his nose and face told of years of overdrinking. The thickening in his waist spoke of more overindulgences.

"You still believe that little cock teaser, she's nothing but a slut, Mike. You'd better open your eyes before you end up just like Todd."

Logan tightened his fist aching to shut the jerk's mouth. Getting arrested would do them little good. He suddenly felt tired. How did this get so messed up? Drugs, murder, rape? For a town with only a thousand people, it sure was turning into something out of a gothic novel.

"What's with him?" Fleming demanded, pointing to the ill medic.

A young man tossed down his cigarette butt and came to attention. "It's the blood, sir; it's his first time."

"Pick up that butt and get your buddy here cleaned up."

"Yes sir, I'll take him inside."

"Don't be a jackass, take him down the road to the gas station or something but do not contaminate my crime scene." Logan rolled his eyes. *Fleming was a real charmer.*

"I can clean him up at the ambulance," the pretty volunteer offered.

"Why are you all still here? Just get in your vehicles and go." Fleming stomped into the house.

Logan ducked back behind the chimney.

The front door slammed. The EMTs took their sick friend to the ambulance. Logan eased around to the front of the house where only the two officers remained. He scooted back and edged around the back of the house until he came to the French doors. He angled his head so he could peer through the curtains.

The house was something out of House Beautiful Magazine, decorated with a combination of high end antiques and modern furnishings. The cool blue of the living room was just visible past the dining room. The blue was supposed to be calming but dark splatters of blood covering the walls destroyed the effect.

"McKenzie ain't this some shit." The chief's voice reverberated off the walls. Logan jump back, startled. He couldn't hear Mike's reply, then his voice became clearer.

"Who called it in?" Mike asked. The dining room curtain moved. Logan ducked into the shadows, his heart tripping.

"Elderly neighbor walking her dog." Logan didn't recognize the voice; it sounded younger. He eased back to the window. He could see the top of the officer's head and recognized one of the sentries from the front of the house. He was telling about the vehicle nearly running the old lady over.

Mike said, "Send your partner over to get a description of the driver, the vehicle, anything she can remember."

"But sir, it's late, don't you think she might be asleep?"

"It's not that late."

"But she's old. Don't old people go to bed early?"

"Would you be sleeping after finding your neighbor shot in the head?"

"When Todd wakes up, he'll tell you, it was that Grimes girl," the chief huffed.

"If he wakes up, we'll be lucky if he remembers anything."

"I'm going to issue an apprehend order for the girl."

"Don't you think that's a little premature? We need to gather more evidence. Have you considered, whoever shot Todd might try again."

Fleming sighed. "Yeah, we may need to let everyone think Todd died. If the killer finds out he survived, she might come back to finish the job." He raised his brow. "That might be the way to catch her."

Mike sighed. "Are you forgetting about the fire at her house?"

Fleming waved. "Part of her plan to throw us off."

Mike didn't respond. He pulled on a fresh pair of latex gloves and leaned close to inspect the hole where a bullet lodged in the plaster. "Looks like a large caliber, maybe a 357?"

"Todd owns a 357 Magnum," Fleming said. "I was with him when he bought it at a gun show a few years ago. Big hunkin' gun, a real man's weapon."

"Do you know where he kept it?"

Fleming's reply was muffled. "Yeah, I think he kept it in his office. I'll check and see if it's still there."

"Don't touch anything, just make sure it's where it is supposed to be."

"I'm not some rookie still wet behind the ears, McKenzie," the chief grumbled, his voice fading. Logan stood and tried to see more.

The young officer returned.

"Has anyone notified his mother?" Mike asked.

The rookie shook his head. "No sir, we were waiting for you or the chief to arrive."

"Get someone on it. I don't want them coming home to find him like this."

Logan noticed a dining chair turned on its side; an expensive looking vase lay shattered near the body.

Mike took pictures with his cell phone. "Looks like there was a struggle—"

"You think he surprised a burglar?" the younger man asked.

"Any sign of forced entry?"

Frustrated, Logan tried to hear what the other officer said.

Mike moved closer to the glass doors and pushed back the curtains to check the locks. "Look around, check windows and doors. He has an alarm system, was it activated?"

"I don't think so." The rookie hurried to check the windows and doors.

Mike tapped the door and pointed.

Logan pushed away from the brick and met Mike's eyes.

"The gun's gone!" Chief Fleming said, coming into the dining room.

Mike dropped the curtain, letting it fall closed.

Logan hesitated.

Breathless, Fleming said, "The box he kept it in was on the floor in the office, open and on its side."

"Did you get a picture of it?"

"Of course," the older man sounded offended.

"Polly and the children are gone," Fleming said, his voice becoming stronger. "I bet that Grimes girl kidnapped her—"

"Hey, ho, you there!"

Logan turned to see the other young officer returning from his mission. "Damn." He sprinted around the back of the house.

The officer called out. "Hey stop!"

Logan kept running.

He burst out of the shrubbery, his father gone. "Damn." He sprinted to the next block. Lights out, Sam pulled up beside him. "Need a ride?"

Logan jumped into the back seat.

"What happened?"

"Deputy spotted me."

Sam waited until he was turning on the highway before flipping his headlights on. "No one's following us. You must have outrun him."

Logan gasped, "He was out of shape." Leaning over the seat, he said, "That was too close."

"Were you able to find out anything?"

Logan told him what he'd heard and seen. "We need to get back to Rae, this is getting ready to get nasty."

Chapter 46

Rae pulled out her cell phone to answer the call.

Monroe reached for it. "You can't have a cell phone. They can track it."

"I watch TV, that's why we bought these." Rae held up the disposable phone. "I'm not stupid. Only Logan and my brother Billy have this number. Billy and Logan both have burner phones, too."

"Not everything you see on CSI is real, you know."

Rae waved her hand and answered the phone. "Hello."

"Hey," Billy said. "You okay?"

"Yes, I was hoping you were Logan."

"Logan, I thought he was with you?"

"He went to see what he could learn about Todd."

"Then you know?"

"Mike was here when he got the call. Is there any news on Polly and the kids?"

"The kids are with Polly's parents but Mike just called to get the information on Polly's car." Billy told her what Mike had said over the phone earlier.

"Do they think she shot Todd?" Rae asked staring at the news.

"Polly's not a killer."

"Todd's not dead, at least not yet."

"Shit, well the news is telling everyone you murdered him."

Rae stared at the television. Her photo came up with a list of numbers to call.

Monroe opened the door and Logan rushed inside. "Shit, I think I've lost ten years of my life."

"Hold on," Rae said. "You okay?"

Logan nodded and asked, "You talking to Billy?"

"Yeah, he was checking to see if I'd heard about Todd."

Holding out his hand, Logan said, "Let me talk to him."

Rae nodded and handed him the phone. "Have you talked to Mike?"

"Yeah, he asked about Polly's car."

Logan said, "Is that all, nothing about the guy who drove away and nearly ran over one of the neighbors and her dog?"

 "He did ask about a burgundy truck."

"The same one that tried to run us down at the hospital?" Logan glanced at Monroe.

Monroe asked, "Do they have a license plate number? Or know the make or model?"

Logan asked. Rae handed him the hotel stationary and pen.

Billy said, "1990s model GMC, partial license plate the witness gave matched a truck we had in the shop for Cole Adams, plate number BWE524."

Logan wrote it down. "He hit that pole kinda hard."

Billy agreed. "Wouldn't be surprised if he damaged the radiator."

Monroe's phone rang. "Monroe."

"McKenzie."

Logan looked up, when he heard Mike's voice and wanted to hear what he told the agent. "Thanks Billy, we'll call as soon as we can."

"Todd Bryant was shot with what appears to be a large caliber, we suspect a 357."

"His own gun?" Monroe asked.

"Logan tell you that?"

"No, I just know there's one registered to him."

Mike paused. "And why do you know that?"

Monroe hesitated. "It may have been used in another murder."

"This just gets more fun as we speak. Tell Logan he's freaking lucky, the deputy believed he was one of the news reporters. They caught a guy sneaking around shortly after he was spotted and made an assumption it was him, otherwise he could be deeper in the crapper than he already is."

Monroe scowled at Logan. "Yeah, he came in just a few minutes ago. What can you tell me?" The agent put the phone on speaker.

"Devin Kinnion was seen driving away shortly after the shooting."

"How does this affect my investigation?" Monroe took a seat at the little table in front of the window. Moving the curtains, he glanced out. Satisfied, he straightened them and returned his attention to the phone.

"The chief is already trying to pin this on Rae Lynne."

"I see."

"No, I don't think you do. This is unraveling, the two, known-rapist have self-destructed. There is only one more out there. Tell me Special Agent, do you think he's cleaning house?" Mike asked. "Or is someone else?"

"Who do you have in mind?" Agent Monroe asked.

"How about your informant? Do you think he could have taken things into his own hands?"

"No, it's not him," he said.

"How can you be sure he's trustworthy?"

Monroe sighed. "Because he's Malcolm Bryant."

"Todd's father?" Mike's voice lowered. "And you're just telling me this now?"

"You didn't need to know and I needed to protect my source. I'm sure you can respect that." Special Agent Monroe said.

"Yeah, but the shit is about to hit the fan, you might want to warn him."

"He's safe, but I'm worried about Logan and Rae."

"I am, too." Mike sighed.

"Tell him about the radiator," Logan suggested.

Monroe repeated what Billy had told them earlier.

"Well, let's hope we catch a break in all this."

"I'm moving to a more secure location. I'll call when we're settled. If there's a problem, leave a message."

"I gotta go." The line went dead.

Logan and Rae stared at the agent.

Monroe shook his head. "We need to find another place."

"Why?" Rae crossed her arms.

"Because your boyfriend went out and possibly led someone back here."

"I wasn't followed. Sam and I rode around before returning."

"I keep telling you, television doesn't always get it right. And sometimes the bad guys just get fucking lucky."

Chapter 47

Logan waited until Rae went to take a shower before confronting Agent Monroe. "What aren't you telling us?"

Monroe turned from the window. "What makes you think I'm not telling you something?"

Logan crossed his arms and waited. "You keep looking out the window."

"The other agent is supposed to be on his way with oxygen and medicine..." He glanced out the window. "I think I'm getting paranoid."

Shaking his head, Logan said, "If you've got a feeling, share it with us. I learned a long time ago to listen to that small voice in my head."

Monroe looked at him. "And what did that voice tell you about Todd?"

"That he's an asshole."

Monroe nodded and heaved a sigh. "If Todd was a spoiled asshole, his mother is the queen bitch."

Logan said, "Yeah?"

"If she's really the head of this cartel, then by trying to kill the prince, someone has either staged a coup or made a royal mistake. Either way we're in the middle of a war."

Logan raised his eyes upward, and said, "If Fleming is blaming Rae, then it won't be long before someone comes looking for her."

The agent nodded. "Money will soothe fractured morality and encourage betrayal."

"And what she can't purchase, she'll bully and threaten," Logan said.

Monroe nodded. "This is about to go nuclear."

Logan nodded. "Rae's in the shower."

"You may want to tell her to get ready. I think it's time to go." He looked out.

"I'm going to check the area. Keep this door locked."

Logan exhaled. "We'll be ready to go when you are."

Monroe slipped silently from the room into the deepening darkness.

Rae was so tired. Her mind was numb. Too bad her shoulders weren't. Her back felt as if someone had tried to twist her into a pretzel. She turned the shower on as hot as she could stand it with the shower massage turned to high and stood under the spray. She let the water pound her tight muscles until the knots in her back loosened.

She heard the door open. Footsteps tapped against the tiled floor. "Rae?" Logan's deep voice filled the small bathroom. "We have to go."

"Can I finish my shower?"

"If you hurry. I'm going to get our things together. Monroe is looking around outside."

She sighed. "I don't guess you have time to join me?"

"I wish, soon love, let's get somewhere safe first."

Rae washed and dressed in record time. Tying her wet hair in a scrunchie, she ignored the dampness at the back of her tee shirt. At least she no longer smelled like a barbeque pit.

"We need to go!" Monroe shouted rushing into the room.

Logan and Rae were finishing their packing. "What's wrong?" she asked.

"White panel delivery van circling the parking lot," Monroe said grabbing his laptop and overnight case. "Let's go."

Rae looked at Logan, but he just gave her a tight nod. She zipped her duffle and hoisted it on her shoulder. "Okay."

Agent Monroe flipped off the lights in the main living/sleeping area, leaving only the one on in the bathroom. He pushed the curtain open a fraction to see out. Nothing. "It looks clear. Let's do this. I'll get the car and drive as close as I can. You wait here until I'm up to the room."

Rae clasped Logan's hand.

The minutes seemed interminable as they waited for Monroe. Rae was nearly vibrating out of her skin, her nerves pulled so tight. When the dark blue sedan pulled up in front of the room, Logan said, "Let me go first."

Rae shook her head. "Together, it's more choices."

He nodded.

They rushed out the door Logan just a step ahead of her. A shot reverberated in the silence of the parking lot. Logan grabbed her hand and pulled her into the back seat. She yanked the door closed as Monroe shoved his foot on the gas, propelling them forward.

"Are you hurt?" Monroe asked when they'd reached the highway.

"Just terrified," Rae answered. Turning to Logan she saw blood staining the sleeve of his shirt. "Shit, Logan was hit."

"It's just a flesh wound but it hurts like a mother…"

"First aid kit under the seat," Monroe said.

Rae located it and examined the wound as they bumped along. "Hold steady, I can't do a thing with you jarring us around."

"I'm fine, just get us away from that psycho," Logan said.

Rae poured antiseptic into the wound.

"Shit!" Logan exclaimed between clenched teeth.

"No bullet, that's good." Rae ignored his protests. Slathering antibiotic cream into the wound she bound it with gauze and taped it. "There, just a flesh wound." She leaned back against the seat and burst into tears.

"I'm okay." Logan pulled her into his arms.

"You got shot."

Monroe swerved, sliding them across the seat.

"What the hell?" Logan held her tight.

Rae looked up to see a white van barreling into their side. Pushing Logan to the floorboard she fell on top of him as the van scraped against the side of the sedan and bounced off.

"Hold on!" Monroe shouted and made a sharp turn to the left followed by a few more turns until he slowed and the road became smoother. "I think I lost him."

Rae crawled onto the seat and asked. "Who was it?"

Monroe shook his head. "I never saw a face."

Logan eased onto the seat.

"You okay?" Monroe glanced in the review mirror.

He'd bled through his bandage.

"Let me see." Rae found a couple of butterfly strips and closed the wound, added a pad of gauze for pressure and taped it again. "If you don't do anything strenuous it should hold."

Logan grinned and pulled her against his side. "If I do, you'll patch me up again."

Her smile was fake as worry crept inside her, gnawing at the momentary sense of peace. *I could've gotten him killed.* The realization left her trembling.

Chapter 48

"I don't know where the heck we are but we're here." Monroe turned into the drive of a little campground. Each of the cabins looked like they were leftovers from an old Daniel Boone movie made in the fifties. "I'm going to get you guys settled and then see if I can get up with McKenzie." He parked in front of the first cabin where the sign out front said lodge registration. He turned to look at them. "You two okay?"

Rae nodded. She'd dozed but still felt groggy and out of sorts. "Is there some place to eat here?"

"I'll see." He got out and went into the office.

Logan groaned, his arm bleeding again. Rae checked the first aid kit for superglue, remembering Billy had used it once when he'd cut his leg on a piece of metal.

"You should probably get stitches," she said, using the glue to hold the edges of the wound together.

"Is there any water? My mouth is dry."

He'd lost a lot of blood. She leaned over the seat and pulled a warm bottle of water from the bag of groceries Monroe had bought earlier. Finding more gauze and tape, she put a fresh bandage over the glue and secured it. "I'm no nurse, but maybe this will hold."

"You can give me a sponge bath when we get to the room," Logan said, teasing a smile out of her.

Monroe opened the door and crawled in before she could reply. "All set, I told him you were an almost famous rock star who didn't want anyone knowing you'd gotten hitched. You'd gotten too drunk at the reception to make your flight, so we were sending you to the middle of nowhere for your honeymoon."

Rae rolled her eyes. "So, which one of us is the infamous rock star?"

Monroe grinned in the rearview mirror as he put the car in drive. "You, of course. With that pink hair, I'm sure he'll believe it."

"Unless he's watched the news and seen my face plastered all over the place."

"It'll be okay," Logan whispered.

Monroe nodded. "Just stay inside."

Monroe left them at the cabin while he went to stock up on groceries and linens. Seemed the cabin was only semi-furnished.

Rae was glad for the reprieve. She dialed Billy's number while Logan dozed on the couch. No signal. "Shoot." She turned on the ancient television but only found two stations that worked.

She left the news playing as she examined the cabin. It was small, the living and kitchen areas were in the first room and the sleeping area was partitioned off, giving it the illusion of privacy. It was clean, if dated, but there was a certain charm to it that appealed to her. She wished for her art supplies, even if just a sketch pad.

Her stomach growled. She found coffee packs and filters in a basket in the kitchen and fixed a pot. Monroe had bought a few supplies earlier, not wanting to stop anywhere to eat in case they were spotted. Although Rae didn't think drive-thru would have hurt anything, he'd worried about cameras.

She found cookies and dried fruit, a pack of nuts and some jerky. "Not exactly a four-star breakfast but it's better than nothing." She arranged everything on a plate and set it all on the coffee table in front of the sofa where Logan dozed.

She fixed two mugs of coffee and brought them into the living area. "Hey, you hungry? You need to rebuild your blood."

Logan opened his eyes and smiled. "I'm fine, is that coffee? Oh, I love you! Nurse, sex goddess and barista, what more could a man want?" He sipped the coffee and made a gagging sound. "Sugar?"

Rae handed him a couple of packs. "You were saying?"

He grinned. "Okay, almost perfect." He stirred in the sugar. "Did you get up with Billy?"

Shaking her head, she told him. "No signal. Only two channels on the television and…"

Logan pointed to the TV. "Look!"

Setting down her coffee, she turned up the volume and eased onto the couch beside him.

The newscaster said, "The truck seen leaving the home of murder-victim Mayor Bryant has been discovered near the old phosphate mine off Old Bay Road. No sign, as yet of the driver. Let's go to Jason Michaels at the scene. Jason, what can you tell us?"

"Well Walter, the police have the road blocked and right now they're waiting for the forensics team to arrive."

"Do we know yet why the suspect abandoned the truck?"

"Looks like it may have overheated." Jason replied. "One of the officers said something about a radiator." The camera pans to a pair of officers propped against a set of saw horses used to block the road. The burgundy truck was just visible past the blockade. "Someone mentioned it may have been in a previous accident. Witnesses claim murder suspect Rae Lynne Grimes was nearly run down while escaping from the hospital. You'll remember a few years ago, she accused Mayor Bryant of rape." The reporter went on to tell how Devin was sent to prison but locals believed the rape charges were bogus.

Rae glowered at the television.

Logan turned the volume down and eased back beside her. He reached for her hand.

Rae leaned into him. He wrapped his good arm around her and they dozed off together.

When Rae next woke, her coffee was cold, and Mike was on the screen.

Logan was standing at the TV increasing the volume.

Mike looked as tired as she felt. As he walked up to the site, a reporter made snide comments about his late arrival. CSI Wade Matthews was getting suited up just inside the barricade. The reporter turned his attention to the forensics team.

The camera showed the two men as they walked towards the truck.

Engrossed in the news they barely noticed when Monroe entered. He was carrying several bags. "Want to give me a hand?" They both hurried to relieve him of his burdens.

Logan followed him back outside and they returned with another arm load.

Rae demanded. "How long do you think we'll be here?"

Monroe shrugged. "Until it's safe for you to go back to Leeward."

Rae's stomach plummeted at the sight of all the supplies. "I can't. I can't stay gone this long." She waved to encompass the amount of food and stuff. "There's no cell signal, I can't contact my family. I don't know if they're okay or what?" She tried to control the panic. She took deep breaths and let them out slowly.

"I talked to your brother, everyone is okay. Dana and her mom are staying with your dad at the campground. I don't know what's happened with your stepmother, she's disappeared. Billy is between the shop and the camp. He's been helping Mike with some of the investigation."

"Connie's disappeared?"

"We think she may be hiding out with Devin," he explained.

Logan said around a mouthful of apple. "They found the truck."

Monroe nodded. "Yeah, I talked to McKenzie. They found a fingerprint. We're hoping it leads us to Devin."

"Do you think he's the shooter?"

"After the white van last night? I don't know. We won't know anything until we find him."

"Is Rae still a suspect?"

Reluctantly, he nodded. "I'm afraid so. Elva Bryant doesn't want to believe you didn't do it. And right now, she's still pulling the strings."

***

The news flashed to the Leeward Town Hall. "Logan!" Rae put their glasses on the table in front of the television.

Logan hurried to set their lunch down and leaned over to turn up the volume on the old television set.

They'd been holed up in the cabin for two days. Rae wasn't complaining, they'd found some interesting ways to entertain themselves. She blushed, remembering how they'd spent the morning.

Logan met her gaze and raised his brow, smirking with male pride.

Rae rolled her eyes, it was obvious he knew the path her thoughts had traveled.

He eased down on the old sofa beside her. He was too tall for the worn furniture, but he had a lanky grace that was sexy and soothing. He leaned over, draping his arm around behind her. "I need fortification if we're going to have a repeat session."

"Eat your dinner, stud." If not for the anxiety of expecting a gun man to blow them away in their sleep or the fear the police would show up at any time to arrest her, Rae would have enjoyed the time alone with Logan.

He was a sensitive lover, teaching her to savor each moment and let the intensity build. Each caress was a gentle pairing of rough callused hands and gentle touches. His kisses were succulent delights from the sweet tender ones to the mind-blowing panty melts.

The commercial ended and the news returned to the town hall. Nodding to the television, Rae said, "That's Todd's mother."

Elva Bryant stood in front of town hall giving an interview with the Channel Seven News. "I have just learned that Devin Kinnion and my daughter-in-law, Polly Bryant, were having an affair. I believe they conspired to kill my son." Her voice broke and Rae wondered if the emotion was real. Elva Bryant looked more like a frail grandmother than the crime-boss the SBI believed her to be. "My son, Mayor Todd Bryant had a glorious future ahead of him. He often spoke of one day becoming president of the United States." She blinked back tears. "I am asking your help to bring these two to justice. If anyone knows where they are hiding, please let me know or call Chief Von Fleming." She gave out the numbers as Fleming joined her in front of the camera.

Rae turned to Logan, grabbing his hand. "Does that mean it's safe to go back home?"

"Is it true Mayor Bryant abused his wife?"

"We heard she was forced to marry him."

The reporters were shouting questions and accusations. Elva was losing her composure. "Polly was a nobody before she married my son. She got pregnant to trap him into marriage."

"It's all that Rae Lynne Grimes' fault," Fleming grumbled.

Elva glared at the chief.

The reporters smelled blood in the water and circling, they threw out questions in a feeding frenzy.

"Did Todd rape Rae Lynne Grimes?"

"Is it true she was only fourteen?"

Mike arrived on the scene amid the shouts of the reporters. He ignored the questions as he strode past.

One of the young officers arrived and tried to herd the news reporters and camera crew away but they were a blood thirsty lot.

Another officer and a county deputy arrived but the news people were like piranha swarming.

There were too many to corral them all.

Chief Fleming rushed towards Mike shouting, "I want that woman arrested."

Mike shook his head. "Chief, for what? She's a victim here, too."

The Chief glared at him. "I don't need your permission to arrest someone."

The news feed abruptly ended, the television going black before a commercial blared.

Chapter 49

"We need to get back home," Rae said. "When is Monroe supposed to check back with us?"

Logan glanced at the clock. "In an hour."

"All right, I'm going to start packing. If he's not here when I'm done, I'm finding my own way out of here."

"Rae, let's be reasonable. He put us here to protect us."

"No, he put us here to get me out of the way. If Fleming wants to mess with me, then he'd better pack a picnic because I'm gonna give as good as he does. I'm tired of hiding."

"Rae, let's talk to Monroe first before we do anything…"

"I'll talk to him but if he doesn't say what I want to hear, I'm on my own. You can come or stay whatever you want Logan, but I can't just sit here and let everything go wonky without me. Todd's dead or dying, Elva's blaming Devin and Polly. I think it's safe for me to go back home."

"And the third rapist?"

She took a deep shuddering breath. "Who's to say he's even still a part of this thing?"

Logan sighed. "I'll do the laundry." He kissed her cheek. "I'm becoming domesticated."

"You do look really hot in an apron."

Monroe grumbled all the way back to Leeward. "I promised your mother I'd keep you safe."

Rae shook her head. "My mother?"

"You don't understand how long this investigation has been going on…"

"About twenty years?" She sneered. "Because that's how long she's been gone."

"I'm sorry Rae, there's a lot you don't understand."

"I understand my mother abandoned me and ran off with a married man. What else is there to know?"

"She went to the FBI when she first left Leeward. Elva was expecting it. She got rid of the evidence."

"Evidence? What are you talking about?" Rae demanded.

"The reason your mother had to leave town. She saw Elva Bryant murder a man." He sighed. "Your mother was trying to find out what happened to her cousin and a group of young Mexican women. She went to Malcolm for help. Independently, they went to check out a seafood house down on the river. They found a couple of young women being held captive. Elva shot a man and we believe she loaded him and the girls onto a boat. We've never found any evidence or any bodies. The seafood house burned to the ground shortly after your mother left town.

"With no evidence, the police wouldn't listen. Elva turned it around and made it sound like Malcolm and Marisol were just trying to take her money and get her out of the way. She played the poor injured wife."

"What about the man's family?" Rae asked. "The man she shot?"

"No one cared enough to ask questions."

"So, it was their word against hers?"

Monroe nodded. "Pretty much."

"So why didn't they just come back?"

"Threats."

Rae shrugged. "Elva's just one woman."

"But she had ties to law enforcement and local politicians. They weren't sure how far her power had corrupted. She even had friends in state government."

"You can't tell me my mother couldn't find a way to get in touch with me in twenty years?"

Monroe sighed. "She was afraid."

"Of Elva Bryant?"

"Yes, and you."

"Me?"

"She was afraid you wouldn't want to see her." Monroe glanced at her. "They've never stopped trying to bring Elva down."

"It's taken twenty years?"

Monroe nodded. "Elva was good, but her boy got sloppy. He pissed in his own pool."

"Stop the car!"

Monroe pulled off onto the side of the road.

Rae shoved the door open and jumped out.

"Rae?"

"Ezekiel said something the night of our date. He said he'd treat me better than the others?" She turned to Logan. "Was he part of that, of the sex trafficking?"

Monroe leaned on the roof of the car.

Rae turned back to him and demanded. "Was Ezekiel La Port part of that group?"

He nodded. "We believe he used the art show to move people and drugs around."

"Fuck!" She paced up and down the side of the road. "Fuck, this is much worse than…"

"Rae Lynne?" Logan followed her.

"I think I'm going to be sick."

"We believe Todd loaned Polly to men and women he wished to form alliances with…"

Rae looked at Logan. "Did he ever offer you his wife?"

Logan shook his head. "No, but there were women at his business meetings who were obviously there for sex. I never stayed long enough to find out."

"Would you recognize any of the women if I showed you some pictures?" Monroe asked.

"I think so. To tell you the truth Monroe, I don't know." He met his gaze and nodded. "I'll try." Taking Rae's hand, he said, "Rae, we need to go. It's not safe here on the side of the road."

She looked from one to the other and sighed. "This is seriously messed up."

She returned to the car. "Okay, let's go."

Chapter 50

Rae awoke when the car stopped. She was splayed on Logan's chest. "Where are we?"

"Across the river from your camp." Monroe explained. "I don't want to carry you home just yet. My gut tells me we're missing something."

"Whose house is this?" Logan asked as they climbed out of the car.

Rae walked around staring at the camp. It seemed familiar. An old fire pit near the water's edge made her head spin. The trees had been timbered, opening it up to the river. She could see the roofs of the camp in the distance. She started to hyperventilate. Panting, she struggled for air. "You brought me here?" Her voice cracked on a sob.

Logan demanded, "What the fuck?" He reached for her, pulling the inhaler from his pocket. "Slow Rae, breath in, breath out. Here, sit down and catch your breath." He turned to Monroe. "Who told you about this place?"

Monroe shook his head. "I-my partner—what's wrong?"

She put her head between her knees and sobbed. "This is where it happened, this is where they took me."

"Are you sure?"

She nodded. "It's more open." She pointed in the direction of her house. "There were trees there, I didn't know it was this close to my papa's house." She started to sob.

Monroe's eyes widened. He started shouting into his cell phone. "What was this supposed to be?" He cursed whomever was on the other end of the line. "Do you know where we are?" He walked away screaming and waving his hands.

Between sobs, Rae told Logan about that night. "I had a little crush on my new step-brother." A sigh shuddered from her lips. "Billy was gone, I think he was at camp or something." She gave him a watery smile. "He was a real Boy Scout."

Logan held her hand his grip, reassuring.

"Devin invited me to a party. The camp belonged to some friend of Devin's, or maybe Todd's, I can't recall. We were drinking and listening to music and I got up to dance." She stood up, her legs shaky. It felt as if it were just yesterday. She stumbled, turning to take it all in.

"Rae maybe you better sit down." Logan grabbed her arm to steady her.

"I was this close to my house and didn't even know it." She gasped and fought to keep her breathing even. "I bet I could have swam to it." She shuddered. Looking around she started naming the people who were here. "Mike was here. He made Jenna leave. Dana came with them, so she left when they did. She tried to talk me into leaving but I'd come with Devin…" she nodded. "Mike testified for me—at the trial." She took a deep breath and let it out. "We tried to give them directions to this place but we were never able to find it."

"Or maybe they didn't look that hard, you did say the chief was on the Bryant payroll."

Rae wandered towards the house. "It looks run down now, it wasn't this bad then." She put her hand on the door knob.

Monroe was still shouting.

Logan said, "Are you sure you want to do this?"

She nodded and pushed it open. It was dark and smelled of mold and urine. "Logan?" She reached for his hand. Watching her feet, she stepped down.

"Watch out!" Logan pulled her back. Fishing line was strung from one side of the shack to the other.

A shuffling sounded from the shadows. Rae strained to see. Stepping carefully over the line, she walked gingerly into the old fishing camp. Boards creaked beneath her feet. She stepped and the crack sounded like a gun shot in the silence. She froze. Logan held tight to her arm, the only thing keeping her from falling or twisting her ankle. More shuffling followed by a scraping sound. Afraid to move, Rae turned to Logan.

He put his finger to his lips and moved her behind him. Watching each step, he led her to the back of the cabin to what was once a bedroom.

At the threshold Rae gasped. "Here," she whispered. "This is where..."

Muffled moaning and scraping, the stench of urine and blood and something rotting nearly suffocated them as they entered the small, dark room. Rae didn't think it could get any darker, but this room seemed absent of any light. She clutched Logan's arm. "Someone's here."

A frantic scraping and moaning.

Logan led her around the perimeter of the room. He stopped and yanked at a piece of cloth, the sound of tearing fabric and the sudden flood of light filled the room.

Rae blinked. Seeing the body on the floor, she screamed and reached for Logan. "Devin?"

Devin groaned. He was hardly recognizable.

"Oh, dear lord, who did this to you?" She knelt and tried to untie him. He was tied arm and leg to the chair, his mouth gagged. Blood matted his hair and streaked his face and he smelled. Rae pulled her shirt up over her nose. Her fingers fumbled with the knots.

"Here, let me see." Logan squatted beside them and using a small pocket knife, sawed the ropes in two. Then the gag. When he was free of the chair, Devin collapsed to the floor.

"He needs an ambulance." Rae pushed at the door but it wasn't an exit. The door swung open. The cupboard was filled with clothes, pictures and bones. Rae screamed.

Logan leapt to his feet. "Oh, dear God." He clutched her to his chest. "We've got to get out of here."

Monroe called, "Where are you?" His footsteps crashed through the fragile wood of the house.

Logan shouted, "Watch out for the fishing line."

"Ugh," Monroe groaned, a light flashed and the smell of gasoline filled the air. "Ah fuck."

Logan pulled the agent into the room.

There was a whoosh and fire spread across the front of the house.

They pushed the door shut.

"I hope there's another way out," Monroe said looking around the macabre bedroom.

"We're getting ready to make one." Logan pointed. "That wall looks weak, what do you say?"

"We'll either get out or bring it down on our heads. Is that Devin Kinnion? What the fuck is that?" He gaped at the shelves filled with haunting souvenirs.

"The trophy room?"

Smoke slid under the bedroom door.

Logan and Monroe nodded to each other. "Let's do this." They ran the short distance across the room and put their shoulders against the wall.

Rae helped Devin to sit up. He was weak and disoriented.

They ran again, shaking the whole house.

A third time.

A board cracked.

The room got warmer. The door smoldered.

They ran again, falling through the wall. They scurried to their feet and pulled at the boards widening the hole. Logan ran back in and lifted an unconscious Devin into his arms. He carried him from the house.

Monroe started grabbing stuff from the trophy room.

"What are you doing?" Rae demanded. "We need to get out of here."

"If this stuff burns up, they'll never get any justice."

Rae prayed for strength and grabbed what she could. She tried not to think about what she was touching, who these people were or what had happened to them.

Logan barreled into the room screaming. "Out, both of you! This room is on fire and it's going fast." He coughed and picked up the nearest stack of evidence and threw it outside. He pushed Rae and Monroe through the hole and dropped to the ground rolling the flames from his shirt.

"What the hell is that?" a familiar voice shouted.

Rae looked up to see her father coming up the lawn. She dropped her macabre treasures and ran to him. "Daddy!" She threw herself at him and cried, wishing she could forget all she'd seen. "Devin's hurt."

Fire trucks, ambulances and police vehicles crowded the lawn.

Dana and Ms. Sandy were slower coming across the creek. "Rae, you're okay." Dana hugged her tight. "I thought I saw you and then we saw smoke." She started to cry. "This was it, wasn't it? This was where it all happened."

Rae nodded.

"I remember." She choked back a sob. "Oh God, I remember that night. I-I went home with Jenna and Mike. You wanted to stay."

Rae swallowed. "I had a crush on Devin and thought he might kiss me." She laughed and blinked back tears, shaking her head, she said, "He didn't kiss me." Her voice cracked.

Dana wiped her tears. "I bet you could get a kiss from him now."

Rae glanced at her stepbrother laying on the ground. The two girls shook their heads and shuddered.

Chapter 51

Rae shifted from cheek to cheek in the hard, plastic chair. She was exhausted, hungry and grimy. Mike came in and she leapt to her feet. "Can I please go home now?"

Mike shook his head. "Sorry Rae, but we need to get your statement."

Narrowing her eyes, she said, "Fleming wants you to charge me, doesn't he?"

"Monroe's talking to him."

"Still," she said with a huff. "Really Mike, I stink, I'm starving and I'm so tired."

"I can help with the hunger, what would you like?"

She rolled her eyes. "To go home."

"Rae?"

"Fine, a cheese burger and fries."

He made a call and placed the order. "What do you want to drink?"

"Coffee shake?"

He repeated her answer and disconnected.

"How's Devin?" She plopped back down in the chair.

Shaking his head, Mike said, "He's dehydrated, his wounds infected, they've got him on some strong antibiotics and a pain killer cocktail that would send a horse to the moon." He sighed. "Good lord, what was done to him? I'm always amazed at the inhumanity of humans. He's not coherent enough to give a statement. The doctor seems to think he'll recover, at least physically, thanks to you and Logan."

She shrugged. "We couldn't leave him there." Chewing her bottom lip, she asked, "What about the things we saved from the cabin?"

He shook his head. "I don't know. Monroe is handling that, he had everything sent to a forensics lab in Raleigh. We're not equipped to handle something like that here."

The young cop she'd seen on television entered with a bag of savory goodness and a creamy, delicious shake. "Oh, I love you," she exclaimed reaching for the food.

He blushed to his roots.

"That's enough Johnson. Why don't you see if her boyfriend's here? You remember: big, red-head, built like he could crush you with his bare hands?"

Johnson lowered his head and rushed out the door.

Rae grabbed a handful of fries and stuffed them in her mouth.

Logan came in and smiled. "Well, this is a good sign, they're finally feeding you." He kissed her forehead.

She sniffed and frowned. "How is it you've had a shower?"

"I've got a good lawyer and I'm nobody. You on the other hand are the infamous Rae Lynne Grimes, notorious trouble maker and champion of the weak."

Rae snorted the shake she was sipping and coughed.

"They're working on getting you out of here." Logan rubbed her back until she quit coughing.

Fleming pushed into the room pointing at Rae, he said, "You're not getting away with it, I'll see to it. I don't care how many fancy lawyers you screw."

Logan stiffened. He turned to confront the chief. "Excuse me? Don't you ever disrespect this woman again."

"You don't scare me cowboy." Fleming puffed out his chest and reached for his sidearm.

He patted his side for his weapon. Finding his holster empty he spun around and found himself face to face with the county sheriff.

"Well, how about me?" Sheriff Adams handed the chief's gun to one of his deputies.

"What do you think you're doing Adams?" Fleming demanded.

"Von Ross Fleming, you are under arrest for extortion, taking sexual liberties with minors and accepting bribes," Sheriff Adams said. "There are other charges pending but these are enough to see you locked up."

Fleming paled. "Funny joke, now get the fuck out of my station."

Adams presented the chief with a writ of arrest. "Ms. Polly Bryant kept some interesting files, videos and a very enlightening journal in her bedroom. You'll be lucky to see parole in forty years."

"Polly would never testify against me," the chief shouted.

"No, but I would." A tall thin man in his fifties, handsome with silver hair and gray eyes stepped forward, Monroe at his side.

Rae knew this must be Malcolm Bryant. He reminded her of Dick Van Dyke. She'd never have imagined him as Todd's father.

"What are you doing back in Leeward?" the chief spat.

"Cleaning out the trash." Malcolm smiled, and Rae shivered, seeing the family resemblance.

"I'm chief of police, you can't…" Fleming attempted to push his way from the office. The deputies stepped in his way, stopping him. "You're not lily-white either, Mac. Don't forget, I know stuff. I'll see you behind bars with me."

"Remember that right to remain silent, exercise it." Adams shoved him around and locked handcuffs on him while one of his deputies read him his Miranda rights.

Rae took a bite of her cheese burger and sighed. "Does that mean I can get a shower without worrying I'll drop the soap?"

"You can but I don't think the chief will be as lucky," Logan said and grinned at her.

They watched as the sheriff and deputies escorted the snarling chief down the hall. Monroe cleared his throat.

"Well, let me finish eating and I'll be ready to go." She shoved the burger in her mouth nearly taking half in one bite. She wouldn't meet the older man's gaze. She knew he watched her, but she wasn't ready to deal with him yet. Malcolm was the one who'd taken her mother away. He was also the father of her childhood tormentor. She wasn't strong enough to deal with him just yet.

"I thought you'd want to get Malcolm's statement and permission to search his properties," Monroe smiled. "He and Elva were still married so without a will her property is his property."

Mike stood and clasped the Malcolm's hand. "Well now, that would save us some hassle with a few judges."

"We'll just wait out front," Monroe said, and the two men shuffled away.

Rae glanced up and met Mike's disapproval. Shaking her head, she said, "Don't start Mike, it's been a long few weeks."

Mike grimaced. "Go home, get some sleep and after I've talked to Devin I'll call you."

Rae paled and stopped eating. Feeling suddenly queasy, she asked, "You don't think the chief was the…was the other guy in the video?"

Mike paled.

She grabbed his trashcan and lost the burger.

Mike pulled the notes she'd given him from his drawer and compared it to a paper on his desk. "I don't think he wrote these notes."

Logan handed her a cup of water.

"And even ten years ago, the chief would have been packing on the pounds. I don't think he could have been the one in the video."

Rae shook her head. "He wasn't fat then."

Mike frowned at her.

"Don't you remember? He came out to the school and flirted with the cheerleaders. He asked them to do a music video and it got back to someone's mama and she threw a fit because she knew what he really wanted. Fleming was a known pervert who preyed on young girls. He only got elected because the Bryant family backed him."

Mike eased back in his chair and nodded. "Yeah, but that doesn't mean…"

"We need to look at both videos again," Rae said.

Mike and Logan both said, "No!"

"I'll do it with or without you. I still have my copy. I saved it in just case …"

Mike nodded. "Fine, I'll look at the videos but without you. I just don't think you need to do this right now. Damn it Rae, you've been through enough."

"Mike, I appreciate you trying to protect me, but I've lived with this for ten years. I see it every time I close my eyes." She blinked back tears. "When we were at the camp that was the first time I really remembered that night, not just the video."

Logan squeezed her hand.

Taking a deep breath Rae said, "Don't you understand? I need to close this chapter of my life."

S L Hollister   Chrome Pink   265

Chapter 52

The men didn't like it but that was just too frigging bad, Rae thought as they squeezed into the little room used for storing contraband and evidence. Mike didn't want to view the tape where anyone else could see it. *Is that because he's on the tape?* She shook her head. *He's just trying to protect me.*

Logan and Mike had hoped that after a good night's sleep she would change her mind, but she was determined find out the truth.

The metal folding chair were becoming more uncomfortable the longer they sat on them. "We're not getting anywhere, Rae let's turn it off," Mike suggested after the fourth pass.

The video was grainy, out of focus and of poor quality. It hadn't held up well. Rae tried to look at the three men objectively but it was difficult. Her stomach churned, and she felt feverish watching them go through with the act. Each time she watched, she put a little more distance between herself and the girl in the video. She was hoping to see something that would tell her the identity of the third guy. "One more time Mike, but fast forward to the third guy, after he finishes with me." She swallows. "There was something, he looked toward the camera."

Average height, average weight and hair, probably brown, eye color unknown and there was no real clue to his age. Everything was in shadow and the boys were all tanned. No one stood out as too light or too dark. "Is there any way to zoom in and see what color his eyes are?"

"I can send it to Raleigh, they have some excellent computer people. Maybe they can pull something off of the video we can't." Mike stopped the video and turned off the monitor. "It's not the chief but I can't tell who it could be," Mike said and sighed. "I'm pretty sure which one is Todd and which is Devin, but that doesn't help much. With their faces covered, it's still all she said-he said."

Rae nodded. "Okay, pack it up, I'm done."

Logan squeezed her hand. She was thankful for his silent support. She didn't think she could make small talk. She felt dirty and sick.

They'd wasted their time and it had given them no clue to the third rapist. She couldn't rule out anyone. It could be Phil or Jorge, or even Mike. They were all about the same height and weight. Her head and her stomach both felt as if she'd just come off a carnival ride. She leaned against Logan for comfort and support. "Thank you for doing that with me. I know you didn't really want to."

Logan squeezed her shoulder. "Rae, I hate what happened to you." His voice choked. "I can't believe you even allow me to touch you after that."

"Are you ashamed of me?" She glanced up determined to face his scorn.

"Ashamed, oh my God, Rae, I am so proud of you. Of what it took for you to survive that…" he swallowed, turning her to face him. "I'm honored you trust me enough to include me. As difficult as it was for me to watch, I…" he shook his head. "It had to be harder for you. I'm here Rae, whatever you need."

"I just thought with a couple of suspects, I could figure it out."

He rubbed her shoulder. "I'm sorry Rae, I was hoping you could too."

Chapter 53

"Devin's not changing his statement," Mike said pacing Rae's patio. He looked as if he'd not slept in since this mess started. "He says he doesn't know who brought him to the shack. He was hit on the back of the head and when he woke, he was tied to the chair."

Rae felt guilty for entertaining the idea that Mike could be a suspect for the third rapist. *It could be anyone!* No, she thought, it couldn't be Mike or her brother, and definitely not Logan. She realized there were people she could trust. Her circle was widening. She stretched her pinky out and stroked Logan's hand, just needing to feel that connection to know she was no longer alone.

Mike shoved his hands through his already tousled hair, bringing them around behind his head, to rub his neck. His tension was palpable. "He claims the coach was still alive when he left him."

"You don't believe him?" Rae stood and filled a glass with ice water and set it on the table. She motioned him to sit.

Mike dropped into the patio chair and clutched the water glass. He guzzled the cool liquid as if he'd walked through a desert. "I don't think he's telling us everything." He sighed, setting the glass down. He leaned his elbows on the table and propped his chin in his hands.

"What if he is telling the truth?" Perching on the edge of her seat, Rae played Devil's advocate.

Mike scowled at her. "You think I haven't thought of that?"

She shrugged. "It would be easier to blame him and be done with it."

"If he didn't kill the coach but left him on the side of the road injured, then someone came along and committed murder in the first."

"Devin was drunk, and from what everyone has been telling me, he's been staying that way. He takes the company truck and has a hit and run. Who would he turn to for help?"

Mike looked up and met her eyes. "Todd."

She nodded. "Or his mama but I think this has Todd's marks all over it."

He pushed back his chair and nodded. "Okay but then why wouldn't he just tell us since he thought Todd was dead?"

She shrugged. "I don't know. Is Todd still in a coma?"

Mike nodded. "I doubt he'll come out of it. Devin is very likely facing murder charges. He says he didn't shoot Todd. There was no gun powder on his clothes when we found him."

"Yeah, but that was a long time after Todd's shooting."

"He had blood that matched Todd's on his clothes."

"So, was it splatter."

"He was there but maybe he didn't pull the trigger."

Mike nodded. "The ADA says there's enough evidence to convict him of Coach Evans' death, but not enough for a murder charge. He'll probably be charged with leaving the scene of an accident."

Rae toyed with her coffee, her mind spinning. She still didn't have her footing. Her hands trembled and she slid them beneath her thighs to still them. "Still nothing on Polly?"

He shook his head. "Elva Bryant is fighting for custody of the children."

Rae glanced up, her thoughts reflected in Mike's weary gaze. He looked away. "Polly's parents have temporary custody. They've put in a counter suit, but money talks."

She sighed. "Those kids don't deserve a life sentence with Mafia Granny."

"The town has gone crazy. People are coming out of the woodwork with claims against the chief and Todd. The ADA is busy building a case. Several women have come forward to say the chief coerced them to have sex to keep themselves or someone they cared about out of trouble. Sometimes the trouble was fabricated, sometimes it was real. Others have claimed he took bribes, insurance money, or made threats against them. Some of these claims are going back twenty years." He shook his head.

"You need to quit referring to Fleming as chief. You're the chief now."

"Interim."

"You're not going to take the job permanently?"

He sighed. "Afghanistan is starting to look more peaceful than Leeward, North Carolina."

She nodded. "You thinking of going active?"

"Logan building his dog house?" Mike asked, changing the subject. He nodded to the new construction where her studio used to be.

Rae smiled, glancing over her shoulder. "So far he's not needed one."

Logan leaned in and kissed her nose. "I guess that's my cue to get back to work."

She watched him walk away enjoying the way he filled out his jeans.

Mike acted guilty, refusing to meet her eyes. She studied her old friend. He'd had an alibi that night, Jenna and Dana had gone home with him. "Phil?"

He turned his head to see Phil's house. It wasn't visible through the trees. "He owned the camp but it looks like he sold it to Todd years ago." He shook his head. "We have nothing on him."

Rae reached for the water pitcher and poured herself a glass. Her hands shaking. Phil was her friend. Could he have really participated in her rape?

"Looks like I'm going to have to make another trip to hardware store." Logan's hand stiffened on Rae's shoulder as a shadow moved around the side of the house. They both relaxed when they recognized Agent Monroe.

Mike's hand eased away from his gun. They were all jumpy.

"You folks don't answer your doors?"

Rae slid her seat back, rising to greet the agent. "Pete, most folks around here just holler to be sure everyone's dressed and let themselves in." She hugged him. "You look tired. Can I get you some coffee or something?"

"You do know my real name's not Pete, right?"

"At least she didn't call you Ditchwater." Logan grasped his hand and eased his large frame into one of the metal and canvas chairs that circled the outdoor table. Rae wasn't sure if it was the man or the chair that groaned. Logan was tired too. None of them were sleeping much lately.

Rae smiled. These men would keep her safe. "Sorry, Jake."

"Coffee if you have some," Monroe said pulling out a chair to join them.

Rae hurried to fetch a cup and the coffee pot. She poured and set the cup in front of him. "What's troubling you?"

Monroe sipped his coffee.

Rae took her seat across from him.

"The FBI has stepped in. They've offered Devin immunity if he testifies. His mother is asking for witness protection."

"She plans to go with him?" Logan asked.

Monroe nodded, his eyes searched Rae Lynne's face.

"My dad has filed for divorce."

Logan's big hand enveloped hers. She turned her hand over so their palms touched. His callused hand offered strength and comfort. Rae feared becoming dependent on it.

"I guess I'm heading back to Raleigh." Monroe took another sip of coffee.

"You'll come back, we've kinda begun to think of you as a friend," Rae said with a grin.

"Been a while since I made new friends."

"Then take some time off. Come back here, I'll take you fishing."

"I'll take you up on it." Monroe stood, shook hands with the men and hugged Rae.

"Don't go getting any ideas about my girl," Logan said, putting his arm around her waist.

"I don't know Red, she offered to take me fishing. I may have to woo her away from you." The agent winked.

"I'm building her a new studio, I think that trumps fishing." Logan leaned in to kiss her.

Monroe grinned. "We'll have to see."

Logan stroked a rough finger gently over her cheek. "I need to head to the hardware store before they close. You want to come?"

Staring into his eyes, she worried. *How much longer will he stay?* "I'm going to work on the sculpture for the Town Hall."

Logan gave her another kiss and ran to catch up with Monroe.

Mike stood. "I guess I might as well head out, too. Thanks Rae, for everything."

She gave him a hug. Stepping back, she studied the bags around his eyes, the droop of his shoulders and the gray color of his usually tanned skin. "Are you okay?"

He nodded. "Just tired."

His radio crackled. "McKenzie?"

The voice on the other end went in and out. Mike called from his cell. "Repeat that."

Rae couldn't hear what was being said, but the look on his face did not bode well.

"Elva Bryant was found murdered in her bed."

"What?" Rae followed him to his car. "How, who…"

"I don't know, the cleaning lady let herself in, when she went to change Ms. Bryant's sheets, she found her. Her throat was slit."

"Holy shit." Rae put her hand to her throat.

"I gotta run, you okay here by yourself?" He looked around, frowning.

"Yeah Mike, I'm fine. Logan will be back shortly."

He hugged her. "Call if you need me."

"Go." She watched until his car was out of sight. Her stomach churned. She looked to Phil's house trying to see through the thick trees that separated the two properties, wondering if he was home. She shivered. "What's going on in this town?"

She went back to the patio and picked up her coffee mug. The coffee was cold and felt like acid in her stomach. Nervous, she cleared the table and returned to her sculpture. She tried to work but her thoughts kept drifting. Rae had been awarded the commission for the Veteran's Memorial Garden. Logan's company would build the retaining walls and pave the walk ways. She struggled to find that place of comfort that came when she worked.

"I can't believe they gave you the commission for the veteran's garden statue."

Rae whirled around and came face to face with Polly Bryant. "Oh my God,

Pol, where have you been? Are you all right?" She reached out to hug her but stopped.

"Isn't that sweet." Polly rolled her pale eyes. "I'm gone a few weeks and everything goes to shit. The stupid chief gets himself arrested. The Junior Women give you the commission and my bitch of a mother-in-law tries to steal my kids."

"Elva's dead," Rae whispered. Polly looked like a homeless woman. Her skin was too tight and her eyes heavy with dark circles. Rae had never seen her so disheveled. Her clothes were dirty and too big for her gaunt frame.

"Of course, the witch is dead. Do you think I'd let her get her hands on my children?"

"Polly, you look—unwell. Let me call someone, get you some help." She pulled her cell phone from the pocket of her jean shorts.

"Shut up Rae Lynne and drop the phone." Polly held a large gun in her thin, pale hands.

Rae licked her lips as she gaped at the 357. She hit send on her phone, not sure who she'd called last, but prayed they'd send help. "Polly? What are you doing? Put the gun down, let me help you." She spoke loud enunciating carefully.

Polly waved the gun. "Once again you ruined everything. God, you couldn't just leave us alone, could you? I should have killed you years ago. Do you know what he did to me? What he made me do?" The gun wobbled in her hand. "He promised we'd go to the White House. I was going to be the First Lady. I put up with everything—the abuse, the partying and the running around because he promised me! He pimped me out, Rae Lynne. Did you hear that? He pimped me out to his friends. I was his special treat to anyone he needed to keep quiet or make extra happy. I became his whore." Her shoulders sagged and for a moment Rae thought she'd drop the gun. She started forward.

Polly stiffened. "Don't!" She raised the gun. "I swear Rae Lynne, I'll shoot you."

"Polly, you don't want to shoot me. We were friends once. We could be again."

Polly shook her head, her voice rising. "We were never friends. Todd told me how you used me. You didn't really care about me. You just needed someone good to make you look good." She laughed, the sound chilling. "Turns out I'm not as good as everyone thought."

Polly gazed out across the river, her hands trembling. "I tried to make him love me. We were doing okay, too, until you came back. You ruined everything! Just like in high school. Everyone loved Rae Lynne. Todd was obsessed with you. They all were."

Rae eased a step closer.

"Why didn't you just leave? I sent you all those notes! I thought you'd get the hint, are you stupid or something?" Polly tightened her grip on the gun. "He blamed you for everything that went wrong in his life. He even blamed you for his having to marry me. I used his obsession with you to keep him around. How sick is that?

"Your mother tempted his dad into leaving. He was the only one who could keep Elva in check. She was the real monster. She sold children." Straightening to her full height, she glowered at Rae.

Rae saw the craziness in her eyes and wondered if she'd always been this way.

"She called me weak but, she'll rot in hell, for underestimating me."

Rae worried she was on her own. If she was going to survive she had to think fast. "Polly, you were always so smart and had it all together. You didn't need us like we needed you. But Todd was wrong, we were friends. We were part of a team. Don't you miss that? Being with the girls. Having friends. Please, put the gun down. We can talk about this."

"It's too late for talking. I gotta clean up a few loose ends, then I'll be on my way," Polly aimed at Rae's chest. "So, did you ever figure it out? The third rapist, do you know who he is?" Polly asked, a ghoulish grin stretching her taunt face.

"You know?"

"I've always known. Damn Rae, for all of your college education, you're not very smart." Polly laughed, she was enjoying her one-upmanship. "I thought for sure you'd figure it out once I gave poor ole Ezekiel that designer drug." She grinned, looking smug. "He thought he could blackmail me after I paid him to go out with you."

Rae gasped in surprise.

Polly nodded. "He got greedy, but that's a man for you. Never satisfied." Polly blinked, her fatigue obvious, her arm drooping with the weight of the gun. "Even my secret lover wanted more. He let his desire for me ruin a good thing. He thought if Todd was gone, we could be together. He didn't get it. I could never be his. He would always be just the clean-up man." Polly was babbling. Rae needed her to keep talking and maybe, if she were lucky, help would arrive. "He designed the drugs, cleaned up their messes and even helped on some of their more exciting activities. They let him watch and they even let him participate, just like that night with you. Still no guess? Oh well, it looks like you'll die in your ignorance." Polly raised the weapon.

Rae dove behind the statue.

A shot punctuated the air.

Rae darted to the patio.

Another shot.

Rae looked down, she'd not been hit. She turned to see Polly crumple to the ground like a paper doll in the rain.

Rae ran to her side, falling to her knees. "Polly!"

Polly tried to speak but blood bubbled in her mouth and trickled from her chapped lips. She looked frantic, her eyes shifting behind Rae—warning.

Rae grabbed Polly's gun and turned to see Phillip Archer setting down his rifle. His pale face looked even whiter. Rae gawked at him as she gripped the gun.

He stepped closer. "I loved her," he whispered.

Rae glanced down. Polly stared up with unfocused eyes.

Phil knelt beside her, reaching for Polly's hand. "I couldn't let her kill you."

Rae stood, her hands shaking. She gripped the gun and glared at Phil. She swallowed the bile that filled her throat. Her heart pounded so loud she could hardly hear.

Phil held Polly's hand, tears sliding down his cheeks. "I'm so sorry, love."

Polly whispered his name and something else. It sounded like 'clean up man'.

Blood bubbled on her lips, Rae sprinted for her phone and dialed 9-1-1.

Phil watched her, his expression cold.

Logan shouted her name. Forgetting her fears, Rae ran to him, dropping the gun and her phone, she threw herself against him, clinging and crying.

Logan held her as if afraid she'd be swept away. "Rae, oh God, Rae, I heard it all. I couldn't get turned around fast enough. I was so afraid." He trembled, tears dampened her skin and Rae realized they weren't hers.

She pulled back and looked into Logan's eyes. Putting her hands to his cheeks she brushed her lips over his. "I'm fine, I'm fine."

"You weren't hurt?" He moved his hands over her searching for wounds.

She glanced over her shoulder and shuddered. "Phil saved me."

Logan looked to where Phil knelt, still holding Polly's hand.

"He was in love with her," she told him.

Logan pulled her close. "Oh God, Rae, never scare me like that again."

"The phone?"

He nodded. "Mike called, a neighbor saw Polly leaving Elva's house." He gave her a squeeze. Rae wasn't sure if it was to reassure her or himself. "Then you called, I was trying to get back. I—"

Mike came rushing into view, his weapon drawn. Seeing them he asked, "You guys okay?" At their nod, he hurried to Phil and Polly.

Phil looked up and whispered something but Rae was too far away to hear. Mike holstered his weapon and patted Phil on the shoulder.

Detective Monroe arrived. "What happened?"

Rae told him what Polly had said.

Mike called the rescue squad and they arrived with the county coroner, a deputy and Officer Claudio. Polly was dead. Mike gave orders for evidence to be collected, then joined them on the patio.

Rae sat in Logan's lap resting her head on his shoulder.

"I'll need you to come down to the station and make a statement. Phil said he'd come down as soon as they take the body away."

Rae glanced to where the EMTs were bagging the body. She shifted her attention to Phil. He stood watching the EMTs bag Polly's body and the expression on his face wasn't that of a man grieving. He looked almost happy. Something turned in the pit of her stomach. *It's him.* He turned, and she saw it in his eyes. She knew the truth. Phil was the third rapist. Rae clutched her stomach and retched.

The bodies and evidence discovered in the old fishing shack dated back ten years. It was believed that Todd was a serial rapist and killer, using the date rape drugs to incapacitate his victims. He'd moved on from rape and mental torture to rape and murder. The torture his victims had suffered before death was unbelievable. Rae was glad to finally have some closure. "What about Phil? Is he my other rapist?"

Mike shook his head. "There's no evidence, other than the fact that the shack once belonged to his family."

"I know it's him," Rae said.

Mike sighed. "I'm sorry Rae, without proof there's nothing we can do."

"Polly said."

"She was deranged, Rae. Without proof, we have no case." Mike touched her shoulder. "I'll keep an eye on him, but truthfully, Rae, I just can't see him in that role."

"Will Todd stand trial?"

He sighed. "I don't know. He doesn't remember anything. His father will be taking care of him." He shook his head. "I don't know if the DA can make a conviction stick, especially now."

Chapter 54

Cupid's Zone was bustling. People crowded around every table, gathered in groups and drifted out onto the lawn. Dana was busy with last minute errands for the poker run. Rae sat alone, waiting. Running her finger through the condensation on the water glass, she watched without seeing as people came and went. Rae was resigned to keep her promise, one last date to fulfill her obligation but her heart wasn't in it.

She'd said good bye to Logan. He'd left for a job promising to return but Rae knew it was over. She'd been expecting it. The breakup was inevitable. She'd started distancing herself, protecting her heart was necessary to survival. *God Rae, you're such a screw up. Just tell him how you feel. Be brave for once.* She blinked away tears. *It's too late, he's gone.* She couldn't blame him. Rae picked up the glass and sipped, not that she was thirsty, she just needed something to do with her hands. The cool liquid refreshed her parched throat.

She gripped the glass, staring into the ripples of water and ice. The past few months had been hectic between the poker run, the murders, running…seemed that's all she'd ever done—run.

Rae felt centuries old not the twenty-five it said on her birth certificate. *Happy birthday to me.* She'd nearly forgot it was her birthday. Her heart pounded, the thoughts swimming in her head anything but happy. No one remembered. *It doesn't matter.* She wasn't in the mood to celebrate anyway.

Dana rushed around gathering the riders for the poker run. Rae had hoped to ride but she'd sold her bike to pay for the repairs to the Harley. She wouldn't dwell on it. Just one more thing she'd lost. She focused instead on the people around her. Everyone seemed so normal. Her dad was laughing and flirting with Ms. Sandy. She smiled. Her relationship with her father was better than it had ever been.

Buddy had filed for divorce. They'd not heard from Connie since Devin agreed to turn state's evidence. He claimed to have proof the Bryant family was selling everything from drugs to people. Rae still couldn't be sure Phil was the third rapist. Like Mike said, there was nothing to substantiate her theory but she couldn't shake the certainty. She brushed her hands over her arms to dispel the chill bumps. Phil was gone. He'd left town as soon as he'd been exonerated in Polly's death. She glanced around, knowing he wouldn't be at the poker run. She couldn't shake the feeling of being watched. She'd had that feeling a lot lately.

Buddy's booming laugh filled the crowded room. Rae lifted her hand and waved when he caught her staring. He surprised her with his handsome smile. He seemed younger, happier. Ms. Sandy was good for him.

Rae glanced at the clock and sighed. She wished her date would hurry up or call if he wasn't coming. She wanted this to be over. Dana hadn't told her anything about him. She pushed back her chair and stood. She couldn't do this. The door opened. Sunlight burned the familiar image in silhouette. Rae stood, her heart beating in double time. She stumbled forward. "I thought you were gone…" She bit her lip, looking up at him with fear and hope. "I promised Dana—" her words faltered. He looked so good. "What are you doing here?" She wanted to touch him, to tell him. Tears clogged her throat Her emotions were intense and frightening. *He's just another addiction.*

"You wanted to see how we feel about each other. Well, I don't need time to know how I feel about you, Rae Lynne, I love you."

"Logan," she choked, trembling. "I'm-I'm on a date." She fisted her hands to keep from reaching for him.

He nodded. "I joined Cupid's Zone."

Rae frowned up at him. "You?"

"I told your friend I'd join her stupid dating club if that's what it took to be your last date."

Rae grunted a sound between a laugh and a cry. "Logan?"

He strode towards her. "She made me agree to three dates."

Her teeth clamped down on her bottom lip.

"But she promised me, they could all be with you." He held out his hand to her.

"How about it, Rae, will you be my date?"

She threw her arms around him. "Oh Logan, I-I love you, too." She cried against his neck. "You're taking your life in your hands dating me. My dates don't fare well."

He pulled her against him, letting her slide down his length. She could feel his erection against her belly and blushed. He grinned. "I believe in living dangerously, Happy Birthday, Rae."

The crowd shouted, SURPRISE! Dana wheeled out a cake. The crowd began to sing.

Shaking her head, Rae tried not to laugh but it bubbled out with his name on her lips. "Logan?"

He raised a brow and offered his hand. "Yes, and you are?"

Laughing she wrapped her arms about his neck and introduced herself. "Your worst nightmare." She kissed his ear. "You are a glutton for punishment."

The poker run was an amazing success bringing biker clubs from all over the east coast. The ending ceremony at Cupid's Zone was standing room only.

Jenna and her staff from the Depot catered the dinner with North Carolina pulled pork barbeque, grilled chicken and all the fixings. Several ladies sold baked goods along with canned pickles and jellies. All the proceeds would go to breast cancer awareness. The streets of Leeward were filled with every kind of bike from modern crotch-rockets to vintage Harleys.

Rae was glad the weather wasn't too warm and the threat of a hurricane passed without incident. It had been a perfect day for a ride even if she had to ride on the back of Logan's bike. She wouldn't admit to liking it. As the day started to fade she could feel a chill in the air, fall would soon be upon them. She huddled close to Logan, relaxing into his embrace. The freedom of being with him warmed more than her goose bumped skin.

"You need a jacket?" Logan's deep baritone vibrated her ear pressed against his chest. He rubbed her arms, sending shivers of excitement across her nerves.

Rae sighed, shaking her head she buried her nose in his shirt inhaling the spicy, male scent of him. "No, I'll be fine, I think they're getting ready to announce the winners."

He tightened his arms around her and propped his chin on top of her head. "Did I tell you how awesome you are?"

Rae turned in his arms smiling up at him. Only Logan's strong, steady embrace kept her tethered to earth, a lightness she'd not felt since her childhood lifted her heart. "And what did I do to deserve this compliment?"

A lift of his brow and a mischievous grin was interrupted when Dana took the stage.

Rae turned her attention to her friend, giving a shrill whistle, she shouted, "Yay Dana!"

Dana grinned and began. "The winning poker hand is…" The crowd cheered and slapped the winner on the back. She named the club who raised the most money followed by the winner of the best bike contest and finally the time came to announce the winner of the Pink Harley.

"The winner of the 1957 Harley Motor cycle painted this lovely pink by my best friend and co-hostess Rae Lynne Grimes is—" Dana put her hand in the pot and pulled out a ticket. She read it and laughed. "Mr. Buddy Grimes!" She shouted.

People gasped as silence descended.

Logan started clapping, Rae joined him and others followed. The grumblers were soon drowned out.

Ms. Sandy standing beside Buddy, poked him.

Buddy pointed to his chest, mouthing, "Me?"

Sandy gave him a little push towards the stage.

Rae whistled again. "Way to go dad!"

Buddy made his way to the podium. He stumbled coming up on the make-shift stage. "As many tickets as I bought I coulda paid for a new Harley," he grumbled, accepting the keys from Dana.

Dana gave him a quick hug. "You want to say anything?'

Buddy cleared his throat. "I am a man of few words but I have never been prouder of these two girls. They worked hard putting on this shindig. My daughter, Rae Lynne Grimes and the lovely, Dana Windley, deserve your applause. Not only did my daughter paint the bike, she restored it too. Come here honey, this is my daughter, Rae Lynne Grimes." He hugged her as she stepped on the stage. "I am very proud of you."

Rae fought back tears as she returned the gesture. "You going to let me ride your bike, Pop?"

He grunted. "Not very likely, you already wrecked it once."

Rae pouted but grinned when she saw the humor in her father's eyes. This was the man her mother fell in love with.

He grinned and led her off the stage.

Dana said, "Stick around and enjoy the band. We all deserve to celebrate a great fundraiser!"

The band tuned up, tables were moved. Logan waved to her pointing to the door and his parents.

Rae nodded and grabbed Dana's hand. "Come, I want you to meet Logan's parents." Rae dragged Dana to the front door. "I'm so glad you all came." She embraced each in turn.

Logan made the introductions.

Dana stared at Sam, studying him with an eerie intensity. "You look familiar."

Rae glanced between her friend and her lover's stepfather. "Dana?"

Sam smiled, trying to hide his discomfort. "Perhaps I have one of those faces?"

Dana eyes widened. "I swear I've seen you—a picture, you were in the Army."

Sam said, "Marines."

Dana chewed at her lip. She turned to Logan. "Sam Birdsong?"

Logan nodded. "I took Sam's name."

The color leached from Dana's face. She darted between Rae and Logan.

"Dana?" Rae called. Returning her attention to her guests, she said, "I-excuse me. I'm not sure what's wrong." She hurried after Dana.

Rae caught up to Dana as she was dragging her mother to the front door, Buddy in tow. "What's going on?" Rae whispered.

Buddy lifted his shoulder with a shake of his head.

Dana stopped Ms. Sandy in front of Sam. "Is this him, mom. Is this my father?"

Sandy gaped up at Sam and paled. She reached for Buddy's hand.

Buddy put his arm around her shoulder. "Sandy, are you okay?"

"Oh my God, Sam?" Her voice was thin and high.

Sam's pallor grayed as he looked from Sandy to Dana. The big man trembled, tears streaming down his ebony cheeks. "How? You're dead. Your brother…" He turned his hazel eyes to Dana and whispered, "Daniela?"

She nodded tears streaming down her own face. "No one calls me that."

Sam reached out and touched her face. "I thought you were dead. Robbie said you were in an accident."

Dana nodded, staring up at him. "Why would Uncle Robbie say that?"

Sandy whispered, her voice hollow with emotion, "You know why? The same reason we left Georgia."

"Why didn't you wait for me?" Sam asked his face contorting with anger.

Sandy sighed, closing her eyes. "I did, after we got out of the hospital. There really was an accident." She put her hand on Dana's back rubbing circles comforting both of them. "I went to the base but you'd already deployed. I had nowhere to turn, since we weren't married…"

"And Windley?" He interrupted.

She sighed. "Tom, he helped me get away from my family. He adopted Dana, Daniela," she swallowed.

"Your neighbor, the old guy who was always helping you?"

She nodded. "He died the year after we moved here. He was a good man."

"Tom could have found out," Sam said. "He could have gotten word to me."

Sandy tightened her jaw. "He helped us."

"He wanted you for himself."

"We thought you didn't want us," Dana said taking his hand.

Sam looked down at their joined hands and he said, "I blamed myself. That sonofabitch, I can't believe—"

"Uncle Robbie's dead." Dana looked into her father's eyes. "He died in a car accident."

"My sweet baby girl, all these years lost. I thought you were dead. Lillie can you believe it? My daughter—"

Lillie nodded and looked up at her husband, a sad smile on her face. "Yes darling, she's alive and so is her mother." Lillie narrowed her eyes as she met Sandy's.

Sandy nodded and leaned into Buddy's embrace. "It's been over twenty years."

Rae looked from her lover to her best friend, torn between them. She closed her eyes, resigned to the chaos that was her life. She was afraid of losing them both.

Logan gripped her hand and pulled her into his arms. "You won't lose us," he whispered knowing her thoughts. "We'll figure this out."

Rae clung to the fragile thread of hope but she wasn't so sure.

Coming Soon...

The sequel to Chrome Pink

White Gold

Dana Windley, a black girl raised by her white mother must learn what it truly means to be biracial in a rural, southern community.

Suddenly reunited with the father she's never known, Dana is torn between the mother who has protected her all of her life and the man who thought she was dead.

Dana creates her identity and her place in the community of Leeward, North Carolina. She believes she can have it all, if she is willing to work for it. Only that one elusive dream, her perfect love story defies her efforts.

SBI Agent Jake Monroe seeks the truth. On forced leave, he searches for the evidence he needs to prove his theory of drug and human trafficking in Leeward, North Carolina. But he isn't the only one trying to unmask a monster. Which monster will be more frightening.

Together, Dana and Jake discover more secrets, but the worst kept secret is their attraction to each other. Can they save each other from those who wish to silence them, or will they be too late?

Prologue
Nursing Home in Columbus, Georgia
Late August

The lunch tray crashed to the floor startling the other patients.

"Mr. Clinton, is everything okay?" The dark-skinned nurse rushed to the old man's side.

Henry Clinton snarled at the woman. "No, it's not okay," he mimicked. "She's supposed to be dead."

The plastic tray fell short of the television, landing on the dingy linoleum floor splattering food across the front of the dining room. "They lied to me," he growled glaring at the television.

"Let's get you cleaned up and I'll get you another tray…"

"I don't need your nasty black ass in my face. I told you, stay away from me." He struggled to his feet.

The nurse motioned for an orderly to assist the old man.

The young janitor moved forward to clean up the mess. He studied the television. It was one of the local channels from up the coast. He listened as he mopped. The news anchor was talking about a young woman who'd been reunited with her father after twenty years apart. He didn't recognize either of them, but the older woman standing slightly behind the girl reminded him of the picture his father used to carry in his wallet. It was the one he now carried in his own wallet.

"She was supposed to have died in that car crash," Henry Clinton mumbled as the orderly helped him from his chair. "That damned son of mine, if he wasn't already dead, I'd kill him myself." He snorted. "It's ironic, isn't it? My Robbie died in a car accident." He shuffled to the television pointing a gnarled finger at the big, black man on the screen. "That buck defiled my little girl. Their abomination doesn't deserve to live." He beat his fist against the screen until the orderly pulled him away and led him back to his room.

About the Author

Learning to read released Sherri's imagination and her dreams of being a writer took flight. She fell in love with love and wrote her first romance in fifth grade. Her eighth-grade teacher called Agatha Christie. *The Secret Garden*, the stories of Sherlock Holmes, and the bodice rippers of the seventies and eighties influenced her own tales of romance and adventure.

For years Sherri hid her stories in notebooks in her closet. After discovering her own romantic hero and raising a house full of heroes, she dreamed of publishing those stories. With the encouragement of family and friends she began the journey of learning the craft and business of writing.

After winning the Ann Peach Scholarship for new writers and attending her second Romantic Times Readers and Writers Convention, Sherri joined Romance Writers of America and her local chapter. She took over hosting the monthly book in a week competition in 2015. She has been a member of her local writers' group, Pamlico Writers' Group, off and on for fifteen years. Sherri joined the steering committee for the annual writers' conference in 2013. In 2015, she became the chairperson of the Pamlico Writers' Group and in 2017 she took over as chairperson of the conference steering committee.

Check Sherri out at sherrilhollister.com, Twitter @Jeanelia1964 or on Facebook @sjlhollisterwriter.

Made in the USA
Columbia, SC
20 March 2019